Hannah's Left Hook

To Eric Rutan

Best Wishes

Your writing friend

Brian Mc.....

Hannah's Left Hook

Brian McKeown

GARLAND PRESS
Shrewsbury, Massachusetts

Designed and composed in Warnock Pro at Hobblebush Books, Brookline, New Hampshire (www.hobblebush.com)

Printed in the United States of America

ISBN 978-1-940782-00-3
Library of Congress Control Number: 2014930342

Published by:

GARLAND PRESS
P.O. Box 4142 · Shrewsbury, MA 01545

www.garlandpress.com

To my mother, Lilly, with love

Acknowledgments

This novel would never have seen the light of day if Laurel Dile King of Garland Press had not taught me, with incredible patience, how to transform a collection of embellished anecdotes into a complete manuscript. I shall always be indebted to her. Warm thanks for their support are also due to my wife Sue, my daughter Joanne, my uncle Peter, and my sister Valerie. I am also grateful to my writing colleagues at the Worcester Art Museum, who provided meaningful critiques over the last three years: Sam Paradise, Lauren Sheridan, Annie Hill, Laura Tomasko, Marcia Lagerwey, and also Elaine Cowen.

Hannah's Left Hook

Prologue

"You've never been clobbered until you've been clobbered by Hannah Corcoran's left hook, and I should know."
The Most Reverend, Archbishop Michael Mosley

If there was one aspect that all the victims of Hannah Corcoran's left hook could agree on, it was that not one of them saw it coming. Another aspect, of course, was that the wallop hurt like hell, obvious to even the most casual onlooker. Hannah would move her hand slowly behind her back, clench her fist, and somehow transfer all the pent-up energy, of her entire body, into her left arm. There was no indication to the victim that his clock was about to be well and truly cleaned. You could not read it in her eyes. You could not sense it in her demeanor.

The swiftness and ferocity of the blow itself was a sight to behold. Mostly, Hannah aimed for the right cheekbone. The blow turned the recipient's head to the left, as her fist continued its path of destruction onto the nose and lower eye socket. With a spurt of blood and a startled cry, the victim would drop to the ground like a guillotined Frenchman's head.

Being a proud woman of high standards, Hannah generally tried to avoid hitting the chin or the mouth, because she didn't want to permanently injure anyone, not physically anyway, or cause the loss of any teeth—good dentists were few and far between. A bloody nose and a black eye were usually the worst outcome. But on other occasions, when her blood boiled over or when someone laid a hand on her, her aim was straight on, full in the face, with the intent of long-term damage. In either event, the victim's self-esteem was permanently bruised, because the man—and it was always a man—had to carry forever after the humiliation of being decked by such a compact woman.

Don't get the impression that Hannah was some violent maniac who slugged anyone who annoyed her. The left hook appeared on a dozen or so occasions and only in her prime. For most of her eighty years, Hannah was a God-fearing, hard-working matriarch, always in charge. Yes, Hannah was always in charge.

She never punched any of her six children at any age. She did slap them, of course, and while a slap from Hannah was not as legendary as her hook, it could knock the sass out of you for a month or two. But slapping kids was part of the culture in those days, being considered an important part of the character-building process.

Hannah's left hook generally appeared when the situation warranted it, when a serious argument had reached an impasse. But on several famous occasions, when she had vengeance in mind, it opened and closed the argument with few words being spoken. Some folks maintained that Hannah never clobbered anyone who didn't deserve it.

That will be for you to decide.

Chapter One

═ 1916 ═

The Hook's Debut

People said that Pat O'Malley lived to be ninety-five, though no one knew for sure. Even Pat himself had forgotten how old he was, but one thing he did remember, clear as a bell, was the day Hannah Corcoran's left hook made its first public appearance, way back in the spring of 1916. Any evening after seven, you could find old Pat in the corner of the Garrick Snug Public House, and you only needed to buy him a glass of Birkenhead Brewery brown ale for him to recount the whole incident in graphic detail. After all, he should know, being the last surviving witness.

He would start by telling you that it happened in late May, the day after old Mrs. Duff from Cathcart Street died in her sleep. Mrs. Duff's daughter sent for Hannah to wash the body. Together the two women dressed the old lady in her Sunday frock, finally laying her out in the parlor, all clean and peaceful, for the wake the next day. The family gave Hannah a silver shilling for her efforts.

Now, some folks said that washing dead bodies was a grue-some way to earn a few extra coppers. Not Hannah. To her, it was an essential part of preparing the departed to meet Holy God in heaven, because if you are to stand before your maker dressed in your best clothes, you don't want a grimy body underneath. After all, a person must show proper respect. Hannah treated the process as if it were part of a religious ceremony, and she insisted that many a time the spirit would tarry in the body for a while before departing to the hereafter. On more than one occasion she swore that she felt a *whoosh* as the spirit flew by.

Of course it wasn't all spiritual. The money earned washing bodies came in handy when you had three young daughters to feed, and a blind mother to tend, with no help from your drunken wretch of a husband. Times were hard and money was scarce. Over in France, the lads lay slain in the trenches by the thousands—good young lads, Catholic and Protestant alike, with many thousands yet to fall. In the port of Birkenhead, on the southern banks of the River Mersey in northwest England, where Hannah spent her entire life, many lads joined the Merchant Navy, only to perish in the bitter cold of the North Atlantic, their ships torpedoed by lurking German submarines.

Sorrow touched every family. Masses were said, and prayers were prayed for loved ones to come home alive. Hannah prayed for the two brothers she had raised, the one still alive and the one who was killed at the battle of Marne. But she never prayed for the life of her husband, John Luxton, who served in the Royal Navy. Instead, she secretly prayed the Germans would kill him. She cursed the day she weakened and agreed to marry him, in a search for security in her young life, even though she knew in her heart he was a brute of a man. Hannah never revealed in the confessional that she prayed her husband would die, because she never considered it a sin. To Hannah, the definition of a sin was negotiable between herself and God.

That fateful day, clutching her purse with the shilling inside, Hannah rushed to the shops before they closed. It was tripe from the offal shop, spuds from the greengrocer's, and then up St. Anne Street toward home. Home was the Birkenhead Docklands. Irish immigrants had settled there for the past three generations, when Liverpool, on the north side of the river, ran out of space, and they built the terraced houses and dock cottages that were their humble homes.

Hannah turned left onto Price Street, passing the Lord Wellington Arms, where a group of dock laborers waited for the pub to open. Some of them whistled at her as she passed, but that sort of attention never ruffled Hannah—she was used to it. She had the type of figure that caused men to look twice, and together with her wealth of raven hair and high, shiny cheeks, she was a fine colleen, indeed. The Scots would call her bonnie, the Irish would call her beguiling, but in this part of England she was known as a bobby-dazzler.

Hannah's father passed away when she was just twelve. Cataracts stole her mother's eyesight shortly thereafter, leaving Hannah to raise her three younger siblings, thus curtailing her childhood. At seventeen, she married John Luxton, six years her senior, because he had a steady job. Now, at twenty-four, Hannah had reached her prime. She was five feet six inches in her stocking feet, 130 pounds of pure energy, sacrificing grace for speed, a whirling dervish of a woman.

She had almost reached her house when she was met by her eldest, Eileen, rushing toward her in a right state. "Mam, Mam!" Eileen cried, "Come quick! It's Granma!"

Inside the house, Hannah found her mother, blind Granma White, sprawled in a corner of the kitchen, one hand to her bloodied forehead, the other clutching her rosary. Hannah lit the kitchen gaslight to examine her mother's wound.

"There's a lot of blood, Ma, but I don't think it's deep." Hannah turned to Eileen. "Go fetch yer great uncle Charlie and tell him to bring his stitchin' bag. Hurry!"

Uncle Charlie, who had learned to stitch wounds in the Sudan war, ran over from across the street. He helped Hannah lift Granma White to her feet, still holding a dish towel to her head. They lowered her onto the horse hair sofa in the back room, as Hannah's two youngest, Doris and Vera, looked on, wide-eyed. To lift Granma White required considerable leverage, as she was a big woman, not fat, but built tall and wide, like a heavyweight boxer. Yet for all her bulk, Granma White was a gentle soul. In a subdued tone, she explained what had taken place.

"It was John Luxton. He came home on leave this afternoon, and I caught him red-handed riflin' through me purse. When I told him to leave it, he belted me one, knockin' me over such that I caught me head on the corner of the table."

Hannah sat down, closed her eyes, and uttered an angry snort. "That bastard."

Uncle Charlie examined his sister's wound and gave his opinion. "Doesn't need stitchin'. I'll just staunch the bleedin', put some salve on it, and bandage it up. You'll be as right as a five-pound note in no time. Then I'll go find that John Luxton and give him a good thrashin.'"

Hannah knew that Uncle Charlie's thrashing days were long past. "No, this is my problem," Hannah said. "I brought John Luxton into this family, so I'll settle this score."

Full of venom and vengeance, she set off to find her husband.

❖

Hannah strode into the Conway Arms like Robin Hood bursting into the Sheriff of Nottingham's banquet hall. She stood in the middle of the pub, fists clenched, teeth clenched, and the whole room full of dock laborers and servicemen on leave went quiet, all eyes on her.

"No women allowed in this pub!" the barkeeper shouted.

"Shut yer gob, John Docherty," Hannah replied, "or I'll be washin' *your* body in the mornin'." She turned to address the pub patrons. "Now, who's seen John Luxton today?"

Everyone kept silent, but then a sailor with a greasy beard said, "He was here earlier, then left to get some money. After that I don't know. Maybe the Garrick Snug." Hannah spun around and was gone as abruptly as she came, leaving a pubful of men thankful that they were not her husband at that particular moment.

You could walk from the tip of Cornwall to the Scottish Highlands and be hard pressed to find a pub as small as the Garrick Snug. It had no tables or chairs and, on a payday night, maybe thirty men at best could cram into it, shoulder-to-shoulder with barely room to lift a pint of ale. Roll-your-own cigarettes, packed with nasty tobacco, put out a black smoke as thick as oxtail soup. The smell of tobacco and sweat could peel off the wallpaper, if the place had any.

Hannah's entrance had the same effect as it had at the Conway Arms. Every man turned to look at her—the only woman to ever enter the place. (No other woman would come in again until forty-three years later, and that, too, would be Hannah.) She jostled through the crowd, toward the bar where her husband stood, propped up on one elbow, in his sailor's uniform, surrounded by shipmates. His lips seemed to be forming a "What," but not a word escaped his mouth.

Like a bolt of lightning, Hannah's fist flew out of nowhere, into his face. The terrifying blow caused men nearby to be splattered with nose blood. Thus was the debut of the famous left hook.

John Luxton reeled backwards, arms flailing, knocking glasses of ale off the bar, and bouncing off men close by, until he dropped with a thud onto the wooden floor. There he lay, moaning.

A docker said, "Good God, did you see that!" All eyes turned from his prostrate body to Hannah. Her frame no longer quivered with rage.

"He knocked over me blind mother, causing her head to be cut open," she said. "Then he stole coppers from her purse for beer money." The Garrick Snug stayed silent.

Hannah looked down at her husband, still moaning on the floor, splattered with blood. "Done and dusted," she said.

She strode out through the passage the men had made for her, and passed Pat O'Malley at the door. "Evenin', Pat," Hannah said with a nod.

He nodded back. "Evenin', Hannah. That's one hell of a punch yer got there!" Hannah made a fist and looked down at it with a wide smile.

The tiger was out of the cage.

Chapter Two

⟹ 1916 ⟸

Destitute

Hannah scraped the burnt parts off a piece of toast, spread Stork margarine on it, cut it in half, and plopped it on the plate in front of her mother.

"Here's yer breakfast," Hannah said. "How's yer head this mornin'?"

Granma White put her hand over the wound and adjusted the bandage slightly. "So down he went with just one punch? Incredible."

"Just one," Hannah replied.

"Where did that come from?"

Hannah shrugged. "Beats me. I never knew I had it in me. I trembled with rage when I walked in that pub, but when I saw him standin' there, carousin' and laughin', all feelin' left me. I knew what to do and I did it. When I left it was as if somethin' that was lodged in my throat for the last seven years dissolved away. I could breathe again."

With a bemused expression, Granma White said, "Well, I'll tell yer where it comes from—yer father, God rest his soul, that's where. I've never told yer this, but he was an amateur boxer in his youth. Bantam weight champion of County Wexford, and a wicked left hook was his signature."

"Oh Ma, you just made that up!"

"Yes, you're right. I can't help it. It's the Irish in me."

"Maybe, just maybe," Hannah said, "it comes from all the scrubbin' I've done with me left hand—scrubbin' house floors, scrubbin' church floors, scrubbin' kids, scrubbin' the dead."

"You're just an auld scrubber." Granma White chuckled. "Now go and make yer mother another cuppa—me head is really startin' to hurt again."

8

Granma White poured her tea from the cup into the saucer, blew on it to cool it down, and then poured it back into the cup. "Saucered and blowed," she said. Hannah had seen her mother perform this ritual a thousand times, without ever spilling a drop. She supposed being blind made your other senses sharper. Either that or her mother had fooled her all those years and could see as well as an alley cat.

Granma White sipped her tea. "What will you do if John Luxton comes back to look for yer? He must be as mad as a one-armed Chinaman after you humiliated him in front of all his cronies."

"Then I'll slug him again," Hannah said, punching the air, "but I doubt he'll chance it. Eat your toast, Mother, before it gets cold."

"As far as that man's concerned, it's good riddance to bad rubbish," Granma White said, taking a bite of her toast.

"No jam?" she asked.

Hannah sighed. "Not this week."

❖

John Luxton had no time to dwell on his humiliation, for the next day he was recalled to his ship, the light cruiser HMS *Chester*. He took the train to Scapa Flow Naval Base in Scotland to join the British North Sea Fleet. Rumor had it that the German High Seas Fleet might at last come out of its harbor. That meant John Luxton would soon come up against an antagonist as fearsome as Hannah, in the form of Kaiser Wilhelm II, Emperor of Germany, King of Prussia, and grandson of Queen Victoria, no less.

Except for his predatory submarines, Kaiser Wilhelm's obsession for his magnificent new fleet was such that he wouldn't allow any of the ships to leave port lest they get scratched. Eventually, after two years of war, he relented to the pressure from his admirals, and with reluctance, gave the order for his fleet to sail and destroy the enemy.

On the thirty-first of May, 1916, out from Wilhelmshaven the proud German Fleet sailed—sleek destroyers, powerful cruisers, mighty Dreadnought battleships—all manned by the finest officers and crew that Germany could produce. Twenty minutes later, having intercepted and decoded all the German signals, the British Fleet left Scapa Flow. The two mighty armadas collided in the North Sea off the coast of the Danish peninsula, Jutland. Two hundred fifty warships locked horns in the greatest naval battle in history. At stake was no less than the mastery of the high seas.

HMS *Chester*, part of Admiral Hood's Third Battle Cruiser Squadron, was positioned at the end of a line of six similar cruisers, slicing south by southeast at full steam through the North Sea. Able Seaman John Luxton came out of the head, buttoning his fly on his way back to his gun turret. He leaned over the side of the ship next to a young officer who was peering through binoculars into the mist.

"What do you see, sir?"

"The Huns are out there in force," the officer replied.

The air was filled with the sound of faraway guns, as they lobbed huge shells at each other, and the terrible crash when a shell hit home. In the distance, Luxton could see the flashes of guns break the mist, and the thick white smoke from burning ships.

The officer looked at his watch and winced. "The battle started about 2:30 p.m., and it's 5:30 p.m. now. I just hope to God that we get into the fray, because I don't want to miss this one. This is another Trafalgar, Seaman, believe me. This will be the clash of the Titans— the battle that we've waited for these two long years. This will be something to tell your grandchildren."

John Luxton grimaced. Just another middle-class officer prick, he thought, anxious to get his head blown off.

Luxton strode back to his gun turret as the Klaxon horn sounded "Battle Stations." Lookouts had spotted an enemy cruiser to starboard and HMS *Chester* peeled off to engage. Having sighted the line of British cruisers, the German warship turned about with *Chester* in pursuit, gaining on her steadily, blasting at her with the forward guns. But as the mist lifted, Captain Roberts of the *Chester* gasped as several ghost-like forms appeared aft of his quarry. He was steering directly into an enemy cruiser squadron, and doom washed over him.

Captain Roberts frantically swung his ship about as a bursting shell smashed into the hull of his vessel—then another and another. He zigzagged northeastward with four German cruisers on his heels and only his aft gun still in action. The wall of water thrown up by exploding shells engulfed the British ship as it continued its deadly dance, with enemy shells still hitting home. Despite the appalling damage and the death of half its crew, *Chester* kept steaming along.

It was a new ship, fast and strong, built with thick British steel at the Birkenhead Shipyard.

John Luxton shook his head as he regained consciousness. A terrible whirring noise overpowered his brain. He was blinded and deafened, and the smell of cordite filled his nostrils. He gasped for air. Am I dead? was his first thought.

Feeling slowly returned to his nerves, and he realized that he was lying on cold steel, with some sort of soft, heavy weight on top of him. Using his one free hand, he managed to push the weight over and off, and recognized the object as the body of a fellow sailor. John Luxton pulled his hand back onto his stomach and felt something wet and slimy, like a piece of fresh tripe. I hope that isn't *my* innards, he thought.

More senses returned: the sound of the guns, the movement of the ship, the smell of melted metal, and the terrible pain in the back of his head. John Luxton staggered to his feet, and looked in horror at the half-destroyed gun turret. Good God in heaven, he thought, how did I survive this? He found his way out of the turret and onto the deck. Smoke was everywhere. It appeared as if the entire vessel was ablaze. Stumbling toward the side of the ship, he reached the rail and threw up.

As he peered aft through the smoke, Luxton could make out the German cruisers in pursuit. Forward he could see British ships approaching from the portside. On hearing all the gunfire, Admiral Hood had turned his squadron around, with all guns blasting away.

HMS *Chester* sailed through the British squadron to safety. John Luxton still gripped the rail and looked to the heavens to thank God that he was still alive. At that moment, a final German shell smashed into the deck of the *Chester*. And where John Luxton once stood, he stood no more.

❖

Two days later, Hannah queued up at Jones' offal shop, behind Winnie O'Connor, as she waited her turn and counted her coppers. Richard Jones had the look of an archetypical butcher. His bloody apron covered his overweight gut, and his rolled-up shirt sleeves revealed muscled arms made thick by years of chopping up dead animals. It made Hannah wonder why the man wasn't in uniform. His head sprouted a nest of jet-black hair, matched with thick eyebrows and hairy hands. He sneered when he spoke, in a sharp Welsh accent that revealed contempt for all his customers. As far as he was concerned, if you had to eat offal, then you were the dregs at the bottom of the social barrel.

"Two pounds of best beef liver," the butcher said, as he rolled the meat in a piece of greased paper and slapped it down on the counter. "That will be three pence, missus."

Winnie O'Connor leaned in toward the counter. "That doesn't look like two pounds to me."

Butcher Jones shot her a menacing look. "What did you say, missus?"

In a sheepish voice, she responded, "I asked for two pounds of beef liver, and that doesn't look like two pounds to me."

"It's two pounds. Do you want it or don't you? If you don't, then clear off. There are other customers waitin'."

"It's not two pounds," Hannah chimed in. "Yer had a finger on the scale—I saw it."

The Butcher's face turned scarlet. "What? Are you calling me a cheat, you Irish trollop? Who the hell are you? Get the hell out of my shop, right now!" His outburst won no friends in a queue comprised of Irish Catholic housewives.

Hannah shrugged. "Weigh it again and prove me wrong. This time without the help of yer finger."

"Get out of my shop now, both of you!" The butcher rounded the counter, grabbed Winnie by the back of her coat, and pushed other women in line out of his way as he shoved her out the door. She stumbled and fell onto the pavement, twisting her ankle. He turned and grabbed Hannah. Her left fist was already curled behind her back, primed and ready.

For the women in line, the sickening splat was hard to forget. Butcher Jones stood motionless with his back against the counter. A trickle of blood seeped from his nose to mix with the animal blood on his apron. He opened his mouth to speak, but nothing came out. There were red rings of blood around his teeth. Slowly, he turned and walked unsteadily into the back room of his shop.

Five seconds later, Milly Jones, the butcher's wife, stormed out of the back room. She was a little mole of a woman, about half the size of her husband, with a prematurely wrinkled face and rage in her eyes.

"What in God's name is goin' on here!?" Milly asked. "Who did this to my husband?"

"An Irish trollop," Hannah replied.

"I'll slice her in two!" Milly picked up a cleaver and charged at Hannah, who bounded out of the door. Hannah leapt over Winnie, who was being helped up from the pavement by two other women. Milly Jones crashed into them, landing face down, with her skirt pulled high up her skinny legs. Hannah jammed her foot down on Milly's wrist. She bent down and pried the cleaver out of Millie's hand.

"Calm down, Milly. Yer husband will mend well enough. Look, if yer gonna marry a Protestant, and a Welsh one to boot, yer should expect the occasional fracas."

The incident could have ended there, but the proceedings on the pavement had been witnessed by a bobby walking his beat, on the other side of the street. He dashed across, pulling out his truncheon as he ran, as if drawing his trusty sword to chase off Viking marauders. The policeman placed his truncheon on Hannah's shoulder and carefully took the cleaver from her hand.

"It's not my cleaver," said Hannah. "Take yer stick off me, or I'll shove it where the monkey keeps his nuts."

"I know it's not your cleaver. I saw that woman come at you," the policeman said, slowly removing his truncheon. He bent down to talk to Milly Jones, who now sat on the pavement nursing a scraped knee.

"Okay, missus, I know the sign on your shop says 'Family Butcher' but I think you may have misinterpreted its meaning." He looked around at the small crowd that had gathered. "Right. Will someone tell me what happened here?"

Up spoke Mary O'Neil. "We caught the butcher palming his scales and when we accused him, he went berserk, throwin' Winnie out onto the pavement. He would have done the same to Hannah, but she clobbered him in self-defense. Along comes Milly, his wife, who throws a fit and charges at Hannah with that cleaver. I think hot heads must run in the family."

"She wouldn't have hurt me," Hannah said. "She was just sticking up for her husband. Milly and me are old school chums—she was a bit high-strung even then. Don't make too much of this, Constable. It's no more than a little squabble."

"So nobody's pressing charges?" the policeman asked.

"No. We wouldn't know how," Winnie O'Connor said.

The policeman put his truncheon back on his belt. "Right then, I don't want to hear of any more shenanigans from you ladies. I'll have enough trouble with yer husbands when they get home from the war."

When the policeman had gone a good ways, Winnie whispered to Hannah, "I didn't know you and Milly Jones are friends."

"We're not—I hardly know the woman," Hannah replied. "But with a husband like that, she doesn't need more trouble."

❖

Hannah trudged home without any meat. She made a pot of tea and sat with her mother in the kitchen. Hannah bounced little Vera on her knee.

"What meat did you get?" Granma White asked, as she saucered her tea.

"None. I'll get some from the Haymarket later. We can't shop at the offal shop any more."

"And why?"

"I clobbered Richard Jones, the butcher."

"What is this, a new hobby?"

"He manhandled me, so I slugged him." Hannah pulled her head back, closed her eyes and grinned. "You should have seen the look on the poor man's face."

Hannah jumped from her chair. "Hold little Vera for me. Doris is napping, and I'll be back before Eileen gets home from school." She set off down Price Street, with a spring in her step, toward the Birkenhead Haymarket.

❖

There is no town quite like Birkenhead in the whole of England. For a thousand years it was an innocuous village on the Wirral Peninsula, sandwiched between the River Mersey to the north and the River Dee to the south. When the booming port of Liverpool ran out of room, the shipping magnates looked across the Mersey for cheap expansion. In no more than a decade Birkenhead had become a major industrial center.

First there came the docks, miles of them, opened in 1847. Then Scotsman John Laird, one of the fierce businessmen who drove the Industrial Revolution, built a shipyard down the Chester Road. A couple of miles further east, William Lever, a man ahead of his time, sited his Sunlight Soap factory.

The street that Hannah now walked down was built at the same time as all the other streets near the river. The Irish laborers who lived there had left their fields to come over and work the docks, build the ships, and make the soap.

Hannah approached the Haymarket, bounding past tenement houses, pubs, second-hand clothing stores, pawn shops, and a Catholic church named after a long-dead martyr. If one could take this part of Birkenhead and drop it in the middle of Dublin, no one would be any the wiser.

The dreary streets of the working class ran in a semicircle from the docks to the shipyard. Layered next to them stood the middle-class houses, semi-detached and detached, with their small lawns, their greenhouses, and their snobby pretentions. The final layer was the mansions of the nobs and bosses, who the working class called gaffers, with their high walls, servants, and guard dogs. Liverpool businessmen and other white-collar workers found it more expedient to live on the Wirral Peninsula than in the crowded outskirts of Liverpool. They crossed the Mersey each day by ferry boat, sometimes returning by a railway that ran under the river, emerging in Birkenhead, fanning out to the suburbs. An extensive tram service ran throughout the town to aid the daily commute.

Before Hannah reached the Haymarket, she stopped in the public library next door. Reading was Hannah's pleasure. Reading history was her passion, a passion she had developed by reading to her mother more evenings than she could remember.

"If you don't know history, how can you know your place in it?" Granma White would often pontificate.

"If you say so, Ma," Hannah would reply. Hannah left the library to the booming sound of the one o'clock gun. The gun was a Russian cannon captured at the battle of Balaclava during the Crimean War, now fired every day from the observatory on Bidston Hill, as a signal for all the ships on the River Mersey to synchronize their chronometers.

Finally, Hannah entered the Haymarket, a boisterous shopping Mecca, jam-packed with more than a hundred stalls, inside and out, selling just about everything, except perhaps, hay. It was here that Michael Marks had opened his penny bazaar, which he built into the department store empire, Marks and Spencer. In addition to the stalls, people sold all sorts of items from the backs of lorries or out of push carts. Some of them were slicksters who would pinch your boots then sell them back to you. Signs hung in all the aisles, warning shoppers to beware of pickpockets; although in reality, the signs were a warning to the pickpockets, because anyone caught stealing in the Haymarket could count themselves lucky if they still had all their teeth by the time the bobbies came to rescue them.

Everywhere Hannah went in the Haymarket she could smell fish. Everything was negotiable, especially the fish. After a bit of haggling, Hannah bought some beef tongue from one of the many butcher shops, and some wool for her mother's knitting. There were no white collars here in the market, no nobs either—they shopped in Grange Road or Liverpool. This market, with its wonderful earthy atmosphere, was meant for the likes of Hannah and her people—hardworking, hard-drinking, God-fearing, salt-of-the-earth folk who rarely took life seriously. They were poor, but they hardly knew it because they never had anything to compare themselves to.

"Hey, Hannah," yelled Mrs. Smith from Laird Street, "I hear yer punched the butcher on Price Street. Come over and smack me old man a bit. The old bugger's getting a bit too cranky."

Good God, thought Hannah, how fast did that get around?

❖

The next morning, Hannah helped the undertaker on Conway Street prepare some souls to meet their maker. When she got home, a black-edged telegram sat unopened on the kitchen table.

"A telegram came," her mother said.

Hannah gulped. "I can see that. Who's it for, you or me?"

"It's for you, thank God. I couldn't bear to lose another son."

Hannah opened it. It began "The Admiralty regrets. . . ."

"Well?" said Granma White.

"Missing, presumed dead." Hannah said. She folded the telegram neatly and, with a deep sigh, put it back into its envelope and placed it gently back onto the table. She picked up baby Vera and kissed her forehead, holding her there while she tried to cry silently, so her mother would not hear her.

"Yer cryin' over John Luxton?" her mother asked. "God rest his soul?"

"I'm not cryin' over John Luxton. I'm cryin' for my girls who'll have no father. I must go to the church. I'll talk to Eileen and Doris when I come home." She kissed the baby again and handed her over to her mother.

Hannah threw on her faded green coat and made her way to Saint Lawrence's Church in a drizzling rain. Kneeling at the front pew, she gazed up at the altar, behind which hung a huge wooden crucifix, vividly painted in colors of flesh, red, and white. Blood seeping from his head, hands, side, and feet, the twelve-foot Savior looked down on Hannah with eyes of agony.

She clasped her hands and bowed her head. "Please forgive me, God. I didn't mean it when I prayed for him to die. I just wanted him to go away." Then she deftly shifted the blame. "Being God, I would'a thought you knew I wasn't serious—just angry. It wasn't too bad in the early days. After all, he is the father of me children and he wasn't a bad father. It was the drink that changed him, but I didn't mean for him to die." Hannah took a breath to collect her thoughts.

"I blame that fat Tory pig for all this—for this terrible war. He cares nothing for us but to build his ambitions and his empire."

To Hannah, all the evils of the ruling class, in their oppression of the working class, were personified in the form of one aristocratic politician: First Lord of the Admiralty, the Right Honorable Winston Spencer Churchill, M.P.

Hannah left the church as quickly as she had entered, still caught in the rain, as she raced off to the dole office to sign up for a widow's pension.

When Hannah returned home, she found her mother, Uncle Charlie, and Father Flaherty, Saint Lawrence's parish priest, yapping around the kitchen table, sipping Uncle Charlie's illicit, homemade potato whiskey.

"Good heavens, girl," Uncle Charlie said. "You're wet through. Where have you been?"

"I suppose my mother has told you that I'm a widow." Uncle Charlie and the priest nodded.

"God rest his mortal soul," the Priest said.

Hannah took off her wet coat, shivered, and pulled a shawl over her shoulders. "Have you and the girls eaten?" she asked her mother.

"Yes, Charlie brought over fish and chips from the Beckwith Street chippie. We saved some for yer."

Hannah told them she'd been to the dole office, waiting in a queue that stretched outside the building. The office was running out of money, she told the group, because so many were slain. She would have to go back with her marriage certificate, the death certificate, birth certificates of all the family, and John Luxton's services pay book. Hannah bowed her head. "His pay book is at the bottom of the North Sea." The woman at the office had told her that without the pay book, it could take three months to process her widow's pension request.

Granma White asked, "What does *presumed killed* mean, anyway?"

"It means they never found his body. He either drowned or was blown off the ship by an explosion," Uncle Charlie said. "The newspapers say it was a mighty battle with many lives lost."

"Who won?" Granma White asked.

"It's hard to tell. The Germans might believe they won because they sunk more ships. On the other hand, the Admiralty declared a victory because the German ships turned about and scampered back home with our ships on their tails."

"Who is master of the seas?" Granma White asked.

"I suppose we still are," said Charlie.

"Then we won," she said. "In any battle in history, the victor is not the one who suffers least casualties—it's the one who's left in possession of the battlefield."

Hannah pulled her shawl tighter over her shoulders. "It's chilly in here. We have no coal left, do we?" she asked her mother. "And we already owe three weeks rent. I can barely make enough washing bodies to keep us in food." She surveyed her dingy little kitchen—the cold stone floor, the smell of cooking grease, the grubby whitewashed walls. The sticky fly paper hanging from the ceiling was covered in little black victims, with hardly a space left. I'm so poor, I can't even afford new flypaper, she thought.

Hannah covered her face with her hands and whispered through her fingers. "Without a pension we are destitute." A cloud of silence fell over the group.

Father Flaherty finally spoke. "So many of my parishioners are destitute, it's a crime. I hear they're opening two new poorhouses. The church's poor box is empty, but I'm going to the convent tomorrow, and perhaps the Little Sisters of the Poor can help you."

"We'll not see you starve," Uncle Charlie said.

"Thank you, Charlie, but you barely have enough to feed yer own family," Hannah said.

"I have a few shillings put by," Granma White said. Hannah grasped her mother's left hand to look at her fingers.

"Oh mother, you've pawned yer wedding ring again."

"It's not so important," Granma White said.

Solemnly, Hannah looked around the table. "I'm grateful fer yer offers but I'm the sole head of this family now, and we'll not survive on charity."

I may be proud, Hannah thought, but as long as breath is in me, this family will not end up in the poorhouse. I'll keep my mother and children with food in their bellies—good food, not scraps or tripe. They'll not shiver in their beds, or go to school in rags. As God is my judge, no snotty bureaucrat, no fat Tory politician, no rich bastard of a landlord will hurt them. I'll find a way.

Later that night, Hannah mounted the stairs to bed, quietly, so she wouldn't wake Eileen or Doris, who shared her bed. By the light of her candle she could see Eileen's shoes on the floor. She picked them up. They were soaked through. Turning them over, she could see the shilling-sized holes in the soles. Inside each shoe the pieces of cardboard that blocked the holes were soggy and warped. A child could catch her death of cold in these shoes, she thought. Hannah blew out the candle, got into bed and whispered to herself, "God help anyone who gets in my way."

Chapter Three

⟹ 1916 ⟸

The Shipyard

The next morning, Hannah put on her best dress, pulled John Luxton's old bicycle out of the shed, and pedaled the two miles to the Birkenhead Shipyard, Cammell Laird. In the hiring office, she stood in front of the desk of the hiring manager, Percy Thompson, a gangly man with a drooping face and an empty jacket sleeve by his side. He looked up at Hannah from his ledger.

"Wrong place, missus. Office work is the green building." He spoke with a strong Merseyside accent. Hannah smiled. He's one of us, she thought.

"I don't want office work. I can't do office work. I want a man's job, at a man's pay."

"That's a laugh. Unless you're a welder or a boilermaker, the only jobs we're short of are laborers, and that's hard bloody work, luv. It's not fer women. And you'll never get any job that's paid the same as a man—I'll tell yer that fer nowt."

"Why not?"

"Because men have families to feed."

Hannah bristled. "Why the hell do yer think I'm standin' here? My husband's killed in the war. I've three children and no pension. I'm strong and I'm healthy, and you'll get a fair day's work from me." Hannah caught a glimpse of sympathy in his expression. He leaned back in his chair, chewing his bottom lip as he wrestled with a decision.

"Well yer have the mouth of a laborer, that's for sure." He slammed the only hand he had, on his desk, and stood up. "All right, missus, wait here while I go check with the big bosses. We really are desperate for laborers."

Hannah sat down on a nearby bench. Workmen and office women came and went; each looked at her curiously. Time passed such that Hannah thought Percy had forgotten about her, until an office girl came in and gave her a cup of tea and a cheese sandwich. "He'll be back," she assured her. "He's tryin' to get to the top bosses."

Meanwhile, Percy had finally managed to get some time with the two most important men in the shipyard: General Manager Robin Frobisher, a tough-faced, no-nonsense taskmaster; and Managing Director John MacGregor, a young idealist, full of energy, and grandson of the shipyard's founder. They listened, stony-faced, while Percy pleaded Hannah's case.

"Look sirs, this could be the answer to our labor shortage. With all the young laborers off to the war, where else will we find enough labor to meet our building schedule? Do we import Chinese or Russians, maybe? Yet right here, in this area, we have an untapped labor source—young women, thousands of 'em, with their menfolk off fightin' the Hun, desperate to feed their hungry children. Why not give it a try?"

Robin Frobisher took off his spectacles and placed them on the table in front of him. He put his elbows on the table and clasped his fingers together. Percy knew that was a bad sign—Frobisher was about to give him a lecture.

"Look, Thompson, it's unseemly, women working as laborers. It's not Christian, either. Women are meant for the kitchen and the nursery. They are simply not equipped with either the physical strength or the mental capacity to perform the type of work that we need. And who will look after the children while they're at work here?" He paused to put on his spectacles. "I'm sorry this woman has fallen on hard times. This damn war has been a tragedy for many people." Percy nodded. He was aware that Frobisher had lost one of his sons at the battle of Mons.

"Maybe she can serve food in the canteen, if there's a job available." Frobisher paused again. "Frankly, Thompson, I'm surprised that you've brought this foolish suggestion to us. I would have thought you had better things to do."

Percy winced at the rebuke. For a brief moment he considered firing back with sarcasm, but he quickly thought better of it. "Sir, these women are made of stern stuff. They come from the stock of Irish farm women who toiled in the fields from dawn to dusk, with their youngest tied to their backs. They survived when the weaker ones died off. There's nothing frail or squeamish about them. As for their children, they'll attend school during the day and play out in the streets in the evening, as they always do. At least we can let them play with food in their bellies."

John MacGregor nodded in agreement, then turned to address his fellow manager. "Look Robin, our situation is critical and grows worse each week. German subs sink more cargo ships than the shipyards can build. Without food and munitions from America and Canada, it won't be long before it's not only street urchins that starve, but the entire nation, and then we'll have no option but sur-render. We must try anything and everything to build more ships, so go ahead, let Thompson hire this woman as a laborer, then more like her. We will give it a one month trial period and monitor it closely."

"Your decision then, John—not mine," Frobisher said, as he glow-ered at Percy, who realized that he had just made a powerful enemy for himself and Hannah.

◆

Hannah rose from the bench when Percy returned. She could see from the smile on his face that he had been successful.

"All right, missus," he said, "yer start at seven in the mornin', finish at six in the evenin', a half hour break at noon, two ten-minute tea breaks. Most evenings there will be overtime if you want it. Your pay is fifteen shillings per week. No special considerations because yer a woman, and I wanna hear no complaints from the men that you're not pullin' yer weight. Nor do I wanna hear any whinin' from yer—no talk of unions, no excuses because it's that time of the month, no emancipation nonsense, and no complaints if yer groped, or pinched, or whistled at."

"I can take care of myself," Hannah replied.

"Are you the woman who decked her husband in the Garrick Snug, by any chance?"

"That's me."

Percy smiled in approval. "Then I guess you *can* take care of yer self. But listen, Hannah, be aware that you're on a trial period, so if it works out, the door will be open for more women like you."

"Am I gettin' paid the same as the men?"

"Fat chance," Percy said. "But it's more than you'll get anywhere else in this town."

"That I know." Hannah nodded. "I'll see you at seven tomorrow." As he watched her walk away, Percy Thompson grimaced and thought, *My God, what was I thinkin'? I've just bet my job on that woman!*

◆

Cycling home, Hannah felt uneasy. She had the employment that she sought, at a wartime pay that would provide well for her family. But if she failed it would prevent other women from getting the same chance, and that was a responsibility that she had neither foreseen nor wanted.

That evening, Hannah pulled John Luxton's workman's overalls from the cupboard and took in the arms and legs to fit her. The overalls hung like a bag on her frame, which was exactly what she aimed for. The last thing she needed in her new job was to draw attention to her female shape.

◆

Next morning, with the sun barely up, Hannah joined the thousands of workers headed toward the shipyard gates. She wore an old coat wrapped over her modified overalls and a thin cotton scarf that her mother had donated. Her hair was pulled up into a bun. Her clothes kept her from the slight morning chill, but didn't disguise the fact that she was a woman. Even riding her husband's bicycle failed to convince anyone that she wasn't who she was. It was considered unbefitting, at any level of society, for a woman to ride a man's bicycle. To Hannah, it was tram fare saved.

Arriving at the shipyard's huge wooden gates, Hannah checked in at the policemen's hut and moved on to the hiring office. Through the crowd of men, Percy spotted her.

"Wait outside, Hannah. Someone will be with yer in a minute."

She walked outside and leaned against a wall. The sight before her overwhelmed her senses: a throbbing panorama of a shipyard

23

at full capacity and human industry in every shade of gray. Lorries, big and small, some carrying huge slabs of bright steel, discharged their loads, while many more outside the gates waited their turn. Thousands of men scurried to their work: boilermakers, carpenters, drillers, plumbers, riveters, electricians, painters, fitters, engineers, draughtsmen, riggers, office workers—an endless array of trades.

Huge cranes hovered over everything like giants waiting to snatch up their prey. Welding torches flashed their short lightning bursts, spraying yellow sparks back at the welders. The smell of burning metal and petroleum consumed the air, while enormous amounts of pulsating energy from men and machines fed the monstrous steel amalgamation. Foremen, with their white shirts and cloth neckties, oversaw the whole, like Pharaoh's guards, jig-sawing each part together to produce the final magnificent product: an ocean-going ship.

Ships, big and small, warships and merchant ships, in various embryonic stages, stretched down wet and dry docks of the River Mersey. A behemoth amongst them all, a mighty Dreadnought battleship awaited final inspection. Her giant guns attested to the fact that she was the most mobile and deadly killing machine yet devised by man, capable of lobbing huge shells from horizon to horizon or razing a port city to ashes in an afternoon.

I'm now a part of this, Hannah thought. She asked Saint Anthony to give her the strength to gain the men's respect. Out of nowhere, a lonely chestnut horse came racing through the shipyard, just feet away from where she stood. She imagined it must have escaped from the harness of a local trader. The terrified animal, a leftover from another century, swerved to avoid lorries and men, in an effort to find a safety that didn't exist. You poor creature, Hannah thought. God help us both.

A voice brought her down to earth. "Are you Hannah Luxton?" A round little man with a weather-beaten face smiled at her. "Terry McCartney's the name. I'm a driller, and you've been assigned to me as a driller's mate. Let's get a cuppa in the canteen, and I'll tell you yer responsibilities. It's allowed on your first day."

As they walked together, Hannah noticed his slight limp. "What's in all the big long buildings?" she asked.

"They're called sheds. They hold workshops, and each skill has its own shed: drillers' shed, plumbers' shed, and so on."

Hannah put her elbows on the table and clasped her fingers together. "Does it bother you havin' a female as your driller's mate?" she asked.

"Don't be daft," Terry replied. "I get to work with an attractive lady all day, instead of some dodderin' old geezer smellin' of stale beer and pickled onions. I'll be the envy of all my workmates." Terry turned serious. "Here's how it is, Hannah. I'll teach you all I know about drilling steel, and how to survive in this shipyard, so listen carefully. Most of the steel that comes into the yard has been pre-drilled for rivets at the foundry. We drillers do the rest, either in the drillers' shed or on board the vessels. I'll teach you how to drill a hole as straight as a hangman's rope." Hannah smiled at the thought of it.

Terry continued. "The large holes will take the two-handed drill. We work that together, so I hope you're stronger than yer look. You'll sharpen the drill bits every morning," he continued, "and yer'll learn to mark out an exact drilling location. Okay so far?" Hannah nodded.

"A lot of tradesmen won't share their knowledge with their laborers because the more others know, the more competition there is for their jobs. Not me. I'll teach you everything I've learned."

"I thank yer for that," Hannah said. "But why would yer do it if it puts your job in jeopardy?"

"We've got a war to win," he replied. "Nothin' else matters."

"How long have yer been a driller?"

"Just over a year. Before that, I was a merchant seaman running the gauntlet across the North Atlantic. My ship was torpedoed from under me. Me and my mates spent four days in an open lifeboat before a destroyer picked us up. I was lucky, 'cept for losing a couple of toes to frostbite."

"Another cuppa?" asked Hannah. Terry pushed his cup forward.

"First lesson," he continued. "Safety. A shipyard is a dangerous place. Every day, someone is injured. There're many deaths, which is why ambulances are always on stand-by at the shipyard gates. The most danger is in the staging—that's the platforms built so people can work off the ground. We'll spend a lot of time on staging. If it feels shaky, get off and don't get back on until it's stable. Understand?" Hannah nodded.

"Second, is the electric. Don't trust any electric connection. Many electricians are not qualified, so always check the connections before you plug in your drill. I'll show yer how."

They left the canteen and walked toward the quays. Passing workmen nodded at Terry, but did a double take when they saw Hannah. One fellow driller stopped them, pointed at Hannah, and asked Terry, "Where can I get one of those?" Hannah smiled.

"Yer too ugly," Terry replied. They turned a corner toward the drillers' shed.

Hannah asked, "Who do yer report to?"

"Workers report to charge hands, who report to supervisors, who report to foremen. Beware the foremen. They may talk like us, but their allegiance is to the bosses. You can't be a foreman unless yer a registered bastard." Hannah grinned.

"There are three types of workers—skilled, like carpenters and plumbers, semi-skilled like drillers and crane drivers, and last, I'm afraid, are laborers like you. These are the men—I mean people— who have no skill to offer, only muscle. Still, if you're a quick learner, you could be promoted to driller, and that would mean more money. In wartime, skilled and semi-skilled shipbuilders are given deferred status—which means they can't join up even if they wanted to—and laborers are not. Any more questions?"

"Sure," said Hannah. "Do yer smile all the time?"

"Only when I'm awake. When I'm asleep, I snore!"

Hannah laughed. "I think we're going to get along just fine."

◆

There were no easy jobs in the shipyard, Hannah soon learned. It was a continuous, hard slog. During wartime, discipline was a little more slack because skilled people were scarce, but during peacetime, you could be sacked for the slightest infraction: smoking, chatting, taking too long in the toilets, or making tea—even though tea was the fuel that kept the men going.

It was tea during the day and beer at night, although sometimes the call of beer during the day was so powerful that men went "over-the-wall." This involved scaling the eight-foot wall that surrounded the port side of the shipyard, even in places where it was reinforced by barbed wire, and heading for the nearest pub, then climbing back when the call had died to a murmur. Going "over-the-wall" meant instant dismissal if you were caught. Hannah could never understand why a man would risk his livelihood for a glass of beer.

Terry and Hannah got along famously. He was easygoing and always cheerful. She would traipse after him as he limped along the quays, moving from ship to ship. He carried his metal tool box; she carried the heavy electric drill slung over one shoulder, with a large coil of electrical cable over the other, and a smaller drill in each hand. She looked like a Roman slave girl, but she refused any help from Terry to lighten her load. "If a man can do it, so can I. That's what I promised Percy Thompson."

❖

Hannah sat on the hard deck in the engine room of a frigate, with her boots pressed up against a steel bulkhead. She marked off the locations before she drilled ten small pilot holes into the bulkhead. She then fitted a one-inch drill bit into the big shoulder drill, grasped the side grip with her right hand, the front grip with her left, positioned her left shoulder against the shoulder pad, and fired up the drill.

Hannah carefully positioned the drill bit over a pilot hole and pushed. "Keep it straight," Terry said. The drill bit took, biting into the steel.

"Constant pressure," Terry said.

Vibrations began to pulsate through her left arm and shoulder, gradually spreading throughout her entire body.

"Fight the torque! Fight the torque!" Terry said.

Hannah gritted her teeth. Shards of twisted metal peeled away, black smoke spewed from the drill bit, the smell of burning steel filled her nostrils. Hannah held firm. The solid muscle of her left arm, the same muscle that drove the fist of doom, forced the drill slowly but surely into the screaming steel.

"It's Hannah against the Birkenhead Steel Foundry!" Terry yelled. "It's Hannah against the Sheffield Steel Company!" he roared. With a shuddering jerk, the drill bit crashed through the bulkhead to the other side. Hannah pulled the drill back, switched it off, and bowed her head.

"And the winner is!" Terry yelled, "HANNAH, THE BIRKENHEAD BOMBSHELL!"

Hannah sweated like a horse that had just won the derby. Her muscles ached, and her head throbbed, yet she managed a slight smile.

"Yer a natural," Terry said, as he helped her up from the deck. "That's one down, nine more to go."

◆

Hannah tried to get home each night to spend at least an hour with the girls before they were abed. There was no one to cook, so they ate a lot of fish and chips or sardines on toast for supper. Eight-year-old Eileen assumed the role of mother. She washed and fed her sisters, shepherded Doris to Saint Lawrence's kindergarten each day, and looked out for them and her grandmother. This is not what I want for my eldest, Hannah thought. I don't want her childhood stolen as mine was, but for now, I have no choice. Hannah would try to read a story to the girls before they slept, but often she fell asleep before they did. Granma White would usher her exhausted daughter to her bedroom, and then return to tell the girls a tall tale of leprechauns and pixies.

◆

The ten minutes the shipyard allowed for tea breaks included the time not only to drink the tea, but also to make it. One morning when Hannah was slow to get the Primus stove primed, a foreman announced that the ten minutes were up and kicked the tin can off the stove. Boiling water splashed against her legs. She pulled her overall pants out quickly to avoid being scalded. The foreman walked away and Hannah followed after him. She curled her left fist behind her back.

He spun around to face her. "Yer got a problem?" he asked.

Hannah took a deep breath. "No, sir," she said, as her fist uncurled.

"Then get on with yer work, woman."

Aside from this incident, the workmen treated Hannah with unusual deference. She expected to be the butt of jokes, or to be whistled at, or at least to be snickered at behind her back. Instead, they were friendly and respectful toward her, in a standoffish sort of way, as they might be toward a foreman.

"Stands to reason," Terry told her. "They all know yer situation. They have brothers, relatives, close friends over in the trenches, sacrificing their lives for king and country, while they stay safe at home, workin' for good money. They know that their work is important for the war effort, but it's not the same as fightin' or dyin'. They're not allowed to join up even if they wanted to, yet they still feel the guilt.

"Then you come along, doin' a man's work to save yer family from the poorhouse, with your husband killed in a great battle. You're the living embodiment of their guilt. They'll never let yer be part of their brotherhood."

❖

One evening, when Hannah had finished her shift, she had barely cycled through the dockyard gates when she heard someone shout her name, causing her to stop and look around. An older man on his bicycle pulled up beside her. He had a ruddy Irish complexion shining out from a drab flat hat and dirty gray overcoat, which was the standard dress code for the working man of the time.

"My name is Gerry, Gerry McCormack," he began. "This is me wife's bicycle." It was colored light blue with shiny chrome handlebars and a wicker basket. "She died about a year ago, of consumption," he said. "You can have her bike."

Hannah was startled. "It's almost new. Look, I couldn't afford—"

He cut her off. "No, it's yours fer free. I could sell it, but I'd rather you have it." He paused for a deep sigh. "My wife was a lot like you—strong-minded, would do anything for the kids, a good Catholic mother and wife. She would want yer to have this bike. A woman shouldn't have to ride around on a man's bicycle."

"You don't even know me," Hannah said.

"I know *of* you. Everyone does," he replied.

Hannah grasped his hand. "God bless yer. I think I'll call it the Blue Angel."

They swapped bicycles and rode away—Gerry McCormack on John Luxton's rusty old bike and Hannah on the Blue Angel.

◆

Thursday was payday in the shipyard, and at quitting time long queues formed at the pay windows. Hannah stood in line calculating the money she had earned that week. Let's see, she thought, fifteen shillings, plus ten hours overtime at time and a half, minus taxes.

When Hannah reached the pay window she opened the small white package and counted the coins. She poked her head back into the pay window. "Hey, I'm shy five shillings!"

"Can't help yer, luv," said the pay clerk. "Go round to the office and ask for Tommy O'Rourke—he'll sort it out."

In the pay office, Hannah stood in a queue again, on one side of a wooden counter with a small gate at one end, which led into the office proper. Tommy O'Rourke was on the other side of the counter, feverishly working on claimed discrepancies in the men's pay. Like most of the men that worked with the women in the office, he was small and frail—too weak to work on building ships and too old to fight in a war.

Tommy studied the previous week's time books. He looked up at Hannah. "Looks like yer were docked for being late three days last week."

"That's a mistake. I was never late."

"Says here that yer were."

"Well, it's wrong. I've been workin' here now for three weeks and never late once. What's goin' on?" Hannah's face reddened.

"I can only go by when the time keeper clocks yer in." He pointed to the time book. "Best you go upstairs and see Mr. Dalglish, the office manager, and lodge a complaint."

Office manager Roger Dalglish fancied himself a dapper man of sophisticated tastes. Coming from a working-class background, he didn't fool anyone. He intimidated the women in the department and ran roughshod over the men. He was frequently rough, gruff, foul-mouthed, and threatening. He didn't hesitate to sack someone for a small infraction, stating that it hurt him to do it, but no one believed him. Barrel-chested, fifty years old and balding, his physique was still imposing. You didn't want to cross him if you could avoid it. A small group of sycophant underlings fed his ego. They called him "sir" to his face and "Roger Ratbag" behind his back.

A prissy secretary sat at her desk in front of Dalglish's office. She peered over her glasses at Hannah, with obvious distain.

"Can I help you?"

"I need to see Mr. Dalglish. I'm shy with me pay."

"Really," she said with a sigh of boredom. "Do you have an appointment?" Hannah shook her head. "Then wait." Hannah looked around for a chair. "Don't sit down," the secretary ordered. "Your overalls are filthy."

After fifteen minutes, Dalglish emerged from his office with another man. They shook hands and the other man left. Dalglish turned to Hannah and looked her up and down. "You must be that new woman laborer."

"Right," said Hannah, as a twinge of uncertainty flashed in her head. Something in his countenance made her think she might be making a dreadful mistake.

"Come on in." He beckoned Hannah toward his office. The room smelled like armpits. Dalglish followed her in, closed the door, locked it, and put the key in his pocket.

Oh God, Hannah thought, what a fool I am!

Dalglish chuckled and moved toward her. "It's true what they say about you. You're a juicy little plum."

Hannah backed away. She could see the menace in his eyes. "Don't come near me."

"Now, don't be stupid, woman." He moved closer. "Here's how it works. You give me somethin', I'll give you somethin'. Make me happy and yer pay will never be docked again, even if you *are* late. It's as simple as that."

"Slimy pig!" Hannah said, now standing her ground. She shook her right fist at him.

"What? Are yer gonna clout me?" He laughed. "I heard yer clouted yer husband before he went off to die in the war. Give it a try, you Irish whore. I like 'em feisty."

He moved toward her again. She swung her right fist at him. He stepped back to his left to catch her right arm in mid-swing, but then realized too late that it was a feint.

Hannah's left hook smashed into his cheek. He staggered backwards, steadying himself on his metal desk, clutching his cheekbone.

"Now yer know I'm a southpaw, yer gormless maggot. You walked right into it."

Still clutching his face, Dalglish barked through the pain. "You bitch. You friggin' bitch. I'll break yer friggin' neck!"

"Language," Hannah said. She took two steps forward and hit him again with her left, this time harder and full into his nose. Roger Dalglish went down and stayed down.

Hannah took the key from his pocket and opened the door. The secretary stood pressed against her desk. "What . . . what was that noise?"

"Did yer hear him lock the door?" Hannah demanded.

The secretary wrung her hands nervously. "Do you mean when you went in?"

"Of course that's what I mean! Did yer hear him lock the door? Yes or no?"

"Yes."

"Then yer a witness. Hold out yer hand, palm up."

She held out a shaky hand, and Hannah dropped the key into it.

"Yer might need a stretcher," Hannah said calmly, nodding to the office door behind her, then walking toward the stairs.

"Wait!" the secretary said.

Hannah turned. "What is it?"

"Thank you," she said. "Thank you a lot."

◆

Tommy O'Rourke looked surprised to see Hannah back so soon. "Are yer all right, luv?"

"Yer snivelin' little rat, yer set me up." Hannah opened the wooden gate that separated them and walked inside the office proper. The other office workers stood up to witness the confrontation. The old man stepped back and held his hands to his chest.

"I'm sorry, luv. I'm really sorry," he stammered. "I had no choice. He would have fired me if I didn't do what he asked. Punched me, then fired me. He told me he would."

Hannah pushed him aside. The old man toppled back against a filing cabinet, then slid to the floor. A female worker helped him to his feet.

"He's an old man," she said. "You could have hurt him."

"He knew what he was doing. He's lucky I didn't punch him." Hannah looked around at the office workers still staring at her. "Yer all knew, didn't yer? And I'm sure I wasn't the first. I'll bet none of yer ever reported Dalglish, yer load of bloody cowards. Now, who do I see about gettin' the money that's owed me?"

◈

Roger Dalglish was fired over the incident. Tommy O'Rourke got off with a two-week suspension. Robin Frobisher wanted to fire Hannah also, on the grounds that if she hadn't been hired, the incident wouldn't have taken place. He changed his mind when it was pointed out to him that she had become an instant hero among the shipyard workers, who would have rioted had she been disciplined in any way.

Hannah had stood up to a hated manager and dropped him like a lump of lead. Now wherever she went in the shipyard she was hailed by the men. They would yell at her and wave, or punch a left fist into the air as a salute. "Hannah the Hammer" they called her. Charge hands would jokingly use her name as a threat to spur on the workers. "Get crackin', yer lazy bastards, or I'll get Hannah the Hammer to sort yer out."

◈

By mid summer, five hundred women were working as laborers at the shipyard, pushing up productivity way beyond the expectations of a delighted management. Hannah became their unofficial leader—another responsibility she never wanted. Management consulted her on all female matters, and she found little opposition in persuading them to construct additional ladies bathrooms, to provide free female overalls and hairnets, and to allow flexible hours for those women with young children. Hannah also let it be known that any man accused of trying it on with a female worker would need to explain his actions to her left fist.

Chapter Four

= 1917 =

Ally for Life

The mild winter that began in 1916 turned harsh the following year, as if nature was trying to balance things out. Terry and Hannah tried to work in the drillers' shed as much as possible, where most of the muscle required for hard drilling was performed by steam-driven machines, and where the cold wind blowing off the Irish Sea couldn't find them. When they had to work on ships in the dock, out on the open deck, most of February was brass monkey weather.

Terry and Hannah toiled all day on a spanking new destroyer, drilling holes in stanchions, through which electricians would run cables. The launch was just three days away so they worked late. Whey they emerged onto the upper deck into a moonless evening, the only lights that lit their way off the ship were the ship's auxiliary night lights, so Terry and Hannah stepped carefully.

Hannah looked over the side of the ship, onto the quay, deserted except for a lonely bobby making his rounds. The bobby stopped abruptly and gave three loud blasts on his whistle. He drew his truncheon, lit his flashlight, and ran into the darkness of a storage shed at the end of the quay. Hannah couldn't see what happened in the shed, but the sound of a scuffle was obvious and ended with a shuddering cry of pain. In the darkness, she could just discern two men as they dragged the bobby across the quay and threw him into the water. The men turned and ran, disappearing into the gloom.

"Good God, Terry, did yer see that!? Two blokes just threw a policeman into the water. I think he was unconscious!"

"I saw it!" Terry scrambled, as best he could, over to the nearest lifebelt, attached to the side of a bulkhead, and pulled it down. "Jesus, this is heavy."

Hannah gave him a hand, and they carried the lifebelt to the quay side of the ship, and then on the count of three, threw it over the side. It landed on the quay with a thud.

Terry yelled at Hannah, "Go get him, luv. You're the fast one. I'll get help!"

Hannah took off, skipped round barely-visible obstacles, and slid down stairways using the handrails, hardly touching the steps.

Terry yelled after her. "He won't survive long in that icy water." Hannah reached the gangway and charged down it like a crazed banshee. Rounding onto the quay, she grabbed the lifebelt and half carried it, half dragged it, down to where the quay ended.

"Where are you?" she yelled into the blackness of the water. "Where are you?"

"Help! Help! I can't swim," came the frantic response.

Thank God he's conscious, Hannah thought. She heaved the lifebelt into the water, toward the voice.

"Grab the lifebelt!" she said.

"Where is it? I can't see it!"

He began splashing, and Hannah could now make out the bobby in the water, about ten feet from the side of the dock.

"I'm drowning!" he screamed. "I can't see."

"Turn around. The lifebelt is behind you—five feet away," Hannah said. "Keep calm. Flap your arms like you're flying and kick your legs like you're pedaling a bicycle."

"I can't turn. I can't swim!"

"Damn you, Copper!" Hannah said. She pulled off her boots, threw off her overcoat, and jumped into the freezing water. The icy shock hit her like a bolt of lightning; she fought hard to ward off a scream. She surfaced, coughing, spitting dirty dock water. The lifebelt was within grabbing distance. Hannah pushed it toward the drowning man. Both of them grabbed it at the same time.

"Just hold on. Help is on the way." He pulled the lifebelt down as if he was trying to climb onto it, which pushed it down into the water. "Stop that!" Hannah said. "You'll drown both of us, you idiot! Calm down."

Soon they heard the sound of many boots running toward them along the quay.

"Over here," Hannah called out.

Four beams of light shone on them. "Here's a rope—grab it!"

Hannah tied the rope around the lifebelt and she and the policeman held onto it as they were pulled toward the quay. More ropes were thrown; strong hands came down and pulled them out of the water.

Hannah was surrounded by policemen. The shipyard ambulance arrived with towels and blankets. She took off her wet clothes in the privacy of the ambulance and wrapped her shivering body in the coarse blankets. The bobby was brought into the ambulance on a stretcher, accompanied by a nurse, who bandaged his head.

"How are yer?" Hannah asked as he turned his head to face her.

"Thank you for rescuing me," he said with a weak voice.

"You're welcome. So, what happened?"

"I saw one feller in the shed jimmying open a crate, but I didn't see the other feller come up behind me. They beat me with my own truncheon," he said, as if it were a great disgrace.

"Did yer get a good look at 'em?" Hannah asked.

"No, it was too dark. Did you?"

"Me neither, but one of them was a good three inches taller than the other, and stockier."

"What's your name, luv?" He gripped his side and grimaced in pain.

"Hannah Luxton. What's yours?"

"Ah, Hannah the Hammer. I might have known. My name's Mathew Baker. I owe you my life, Hannah Luxton. I'm sorry I panicked in the water. I had blood running into my eyes. I can't swim, you see."

"That makes two of us," Hannah said.

❖

There was nothing in the newspapers about the incident, to Hannah's disappointment. She was hoping for some public recognition for her part in the drama. Two days later, however, the *Liverpool Echo* and the *Birkenhead News* reported that a shipyard policeman had gone missing, and foul play was suspected.

"What's goin' on?" she asked the police sergeant at the dock gates.

He whispered in her ear. "The papers printed what we asked them to print. If they think it's safe, we're hoping those two fellers will come back. Keep it to yerself."

"Ilow's the bobby?"

"He has two broken ribs and a gash to his forehead. He'll be fine."

Three days later, two young louts dragged welder's mate Margie McDonnell into a freighter crew cabin and tried to ravish her. She fought them off until a bosun's mate arrived to find out the cause of the bother. Margie escaped with her virtue intact, at the expense of a fat lip, a torn blouse, and a missing chunk of hair.

"Would yer recognize 'em if you saw 'em again?" Hannah asked the next day.

"Sure would," Margie said. "One was tall and one was short—young fellers, mean and nasty. The tall one wore a red scarf and the small one had really bad teeth. I don't think they're from 'round here—they spoke more Liverpool than Birkenhead."

There's a difference? Hannah wondered. "If yer see 'em again, get a policeman or come and get me, tout bloody suite."

A few days later, Margie sought out Hannah in the shed. "Quick," she said. "Those two fellers are out in number eight warehouse."

Inside the warehouse, Hannah quickly spotted them. She looked them over. Eighteen, maybe nineteen, she thought. The taller one wore a red scarf and a docker's flat cap, turned at an angle over his acne-spotted face. The smaller one looked mean, like he was born looking for trouble. Hannah followed them as they sneaked behind a stack of wooden pallets and lit up a cigarette.

"You'll be fired on the spot if a foreman catches yer smokin', particularly in a warehouse," Hannah said.

"Bugger off," said the small one.

"Language." Hannah moved within striking distance of him, her left arm poised behind her back. "Are youse the lads that attacked Margie McDonnell?"

"She asked fer it." The smaller one grinned. "You could tell she wanted it, but then she got all coy and changed her mind."

"So you beat her up?"

He pushed his face up close to Hannah's and looked her up and down like she was a piece of meat. "Yer gotta smack 'em around a bit, otherwise they get uppity. Yer should know that." He paused and pulled back a step. "Wait, are you the skirt that goes 'round punchin' auld fellas?"

"Not necessarily. I punch young ones, too."

"Well, come and try it on me, missus—I'll beat the snot out of yer."

Hannah spun around and smashed her fist into the tall thug's face. With a spurt of blood and a yelp, he staggered backward into the arms of a couple of welders who had approached to witness the proceedings.

Hannah turned back to the short one and smiled. "Now, where were we?"

He stood there for a few seconds in awe of the effect of Hannah's punch, weighing his options. Then he turned tail and bolted out of the warehouse. Hannah ran after him.

"Go get him, Hannah!" the welders yelled.

Hannah chased him down the dockside as he dodged and swerved around men, machines, and cargo. It was a great spectacle—a nasty young lout hotly pursued by a fine Irish colleen with vengeance in her eyes. Workers cheered her on like a filly in a horse race. Some jumped in front of Hannah's quarry to slow him down. Hannah was exhilarated. She had forgotten how wonderfully free it felt to run, just run, like she had a few nights ago on the quay, like she had when she was a girl.

The lout rounded a corner of the fitters' shed, tripped on a loose cobblestone, and fell smack-dab in front of a bevy of startled managers. Robin Frobisher and John McGregor were among them. Hannah rounded the corner as the lad tried to get up. A swift kick in the backside knocked him down again.

"What in heaven's name is going on?" John McGregor asked. Hannah dragged up her prey, holding him by the collar of his coat. She gasped for breath. "He and his mate . . . he and his mate . . . this weasel . . . tried to ravish Margie McDonnell, a welder's mate, yesterday."

"Well this is a job for the police, then," Robin Frobisher said. As if on cue, two shipyard bobbies appeared and took hold of Hannah's catch. Like a dog with a rabbit, she was reluctant to let him go—after all, she had done all the hard work.

"You said there were two of them," Frobisher said, looking around.

"Where is the other one?" As soon as Frobisher's head was turned, Hannah brought out the hammer. Her fist in the captured lad's face made a sharp splat, like the sound of a wet rag thrown on a piece of metal. As the lad cried out, Frobisher swung back around to see that the two bobbies had to hold him upright. Blood oozed from his nose.

"Did you just punch him!?" Frobisher asked Hannah.

"Yes, sir."

"Why?" he demanded.

"He was trying to escape."

"No he wasn't," said one of the bobbies.

"Well, he was thinkin' about it," Hannah said. She could see that Frobisher didn't appreciate her flippancy.

"Look, Mrs. Luxton, you have to stop this violence. It is not the way to resolve these incidents. There is a process of law that must be followed. You set yourself up as judge, jury, and executioner—without evidence, without investigation, without witnesses. How do you know that you have the right man?"

"Mainly because he told me he did it." Hannah cleared her throat and adopted a more serious tone. "Look sir, if yer tellin' me to stop, then I will. But I wouldn't want to be the one to tell a soldier that his wife was ravished while he was away fightin' for his country, and no one did a damn thing about it." Frobisher crossed his arms, about to utter a rebuttal, but Hannah kept going. "You see, sir, the law you talk about is not meant for the likes of us working-class folk—it's meant to keep us down, to keep us in our place. It always has. These women don't trust it. Besides, they fear reprisals if they report an assault.

"But a good smack in the gob—now that's a deterrent that rats like this one understand." Hannah brandished her fist in the direction of the bleeding lad. "Anyway, I think you will find that these are the two thugs that threw the policeman into the dock a few nights ago," Hannah said. "Excuse me now, sirs. I have work to do."

❖

The *Birkenhead News* rescinded its previous article and reported that two men had been charged with attempted murder, and that the policeman had been rescued from the dock by shipyard workers. Hannah's name was not mentioned. It didn't matter much. The police knew that Hannah was the hero. All the shipyard workers knew, and the entire town knew. Hannah's capital couldn't have been higher.

Hannah's life had certainly taken a dramatic turn for the better. Now there was money for new clothes, for decent food, for chocolate and shoes and dolls for the girls, even for black shag tobacco for Granma White's pipe.

More than that, though, Hannah was aware that she was changing, growing into a person who was the center of her own being, not the servant of someone else's. Conquering the shipyard had given her confidence aplenty, with respect from everyone around. People would point her out in the shipyard, in the market, in the park. In just nine months she had transformed herself from an Irish biddy who washed dead bodies, to a force to be reckoned with, a woman of stature.

So many of the female shipyard workers came to Hannah for help with their issues that her drill was taken away and she was plopped at a desk in the office. They gave her a fancy title: "Female Worker Personnel Coordinator." It meant more money, getting home at a decent hour, and more time with the kids. Still, hard as it was to be a laborer, she missed her drills, and she missed Terry, such that sometimes she would sneak away to have lunch with him on the roof of a warehouse.

❖

"I need yer help," Percy Thompson said to Hannah in her office one day. "I need a woman."

Hannah grinned. "Will a black eye do instead?"

"No! I mean I need a woman fer a ferry boat that's bein' launched today. The mayor's daughter was scheduled to launch it, but she's come down with the flu. Only women can launch—it's tradition. She's only a ferry boat, but she still needs a proper launchin'. Can you spare the time?"

Hannah followed Percy to the launching site. "What's the boat's name?" she asked.

"All the Mersey ferry boats are named after flowers: Iris, Daffodil, and so on. This one's to be named Hyacinth."

Hannah stood on the launching platform above an unusually large lunchtime crowd of workers. Percy told her to smash the champagne bottle hard against the hull and say "I name this boat . . . and so on."

"I know what to do—I've seen it done dozens of times."

Then she noticed that painted in large white letters on the boat's shiny black hull was "*Hannah.*" A huge smile lit up her face. She swung the ribbon attached to the bottle of champagne, smashing it on the steel hull.

"I name this boat *Hannah.* May God save her and all who sail in her."

The crowd cheered; Percy hugged her. A lump came into her throat. Hannah the Hammer felt like queen of the world.

A child's voice yelled out, "Hurray for our mam!" In the middle of the crowd, waving wildly, was the whole family: Eileen, Doris, Vera, and Granma White, all chaperoned by Uncle Charlie.

"Waste of good French tipple, if you ask me," Granma White whispered to herself.

❖

A month later, Hannah had wrapped up an exhausting week. After months of haggling, with Robin Frobisher providing his usual opposition, Hannah had finally gained management's agreement to implement a bereavement leave of absence. Any woman who produced a recent black-edged telegram could take a week off work, with pay.

She arrived home to find her front door wide open. She parked the Blue Angel in the hall and walked into the kitchen, where Granma White was sitting on a stool, her fists clenched together on her lap. Eileen and Doris were sitting on the floor in a corner, both sobbing. Hannah stiffened.

"Good God, what's happened?"

"It's little Vera," said Granma White. "She's gone missin.'"

"When!"

"About two hours ago, we think. She must have just wandered off. We've searched everywhere. The police have been notified, and half the street is out lookin' for her. Neighbors have been comin' in and out—that's why we left the door open."

Hannah choked. "Where could she have gone? How did she get out? My God, she's barely two years old."

"I was playin' in the backyard. She must have wandered out the back door," Eileen said, still sobbing. "I'm sorry, Mam. I'm sorry."

Hannah reddened. "You're sorry? You were supposed to look after her. I'm out workin' meself to a shadow, tryin' to keep this family from the poorhouse, and you can't keep an eye on yer little sister! It's not much to ask, is it? She could have been hit by a lorry, or by a train. She could have wandered down by the docks. There are foreign ships down there. They could have taken her." Hannah, with hands on hip, glowered at her daughter. "Was it too much to ask?"

Eileen buried her head in her hands, sobbing uncontrollably.

"Don't blame the child. It was my fault—I wasn't payin' attention," Granma White said.

Hannah closed her eyes tight. Her head swirled with anguish. God, what am I doing to Eileen? Hannah thought. What am I saying? Eileen does everything I ask, without complaint. Why am I causing her such distress? I'm so wrapped up in myself that I'm ignorin' my responsibility as a mother.

Hannah took Eileen in her arms. "I'm sorry, my love. It's not your fault. Yer just a child. I'm ter blame. I shouldn't expect a child so young to look after another child, or my blind mother to know where my children are at all times. Forgive me, my sweet, please." Hannah dried Eileen's eyes with her handkerchief, and then blew her own nose with it.

"I'm goin' out to look for her. Keep the door open." Hannah didn't get very far. She was met at the front door by Mrs. Sweeny from Watson Street.

"Is this your child?" she asked, gently pushing little Vera in front of her. "She's all in one piece."

"I'm hungry," Vera said.

"Thank you, God. Thank you." Hannah swept the little girl in her arms, squeezing and kissing her, while Eileen came running and Granma White came waddling, hands in the air.

"Please come in and have a cuppa," Hannah said. "Where did you find her?"

Mrs. Sweeney explained that she had just come home from work, put her bicycle in the backyard shed, and there was Vera asleep in the dog kennel. Vera had probably wandered through the alley and stopped when she grew tired.

"Where was the dog?" Granma White asked.

"In his kennel, curled up with the child."

"What type of dog?" Hannah asked.

"A black lab, name of Kim."

❖

Hannah tried not to cry in public. She thought it left her vulnerable. But being a woman who lived on the edge of her emotions, she wept more than most, like it or not. Shortly after Mrs. Sweeney left, Hannah sat on her bed and sobbed into her pillow. Granma White stood quietly outside her door, listening to her distress. She gently knocked on the door, and then entered.

Hannah looked up with eyes red and swollen. "I'm sorry. I'm just worn out, mind and body. The children are my responsibility, so I'll look after them from now on. It's clear to me what I have to do."

"What's that?" Granma White asked, as she sidled up next to her daughter on the bed.

"I swore I'd never marry again, but now I have no choice but to find another husband."

"Splendid idea," Granma White declared, with a big grin. "Do yer have anyone in mind?"

"Not really, although there are a couple of fellers down at the shipyard who'd like to step out with me."

"What about Pat O'Malley?"

"He's a good friend, but he's too fond of the drink. Besides, he can't keep a job. I must be more selective this time."

Grandma White shrugged. "Well, they all say that you're a fine looking lass and a great catch for any man 'round here. Though, with this war takin' so many away, it's slim pickin's, that's fer sure. What about Peter Corcoran? I hear he's home from the war. Were you and he not sweet on each other when yer were at school?"

Hannah straightened up. "Yes, we were. Is he injured?"

"I heard he was gassed," Granma White replied.

"Well, I'll find someone, and soon—someone solid and decent. Then I'll quit the shipyard and be a mother again."

A pleasant memory flashed into Hannah's head—the day she and Peter Corcoran played hooky and went fishing off Wallasey Dock. She caught six fish and he none. She rubbed it in all the way home.

Hmm, Peter Corcoran, she thought. Gassed? What a pity.

Chapter Five

≈ 1918 ≈

Peter Corcoran

Whenever Peter Corcoran's name came up in conversation, people would whisper, "He was gassed, you know," as if he had contracted some unspeakable disease. Nothing more was said, as if people knew exactly what it meant. No one ever asked him about it, except Hannah. But being gassed set him apart from the rest of the soldiers returning from World War I. It was a voucher of entitlement, demanding respect and deference. People assumed he would probably be dead within the year, or if not, that he carried some hideous deformity under his clothing.

Peter had no such deformity and would die one day short of his ninetieth birthday, sporting the same full head of shiny black hair he'd had since the day he was born. If the truth be known, Peter felt lucky that he had been gassed, because it debilitated him enough to be granted a medical discharge and sent home early. He reckoned being gassed probably saved his life.

As soon as he arrived home from the war, Peter signed on as a registered dock worker to get his old job back. Next, he rosined up his football boots and let the coach of Saint Lawrence's team know that he was available to play again. The following Sunday, Peter and his teammates lost to the Birkenhead Shipyard, three goals to one, in Birkenhead Park. In those days, every team had a child as a mascot. As luck would have it, Hannah's daughter Eileen was the mascot for the shipyard team, and Hannah and her girls watched the game from the sidelines.

A player kicked the ball out of play, with Peter chasing it, close to the spot where Hannah stood. Peter picked up the ball.

"Good God, Hannah, is that you?"

"Peter Corcoran!" She hugged him, although it was closer to an embrace than a hug, which was all the sign Peter needed. "Thank God you're home safe. I heard yer were gassed."

Peter shrugged. "You look smashin', Hannah."

"Would you two mind if we carry on with the game?" the referee asked. "Or at least give us the ball back."

◆

As a rule, Peter didn't like to hold strong opinions, mainly because he could be wrong. One opinion, of which he was absolutely sure, however, was that Hannah would be the perfect wife for him. He had missed the chance to propose to her years before, and she had gone and married that swaggering bum, John Luxton. Peter bit his lip every time he thought about it. Now, he wasn't going to miss the chance again.

The following Saturday afternoon, Peter and Hannah were enjoying a sunny picnic on Bidston Hill, near the windmill. Peter had brought homemade ginger beer, tangerines, and strawberry jam sandwiches, which impressed Hannah to no end.

"If yer don't mind me askin', why did yer marry John Luxton?"

Hannah thought the question impertinent but didn't overreact, not wanting to ruin the occasion or its possibilities. "I was seventeen years old. I had a blind mother, no father, and I was the eldest of four. We were headed for the workhouse, for God's sake. Then John Luxton came along. He had a job, and he asked me to marry him. Sure, I suspected he was a womanizer and a bully, but my options were limited. Besides, he was handsome, a good dancer, and had a lovely singin' voice."

"Have you been punchin' people, Hannah? The lass I knew had a short fuse but never went around punchin' anyone."

"So you've been checking up on me." Hannah flicked an ant off her sandwich. "I punched John Luxton because he hurt my mother, and I doffed some fellas at the shipyard who were bothering the girls. Turns out I've got this devil of a left hook. Come here so I can give yer a demonstration!"

Peter jumped up. Hannah ran after him. He skirted round the

windmill. Around he went three times, with Hannah close on his heels, until he stopped and turned, and she ran into his arms. He kissed her. It was a gentle kiss, not passionate, almost exploratory, to gauge her reaction. He kissed her again, this time with fervor, this time longer.

"Yer the first girl that I ever kissed," he said, as they walked back to their picnic spot, hand in hand.

"What, just now?"

"No, you daft ninny, when we were at school. Remember?"

"And since then?"

"Since then, yer number seven thousand, one hundred and twelve."

They sat down again on the grass, both smiling inside and out. Feelings planted nine years ago had laid dormant, barely fading, waiting for a sunny day, a windmill, and strawberry jam sandwiches.

He looks the same, Hannah thought. That happy, innocent grin of his. A little slimmer, perhaps. But I wonder if the war has changed him.

"What was the war like? Terrible?" she asked.

"Bloody awful. It was just so. . . ."

"Were you gassed?"

"Yes, but it was just the gas that blinds yer fer a couple of days, not the one that chokes yer to death or the one that burns your skin off. I got a good sniff of it, and it damaged my eyes enough that they sent me home."

Hannah's heart sank. That's all I need, she thought, a blind husband as well as a blind mother. The expression on her face revealed her concern.

Peter quickly jumped in to recover his position. "My eyes have gotten a lot better since then, mind. They'll get no worse. I'm as fit as a butcher's dog." There was a long pause. Peter moved closer to Hannah until their hips were touching.

"I'm sorry about your brother," he said. "I heard he was killed at the Marne."

Hannah let out a deep sigh. "Yer spend all that time raisin' 'em, then that fat Tory pig takes 'em away to get killed." Peter poured her another glass of ginger beer.

"You mean Churchill?"

"Who else? What does he care about the likes of us? Cannon fodder for his empire buildin', that's all we are."

Hannah finished her ginger beer. "Let's talk about somethin' else. So now that yer home in one piece, what are you gonna to do with yer life?"

"Well, I've signed on at the docks, and I've joined the Lawries football team and. . . ."

"And what?"

"And I'm lookin' for a wife. Can yer think of anyone?"

"Ha, who would have yer? You're not much of a catch, yer know. Maybe some old dear would take yer out of pity."

Peter grinned. "If yer think of someone, let me know."

Hannah scratched her chin in mock thought. "All right, kiss me again, to see if I can recommend yer."

❖

That evening, Peter swaggered into the Ram's Head Pub, came up behind the seated Alf Richards, and smacked him on the back of the head.

"How are yer doin' there, me old mate? Can I buy yer a pint of the best?"

"What's up with you?" Alf said. "Yer look like yer lost a penny and found a pound."

"Guess who I'm gonna marry?"

"The Queen of Sheba."

"Better."

"Not Hannah White! Your old sweetheart? You lucky bastard!"

"Hannah White, once Hannah Luxton, soon to be Hannah Corcoran!" Peter said, thumping his chest.

"She's a bonnie lassie, that's fer sure," the bartender said. "That one could tempt the pope. But yer better not step out of line or she'll box yer ears."

"No, it's you lot that needs to show me respect, or I'll send her 'round to sort yer out."

❖

Peter and Alf Richards had been best mates since they started at

Saint Lawrence's School at age five. Wherever Alf went, Peter walked at his shoulder. They played truant together, fished together, chased the girls, and got into trouble together. Alf made the decisions and Peter went along, until things went wrong, and then Peter would point to Alf and say, "He made me do it."

Peter was an only child, raised by his grandparents. Alf, one of eight children, spent a lot of time at Peter's house to enjoy the breathing room. Alf needed an affable sidekick, and Peter needed someone to do the thinking for him. The partnership was perfect.

When World War I broke out, Alf joined the artillery, so of course, Peter joined, too. Alf had learned to drive and delivered bread from Hurst's bakery to the nobs' houses on Saturday mornings. The artillery assigned him to a lorry, and assigned Peter as the driver's mate. Other soldiers would often ask them if they were brothers because they looked so alike. They had the same stocky build and were almost the same height, with slick, jet-black hair, twangy Merseyside accents, and mischievous faces—round and red.

Over in France, Alf and Peter trucked goods from the docks to the front. Being dockers before they joined up, the war was mainly a busman's holiday, except for the part where Germans were trying to kill them. Mostly they carried artillery ammunition, but sometimes it could be rations or blankets. Occasionally they would bus new recruits to the front. All too often, they would bring back their bodies.

In 1917, Alf and Peter were back at Ypres in Flanders, two years after they had both been gassed there. In the meantime they had gone from one battlefield to another, made their deliveries, and tried to stay alive.

Alf stopped the lorry at the side of the bumpy road so Peter could look at the map again, hoping to find something he'd missed.

"We're lost," he said. "I think we must have taken a wrong turn at that last crossroads."

"I don't remember that ruined village over there on our outward journey," Alf said. "And judgin' from all that gunfire, we're too damn close to the German lines for my likin'. I'll head over to the village. Maybe we can find some Tommies and get directions."

"Slowly," Peter said.

The village was a collection of destroyed buildings, with a long street that ended at a distant ruined chateau. Alf inched the lorry slowly down the street until debris stopped them.

Peter peered out of the window. "I don't see a soul."

A crack of rifle fire rang out. The right-hand mirror of the lorry exploded in a shower of glass, and a loud bang came from the engine as if it had been hit with a sledge hammer.

"Mother of God! They're shootin' at us! Reverse—quick!" Peter said.

Alf threw the lorry in reverse and gunned it, zig-zagging backwards like a drunken sailor. He hit a large shell hole, and the lorry lurched over onto its side. Two wheels were off the ground, stuck solid. Alf cut the engine. More bullets hit the still lorry, as Peter flung open his door.

"Alf, are yer hurt?" he yelled.

"No, but I'm stuck. Give me a hand."

Peter slithered out of the door. Lying down on the side of the lorry, he tugged on Alf's arm as Alf wriggled. Finally he was free. Another shot was fired, the bullet coming so close that Peter felt it whiz past his head.

"I smell petrol!" Alf said.

The two men jumped behind the lorry as the firing continued. "We can't stay here," Alf said. "That wall over there! Let's run for it!"

They raced across the road and dived behind a jagged brick wall about four feet high. The lorry burst into flames behind them. Peter carefully stuck his head around the wall, causing two more shots to be fired. One bullet went over his head, and the other hit the wall. Peter ducked back.

"Those shots came from a burnt-out building about sixty or seventy yards down the other side of the road," he said. Several more shots were fired, but this time they came from behind the spot where Peter and Alf were pinned down. "Wait," Peter said, "someone's firin' back at those Jerries. Looks like about fifty yards back the way we came."

"I wish we could join in the firin'," Alf said, as he glanced over at the burning lorry, where they had left their rifles.

Alf turned and shouted, "Hey lads, what outfit are yer?"

"Francais," came the reply.

"They're Frenchies," Alf said.

"Now what do we do?" Peter asked.

"There's not much we can do. Best stay put and let the Jerries and the French shoot it out. If the Jerries win, we surrender. If the French win, then it's Viva la France."

They sat back against the wall and watched the lorry burn. "Shame," Peter said. "Bloody good lorry, that."

"It served us well," Alf added, with a nod of his head.

Ten minutes went by. "Listen, they've stopped shootin'," Peter said. He poked his head around the wall, then quickly pulled it back. "Jesus Christ! Alf, take a look."

Alf peered over the wall. In the distance, at the end of the street, a greenish-yellow cloud billowed.

"Chlorine gas! Coming this way! That stuff will kill us!"

"Our gasmasks are in the lorry!" Peter said.

Alf pulled a dirty old handkerchief out of his back pocket. "Quick Peter, have yer got a handkerchief?"

Peter took out an old rag. Alf removed his helmet and urinated into it, then dipped his handkerchief into the urine until it was soaked, emptying the surplus urine onto the ground. Peter tried to do the same but his helmet was dry.

"C'mon Peter, what's wrong?"

"There's nothing there."

"For Christ's sake, Peter, piss in your helmet!"

"I can't force it! When you can't, you can't." Panic strained Peter's voice as they buttoned up their flies.

"Turn around!" Alf pulled his friend's shoulder. "I'll tie my hand-kerchief on you."

"No, it's yours!"

"Take it now! We don't have much time!"

"No! Please!" Peter said, "You can't do this."

"Yes, yes I can."

"Why!"

"Because I can run faster, you idiot!"

Alf tied his urine-soaked handkerchief around Peter's face, cover-ing his nose and mouth. "This will work. The ammonia in the piss neutralizes the chlorine. Breath through yer nose and run like the clappers of hell!"

The two men darted from their wall and bolted back down the

street. Peter looked behind to see the yellow cloud considerably closer, so he ran faster, passing Alf.

"Pace yerself!" Alf shouted. "This is a one-mile race, not a hundred-yard dash." Peter tripped on a piece of charred timber. They both looked back as Alf hauled Peter to his feet. The cloud was getting closer.

As they ran by a side alley, a dozen French Zouves emerged and ran with them. The Zouves, dressed in blue coats, red pants and caps, were a startling sight to the two Tommies, who were used to the drab khaki of most uniforms. A Zouve officer appeared from the alley, yelling and firing his pistol at his fleeing men. He shot the Zouve running next to Peter, in the back. He's killing his own men, Peter thought. What a bastard!

Joined by more and more desperate soldiers, the retreating group kept going, passing through the British lines until they slowed down a half mile further on. With all the exertion, Peter was having trouble breathing through the handkerchief. He stopped and looked around. The green cloud had gone, either dispersed or blown by the wind in another direction. Alf and Peter sat down near a trench to catch their breath. Around them, pandemonium broke loose. Retreating soldiers, many of them gassed, fell back amidst heavy German shelling.

"Don't take the mask off," Alf said. "Yer might still need it." The pair headed west, away from the Germans and their own troops. They stopped again to catch their breath. Peter pulled the handkerchief from his face.

"It's makin' me gag, Alf. What the hell have yer been drinkin'?"

Right then, a British officer appeared from a trench. "Are you two gassed?" he asked.

"We were back in 1915," Alf began, "but now we—" Peter interrupted Alf by throwing up at the officer's feet.

"You're gassed," the officer declared. "Get over there and see that sergeant." The sergeant bundled them into a lorry along with other gas victims, coughing and gagging in the early throes of asphyxiation.

Alf whispered to Peter, "Don't get too close to these poor buggers. They say the gas can linger in clothes."

The lorry took them several miles away to a medical station. There they waited in line, in a large khaki medical tent, to see a doctor.

"Next," cried the doctor. "One at a time."

"We're together, sir," said Alf.

"Fine. You two were gassed?" The doctor, a small round man, with graying hair, spoke in a voice that was a monotone of depression.

"No, sir. We're with the Royal Field Artillery. On a return trip from the front, our lorry was fired on and we crashed. We were pinned down by snipers until we saw the gas cloud, but we outran it. Me mate here threw up on an officer's boots, who thought he was gassed, but it was the urine handkerchief that caused it. The officer sent us here."

"Urine handkerchiefs are more effective than some of these damn gas masks," the doctor said.

"It was his urine handkerchief, not mine," Peter said. "I couldn't pee, so he gave me his handkerchief."

"Now, that is true friendship," the doctor said.

"You didn't really need it," Alf remarked.

"Yes, but you didn't know that at the time," Peter replied.

"We *were* gassed, though, back in 1915 at the second battle of Ypres," Peter told the doctor, "but it was bromide gas, so we were out of commission for just a couple of days."

"So you survived two gas attacks? That's remarkable. Young men come in here, their lungs bursting; most of them will die. . . ." The doctor held his fist to his mouth and looked at the floor. He continued in a hushed tone. "I became a doctor to cure people, to help them survive, but I can't help these boys. There's nothing I can do. What's the good of being a doctor?"

He straightened up. "But I can help you two. I'm recommending a medical discharge for both of you. I'll put 'gassed' on the discharge forms, which is partially true. You obviously were not meant to die here."

Alf and Peter looked at each other, mouths agape.

"Just one thing," the doctor said. "Don't waste your lives."

❖

The war changed people. Soldiers returning from the front, who had experienced the horror of trench warfare, bore scant resemblance to the same men who left. Their senses had been battered daily—the fear, the mud, the rats and lice, the thirst and hunger, the sight of their comrades being slaughtered. They returned home hardened, angry, and confused.

Not so Peter Corcoran. His character had been built thick as bricks at an early age, so any trauma that befell him had little chance of changing his outlook on life. If his senses had been stretched to the limit by the war, they sprung back like elastic when he returned home.

In stark contrast, Alf Richard's personality was altered forever. His moods swung between sullen and turbulent. His sharp sense of humor needed a couple of beers before it delighted his friends, as it once did. He was haunted with questions. What was the purpose of the war? Why did so many young men have to die? Was God dead, too? Why did the working class of one country fight the working class of another country, when their real enemies were those who ruled them?

Peter would say to him, "For crying out loud, Alf, cheer up. The war's over. We've done our bit, and now we're home, so stop broodin' about it." But Alf was moving away from Peter. He was seeking the company of more thoughtful people and looking for political solutions for the plight of the working man. Still, the sadness Peter felt, as the distance from his old mate grew, didn't prevent him from asking Alf to be the best man at his wedding.

❖

Peter and Hannah were married by Father Flaherty in Saint Lawrence's Church in August of 1918.

"A stout back and a kind heart," Father Flaherty said after the ceremony. "You've made a fine choice this time, Hannah my girl."

Hannah and Peter honeymooned at Blackpool-by-the-Sea for a couple of days, while a neighbor looked after the girls. They did all the activities that working-class couples are programmed to do when on holiday at Blackpool: they walked along the promenade eating fish and chips; they splashed in the sea; they waltzed in the Tower Ballroom; and they went to see Harold Lloyd in the movie house.

Their individual responsibilities in their new partnership were so obvious to both that they went unspoken. Hannah would be the head of the household and would make all of the important decisions, plus most of the trivial ones. She would handle the finances and raise the children. She would only involve Peter in these responsibilities when it was essential. Hannah would also ensure Peter received the maximum amount of peace and quiet that the turmoil of her household could hope to provide. And of course, she would have a hot dinner waiting when he came home from work.

For his part, Peter would work hard and keep his nose clean. Every Thursday he would turn his pay packet over to Hannah. She would then return to him enough money to cover his beer, tobacco, and newspaper needs. And there would be enough for the Tranmere Rovers admission fee (if they were playing at home that week) and a little more, just in case. Peter realized that he was expected to consume no more beer than would make him a bit tipsy, and that occasionally he should be prepared to take on objectionable tasks such as hanging new curtains or clearing the mouse traps. He readily volunteered to amuse the children and take them for walks in the park.

Peter's placid personality was the perfect foil for Hannah's volatility. Moreover, he was the conduit the family used to approach Hannah when a favor was needed or forgiveness was sought. The entire arrangement was tightly wrapped in the intense fondness they held for each other. Only three times in their long marriage would they raise their voices to each other. However, their seamless unity was to be tested by events that would have caused many families to crumble.

Chapter Six

≡ 1922 ≡

The Expanding Family

"Let's see those pearly whites," the photographer said. When Hannah quit working in the shipyard, a few weeks after her honeymoon, the management made a big fuss about her leaving. They brought in a photographer to snap her on the dock with the managers and some of the women laborers, with a mighty battleship as background. They then headed to the boardroom to have individual photos taken with her. Those photos included John McGregor and Percy Thompson, now promoted to Roger Dalglish's job, thanks in no small part to Hannah. Robin Frobisher declined to attend.

John McGregor gave a speech citing how much Hannah had meant to the shipyard in the short time she worked there and how the female labor program had benefitted not only the war effort, but also the prosperity of the town.

"This woman is unique," he said. "Not only will she jump in the dock to save your life, she'll also bash the people who threw you in!" Hannah lapped it up like a kitten with cream. She was always a sucker for a compliment, and lolled her head to one side, as coy as a teenage girl.

McGregor continued, "On behalf of the Birkenhead Shipyard, Cammell Laird, I would like to present you with this plaque commemorating your time here. May your marriage be forever happy and your drill bit always sharp."

After work, Hannah strode over to the Gladstone Arms where many of her workmates had gathered to drink to her health and bid her goodbye. Terry McCartney was there, and Percy Thompson. Constable Mathew Baker attended in civilian clothes, but he made sure Hannah knew that he was now Sergeant Mathew Baker.

"I'll not forget you saved me," Baker said. "One of these days yer gonna need me. Rest assured, Hannah, I'll be there for yer." Hannah tucked that little pledge into the back of her mind as she kissed him on his whiskery cheek.

Margie McDonnell spoke up. "I'm beholdin' to Hannah for openin' the gates of the shipyard to us women, so we can make a decent wage while our fellers are away at war. More important to me, though, is that while my Billy is over there fightin' fer his country, I'm helpin' him in my way by workin' here buildin' ships. Please God, bring him home safe and sound." Margie broke into tears.

Terry McCartney stepped forward. "We had a whip-round, Hannah, and bought yer a little goin' away gift." He gave her an eight-inch-by-six-inch packet wrapped in fancy paper. She removed the paper very carefully to find a wooden box with the words "Drill Bits" etched on top.

"For the best driller's mate since the art of drilling was invented," Terry said. "There are no drill bits inside, though, just a few notes of appreciation from the girls." Hannah undid the metal clasp and opened the box. Her mouth dropped open. The notes were not the little scribbled messages that she expected, but pound notes—a big bundle of them.

"Fifty-four pound in total," Terry said with a grin. "Every girl contributed a few pennies, as did every policeman, and most of the men. The shipyard management matched the total collected."

Hannah was in shock. "For the love of God—it's a king's ransom!"

"Be careful no one steals it off yer on the way home," Percy Thompson joked. "Wait, what am I thinkin'? No one would be daft enough to try!"

"Drinks all round," Hannah declared.

❖

A few weeks later, the Corcoran family moved into 57 Beckwith Street, just one street away from their old house. It was still a tenement, still in the docklands, but considerably larger and more inviting. It had two front entrances, steps going up to the front door, and steps going down to the basement door. The basement was the main living area, which included the living room and the kitchen, such that you could sit by the living room window and watch the legs of people passing by in the street. The children invented a game of putting a name to the legs.

"There goes Mary Pickford," Eileen said.

"And that one must be Fatty Arbuckle," added Doris.

On the first floor was the parlor, kept locked and used only for special occasions, such as a party or a sing-song, sometimes for a wake, also for when important people visited, such as the man from the Prudential.

The front door opened onto a vestibule where bikes or prams could be parked, which led into a wide hallway. There Peter hung a large mirror, and of course, as in every good Catholic house, a container of holy water attached to a picture of the Sacred Heart. Two extra rooms on the second floor allowed Granma White to have her own room and a rocking chair that actually rocked.

The Beckwith Street house also had a larger backyard than the Price Street house, but like all houses in the area, it backed onto an alley, which led to the street. The backyard walls of all the houses were white-washed to make the place a little brighter. Folks could raise chickens or homing pigeons there, and it was where the toilet was located. Best of all, the house had a stoop where Granma White could sit, a blind spectator to the goings-on of the town.

❖

World War I ended with the armistice of November 1918, and those British servicemen lucky enough to have survived came straggling home, only to find a bankrupted country with jobs hard to find, and the oppressive social system still intact. Of course, there were no women laborers working in the shipyard anymore. Their jobs had been reclaimed by returning servicemen.

There was a new sickness about on the European mainland, so Hannah felt it prudent to end her career as a cleaner of the deceased. She made up for the loss of revenue by filling one of the spare rooms in the Beckwith Street house with a lodger.

Every day at 6:40 a.m. Peter walked the half mile to the docks. He always stopped off at Norris' newsagent to buy a *Daily Express*, two ounces of Old Holborn tobacco, cigarette papers, and a box of matches. He joined hundreds of other dock workers converging on a warehouse called "The Shed." The men were careful where they stepped. The air they breathed, together with the tobacco they smoked, caused the dock area to be part of the "Bronchitis Belt," and sputum soiled the pavement.

By seven a.m., The Shed was filled with men looking for work. Officially they were known as stevedores but everyone called them dockers. They stood in tense silence while hatch bosses, atop wooden boxes, selected the gang of men who would work any new cargo ships that had arrived on the previous tide.

If you weren't selected, you had to return the next day. Selection was arbitrary, left to the decision of the hatch bosses. Still, they had to be careful not to continually select friends or relatives, because an unpopular hatch boss could be heaved into the dock. Of course he was always pulled out before he drowned, but the experience was not one to relish. Peter Corcoran almost always got work because he was known to be a hard worker, and his status as a gassed ex-serviceman played more than a little part.

If working in the shipyard, as Hannah had, was tough, it was a doddle, a breeze, compared to working on the docks. This was raw, backbreaking labor, loading boxes onto pallets, unloading them into the ship's hold from 7:00 a.m. to 7:00 p.m., Monday to Friday, half a day on Saturday. Peter earned every precious penny he made.

Despite extensive security, dockers had raised the process of pilfering to an art form, which many believed was passed genetically from father to son. How dockers managed to avoid being caught by the hatch watchmen, or how they smuggled the goods past the dock policemen, remains one of the great mysteries of the time. Of course, dockers never considered it stealing. They thought it was a right to augment their meager pay.

❖

One soggy morning in the autumn of 1918, Peter walked to work with an old friend, Larry McGee, gabbing away about football and politics. Without warning, Larry slipped on the pavement and fell on his head. Peter attempted to lift him, but Larry issued a frightful cackle and fell to the ground again. A group of dockers surrounded the poor man, who had curled up into a fetal position.

"Someone run for the ambulance at the dock gates!" Peter said. "He's banged his head something fierce." Larry gasped for breath, and a blood-tinged froth gushed from his mouth and nose.

"Holy God in heaven!" a docker said. "He's got rabies."

"That's not rabies," another docker interjected. "That's the Spanish flu. I've seen it before. There's nowt we can do—one day yer fine, the next day yer dead. It's spreading everywhere, like a plague from the Bible, and now it's here. God help us all!"

❖

Two days later, Father Flaherty sipped a noontime cup of tea in Hannah's kitchen. "They've closed down the church," he said. "No Mass, no confession, it's the devil's work, all right. The movie houses are shut, the pubs are empty, there are neither trains nor ferries, yet people are still dyin' left and right. It spares the old and kills the young and strong, so someone explain that to me." Hannah shook her head as she poured him another cup.

Granma White joined in. "They say forty million are dead in India alone. Soldiers coming home from the war bring the disease with them. That's how it's spread. The paper advises everyone to stay in their homes until it passes."

"That's fine for them to say," Hannah said, "but what do we eat? How do we work to buy food?" At that point Eileen and Doris came home. "Why are yer home so early?" Hannah asked.

"They've closed the school," Eileen said. "A couple of kids came down with the Spanish flu, so they took them off to the emergency hospital and sent the rest of us home." She sighed. "I'll put the kettle on."

Eileen went into the kitchen and coughed. She coughed again and then poked her head around the door. "Just a cough," she said.

Hannah sat her down and placed a hand on the girl's forehead. "She's got a temperature fer sure."

Eileen twisted her fingers together in nervousness. "Everyone stop looking at me!"

For the next hour, Eileen's cough became worse and more frequent.

Hannah held her hand to comfort her, trying desperately to mask the dread that had overtaken Hannah's brain. Father Flaherty beckoned Hannah into the parlor and put his arm around her shoulders.

"I'm sorry, Hannah, but it does look like the Spanish flu. Her lungs are clogged up with fluid." Father Flaherty shook his head. "Don't let them take her to one of these emergency hospitals. They're not really hospitals—more like quarantine areas, because there's no cure for this scourge. You're there until you recover or die, and you can have no visitors. Those poor children will have to suffer their agonies among strangers, without the comfort of their mams."

The door was slightly ajar and Eileen was outside, listening to every word. She grabbed her mother's arm. "Please, Mam, don't send me to an emergency hospital."

The child's pitiful plea stung Hannah. She wrapped her arms around her daughter and kissed her head. "That will never happen— you'll be with me until you're better."

Pumped with fear and adrenaline, Hannah's mind shot into high gear. She ordered Doris to take all her clothes out of the bedroom that she shared with Eileen. She grabbed extra blankets, a thin pillow, two large towels, her rosary, a cushion, a beaker, and an old bedpan. Little Vera, not understanding the situation, but feeling the dire tension, burst out crying.

"What can I do?" Granma White asked.

"Comfort Vera and Doris," Hannah answered, "and pray to every saint you know."

"Keep her prostrate," Father Flaherty said. "No solids, only fluids." He put his hand in his pocket and took out a Red Cross mask. "Here Hannah, take this for yerself. It's supposed to help."

"No thank you, Father. I want her to see my face."

Hannah bundled Eileen to the child's room and put her to bed, covered her with the extra blankets, and placed the thin pillow under her head. She jammed the towels under the gap at the bottom of the door, pushed a piece of crinkled paper into the keyhole, and cracked open the window slightly to let some air into the room.

Eileen coughed and spluttered, spitting green lung phlegm into the beaker. Her little body shook, her brow was afire, and her breathing heavy. "Am I going to die, Mam?" she asked in a hoarse voice.

"Of course not," Hannah replied, holding Eileen's sweating hand. "But you are ill, sweetheart, so yer must be still and quiet 'til it passes."

Hannah sat on the bed and softly said the rosary. An hour went by, then two, then three. Eileen continued to cough until she fell asleep. She woke after a short while, had a coughing fit, and fell asleep again. The cycle continued into the evening, leaving Hannah with a fearful dilemma. Should she keep the child awake, or should she let her sleep?

Hannah placed the cushion next to the bed and fell to her knees to pray. "Saint Lawrence, I can't recall if I ever asked yer for help before. I reckon God and Jesus and Mary must be swamped right now with millions of prayers from people like me, whose loved ones are in the grip of this terrible plague. So I'm beggin' yer to intercede on my behalf. You know I normally pray to Saint Anthony or Saint Werburgh, but it's not their churches whose floors I scrub. It's not their parishioners whose bodies I clean, and it was not their women-folk who found work at the shipyard because of me. They're yours— all yours."

Hannah placed her hand gently on Eileen's chest. "Saint Lawrence, look at this child, just nine years. Look at her sweet face, her beautiful hair. No mother has a better daughter. She's obedient, never com-plains, helps in every way, never asks for anything. Please, please ask God to spare her. For me. For the work I've done for you. For pity's sake, spare her." She buried her head in her hands and quietly sobbed.

◆

As twilight came, Hannah lit the bedside candle. Soon, Peter opened the bedroom door slightly. "How is she?" he asked.

"Quiet, she's sleeping. Close that door—I want no one else exposed. Talk to me through the keyhole." Hannah removed the paper from the keyhole and pressed her ear up against it.

"There's some fish and chips, a hot cup of tea, and a spot of brandy out here for yer," Peter said. "Granma White says you've been in there since noon. She wants to take yer place for a while."

"Thank her for me, but this is my job. There's no point both of us catching the flu."

"I love you, Hannah Corcoran," he whispered.

"I love you, too," she answered. "Pray for us both."

◆

Darkness enveloped the room as the candle went out. Hannah sat in an old wicker chair and fell asleep, her rosary still in her hand. Next day, she kept the same vigil, feeding Eileen barley broth, wiping her sweat, and singing soft Irish lilts. Eileen showed no signs of improving. Peter placed a chair outside the bedroom, where he sat during the evening, and Granma White sat during the day. There was nothing they could do, but it comforted Hannah to know they were so close, and somehow it helped them to know that she knew. Once again, Hannah fell asleep that night in the whicker chair, her head lolled on one side. Her rosary, with the shine on the beads worn off, dropped to the floor.

The next morning, Hannah woke with the dawn to find Eileen's leg hanging out of the bed. Her chest no longer heaved, and her pillow was stained with mucus. Hannah picked up her leg to put it back in the bed. It was ice cold.

Hannah's body stiffened. She looked up the ceiling and screamed. "Please God, no!"

Eileen's eyes sprang open. "I'm freezin'," she said, in a weak voice. "Close that window, Mam." Hannah fell back into her wicker chair, her hand on her heart. Peter and Granma White burst into the room, expecting the worst.

Hannah broke into a large grin and cried at the same time. "How are you feeling, my sweet?" she asked.

Eileen tried to pull herself up. "I'm cold and I'm hungry, but my cough is gone."

"Stay in your bed—I'll get yer some breakfast."

Hannah put her arms around her husband and her mother. "It's past. My daughter has beaten the devil. You know, I don't think us Catholics give Saint Lawrence half enough credit."

◆

The spare bedroom that Hannah rented out didn't stay spare forever. Her first child with Peter, Lilly, was born in 1922. When Lilly was a baby, people would remark, "Good God, Hannah, she's the spittin' image of yer." As Lilly grew older, the resemblance grew closer yet.

A year later, Hannah delivered a boy at last. He was known as "young Steven," even as an adult. At his christening, Hannah said to Father Flaherty, "I think he's got the look of one for the priesthood, wouldn't you say, Father?"

"He's one for the cloth, without a doubt. I can almost see his halo. And I'll tell you this fer nowt—you and Peter are makin' such beautiful Catholic babies."

Finally, a year after Steven came Grace. Probably because she was the last, the collective jealousy that Vera secretly harbored for her siblings was combined and redirected to become open hostility toward the new baby, which continued as Grace grew. It was something Grace never understood, but she learned to deal with Vera's antagonism by ignoring it, as Peter had done.

As the only boy, young Steven became the center of attention. "Look after your brother," became the first commandment in the Corcoran household. To escape from all the doting he received from the females in the family, young Steven sought his father's companionship. Peter took him fishing and to football games, to prevent him from becoming "sissified."

"Now that you've got yer candidate for the priesthood," Granma White said to Hannah, "and maybe even a nun with little Grace, are yer plannin' on breedin' any more?"

"Is it a problem for yer?" Hannah replied.

"It's your body, daughter," Granma White chuckled. "As long as there's tea in the pot and a place to plunk me backside."

❖

Granma White chuckled a lot. There was no denying she was a large woman, with broad shoulders, a big head, big hands, and a big heart. Only one photograph of her still exists, brittle with time. It's part of a large panoramic photograph of sixty middle-aged and older women, about to embark on a church outing in the summer of 1930. The women are in three rows, standing on the church steps, all wearing dark clothes and fancy hats after the fashion of the day. Hannah sits in the middle of the bottom row, next to Father Flaherty, a spot where the leader might be, and to the far right stands Granma White, towering over all three rows like a Greek Titan. Her solid head is topped by a large gaucho-style hat with black lace trim, pulled over to one side at a cavalier angle.

Despite her English name, Granma White was born in County Wicklow, Ireland. Her husband came to England to find work and to save enough money to send for his wife. She was just twenty-nine when she went blind, condemned to sixty years of darkness. Still, she never complained. The only regret she harbored was that her blindness had placed such a burden on her eldest daughter, Hannah.

The blind lady became a permanent feature of the parish. She could be found sitting on her stoop every day, smoking black shag tobacco from a white clay pipe. She chatted with anyone who cared to pass the time of day and gave out free advice—requested or not—in a cheerful manner.

For tuppence, she would tell your fortune by feeling the bumps on your head. If you had no bumps, she would volunteer to give you a couple with her cane, for an extra penny. Her predictions were surprisingly accurate, so people assumed that a woman who had no sight in the present might well develop the gift of having sight into the future. In reality, she picked up so many tidbits and rumors, sitting there on her stoop, and was smart enough to parley them into a fairly close understanding of the road you were heading down.

When her pipe went out, she would cajole anyone who passed to relight it, being afraid that small embers might fall and burn her clothes if she lit it herself. From all accounts, lighting that pipe was an experience not easily forgotten, as black shag was the harshest tobacco that a three-penny bit could buy. For five minutes, you would hack up all the sludge at the pit of your lungs, yet feel all the better for it. Hannah maintained that black shag tobacco was the reason her mother lived to be ninety.

Granma White was popular with everyone, particularly her grandchildren. Within her limited capabilities, she aided Hannah in raising them, and occasionally would intercede if they wanted Hannah softened up for some reason.

Every night after supper, Hannah or one of her siblings would read to Granma in her bedroom. The tradition was carried on by Hannah's children, like it or not. It wasn't popular with Grace or Steven. Vera hated it because she would stumble over the words, but

Eileen, Doris, and Lilly didn't mind reading. To be alone with their grandmother, snuggled up to her large frame, made them feel warm and safe, even as adults.

First they would read her the news from the daily paper and then finish off with a chapter or two of a library book, usually a nineteenth-century classic. It was not romance or drama that interested Granma White—no Austen or Dickens for her. It was the great adventure novels that she loved; Stevenson, Forrester, and Walter Scott she devoured with gusto. She took an active part, too, cheering for the hero and hissing at the villain. "Don't yer worry, you old pirate," she might comment. "You'll get your comeuppance later." Or she might punch the air and cry, "You go get them Frenchies, Horatio!"

Granma White also loved poetry. Not the sappy, lovey-dovey kind, but the Kipling/Tennyson kind that stirs the fibers and makes you sit up straight. "The Song of Hiawatha" was her favorite, and somewhere in her long ago she had memorized great chunks of it. Without good reason, she would often recite a stanza or two. At the dinner table, for example, she would chirp in, "By the shores of Gitche Gumee / By the shining Big-Sea-Water / Stood the wigwam of Nokomis / Daughter of the Moon, Nokomis."

Eileen would mutter under her breath, "Oh God, here she goes again."

Then Granma White would pronounce, "Longfellow—greatest poet who ever drew breath!" as if she knew them all.

◆

Even though her husband worked all the overtime God sent, these were tough financial days again for Hannah, what with six children, a mother, and a husband to clothe and feed. Still, no one could soak a sixpence like Hannah. She made Peter's wages stretch from Thursday to Tuesday evening, declaring Wednesdays to be holy fasting days, when plain bread was all the family had to eat, except for Peter, who had a full meal. His nourishment was essential to his hard labor, for which the scant finances of the family depended.

On Wednesdays, Hannah would declare, "Tonight for dinner there are two courses—take it or leave it!" Granma White thought that joke got old after a while.

As strapped as they were for money, Hannah remembered those times as happy times, with little strife. With a new husband, a new house, six healthy kids, and her reputation as a champion of the workers still intact, there was much to be thankful for. Except for the Vera-Grace situation, the children of different fathers integrated themselves without any pressure from Hannah. The older children looked out for the younger ones, while Peter loved them all. Overlooking the whole shebang was Granma White, always ready with an objective opinion, a comforting hug, or a piece of well-meaning sarcasm.

❖

After eleven a.m. Mass on Sundays, Hannah, her mother, and Eileen would go home to prepare the Sunday dinner, while Peter took the rest of the clan for a walk in the park. Sunday dinner, the culinary highlight of the week, usually consisted of a ham shank, boiled spuds, cabbage, and carrots, followed by a healthy dose of rice pudding for afters. Haute cuisine it wasn't, but it filled them up and was a welcome break from greasy chip sandwiches, baked beans on toast, and blind scouse, which constituted the fare for the rest of the week. Scouse was a local type of fish or meat stew, and blind scouse was a variation where you could go blind looking for the meat. Merseysiders were known as Scousers by the rest of the country, who usually uttered the appellation with a superior smirk. For their part, Merseysiders were wont to say proudly, "I'm not really English, I'm a Scouser!"

For Peter, there was nothing more pleasant than a stroll through the park on a fine Sunday before dinner. Birkenhead Park, designed by Joseph Paxton, opened in 1847, at the same time the docks opened. A jewel of a park, there was something for everyone. Paths ran through wooded greenery, around miniature hills for the children to climb, bordered by bushes and flower gardens, the equal of any palace in the land. Dogs ran loose, as dogs are meant to do, and young men rowed their sweethearts around the lake, like an image from a Renoir painting. Plump mallards circled while kids fed them stale bread and table scraps, and in the gazebo over the covered bridge, a military band played Sousa marches.

There were sports aplenty, with football, rugby, and cricket, plus lawn bowls for the old folk. You could even watch a baseball game whenever a Yankee ship was in port. Peter would push his daughters on the swings or watch them play on the big black boulders. Strategically placed, the boulders created a twenty-foot-high maze to be clambered over, hidden in, and explored.

The entire park was surrounded by impressive limestone mansions. Joseph Paxton, however, had strategically placed the park so that it was easily accessible to eighty percent of the town's residents. It was the only place where rich and poor could happily mingle and escape from the glitter or the grime.

Peter and his children would finally emerge from the park at the grand entrance, comprised of a grandiose, arched building, where the park superintendent lived. It opened onto a large paved area which would soon feature as an important part in the town's history.

❖

Hannah's left fist remained rusting in its scabbard for several years, mainly because there never was an occasion that really warranted its appearance. Hannah was busy raising the children, managing the household, and helping at the church. She even became a member of the local Labour Party. Though she only had time to attend the bi-weekly meetings, her opinions always found respect. So things were relatively quiet until the football game that no one in the family would ever forget.

Peter continued to play football for Saint Lawrence's parish team, generally with one or more of the family in attendance to cheer him on when the home games were played in Birkenhead Park. On this occasion, the game was the semi-final of a cup game against Saint Anne's of Rock Ferry, so the entire family turned out, including Granma White. Eileen stood next to her grandmother to relate the play-by-play, plus to protect her from any errant footballs that came her way. It was a bright, cloudless day, with two or three hundred spectators along the side lines, cheering for their parish.

Saint Anne's central defender, a large young man with a shock of auburn hair, was obviously more eager to win the game than most of the other players, displayed by the fact that he sliced down any

Lawries player when the opportunity arose. The referee awarded free kicks, each time warning the man for his illegal tactics, but didn't take any further action, despite the jeering of the Lawries supporters.

"What's happenin' now?" Granma White asked.

"The Lawries have a free kick near the half-way line," Eileen replied.

"What's happenin' now?"

"The ball has been passed to that lad from Watson Street."

"You mean the one with the lisp?"

"No, that's his brother."

"What's happenin' now?"

"Our dad's got the ball! C'mon Dad, shoot! Oh dear!"

"What's up?"

"That big red-headed brute has chopped down our dad. The crowd is jeerin' him."

"I'm blind, not deaf. What's happenin' now?"

"The trainer's on the field. He's seein' to our Dad. It looks like his knee is injured. He seems in a lot of pain. Oh, no!"

"What's happenin' now?"

"It's our mam. She's run onto the field. Father Flaherty has run on to catch her. He's too late!"

"Stop! I don't want to know what's happenin' now!"

Hannah examined her left fist. It's not as rusty as I feared, she thought. In fact it appears to work as well as it ever did. She then realized that everyone was staring at her—the players from both teams, the referee, the trainer, and the quieted crowd. The only noise was a muffled moan coming from the redhead kneeling at her feet, holding a hand to his face, with blood seeping through his fingers.

The referee stood rooted to the spot, trying to determine how to handle the precedent that now confronted him: A woman had run out of the crowd, followed by a priest; the woman had slugged one of the players so hard it almost knocked him out. He looked around hoping to see a bobby somewhere.

"What's yer name?" Hannah asked the referee.

"Kenny Masters," he replied, still perplexed.

"Well, Kenny, listen to me. Look at me when I'm talkin' to yer. That's better. Now, most of these players, on both teams, work on the docks or at the shipyard. If they get badly hurt playing football, such that they can't work, they don't get paid. If they don't get paid, there is no food for their families. Nod if you understand."

The referee nodded. Hannah turned and walked back to the sideline to the cheers of the Lawries' supporters. But one group didn't cheer, and that was her family. They had heard about her left hook, of course, but they had never seen it in action. The savagery of the blow shocked them into silence, including Peter and Father Flaherty. This was an aspect of Hannah's personality they could not reconcile.

The manager of the Saint Anne's team told the police that they wanted Hannah charged with assault and battery. Hannah countered by demanding the redhead be charged with the same offense, with both his manager and the referee being arrested for aiding and abetting. In addition, she required that Saint Anne's Parish compensate her for any wages her husband might lose through his injury. Still, the manager of Saint Anne's team pressed charges.

"I'll sort this out for yer," Father Flaherty said, "but I'm gonna need a full bottle of Irish whiskey from yer, for bribing purposes."

Unlike most Irish priests, who were sozzled half of the time, Father Eamon Flaherty was sozzled most of the time. This never bothered any of his parishioners, who considered it small compensation for a life of devotion and celibacy. In a culture where alcohol was an important mainstay, teetotalers were viewed with suspicion and not to be trusted. In fact, Father Flaherty performed his duties with more diligence when he was tipsy, the drink clearing his mind of extraneous twaddle. After a couple of hits of illicit Irish moonshine, called poteen, and a glass or two of unconsecrated communion wine, he could deliver a cracking sermon that would make you want to stand up and cheer, like you were at a Tranmere Rovers football match, rather than in the house of the Lord.

Armed with the bottle of whiskey hidden about his stout person, Father Flaherty rode his bike over to the presbytery at Father Kilbane's of St. Ann's parish. Both priests settled down to resolve the matter, and by a remarkable coincidence, a resolution was reached at the same moment that the last drop of whiskey was consumed. Both priests agreed to instruct their parishioners that the whole business was a wash and everyone should just shut up and move on. Father

Flaherty mounted his bicycle a little shakily as he waved goodbye to his friend.

❖

The Corcoran family sat down for supper that evening with a black cloud hanging overhead. No one spoke as Vera dished out the food. Eventually Hannah broke the silence.

"I know what's bothering all of you. Who will be the first to say something?"

Peter shook his head. "It was one hell of a blow."

"I suppose it was justified," Eileen said. "But it was a ferocious punch."

"It was scary, Mum, very scary," Doris added.

"But where would we all be without it?" Granma White chimed in. "The way I see it, the punch is a weapon of protection, given to your mother by God, in thanks for years of cleaning the floor of his house with her left hand. It has protected us from those who would hurt us—and not just us, others too. I dare say, if God spares her, she will continue to protect us. We are fortunate, indeed, to have her."

Chapter Seven

⇒ 1926 ⇐

General Strike

The last general election had been all bad news as far as Hannah was concerned. Stanley Baldwin had been elected prime minister again, this time with enough votes to form a majority Conservative government.

To make matters worse for the working class, Baldwin brought Winston Churchill into his cabinet as Chancellor of the Exchequer. Both Baldwin and Churchill were alarmed by the growing power of the trade unions. They both could see Communists in their porridge, afraid that the country was headed toward a people's revolution, like that of Bolshevik Russia. Baldwin and Churchill stood so far to the political right, that when they strained to view the political left, it was so distant they couldn't discern between Socialism and Communism. Consequently, the unspoken item at the top of their political agenda, now that they had the power to do it, was to break the backs of the unions, where they believed Communism festered.

Although the Communist Party set up groups in factories and coal mines around the country, they played a small role in the unions' leadership, whose only aim was to improve the pay and working conditions of those they represented.

Hannah knew that the coal miners were even worse off than the dockers and shipyard workers. The men that dug coal out of the ground spent their working day breathing in more coal dust than oxygen, their life expectancy shorter than in any other industry. The work was backbreaking, poorly paid, and dangerous, with cave-ins quite common.

Britain was made of coal. Underneath the lush green grass and the gentle hills, lay huge deposits. Coal was the fuel that powered the Industrial Revolution. In every factory, coal heated the water, which made the steam, which drove the machines. Trains and ships ran on coal, and every citizen, rich or poor, warmed to a coal fire. Mine owners grew rich on the toil of the miners, but if any financial downturn affected coal prices, it was the meager wages of the miners that took the hit.

◈

Several months later, Hannah read that Churchill was putting the country back on the Gold Standard. "Whatever that means," Hannah declared, "it's not gonna be good for anyone who doesn't speak with a plum stone in his mouth."

Because of Churchill's actions, the pound was devalued by ten percent, causing wages to drop again. The miners, already below the poverty line, threatened to strike and asked the prime minister to intervene.

"It's like asking the hangman to tie the noose loosely," Hannah remarked.

Baldwin promised the miners that he would initiate an inquiry into the mining industry, during which the government would subsidize the miners' wages back to the 1925 level, for a period of no less than nine months.

Hannah couldn't believe it. "What's this bastard up to?" she asked anyone who would listen. All such previous independent inquiries had come down in favor of the miners, and that surely couldn't be Baldwin's intent.

◈

The following spring, Hannah ran to the letter box at the end of the street to catch the postman before he emptied its contents. "Phew, just made it," she said as she handed the new postman her letter. He was a young lad, lanky with greased-down hair and a pleasant, freckled face.

"I saw you running, so I waited, madam. We are glad to be of service."

"What's yer name, son?"

"Randall."

"Where are yer from? Not 'round here, I know."

"Suffolk, down South."

"So what are yer doin' in Birkenhead?"

"Just working my way around the country, madam, seeing all the sights." His knitted brows showed that the questions aggravated him.

As he walked away with the post bag on his back, Hannah thought, who names their kid Randall?

A similar encounter took place a week later. Hannah was on her way back from visiting her father's grave in Landigan Cemetery when she struck up a conversation with a tram conductor. This fellow was older than the postman but had the same educated accent, plus he also called her "madam."

When Hannah recounted the incidents to Peter, he told her a couple of young men in suits had been asking a lot of questions around the docks. "The bosses told us they were managers in trainin' and to give them full cooperation."

"Something's strange," Hannah said. "Something stinks."

"It's odd," Peter said. "By the way, did I tell yer that I was promoted to hatch boss yesterday?"

"Why yer rascal, why didn't yer tell me sooner? That's wonderful! That means more security and more money." She jumped in his lap and kissed him.

❖

At the next Labour Party meeting, Hannah brought up the issue of the strangers in town. The Labour Party leader, John Brophy, was skeptical. "So these lads have come from out of town to find work? What makes yer suspect 'em of something shady?"

"Well, first off they both called me 'madam,' not 'missus' or 'luv,' which yer would normally expect to be called by a postman or tram conductor. Then last Sunday I saw 'em both playin' cricket in the park."

"What's suspicious about cricket? It's the national summer game!" Brophy said.

"Not for folks like us," replied Hannah. "We could never play cricket."

"Why not?"

"Well, we could never afford that fancy white get-up and besides, we would chop up the bat for firewood in the winter."

"Of course." Brophy allowed himself a smile. "What was I thinkin'?"

"Another thing," Hannah said, "I saw the two of 'em later, chummin' up with none other than Robin Frobisher, ex-general manager of the shipyard, now a local politician, and more right wing than Ivan the Terrible." Brophy shrugged.

"Look, all I'm sayin' is that suddenly we find middle-class young men comin' to our town to do working-class jobs."

A boilermaker at the back of the room spoke up. "We have a new young man around the steel mill askin' questions. The boss says to give him full cooperation."

"All right," said Brophy. "Everyone should keep their eyes and ears open for new people in town, also for leprechauns and hobgoblins."

When the meeting was over, Hannah approached the leader of the dockers' union, George Newell, and asked him if he knew anyone in the miners' union.

"Yes, I know Frank Hodges, the Miners' Federation secretary."

"Do me a favor. Find out all yer can about coal sales, up or down, and all you can about the major coal customers these days."

❖

At closing time the following Thursday evening, Peter Corcoran came out of the Ram's Head Pub and headed home down Cathcart Street, when a voice behind him called his name. He turned to see, by the light of a street lamp, three well-dressed young men approaching him. One pudgy lad held a lead pipe.

"Are you Hannah Corcoran's husband?" the pudgy one said.

"Who's askin'?" Peter replied.

"We want you to give her a message. Tell her she had better stop asking questions, or we will give her the same beating we might just give you." He tried hard to sound menacing.

Peter grinned. "You boys are not too smart, are yer? Now her suspicions will be verified, and everyone will know there is some conspiracy afoot." The young men drew nearer and surrounded Peter, who now wished he'd kept his mouth shut. At that point, a green Austin sedan pulled up and out jumped Robin Frobisher.

"What's going on?" he asked the group.

"Mr. Frobisher, this is Hannah Corcoran's husband. We thought we might give him a message for his wife."

"With a lead pipe?" Frobisher asked. "What are you, a gang of lower-class thugs? Give me that pipe, Thomas." He snatched the pipe from the pudgy lad. "Now get back to your digs, you stupid fools, before I call the police."

The young men sulked off. Frobisher glowered at Peter and drove away.

◆

"Are you sure they said 'Mr. Frobisher?'" Hannah asked as they sat drinking their night-time cocoa.

Peter nodded. "The man saved me from a beatin'."

"Well, from your description it was Robin Frobisher, all right. Something very fishy is goin' on, and I'm gonna get to the bottom of it, and if they dare to threaten my husband again, they'll taste a plateful of my knuckles, so they will."

The next morning, Hannah waited patiently in the parlor, staring through the window at her front door stoop. Soon, Randall the postman appeared, coming up the street.

"Eileen!" she called. "It's time." Hannah handed Eileen a letter to be posted.

"Do I *have* to do this?" Eileen asked.

"No, you don't, *have to*," Hannah replied, "but I'm asking you to."

Hannah watched through the window as Eileen walked down the street, envelope in hand. What a fine-looking young woman, Hannah thought. What an obliging daughter—my own Mata Hari.

Eileen reached the mail box and handed Randall the envelope, flashing her blue eyes and a sweet smile. "You must be Randall, our new postman. Nice to meet you," she said

"Nice to me me meet you, too," he stuttered, taken aback by this sudden encounter with an attractive young woman.

Eileen returned to the house a few minutes later. "Easy as pie," she told Hannah. "He'll pick me up at six this evening."

Hannah was waiting when Eileen came home from the date about nine. "Well?" Hannah asked.

"Well?" echoed Granma White.

Eileen shrugged. "Dull, dull, dull. Dull as dishwater. We went to Olivetti's for an ice cream and walked through the park, but all he could talk about was politics. I suggested we go to the Ram's Head, where they'll serve women in the lounge if accompanied by a man. He's a right-winger to be sure."

Hannah was elated. "Is that so? Did he tell you why he was here?"

"He sure did. Right after his second pint."

Hannah gave Eileen a bear hug. "That's my girl. Tell me everything he said."

◆

Hannah persuaded John Brophy to allow her to make a presentation at a special Birkenhead Labour Party meeting, convincing him that she had found out about the new people in town. She asked him to ensure that at least one representative of the Trade Union Council be present. The Trade Union Council (TUC) was the national organization to which all the major unions belonged, responsible for negotiating on national union matters with the British government.

The special meeting, held in Saint Lawrence's social club on Bidston Avenue, was packed to the rafters with local Labour Party members, Labour councilors, union leaders, and a solitary TUC representative. Hannah was amazed that through the years of anonymity her reputation as a champion of the working classes was still solid enough to fill a hall.

John Brophy took the podium. He was an austere man with a pasty face and lacked charm, but everyone trusted him because of his dedication to the cause of the working-class people he represented.

"Can yer all hear me?" he yelled.

"The acoustics in this place are a problem," a plumbers' union leader yelled back.

"Thank yer for that," said Brophy. "We've put traps down so we should be rid of them by the weekend." A snicker ran through the audience. He scanned the room, looking at mostly familiar faces, until he spied Alf Richards.

"Mr. Richards, this is a Labour Party meetin', members only. Yer not welcome here. We want no association with Communists."

"I wanna hear what Hannah has to say," Alf said.

"Communists get out!" someone shouted.

"Let him stay," said Hannah. "He might be able to add something." So Alf Richards stayed, although this caused a disapproving scowl from the TUC representative.

Brophy called the meeting to order, introduced the TUC man, a Labour councilor, and finally, Hannah. She stood at the podium and scanned the faces of the all-male audience. Hard, tough faces chiseled by years of toil. "Give us a song, Hannah," a docker shouted. "Let's see that left hook," another added.

"I won't sing for yer," Hannah said, "but I'll gladly demonstrate me left hook. I'll just need a volunteer," which caused a chortle among the audience.

Hannah cleared her throat. "I wish I was here to entertain yer, but what I have to tell yer is deadly serious. One of my girls had a chat with our new postman—one of the young fellas recently arrived in Birkenhead. It turns out that he's a member of The Organization for the Maintenance of Supplies, the OMS. It comprises volunteers trained to take over vital jobs in the event of a general strike. Apparently there are about a hundred thousand of them around the country."

"That organization is rife with Fascists!" Alf Richards shouted.

"Who do they work for? The government?" Brophy asked.

"Not yet, but they will when the general strike occurs," Hannah replied.

"A hundred thousand isn't enough to run the country," Brophy said.

"Yes, but they can provide minimum basic services for the duration of a general strike," she said.

"Why are you talking about a general strike as if it's a foregone conclusion?" the Labour councilor asked, rising to his feet. "The inquiry into the coal mining industry will be out in two weeks, and it may well be positive toward the miners. In any event, negotiations will take place, and if a strike is needed, it will be called for by the TUC."

"I'm sorry," said Hannah, "but the strike is almost certain at this point, and it will be called for by the prime minister and Winston bloody Churchill."

"That makes no sense," Brophy said.

"Listen to George Newell," she replied.

George stood up, a piece of paper in his hand. "Hannah asked me to check on national coal sales for the last nine months. Despite what the mine owners are telling the country, coal sales have actually shown an increase. The biggest single customer right now is the British Navy. Ten times more than they normally order!"

"My God," a party member said, "there must be another war coming, of which we know nothing!"

The Labour councilor slumped back down in his chair. "No," he said with a deep sigh, "the government must be stockpiling coal."

Hannah jumped in. "Exactly. And if they are stockpiling coal, you can bet yer boots they're also stockpiling food and petrol. The inquiry into the mining industry was just a ploy to allow the government nine months to prepare for a general strike. The inquiry is a fix, and I'll betcha the report will recommend a decrease in miners' wages, plus an increase in their work week. The miners will strike, negotiations will break down, and the TUC will have no choice but to call a general strike—exactly how Baldwin and Churchill have planned it."

The room went so quiet you could hear men breath. Every face was stern.

"How long can a general strike last?" asked a union leader.

"How much money do yer have in your strike funds? How much food does yer missus have in the larder?" Hannah replied. "We live from payday to payday. They can hold out—we can't. We'll try to negotiate an end to the strike and lose on every point. The backs of the unions will be broken."

"Who is this woman?" the TUC rep asked the Labour councilor sitting next to him.

"Why, it's Hannah Corcoran," came the reply, as if that explained everything.

"When does the TUC meet next?" Brophy asked.

"Next Friday, a week before the miners' report is published," the TUC man said.

"That's just great." said Brophy. "They've been plannin' fer nine bloody months. The TUC has got a week!"

"What's to be done?" someone asked.

"If the miners strike, our members will strike in sympathy," said

Harry O'Neil, the boilermakers' union leader. "They stood by us in the past."

"There must be something we can do," Brophy said.

"Can you cut lose the miners?" Hannah asked.

"Impossible," said the TUC man. "They are our biggest union and they've suffered enough. It's solidarity among the unions that has got us this far—if they split us now they can beat us piecemeal."

"Then we've already lost," Hannah declared. "Be prepared to work harder, for less money, in worse conditions. All yer have fought for, all yer fathers fought for, will slowly erode away—mark my words. Strikes are not the answer. The only way to improve our lot in life is through the ballot box, to elect a Labour government with a clear majority in Parliament. Only then will we have a nation where the welfare of every citizen will carry the same importance."

Hannah took a deep breath. "Thank yer for listenin'." She stepped down from the stage.

"I'll report what you have said here to Walter Citrine, head of the TUC," said the TUC representative, "but I'm not buying it—too farfetched."

As Hannah passed through the crowd, a docker, Denny Lawson, shouted at her. "Yer sure are surrenderin' easy enough to the bosses. It wouldn't be anythin' to do with yer husband being made up to hatch boss, would it now?" This caused laughter around the room.

Hannah crashed through the crowd to get at Lawson, pushing big men aside, springing over Harry the boilermaker in front of him, with her fist behind her back. She swung at the docker, but he pulled backward, causing her to miss by a mile. She fell into Lawson's arms, who kissed her on the cheek. Hannah gave him a mock slap.

"Next time, Denny Lawson, I won't miss."

"Good God, Denny," said Brophy, "what did yer do that for?"

"What's wrong?" Harry said, puzzled.

Brophy growled. "Every man here would gladly have given up a month's beer money to witness Hannah's left hook hitting its target."

❖

The following Saturday, Hannah, with young Lilly in tow, took the bus to Landigan Cemetery to lay flowers at her father's grave. A steady rain spoiled their visit. It always rains when I'm at this place,

Hannah thought, so why do I always forget me brolly? Mother and child were heading for the exit when they passed a man in a black coat, holding a large black umbrella, staring down at a grave. At first Hannah thought he might be an undertaker, but when he glanced at her, she recognized his face, although he gave no indication he recognized her. Pulling Lilly along, Hannah approached him. She stood at his shoulder and looked down at the grave.

"Is this yer boy, Mr. Frobisher?" she asked.

He glanced at her, then turned back to the grave. "Yes. He would be thirty-one now if he hadn't been killed in the war."

"By all accounts, he was a fine young man."

"That he was. You've no idea how much I miss him." He looked at the little girl, who smiled back at him. "So this is one of your brood."

"Her name is Lilly."

"She's the spitting image."

"So they say."

"You're getting soaked." He held his big umbrella over Hannah and Lilly.

"Thank you for saving my husband from a beating," Hannah said. There was a long silence while Frobisher continued to stare at the grave.

"I know what yer up to," Hannah said. "I know yer plan."

"It doesn't matter if you know, Mrs. Corcoran. It's too late."

"I just don't understand why yer doin' this," Hannah said, as the rain came down harder and the three of them huddled closer together. "You have the money. You have the power. You own the courts, the police, the army, the government. We have crumbs. We only want enough to stay alive, yet you persecute us without mercy. Tell me why."

"You don't understand what's at stake," Frobisher replied. "Each day the unions increase their power. Each day the Communists become more bold. We must force a confrontation before it's too late. If the government backs down in the face of a general strike, power in this country shifts to the unions. To you, to the miners, to the TUC, this is just a straightforward wage dispute. But to Baldwin, Churchill and those you call nobs and bosses, this is a great deal more. With power in the hands of the working class, the peasants, for the first time in two thousand years the country will slide toward Marxism."

"We don't want to run the country. We don't want a revolution,"

81

Hannah said. "It's disaffected middle class and intellectuals that lead revolutions, not working class seekin' a better standard of livin'."

"So you say. But we will always be enemies, Mrs. Corcoran. Socialist leaders like you are our greatest fear."

Hannah sighed and began to walk away. Frobisher stopped her. "Can I give you a ride home?"

"No thanks. Someone might see us, and I've already been accused of collaboration."

He handed her his umbrella. "Then at least take this to keep the child dry."

When they reached the cemetery gates, Hannah turned to see Frobisher still standing there, with his hands plunged into his coat pockets, staring down again at his son's grave.

◆

The mining industry report was released the following week and damned the coal mine owners, but it also called for a reduction in miners' pay, as Hannah had predicted.

On the afternoon of April 30, 1926, the mine owners announced their new terms: thirteen percent pay cuts and an hour extra on the work day. Naturally, the miners rejected it, chanting, "Not a minute on the day, not a penny off the pay." On May first, one million miners turned up for work only to discover they were locked out. The confrontation had begun. The TUC now assumed responsibility for the miners' dispute, calling for immediate talks with the government and threatening to call out the "front ranks" on May 3.

The two sides met at 10 Downing Street on May 2, while the whole country held its breath. Once again the TUC representatives asked the prime minister to arbitrate a solution, still unable to comprehend that he was their enemy. Instead, they gave him even more of an advantage by displaying how anxious they were to avoid a general strike.

The government kept a hard line, giving the TUC little room to maneuver. Then at 11:00 p.m., Baldwin announced that all negotiations were over because workers at the *Daily Mail* newspaper had already started the strike.

Walter Citrine, head of the TUC, scurried across the city of

London to the *Daily Mail* building, only to find that the workers had unofficially walked out. They refused to print the paper's lead article for the next day because it slammed the unions.

Citrine raced back to 10 Downing Street, only to be told that the Prime Minister had gone to bed. The door was closed in his face. He turned and stood motionless on the pavement as a thunderstorm broke, a dark omen of the strife to come. The rain lashed down on him, streaming from the brim of his bowler hat. Too late, he now realized that he and his colleagues had stepped into quicksand. Baldwin had left him no option but to call a general strike. The policeman at the door of number ten said, "Time you moved on, sir."

❖

The next day, the dockers were the first to come out on strike, followed by the railway workers. Then came the builders, the printers, and the iron, steel, chemical, and transport workers. By the end of the day, two million workers had downed tools.

Peter Corcoran, not wanting to go home immediately and listen to Hannah rant on against the TUC leadership, walked over the Duke Street Bridge to Wallasey, with a group of other dockers, to watch a battle cruiser take up position in the River Mersey. It didn't take 'em long, he thought.

Warships were positioned in all the major rivers in the country. All army leave was cancelled, and telegrams went out to all regional centers with the one word—*Action*—as the government's carefully developed plans were implemented. By the end of the second day, regional civil commissions were given dictatorial powers. A state of emergency was declared, followed by the 100,000 members of the OMS offering their services to the Government, many of whom where sworn in as special constables. Inevitably, violence flared between these people and the strikers. The number of strikers had now grown to four million.

Winston Churchill undertook the production of a newspaper, *The British Gazette*, full of propaganda. He praised Benito Mussolini and suggested that machine guns be used on the striking miners. Hannah relegated it to the toilet. In response to the government's civil commissions, the strikers set up local councils of action to organize essential services where they were deemed necessary. By the end of the week, it became clear that the government's plans were ineffective against the well-organized strikers' councils. Nothing moved, nothing was produced, no light shone, without the agreement of the strikers. The country ground to a standstill.

"Good God," Hannah said to Peter, "we've got the bastards. All that needs to be done now is to tie these local councils of action into a national organization with a single coordinated policy."

This never came to pass, chiefly because the TUC leadership was in turmoil. It was frozen into inaction by exaggerated reports that Communist leaders were coming to the fore in important parts of the country.

In Parliament, Baldwin and Churchill railed against the strikers, claiming, "We have been challenged with an alternative government, and we are near to civil war." Although wildly exaggerated, this type of rhetoric made the TUC leaders even more jittery. Meeting with Baldwin again, asking him to simply give the miners their pre-strike wage so the strike could end and the country could return to normal, they found him adamant, without compromise. Squeezed between two unacceptable outcomes, without perspective, Walter Citrine and his TUC colleagues lapsed into impotency.

Two small unions took the TUC to court to prevent being called out on strike, resulting in Judge Astbury concluding that the strike was illegal. This meant the TUC and the unions were liable for huge fines from employers, plus it allowed the government to confiscate all union funds. This was the escape hatch that the TUC leadership used to weasel out of the standoff. They met with the government again, and despite receiving no concessions regarding the victimization of strikers, they totally capitulated and called off the general strike.

The first response from the strikers was disbelief. The second was anger. The workers were prepared to stay out as long as it took, but now they were betrayed by their own leadership.

Hannah fumed throughout the house. "Keep out of her way," said Granma White as she escaped to her room.

"Stinking cowards, spineless jellyfish," Hannah said, a sentiment that was echoed around the country.

"Unconditional Surrender," Churchill's *British Gazette* headline gloated.

The strike had lasted just ten days, but after its official end, workers continued to come out. If a charismatic Labour leader had emerged, the country might well have suffered the revolution the government feared.

◆

All the family had gone to bed except Hannah when John Brophy rang the doorbell.

"It's almost eleven o'clock," Hannah said, leading him into the parlor. "What's going on?" Granma White, her curiosity peaked, came down to brew some tea.

Brophy plopped down on the settee and lit a cigarette. His eyes seemed a bit glazed.

"Have yer had a few drinks?" Hannah asked.

"A couple," he replied. "I've come to tell yer, Hannah, that you were right and I was wrong. You had it sussed out the whole time. You grasped what Baldwin and Churchill were up to from the starting gate, but no one listened to yer. They'll listen to yer now."

"It's a bit late fer that." Hannah slipped an ashtray under his nose. "What are yer really here for, John?"

"We proved that we can sustain a strike. At the same time, we proved that they couldn't run the country without us, even for a week. There's no point havin' a postman if there are twenty postmen on strike ready to stop him delivering the mail. I'm not ready to admit the strike is over. All we lack is strong leadership, someone with courage who can rally the workers, someone who will spit in the face of those that would enslave us. A person, larger than life, with foresight, with strength of mind and strength of gut. Whadda yer say?"

Hannah looked over her shoulder. "Yer don't mean me, do yer?"

"Who better?" said Granma White. "This could be yer time, girl. This could be yer destiny."

"My destiny is to go to the market tomorrow and buy some haddock. Besides, no one knows of me outside of this town."

Granma White reached for her pipe, which she passed to her

daughter to light. "No one knew of Wat Tyler until he led the Peasants' Revolt, back in the fourteenth century," Granma White said.

"I read that Wat Tyler was run through with a sword for his trouble. Anyway, whatever happens, working-class men wouldn't allow a woman to lead them," Hannah said.

"Tell that to the French and Joan of Arc."

"Burned at the stake." Hannah smirked.

"I give up," Granma White said.

"Look John, I can't say I'm not complimented by yer offer," Hannah said, as she poured him some tea. "But yer got the wrong person. There are a dozen reasons. Leadin' the girls at the shipyard during the war was not enough experience fer the job. And what about me fist? The opposition would have a field day with that. Besides, Peter would be fired from the docks, and then who would pay the bills? I've a large family to tend. It wouldn't be fair to them. I'm sorry."

❖

Without leadership, the workers drifted back to work over the course of a week. To the unions, to the Labour movement, to the blue-collar workers of Britain, the strike was an unmitigated disaster. The miners, cast adrift, were locked out for six more months, only to return to a longer work day at less pay. Many miners never got their jobs back; victimization became rampant across other industries. Three thousand strikers were prosecuted and vicious anti-union legislation was introduced. Workers' pay was reduced everywhere and working conditions hardened, resulting in bitterness toward the ruling class that lasted throughout the rest of the century.

It wouldn't be until twenty years later that the Labour Party Hannah spoke of would come to power with a majority government. Hannah's antipathy toward Winston Churchill reached a new high.

Chapter Eight

≡ 1928 ≡

Vera

Vera's primary quality was her meekness. Granma White said that if Jesus was right, and the meek did inherit the earth, then Vera was sure to get half of Europe, with the Isle of Man thrown in. Dominated by Hannah's personality since she was a child, Vera always did as she was told. She had no motivation except for that given to her by her mother, and she never strayed from her devotion to Hannah and Saint Lawrence's Church.

For all her submissiveness, however, Vera could be spiteful, as she was toward little Grace. Her jealousy toward Peter Corcoran, because of his closeness to Hannah, caused her never to accept him as her father, and she would only speak to him through her mother. Peter handled this situation with his usual indifference to the quirks of others.

Unlike her sisters, Vera was not particularly attractive and never felt a need to improve her appearance. "Mousey in looks and subdued in personality," was the way most people described her. She was short of stature, with slumped shoulders and a tendency to the sniffles. If she wasn't cleaning the house or running errands, Vera was over at Saint Lawrence's scrubbing the church floor.

"How lucky you are to have a daughter like Vera, who can help shoulder some of your daily burdens," Father Flaherty said to Hannah.

But his words troubled her. Am I using my daughter to perform the menial jobs, while I socialize? Have I stolen part of her childhood, as part of mine was stolen? she asked herself. Hannah decided it was time to set her butterfly free.

One evening after dinner, Hannah declared, "Vera, I think yer should get a job. Eileen and Doris are both working. It's time you went out into the world, too, and gained some experience and earned some money fer yerself. After all, yer seventeen years old." Peter looked up from his newspaper with surprise but didn't speak.

Vera's mouth gaped open. "What? What? Mam, yer can't mean it! Who will look after yer? Who will do the washin' and ironin'? Who will clean the church? I don't want a job. Please tell me you don't mean it!"

"Don't fret, girl. Everyone has to grow up eventually. It'll be an adventure for yer. Lilly and Grace will help me, and the church can do without our swollen knees for a while. You have a lot to offer. Yer work hard; you're good natured and always willin' to please. I think domestic service would be the ideal job for yer."

Later that night, when Vera was in bed, Granma White asked Hannah, "Are you sure about this? That girl is not the brightest star in the heavens. Do you really need the extra money?"

"That's not true!" Hannah shot back. "She's slow, that's all. And, yes, the extra money would be helpful, but I'm doing this for Vera, so she can experience the world outside this house. Saint Anthony and I will keep an eye on her." Later as she lay in bed, Hannah thought, I hope I'm doing the right thing.

Hannah and Vera scoured the *Birkenhead News* want ads each day, circling the possibilities. "Here's one that suits you," Hannah said.

Girl wanted for live-in domestic service and to provide assistance with four children. Must be hard-working and even-tempered. Previous experience an advantage, but not essential. Sunday's off. Apply Maria Purell, Oxton 7298.

"They don't mind lack of experience, because then they don't have to pay too much. You love kids, spoiled or otherwise. And the woman's name is Maria, which means she's Latin, and that means she's Catholic."

"They're foreign!" Vera exclaimed.

"Don't worry. Before we walk down to the phone box on the corner, we'll write down exactly what yer gonna say to her, just so yer won't stutter."

◆

Ricardo Purell was feeling pleased with himself. Here he was, just forty years old and doing quite well, thank you. Money? He had money and responsibility—lots of it. He was widely respected. Best of all, he had influence. As secretary to the Mexican Consulate in Liverpool, he was the focus of all trading decisions between Mexico and Britain and used his position to benefit both countries.

Ricardo was born on the Rock of Gibraltar. His father was British, his mother Spanish, which made him an expert in the nuances and customs of both cultures. He ingratiated himself with the Mexican authorities, who were anxious to improve their trading status with British industrialists. He presented himself as the conduit to accommodate trade agreements and was able to smooth out any cultural misunderstandings.

Augmenting Ricardo's status was his wife, Maria, an elegant Spanish charmer, admired by both slippery Mexican traders and stodgy British factory owners. She was a potent weapon in social situations, where business deals were often finalized. Maria bore Ricardo four children, all of whom had Spanish forenames at her insistence. He modified his own forename, depending on who he was dealing with—Ricardo for the Mexicans, Richard for the British.

The Purells owned an expensive house in Oxton, a well-to-do suburb of Birkenhead, from where Ricardo commuted each day, via the underground railway, to his office in Liverpool. They also had a live-in servant girl, a necessity for people in their social position. Their current servant had not lived up to their requirements, so Richardo had fired her.

◆

The interview went well. Maria Purell was impressed with Vera's humility and religious fervor—always good characteristics in a domestic servant. Plus, Vera was prepared to accept a low wage. Just seventeen years old, Vera became a live-in maid. She rode away from Hannah's nest on the Blue Angel, totally ill-equipped to deal with the world she was about to enter.

Senor and Senora Purell's home was no more than three miles

89

from Beckwith Street, but it might have been a thousand miles in terms of social status and cultural values. To Vera the house was a palace, full of rooms with names like "study" and "playroom."

"They eat with silver cutlery," Vera told her sisters. "They have two indoor toilets! Their children have lots of shoes, and they leave food on their plates." But what impressed Vera the most was that they had their own telephone. Vera was afraid to answer it, because whoever was calling had to be important, at least a lot more important than she. So Vera would stutter and stammer and sound like an idiot when she had to pick it up.

Eventually Vera settled into her new surroundings. Richard and Maria were more than patient with her. Understanding her naïveté, she was someone they could mold to their own needs. Sometimes when she made a mistake, Richard would put his arm around her shoulders and comfort her. "Don't fret, Vera. This is how you learn."

Vera worked hard: She fetched, polished, cleaned, and answered the door. She was good with the children, who were all well behaved. All her life, Vera was good with children. Maria tried to teach her the art of Spanish cooking, but the chasm between paella and greasy chip sandwiches was too wide to bridge.

"So what is this *scouse* that you eat?" asked Maria.

"Well, ma'am, it's a stew made with fish or meat, potatoes, carrots, and old socks."

"What type of fish?"

"Fish heads, ma'am."

When Maria dressed for a social event, Vera would help her choose her jewelry; then Maria would swirl around her room and pull Vera up to swirl too. They laughed together like debutants at a ball.

On Sundays, Vera would relay to her attentive sisters the events of the week. "Her wardrobe is full of the most wonderful gowns, all made for her by T.J. Hughes in Liverpool. When she dances, she is so elegant, she looks like a Princess of Seville. The Master is such an important man, and so handsome. He always has kind words for me." Vera didn't disclose how lonely she was, or how much she missed the hustle and bustle of Hannah's house.

Ricardo's advances on Vera were slow and gradual—a process

that he had perfected over the years. He started with the fatherly arm around her shoulders, leaving it there for a little longer than he should. It made Vera feel uncomfortable, but she didn't want to be rude. Next, he progressed to a squeeze of her hips, and from there, the risky step to a slap on her bottom. She stayed silent—troubled, but not knowing how to deal with the situation. When he tried to kiss her, she resisted and pushed him away, but he wasn't deterred and tried again. This time she succumbed and offered no resistance, but with no active participation. In truth, she was flattered by his attentions, but she could not admit those feelings to herself. She knew it was very wrong and felt shame.

The inevitable soon occurred. Maria was out shopping in Liverpool, accompanied by three of her children, leaving Ricardo and Vera alone in the house, except for the baby. He waited until she was cleaning a bedroom and saw his opportunity. He took her in his arms and kissed her with a passion that caused her body to tremble. Ricardo was careful to be gentle with her, however, knowing she must be a virgin and not wanting to spoil any further opportunities for himself.

When it was over she lay on the bed, crying softly, because she knew she had encouraged him, because she had wanted it to happen. It was impossible for her to reconcile these emotions with her religious fervor. She had committed a mortal sin. She was an adulteress, and the guilt was of the severest intensity, which only a good Catholic education can provide.

From then on, whenever Ricardo and Vera could sneak the chance, they made love. She didn't understand that she was responding to normal, human hormones. She believed that the devil had captured her soul.

Vera's internal struggle began to change her personality; she became sullen and short-tempered. When Hannah or any of her sisters asked what was bothering her, she would respond that she didn't feel well. Maria noticed the change, too, but she knew exactly what caused it.

One evening, Maria and Ricardo had a stormy argument, which Vera could not help but overhear. Maria yelled at her husband, "Enough! I've had enough of this. She must go! There will be no more girls in this house. You can't keep your hands off them, you pig! If this happens again, I will take the children and return to Espana! She goes immediately."

After Vera packed her bag, she crept down the stairs, in an attempt to secretly slip away, but Maria was at the front door.

Vera bowed her head sheepishly. "I'm so sorry," she said, her voice as fragile as a soap bubble.

Maria pointed a manicured finger at Vera's face. "Never come back."

Vera cycled the three miles back to Hannah's house slowly, her suitcase attached to the front basket. She needed time to think of an excuse.

"Yer fired? Why?" Hannah asked, with arms folded.

"I broke some wine glasses. It was an accident, but the mistress was very angry."

"So they threw yer out at this time of night? They wouldn't let yer stay 'til the mornin'? Tell me the truth, girl. What happened? What bothers yer?"

"Mam, I'm tired and don't feel well. Please, let me go to bed."

❖

Two Sundays later was the day that Lilly, then eight years old, was to be confirmed into the Catholic Church. Hannah had put aside some money to buy a leg of lamb from the market, so a grand Sunday meal was prepared for after the ceremony. Vera volunteered to stay home and cook while everyone was at church. When Hannah reached the church, she realized that she had left the offering envelope at home, so back she headed to the house.

Meanwhile, Vera tried to light the gas stove to cook the lamb but had trouble with the pilot light. She turned on the gas several times without effect, then turned if off again. Finally she took a match and bent down to light the stove by hand. It was at that moment that Hannah arrived back at the house. She found Vera on her knees, with her head in the oven, a slight smell of gas in the room.

Hannah gasped. "Oh my God! Vera!" She grabbed her daughter in a tight bear hug. "What in God's name are yer doin', girl? Holy Mary, mother of God, what are you doin'?"

"I'm tryin' to light the gas," Vera said.

"Whatever is wrong, girl, this is not the answer." Hannah sobbed. "Whatever it is, I'll make it better—that I will. Yer have yer whole life ahead. Takin' yer life is not the answer." Hannah's emotional state intensified. "It's never the answer."

"What? I wasn't tryin' to commit suicide. Mam, please let go of me—you're hurtin' me. I was just tryin' to light the gas."

"Of course you were, dear. Now you and I are going to work this out together. I blame myself, of course. I should never have let yer go out into the world—yer too young and naive. It's my fault. I'll pray to Saint Anthony to intercede with God to forgive me."

Vera let her mother ramble for a while until her emotional intensity ebbed, then they both got up from their knees. She sat her mother down on a chair and fetched a handkerchief for Hannah's eyes and nose.

"I wasn't tryin' to kill myself, Mam, but I'll tell yer what's wrong, because I know yer'll keep on at me until I do." She took a deep breath. "I'm pregnant."

Hannah stopped sniffling. Her demeanor changed to grim. "Who is the fath—?"

"Mr. Purell," Vera interrupted. "I was fired because his wife found out." Hannah sat in stunned silence. Vera sat down at Hannah's knees and wept. "I know it was wrong. I know it was a terrible sin. I let you down, Mam—I'm so sorry. I'm stained for life. I'm an adulteress!"

"No, you're not." Hannah came back to life. "You can't be an adulteress, because yer not married. He's an adulterer, but you have to be married to be an adulteress."

"Are you sure?"

"As God is my witness. Listen, I'll tell you a secret that you have to promise you won't repeat."

"I promise—not a soul."

"I was pregnant with Eileen when I married yer father."

Vera clasped her hands to her mouth. "Oh my God!"

"It happens," Hannah said. "Mary was pregnant when she married Joseph." Hannah rose from her chair. "I'll make some tea, and then we'll decide on what needs to be done."

Vera knew that her mother would never believe that she wasn't trying to commit suicide. Hannah blamed herself and remained convinced, for the rest of her life, that when she entered Saint Lawrence's Church that day, the spirit of Saint Lawrence spun her around and sent her scurrying back home to save her daughter's life.

❖

Maria Purell put another advertisement in the *Birkenhead News,* looking for a replacement servant, this time with the caveat "only mature women may apply."

Hannah hid the Blue Angel by the side hedge so it wouldn't be recognized and knocked on the Purell's door. Maria opened it. Well, missus, Hannah thought, no slime ball is going to ravish my daughter and get away with it.

"I've come about the job," Hannah said.

"Well you're about the right age," Maria said, and invited Hannah into the parlor.

Maria pointed to an expensive Italian armchair. "Please sit down." Hannah remained standing. "Are you the lady who can speak Spanish?" Maria asked.

Hannah nodded. "Is your husband home?"

"Yes, why do you ask?"

Hannah shot out the parlor door, and ran from room to room, while Maria hurried behind her, yelling, "Where are you going? What are you doing?"

Hannah burst into the study, causing Richard Purell to look up sharply from his desk.

"Are you Richard Purell?" she demanded.

"It's Ricardo Purell, and who the hell are you?"

"I'm Hannah Corcoran. Vera Luxton is my daughter. She's pregnant and you're the father, you slimy cockroach. What have yer got to say for yerself?"

Richardo bounced up from his chair. "How dare you," he blurted, "come into my home, you washerwoman, you peasant, and accuse me. . . . I'll call the police right now, have you arrested. Get out! I'll throw you out myself!"

Hannah simmered a few degrees below her boiling point. "She's only seventeen. A sweet, naive girl. Yer took advantage, as if she meant nothin' because she was a servant. You people think yer can treat us like animals. You use us then toss us away like a cigarette butt. And now my daughter is ruined. What type of low life are yer?"

Richardo blustered and threatened again, but Maria had come into the room behind Hannah and cut him off. "Stop, Ricardo! Be a man! Admit what you have done to this woman's daughter, a good Catholic girl."

Assailed now from both sides, Richardo became defensive. "It was her. She seduced me. Besides, how do you know I made her pregnant? It could be any number of dock workers!"

Hannah's left fist went to its action station behind her back, but Maria answered before Hannah could.

"Ricardo, you know that she was an innocent. You promised me that it would never happen again."

Richardo came over to stand face-to-face with Hannah. "I suppose you came here for money."

"I want no money. There is nothing yer have that I want."

"Then why are you here? To embarrass me in front of my wife?"

"No, I've come here to give *you* something."

"And what would that be?"

"This!" But before the fist could begin its deadly journey, Maria stepped between Hannah and her husband and slapped him hard across the face. Ricardo stepped backwards, his hand on his cheek. Hannah stepped the opposite way, her fist still curled. She glared at Maria. "Why did yer do that?"

"What? You don't approve?"

"No. He deserves better." Hannah took two steps forward, and the fist of vengeance smashed into Ricardo's nose with a horrible thud. "That's better," Hannah said.

Maria gasped. Ricardo was on his knees, and his nose dripped blood onto the Turkish carpet. "I'll get some cotton wool and bandages," she said, clearly shaken.

Before she reached the door, Hannah stopped her with a hand on her chest. She pointed an accusing finger at Maria's face. "You bitch. Yer knew what would happen." Hannah spat out her words. "Yer knew, and yet yer still hired my Vera."

Maria lowered her head. "He told me that he would not touch Vera. He promised. I thought it was safe to hire her because. . . ."

"Why?" said Hannah. "Why?"

"Because she was not attractive." With her head still bowed, she said softly, "I am so sorry." Maria looked down at Ricardo, still kneeling on the carpet. "Of course we shall help you financially with the child's upbringing," Maria said.

Hannah shot her an icy glare. "We want none of your money. Vera, myself, and the rest of my family will raise this child. You or your husband will play no part in its life. I don't want the child knowing its father preyed on innocent young women." Hannah slammed the door on her way out.

◆

A couple of weeks went by before Hannah mentioned to Vera that she had called on the Purells, although Vera suspected that she would. "I don't know what yer saw in him, really," Hannah casually remarked.

"Well, he is a handsome man, don't yer think?"

"Are you kiddin'? With a nose like that?"

"Like what?"

"Broken!"

Still, there was a serious problem to be addressed. An unmarried girl who became pregnant brought shame on her family, regardless of the circumstances. So Vera was shipped off to Hannah's brother Billy, who lived in West Derby—a part of Liverpool, where no one would know her.

The baby was stillborn. Vera, cursed like all Catholics with an overwhelming sense of guilt, entered a nearby convent. Two months later, Billy arrived to inform Hannah that Vera had left the convent without taking her vows and had disappeared.

"Just like she did when she was a kid," Eileen said.

◆

"Bless me, Father, for I have sinned." From the other side of the confessional, Father Flaherty recognized Hannah's voice.

"What is it my child?"

"I thought I was doing the right thing for my daughter, but now she is lost, and I have a stillborn child on my conscience. God forgive me."

"Hannah, yer sent your daughter out into the world to spread her wings, but she flew into a spider's web. It was not a sin, just an error in judgment, which any mother could have made. Vera is tougher than yer think—she'll turn up."

◆

Two weeks later, Hannah answered a knock on the front door. Vera, bedraggled and weary, held her worn, old suitcase. Next to her a black Labrador retriever wagged his tail.

"Mam, this dog has followed me. If I come home, can I keep it?"

Tears stung Hannah's eyes. "You drive a hard bargain, but I welcome you with open arms, my sweet."

Hannah tucked Vera back under her wing, where she belonged, where she was happy. She never left again. And for the rest of her life Vera always had a black Labrador companion, and she always named the dog Kim.

Hannah snuggled into bed with Peter that night, pleased that all her charges were safe again, under her roof. There was food in the pantry, coal in the coal hole, and no one ailed. As the decade neared its end, all seemed right with her world. But a chill wind was blowing across the North Atlantic, carrying dire news that would bring turmoil to Hannah's life once again.

Chapter Nine

≡ 1932 ≡

Activist

In October of 1929, three thousand miles to the west, men of fortune threw themselves off tall buildings. They couldn't bear the thought of being poor. A year later, destitute mothers back in Birkenhead stuck their heads in gas ovens. They couldn't bear the thought of watching their children starve. The Great Depression spread its misery throughout the industrialized world like the bubonic plague, and as in every disaster throughout history, it was the poor who took it in the neck.

A tall man in a black suit and trilby hat, face as grim as Lucifer, thumped on the front door of 59 Beckwith Street, home of the Rileys, next-door neighbors of Peter and Hannah Corcoran. When Mrs. Dora Riley opened the door, the man barged in.

"Means test assessor," he said, as he pulled a notebook from his inside pocket. Without another word, he marched from room to room, taking note of every stick of furniture, every carpet, every curtain, every picture on the wall, everything with the slightest value. He rummaged through drawers and emptied the contents of Mrs. Riley's handbag onto the kitchen table. He searched in every possible place where a watch or a necklace might be hidden. Means test assessors put an arbitrary value on any object that could be pawned, which was then subtracted from any unemployment benefit the family might receive.

The assessor looked at his notes. "Says here you have three children: a boy of ten years, a girl six, and a baby. I've seen the boy and girl—where is the baby?"

Dora pointed to the perambulator. "She's asleep."

"Take her out of the pram," he said.

"It will wake her," Dora said. "What's the point?"

"I said take her out of the pram, woman. I want to be sure it's not a doll."

Dora held the baby while the assessor examined the pram. The baby woke and began to cry.

Without changing his dour expression, like a burglar searching for loot, he pulled clothes out of closets, checked every pocket of every coat, and stripped the bed clothes off the bed. Dora held a hand on her underwear drawer. With a grunt, the assessor swept her hand away and rummaged through her unmentionables, while Dora stood next to him, head bowed.

He looked under the bed, where the piss pot was still unemptied from the night before. The assessor pulled it out and peered into it, checking for anything hidden. Dora rushed from the room with the pram, her face crimson with embarrassment, her self-respect destroyed.

Meanwhile, in the backyard, Teddy Riley heaved assorted possessions over the wall to Peter Corcoran in the yard next door. The mangle, the zinc bathtub, Granma's old ottoman, the king's picture, a child's wooden scooter—all disappeared into the Corcoran cellar. A lookout at the end of the street had seen the assessor coming and had spread the word.

"He's gone," said Teddy Riley, "but keep the stuff for a couple of days, Peter, if you don't mind. Sometimes they come back to try and catch you."

"No problem," Peter replied. "Which assessor was it?"

"Councilor Brown, the bastard. They say he enjoys it."

Hannah emerged through the Riley's back door into the yard, ducking under the washing on the line, with her arm around the shoulders of Dora Riley, who sobbed into a handkerchief.

Teddy Riley wrapped his wife in his arms. "Don't despair, luv. We'll get through this."

"I feel as cheap as dirt," she said.

Peter lit a cigarette and asked Teddy, "What's the word down at the shipyard?"

"The last refit finished a week ago," Teddy replied. "There's no work on the books, so I don't know when I'll get my job back. How are you fixed down at the docks?"

Peter shrugged. "They reckon forty percent of Birkenhead dockers are unemployed. Instead of lines of ships waiting for the tide to turn at the mouth of the Mersey, now there's a scant few. Still, I think I'll be safe for a while. On the docks it's last-in, first-out, and excepting for the war, I've worked there since I left school."

"Even if we pass the means test, we only get fifteen shillings a week," Dora Riley said, still sobbing. "How can we live on that?"

The Riley's son, Tommy, appeared from the back door. Gaunt and pale, the boy hid behind his father's back.

"Do you see my lad?" Teddy said. "He's ten years old and as thin as a whippet. Now he's wearing bobby's blues. He went to school with his arse sticking out of his pants and holes in his socks. The school notified the Policemen's Benevolent Fund, which kitted him out in bobby's blues—navy blue coat, navy blue pants, black socks—which is great, except every kid they help gets the same damn uniform. They may as well have tattooed *Poor* on his forehead. The other kids make fun of him, rough him up. It breaks his mother's heart to see him so depressed."

"When's it all goin' to end?" asked Dora. "When are all these politicians going to get off their backsides and fix this state of affairs so we can all get back on our feet?"

"It's a downward spiral, out of control," Hannah said. "It's not that they don't want to fix it—they don't know how. It'll end when we hit rock bottom, and no one knows when that will be. There is one thing they *could* do though, and that's abolish this terrible means test." Hannah took hold of Dora again. "C'mon luv, I'll make yer a cuppa."

❖

At six the next morning, Peter parted the bedroom curtains slightly and looked down at Teddy Riley leaving his house.

"What is it?" Hannah asked with a yawn.

"Teddy Riley, on his way out."

"To go looking for work?" Hannah got out of bed.

"There is no work," Peter answered. "He's goin' to get his papers signed. He can't get any unemployment pay if he doesn't have three signatures a week from firms, showin' he applied for work. It's a government requirement. Problem is, thousands of men are out there looking for someone to sign their papers, and firms have gotten tired of it. Most won't do it anymore."

"So what do they do?" Hannah asked, half listening to young Grace yelling at Lilly in the next room.

"They walk. They walk all day, that's what they do. Teddy told me that yesterday he walked down to the docks, then to the steel foundry, down Conway Street to the abattoir, and then on to the shipyard. Finally, he walked down New Chester Road all the way to the soap factory in Port Sunlight. He walked home in the rain, without one signature."

"It's a shame," said Hannah. "Where's his bike?"

"The first things they pawn are the bikes, as long as their legs are still workin'."

"Well, maybe we can lend him the Blue Angel." Hannah was finally dressed. "I've got to see to the children."

"It's more than a shame. It's a bloody crime!" Peter yelled.

Startled, Hannah stopped and turned around. She had rarely seen Peter this upset. His face flushed, he continued to yell. "Are you blind to all this? Have you not seen the queues outside the pawn shops? Have you not seen men in the streets chasing pigeons for food? Look at the men roaming through the park with nowt to do, with hopelessness in their eyes, stripped of their dignity. Look at the kids, skinny to the bone, no shoes on their feet. Kids dying of pneumonia, diphtheria, tuberculosis."

"Of course I've seen them," Hannah yelled back. "What do you want me to do? I've been in their shoes! I pray for them. I put money in the poor box. But my responsibility is to my family, and that's responsibility enough."

Outside the open bedroom door, Granma White and all the children stood in stunned silence, to witness the first shouting match that their parents had ever had.

"What's come over Peter?" Granma White asked.

Still red with anger, Hannah replied, "I don't know, but I blame Alf Richards for this!"

◆

The next Sunday after Mass, Peter took the children for their usual walk in Birkenhead Park. He stopped at the park entrance on Park Road North to listen to the soapbox orators, but instead of the usual spattering of spectators, this day there were hundreds of people. Several more speakers than usual spouted their spiel, including would-be town councilors, Labour Party leaders, even black-shirted Fascists.

Alf Richards, on his soapbox as usual, had drawn the largest audience by far. Plain-clothes detectives mingled with the crowd, easily identified by their smooth hands and beady eyes. Peter loved to hear his old friend speak, and Alf was in fine voice that day. The two nodded at each other while Alf extorted the unemployed to join him in a march on London.

"Let's tell this government how grim our lives are," he said. "Let's join our fellow brothers and sisters from the Durham coal mines, from Yorkshire and Lancashire mill towns, from the steel mills of the Midlands, from the coal fields of South Wales. Let us all march on London.

"The government shall witness the misery and starvation of the unemployed. They shall hear of the evictions and the degradation. Tomorrow we march. Birkenhead, Birkenhead," he yelled, "who is with me!?"

A great cheer went up. Eleven-year-old Lilly cheered too. "Shush," her father said.

◆

Three days after the argument, tension still simmered in the house. It ratcheted up several notches when Hannah burst into the back room and thrust a paper at Peter.

"What the hell is this!" she said.

"It's a paper! What does it look like?"

"I found it in the toilet."

"Then it's toilet paper!"

"And that's all it's good for—toilet paper. It's *The Daily Worker!* A Communist paper! Are you out of your mind?" Hannah puffed. "If anyone sees you with this, you'll be labeled a Communist and your feet won't touch the pavement when they kick you off the docks. You know that. You'll never find work around here again, and then we'll all join the starving masses." Hannah paused to take a breath. "What will you have accomplished? If you want to be an activist, then you do it when you're a young man, when you've no responsibilities. I know we have two girls working now, but it's a pittance they get. The whole family relies upon your wage, so think twice before you go any further with this." Hannah turned and stormed out.

◈

"A pint of the best, Alf?" Peter asked, looking around at the almost deserted bar of the Ram's Head. Beer money is scarce these days, he thought.

"I can't buy yer one back," Alf said.

"Then I'll buy the second round too." Peter smiled.

"God love yer," said Alf as Peter put a frothy Birkenhead brown ale in front of him.

"I thought you weren't religious," Peter said.

"Yes, I'm an atheist, thank God."

Peter laughed. "You *are* a card, Alf Richards."

Alf took a long swig of his beer, wiped the froth from his mouth with his sleeve, and looked seriously at his old friend. "So how did she take it?"

"She took it like I told yer she would," Peter said. "She's angry. She's afraid that I'll lose my job and so am I. She's shown no sign of wanting to get involved. She'll look after the family, that's all, and everyone else needs to fend for themselves." Peter took a swig of beer. "Look, Alf, I admire you for yer principles, yer courage, and I agree with everything you believe in, but I'm not strong like you. I'm not an activist. I'm not a Communist. I'm just selfish because all I want out of life is a bit of peace and quiet. If yer want Hannah to get involved, then you should ask her yerself."

"Then I'll do just that, if it's all right with you. C'mon, you old scoundrel, let's have a game of darts."

◈

Hannah was surprised when she answered the door. "Alf Richards, want do you want? Peter is at work."

"I know. It's you I want to talk with."

Hannah stiffened. "What in God's name would you want to talk to me about?"

"Can I come in?"

Hannah looked up and down the street. "C'mon in then, before someone sees you." Alf followed her past the parlor, where guests would normally be taken, into the kitchen. He was used to being treated like a criminal.

"I'll make some tea," Hannah said. "It's Alf Richards," she said to her mother, who was sitting at the table.

"Comrade Richards, how goes the battle? How is Comrade Stalin these days?" Granma White grinned.

Alf sat down at the table. "You know, all reports say that the system works well over there in Russia. The workers are in charge. Everyone shares what they have. It's all for one and one for all."

"Well, I've heard different reports," the blind lady replied, "but you believe what you want to believe."

Hannah placed a mug of tea and a plate of shortbread biscuits in front of Alf. Seeing how he eyed the biscuits, she said, "Eat as many as you like." As he munched, Hannah thought back to the time she and Alf were at school together. He was liked by the teachers and admired by the kids. He was the sort of kid that other kids wanted to be seen with. The smart kid, the funny kid, the mature kid—that was Alf. She knew the war had twisted him around and sent him off in a dangerous direction. What a damn shame, she thought.

Finally, Hannah asked, "What're you doing with my Peter?"

"He's my Peter, too. We've been best mates since school. That aside, I'm here because I need help, but not from Peter—from you. We've put together a petition, a series of demands that we want to present to the town council at their next meeting. I'm asking you to present them."

"Who are *we*?" Hannah asked.

"The National Unemployed Workers Movement, the NUWM."

"Isn't that an offshoot of the Communist Party?"

"Yes," Alf Richards said with a sigh, "it's an organization to help the unemployed, but if yer a member of the NUWM, it doesn't mean that yer a member of the Communist Party."

"Still, I want no part of it," Hannah said, folding her arms. "I think you should leave now."

Alf put his hand to his forehead and briefly closed his eyes, but he didn't budge.

"Hannah, I joined the Communist Party back in 1920, after I experienced the horrors of the Great War—a war we fought for the rich, for the aristocrats, for princes and kings. Our men returned home to find nowt had changed for them. The poverty, the oppression, and the rampant unemployment were all still there."

"But why the Communists? Why not the Labour Party?" Hannah asked.

"The Labour Party was insipid and the members fought among themselves. To my mind, the concept of communism was the only idea that offered an answer." Hannah looked away.

Alf told her that he hadn't found permanent employment in sixteen years. He stood outside the dock gates and tried to sell *The Daily Worker*, but rarely did anyone buy it, because they were afraid someone might see them. Sometimes dockers stole his papers and ripped them up. Sometimes they spit on him, and sometimes they punched him.

Alf's voice softened. "Many pubs won't allow me in. I'm a pariah wherever I go, and I'm abused by the very people I'm trying to help. I often wonder why I put myself and my wife through this torment."

"Why do yer?" Granma White asked.

"Because I can't watch my people suffer and do nothing."

Hannah made eye contact with him. There was a short silence. Alf took his last sip of tea, and continued.

"Hannah Corcoran, you're a legend in this town. People look up to yer. They see yer as a champion of the workin' class. I know you're a member of the Labour Party and the Labour councilors respect yer. The Tory councilors are in the majority, although how we let that happen is beyond me, but even they will listen to yer. I've heard yer rage about Winston Churchill and the Tories. So is that just talk? All these years—just talk?"

Hannah broke off eye contact. "If I aid yer, Peter will be judged a Communist by association."

"He hasn't been so far, and everyone knows we're old war pals. The bosses know Peter to be a hard-workin', easy-goin' man who never causes any trouble. Look Hannah, we've been hit by a tidal wave. The property class has gotten wet, but our people are drownin'. Are you going to stand by and watch them drown?" Alf arose. "Thank you for the tea and biscuits. Tell Peter I was here."

An old voice went through Hannah's head. *Help me, I'm drowning! Please help me, I can't swim!* Everything Alf said resonated with her—her neighbors suffering, the respect they had for her, yet she did little to help them. But Alf Richards, the smartest kid in the class, once Peter's best mate, had dedicated his life to the welfare of these people, though all he got in return was derision and scorn. Hannah still remembered the bad times, when an egg was a luxury, when she sent Peter to work with a ham sandwich for lunch but had cut out the middle of the ham, leaving the edges so his mates thought the ham was whole.

"Wait," Hannah said. "All right, I'll present your petition. But I have conditions: You won't talk to Peter again. You won't be seen with him in the pubs, or in the street, or at Tranmere Rovers games. You will totally disassociate yourself from my husband. Agreed?"

Alf bowed his head and issued a deep sigh. "Agreed."

◆

The following Monday, Hannah donned her best dress, polished her shoes, put her raven hair up in a bun, tied it with a red ribbon, and headed over to the park entrance. Her jaw dropped when she saw the crowd. "How many?" she asked Alf.

"I'd say about three thousand. Another couple of thousand are going direct to the town hall from Rock Ferry and New Ferry. They knew you'd be here."

Alf jumped on his soapbox and bellowed through his rusty megaphone. "Hannah Corcoran's here. She's going to lead us to the town hall." The crowd cheered while Hannah scowled at Alf. She hadn't agreed to lead anyone anywhere. Reluctantly, Hannah climbed up on

Alf's soapbox and the cheering grew louder. Alf gave her his rusty old megaphone. She cleared her throat.

"I know that the last two weeks you've marched to the town hall and were turned away. Today, they will listen to us." The cheering could be heard at the other end of the park. "Remember, we are not a mob. Ours is a peaceful demonstration. There will be no intimidation, no violence. But today they will listen to us because we are five thousand strong, because we have reached the end of our patience, because we are desperate."

With banners flying, Hannah and Alf in the lead, chanting "We Want Work," the unemployed began the one-mile march down Conway Street to keep their appointment with the Birkenhead Town Council. When the marchers turned onto Argyle Street, they stopped dead in their tracks. A metal barricade blocked the way to Hamilton Square, behind which a large contingent of policemen was posted, batons in hand.

The marchers continued until they were nose-to-nose with the police. Pushing and shoving escalated to banners being pulled away from protesters and a man being pulled out of the crowd and beaten with batons. The situation was about to explode when a Labour councilor appeared and announced that the council would accept a delegation from the NUWM.

Hannah and Alf came forward.

Birkenhead Town Hall was pillared in the Greco-Roman style, topped by an imposing bell tower. It dominated Hamilton Square, whose center contained neat lawns and flower beds, with a monument at either end—one a statue of John Laird, founder of the shipyard, and the other a memorial to the dead of the Great War. Around the square stood town offices, lawyers' offices, and expensive townhouses.

Alf and Hannah nervously mounted the steps of the town hall and were ushered into the council chamber, a room of polished mahogany and marble busts. Rows of chairs were divided by an aisle into two halves: to the right sat twenty-two Conservative Party councilors, and to the left sat eighteen Labour councilors—in all they represented the 150,000 residents of Birkenhead. The mayor sat at a shiny mahogany table at the front of the room, with town officials on either side.

The office of mayor was an honorary position granted each year to a councilor who had a long record of service to the town. The real political power in the council lay with the leader of the majority party. The present leader was none other than Robin Frobisher, Hannah's old nemesis from the shipyard.

Hannah and Alf were seated at a side table, together with a deputation from the dockers' union. Hannah glanced at Frobisher. Hmm, she thought, he's put on a lot of weight; he's actually beginning to look like Winston Churchill.

At the back of the room, two stenographers and a reporter from the *Birkenhead News* took notes. By a window sat Captain James Driscoll, chief constable of Birkenhead, arms folded across his chest. Hannah noticed that two lady councilors, both of the Tory Party, wore expensive-looking dresses and hats, which made Hannah feel shabby in her best frock. All the male councilors wore dark suits, starched white shirts, and polished shoes, in contrast to the workman's clothes of Alf and the dockers.

The first to speak was the dockers' representative, George Newell, an experienced union man who was used to speaking in this type of environment. He railed against the means test and the fact that the unemployment rate for a single man was ten shillings a week, below the rate of surrounding towns and below the poverty line. The government mandated the means test before any money could be doled out but didn't give the local councils guidelines on how to administer it. He reminded them that each town's council decided the rate of compensation, so it was in their power to increase the rate and reduce the suffering of the unemployed. He didn't tell the council anything they didn't already know.

Next up was Hannah. She was surprised to find her hands quivered. She closed her eyes and prayed to Saint Anthony that she wouldn't let her people or her family down. What if Peter is thrown off the docks? she thought. How will I feed my children? Am I making a terrible mistake? Or has God put me here to speak for his starving children? If so, I must be strong.

"Ah, Mrs. Corcoran," said Robin Frobisher, "it's been a long time since we last met. Now you're an activist, I see. Tell me, do you still punch people?"

"No sir, but I'll make an exception in your case." Some of the Labour councilors snickered behind their hands. The two female councilors looked at Hannah with distain. Frobisher scowled.

"Careful," whispered Alf behind her.

That was a mistake, Hannah thought. I shouldn't let him get to me—the stakes are too high. She cleared her throat and read from a piece of paper.

"I would ask the council to adopt the following four resolutions. First, petition the government to abolish the means test, following the example of Wigan, Sheffield, and the Vale of Leven. Second, increase unemployment benefits by twenty-five percent. Third, provide the unemployed households with boots and clothing and a hundredweight of coal each week. Finally, begin work programs such as road repair and school building, which will reduce the number of unemployed."

"Are these demands or requests?" asked Robin Frobisher.

"Demands," whispered Alf.

"For those of you who support them, they are requests, but for those of you who oppose them, they are demands," Hannah said.

A Labour councilor shouted, "Well said."

The chief constable looked out of the window, concerned that he could hear the crowd in Argyle Street becoming more restless.

Councilor Frobisher removed his spectacles and uncrossed his legs. "Look, Mrs. Corcoran, you can make all the demands that you like, but the means test is not going away. The rates in Birkenhead are comparable to those in neighboring towns, and we simply don't have the money for building programs. The economic problems that we face are worldwide problems. The solution must come from other places." Hannah scowled but held her tongue.

Frobisher continued, "Let me explain it to you with a simple example, so you can understand." Hannah bristled.

"Let's say cowboys on a ranch in Texas raise cattle. When they're ready, they drive them north to Chicago—you've seen the movies. In Chicago they slaughter them, sell the meat, sell some of the hides to McDonald Saddlery in West Kirby, and send them here on a ship that

docks in Birkenhead. McDonald Saddlrey turns the hides into saddles and sends them back to America on a ship made in Birkenhead,
where the saddles are sold to cowboys in Texas. That's how it works.
You see, Americans want good quality saddles at a reasonable price,
and we don't have enough room here to raise all that cattle." He
cleared his throat and continued.

"Now, the Chicago slaughterhouse starts speculating on the
stock market and goes bankrupt. No one sends hides to Birkenhead.
McDonald Saddlery goes bankrupt. Fewer ships come through
Birkenhead. Dockers are laid off. No more ships are built to transport saddles. Ship builders are laid off. Texans have no saddles to herd
their cattle. It's a vicious circle."

"What happens to the cattle?" Hannah asked.

"I don't know," said Frobisher, a bit flustered by the question. "I
suppose they just wander off."

"So what you're sayin'," Hannah said, "is that this economy won't
improve until the cows come home."

The council chamber shook with laughter. Frobisher sat grim-
faced, but Hannah had eased her tension, so now she could say with
confidence what she came to say.

"You've heard enough of the sufferin' of the unemployed in this
town," she began, "so I won't go over it again. I just want to tell you
this—these people are at the end of their rope. Look out the window. The situation is volatile. To those poor people out there, this
is another potato famine. You do nothing while they starve, but this
time they will not stand by. Between 1914 and 1918 they went to war
to protect the interests of the property classes, for the workin' classes
had nothing to lose." She pointed to the window. "Look at that war
memorial out there. On its base is etched *Lest We Forget*. How many
of you have forgotten? The next time we fight, we will fight for our
own interest—not yours."

"Is that a threat?" asked a Tory councilor.

"No, it's a warning," Hannah replied. "You need to act quickly
before the situation gets worse, before blood is spilt."

With that, a heated argument broke out between a Labour councilor
and a Tory councilor. The Tory maintained that the unemployment

rate in Birkenhead was around twenty percent, while the Labour councilor was adamant that the number was closer to forty percent.

Hannah broke in. "I don't understand all these numbers, so maybe you can help me. This year, twenty-nine unemployed committed suicide in Birkenhead. Last year it was sixteen. What's a good number? Last year, one out of every twenty of our children died. This year it looks like it will be one in ten. Is that a good number? I don't know. Please tell me."

Heads bowed among the council members. Alf nodded at Hannah in approval.

Hannah opened her pocketbook and took out a paper bag. She pulled a boy's cap from the bag and tossed it onto the middle of the table.

"That's Tommy Riley's cap, a nice young lad, ten years old, son of my neighbor. He died two days ago of diphtheria. If his parents could afford medicine, or if they could have given him more than stale bread and tea as his nourishment, then maybe. . . ." Hannah's chin trembled. "I gave him the occasional cheese sandwich, but I've six of my own to feed. God help me, I should have done more. What is the number of dead children we're willing to accept? I need to tell his mother."

A solemn silence fell over the proceedings. Hannah put the cap back in the paper bag. "Thank you for listening." Hannah sat down again at the side table. Alf put his arm around her shoulders and could feel her body shaking.

◆

Outside, a fine drizzle was falling on the crowd, which had waited in frustration for two hours. When Alf and Hannah appeared, all went silent. Alf spoke again through his old, rusty megaphone. "The council has debated the first resolution, and has voted to adopt it. They will petition the government to abolish the means test." Loud cheers echoed around the square. Alf continued, "The vote was thirty-nine for, one against."

"Give us his name!" someone shouted.

Alf asked them if they wanted to wait while the council debated the second resolution. The crowd yelled "Yes, Yes, Yes!"

When Hannah and Alf returned to the council chamber, Robin Frobisher was arguing vehemently against an increase in unemployment benefits. He stated that Poor Law abuse was rampant. "These people deliver newspapers. They act as golf caddies. They dig up cockles at Morton Shore, then sell them in the pubs at night. We give them boots, and they pawn them for beer money. They claim they are destitute, but you will find betting slips in their pockets. They spend their time at mid-week football matches and raising expensive racing dogs."

Frobisher glanced at Hannah and then continued. "And these Catholics breed like rabbits, so why should we be expected to feed and clothe their children? I move an amendment to refer this matter to the Public Assistance Committee." Throughout his speech, the Labour councilors hissed.

If ever I wanted to punch someone, it's now, Hannah thought.

Frobisher's amendment passed 22 to 18, following party lines.

◆

Alf Richards, head held low, faced the crowd—wet, tired, and hungry—and told them that the town council had fobbed them off again. "But we will be back," he urged. "The Public Assistance Committee meets here on Wednesday. We need everyone here, and more, to march again."

Local printers refused to print leaflets for the NUWM, afraid of being black-listed, so on Monday night the chalkers were deployed. All over the town and beyond, they chalked on walls, on doors, on pavements, and even on the roads:

NEXT DEMONSRATION—WEDNESDAY NOON—
MEET PARK ENTRANCE

Hannah and Alf were astonished to find ten thousand protesters had turned up to march with them again.

"Mind if I join you?" said a familiar voice.

"Well, Father Flaherty, you're welcome, but won't yer get into trouble?" Hannah asked.

"Better to be in trouble with the Bishop than in trouble with God."

So the priest, the Communist, and Hannah the Hammer set off down Conway Street leading an army of the great unwashed, chanting, singing, waving banners, inspired by the magnitude of their numbers. They now felt they were at least doing something to aid their plight, rather than waiting for their elected officials to act.

Hannah looked across at Alf Richards marching to her left. His head was held high, his chest puffed out, grinning like the Cheshire cat. All these years, she thought, they ignored him. They treated him like horse manure and now they need him. Now he is their leader. She had read about the Russian Revolution, and it struck her that Alf looked like he was leading the proletariat into Red Square, or leading the poor people of Odessa down the Potemkin Steps. Is this what he dreamed about, she thought, all those years in the wilderness? Then she reminded herself that both of those protests had ended with a massacre of the marchers.

Chapter Ten

≡ 1932 ≡

The Riots

Once again the protesters faced the barricades at Argyle Street. Only this time, the NUWM infiltrators had gravely underestimated the number of expected protestors. The police cordon was swept aside, and exuberant demonstrators swamped Hamilton Square.

Standing at the second-floor widow of police headquarters, Chief Constable Driscoll fumed with righteous indignation as he watched his policemen retreat. "This is what you get when you give these people an inch," he growled.

"Couldn't agree more," Councilor Frobisher said, standing next to him. "I'd say your job is on the line, my old friend."

The police had fallen back to form a human barricade in front of the Public Assistance offices, located on the east side of Hamilton Square. The members of the PAC, a subset of the town council, were disturbed, to say the least, by the clamor outside. The Conservative members denied Alf and Hannah entrance to the building and refused to discuss any issue under the duress of an "angry mob." The Conservatives sneaked out the back door under police protection. The chairman of the committee had no choice but to abandon the meeting and refer the issue of increasing the unemployment allowance back to the town council.

Alf Richards told the increasingly turbulent crowd that, once again, they had been fobbed off. In an attempt to clear the demonstrators away from the council buildings, he asked them to march back to the park entrance, where they would decide their next step. The majority of the marchers simply went back to their homes. But still, a couple of thousand had gathered at the meeting place when Alf and Hannah arrived back.

A man climbed on the park railing and yelled, "We've had enough! Councilor Frobisher is the devil who's blocking our cause. I know where he lives—about three miles from here, in Oxton. If we can trudge three miles through Flanders' mud, we can march to his house. Follow me!"

Hannah shouted, "No! No! That would be a grave mistake!" Frustrated and angry, the crowd marched off despite Hannah's plea.

"We've lost control," Hannah said to Alf.

"I know, but we better go with them to head off any mischief."

❖

Back at police headquarters, Chief Constable Driscoll discussed strategy with his inspectors, including Mathew Baker, who was now chief inspector. Also present was Chief Councilor Frobisher.

The chief constable informed the group, "What happened this morning will not happen again—you can bet your pensions on that. There are fifty extra police arriving from Chester as we speak, and Liverpool has offered a hundred more. That should be sufficient to prevent any more demonstrations at the town hall."

"Why don't we bring in the army?" Councilor Frobisher suggested.

"God, no," said Chief Inspector Baker. "The army will bring firearms, and people will get killed. We have to avoid any escalation here."

"How do we do that?" Driscoll asked, in the sarcastic tone he used for subordinates.

"Give them the extra money they ask for," Baker replied.

"And where do you suggest we get that from?" asked Frobisher, glad to double up on Baker.

"I dunno—maybe increase house taxes by, say, five shillings a year. Most people wouldn't begrudge a few coppers a week to help those who suffer." Baker looked into Frobisher's eyes. "Well, my people wouldn't."

Driscoll slapped his palm on his desk. "We will not give in to mob rule while I'm chief constable!"

The phone rang. Driscoll answered it and looked over at Frobisher. "The mob is on its way to your house!"

Frobisher jumped up, knocking his chair over. "Good God! My wife. My grandson. You have to stop them!"

❖

When Hannah and Alf arrived at the Frobisher house, in a swanky part of town, the crowd had already surrounded it.

Hannah jumped up on a small rock wall nearby. "Stop this madness! You're playin' into their hands."

"We want Frobisher!" the crowd yelled.

"Fine, I'll ask if he'll come out to talk to us, but you must hear him out, and no violence."

Hannah rang the doorbell. A woman in her mid-fifties, with a terrified expression on her powdered face, gingerly opened the door.

"I'd like to speak to Councilor Frobisher, please." Hannah said, in a tone as polite as she could muster.

"He's not here. He's out doing town business."

"Thank you. Sorry to have bothered you."

Hannah jumped back on the wall. "Frobisher's not home. Now go back to yer own homes. We'll meet at the park entrance again tomorrow."

A thin man, with a pock-marked nose, pushed to the front and threw a rock through one of Frobisher's windows.

"Stop that, you bloody idiot! Go on, get home, all of yer!"

But it was too late. Three motor coaches full of policemen arrived with a screech of brakes, and out charged the police like a horde of Goths, batons flailing. People fled in all directions. Scores were struck down causing others to fall over them in a panic to escape. Some men rallied and charged back at the police, hurling rocks, flowerpots, anything that could act as a missile. Several policemen were injured, but they eventually routed the charge. A small group of protesters, trapped in the garden of a nearby house, were taking a terrible beating. Alf Richards led a group that dove in to the rescue them. Fists and batons flew indiscriminately until the police backed away. Eventually, over fifty protesters were taken to Birkenhead General Hospital, some with their heads cut open.

Hannah and Alf walked back through the park together with a small band of supporters. No one said a word. The fuse to the powder keg now hissed away. Trepidation replaced optimism, and the mood was dire.

Ahead of them, Hannah spotted the man who threw the stone through Frobisher's window. "Hey you! I want a word."

The man stopped as the group surrounded him. "What do yer want?" He tried to sound composed, but his nervousness showed through.

"Where'd you come from?" Hannah asked. "Where do you work? What's your boss' name?"

"I'm a bricklayer," he stammered.

Hannah grabbed one of his hands. "Not the hands of a bricklayer," she said. "More the hands of a secretary."

Hannah took one step backward, and the famous left fist flew again, right on target. The victim tottered and listed to the left. His flat cap fell off and down he went.

"Good God!" Alf said. "I've heard about that fist, but I've never seen it in action."

"Let's string him up from one of these trees," a young man said.

"You've been watching too many cowboy movies," Hannah replied.

"Hit him again," Alf said.

Hannah knelt down beside him. "Look, if you don't tell us who you really work for, then I'll hand yer over to Wyatt Earp here. If yer tell us the truth, you can walk away. You have me word."

Holding his bloody nose, he took a deep breath and whispered, "I'm an undercover policeman from Liverpool."

"An agent provocateur!" Alf declared.

Hannah grabbed the man by his collar. "You started this whole riot, yer piece of dog shit! Never come back here again. Understand?"

The man nodded and scampered off faster than a rat on wheels.

Word spread quickly of the police brutality at the Frobisher house. Thousands of the unemployed came out of their homes, and the peaceful demonstrators transformed into a furious mob. By the time Alf and Hannah reached the park entrance, a battle between police and protestors was well underway. This time the protestors came armed with hammers, pokers, and rocks. They broke off spikes from the park railings and hurled them at the police, who charged several times but failed to dislodge the mob. How they broke off iron railings is a mystery to this day, but the stumps are still there for all to see.

Throughout the evening, police and protestors clashed as the violence spread into the dockside streets. A mob swept down Grange Road, the main shopping area, smashing windows and looting what they could, mainly food, clothing, and medicine.

Hannah sat in her kitchen while Doris bandaged her right hand. She had tried to punch a policeman, using her right fist for the first time, and had sprained it. As Hannah considered the irony in that, Eileen arrived home to announce that Tommy Cavanaugh, Hannah's cousin, had been arrested for looting.

The next day, violence flared again, as police reinforcements arrived from outlying areas. Peter pleaded with Hannah to stay home, but she knew she couldn't—not when the people she had led were being terrorized and beaten.

First, Hannah cycled to the county courthouse, avoiding debris in the streets and police patrols. She sat in the back of the courtroom as a string of arrested looters were paraded before a local magistrate, until eventually Tommy Cavanaugh was hauled out. Happy, but clueless was the best way to describe Tommy's personality. He smiled and waved at Hannah.

"You are accused of breaking into a store in Grange Road and stealing food. Is that true?" the magistrate asked, in a voice laced with frustration and boredom.

"Yes and no," Tommy replied.

"Which one is it, man?"

"Well yes, I'm accused of breaking into the store, and no, I didn't do it."

"I apprehended him with several other looters, leaving the store with food in his pocket," the arresting policeman chimed in.

"That's a fact," Tommy said. "I came out of the Garrick Snug and was walking home down Grange Road when I passed the co-op and saw the smashed windows, with people inside stealing food. I went inside to find out what was happenin' and noticed some cans of pineapple chunks. I took one, went back out, and that copper arrested me."

"What else did he take?" the magistrate asked the policeman.

"Just the pineapple chunks, sir."

"Were you hungry?" the magistrate asked Tommy.

"No sir, I just fancied some pineapple chunks."

A strange silence fell over the court. The magistrate bit his lip but couldn't help himself. He started with a snicker, which developed into a chuckle, which exploded into a laugh. The whole court then laughed with him, including the policeman, Hannah, and Tommy himself.

"Give this man his pineapple chunks and get him out of here," the Magistrate said.

Tommy was known as "Chunks" Cavanaugh for the rest of his life.

◆

As Hannah cycled away from the courthouse, she passed small groups of rioters going the other way. They waved at her and shouted, "Hannah the Hammer will hammer them all!"

"Where are yer all goin'?" she asked.

"To the landing stage. Coppers from Liverpool are coming over on the ferry!"

Turning the Blue Angel around, Hannah headed toward Woodside where the Mersey ferry boats landed. She cycled down the ramp to the landing stage, where at least a hundred rioters had gathered. "Here comes Hannah!" They shouted and cheered her heartily as she approached. Good God, she thought, I feel like Queen Boadicea riding in on her chariot. Historic analogies were never lost on Hannah.

The rioters had piled up a heap of bricks and stones. In front of the pile strode Robert O'Toole, ex-sergeant major of the 17th Battalion, King's Lancashire Regiment, veteran of the Somme, Passchendaele, and Cambrai. After fourteen years, ex-Sergeant Major O'Toole was back in his element, marching up and down in front of his troops, yelling out instructions, as two ferry boats drew near, choc-a-bloc with police reinforcements.

"Volley fire only, lads, on my order. Throw up, not straight, so we get the buggers in the back of the boat."

Hannah could not help but think of another historical analogy. Fourteen centuries earlier, barbaric Viking raiders had sailed up the mouth of the Mersey, rounded a headland of sparkling birch trees, hence the name Birkenhead, and landed right where she now stood. Civilized Anglo-Saxons, armed with bows and slingshots, waited to fight them off. The trepidation that those Anglo-Saxons felt must have been the same as she felt now.

Hannah asked Sergeant Major O'Toole, who was tracking the ferry boats with a pair of binoculars, if he could make out the names of the boats. "The first one's called *Hannah*," he said. "That's a coincidence—same name as you, ma'am."

Hannah sighed. Her mind flashed back sixteen years to her time in the shipyard, when she launched that ferry boat and the burst of pride she felt when she realized they had named it after her. Ah well, such is life, she thought.

Only one boat at a time could dock at the landing stage. As the *Hannah* approached, Sergeant Major O'Toole yelled "Ready, fire," and a hail of rocks and bricks rained down on the boat and its occupants. "Ready, fire," said the Sergeant Major again, then "Fire at will." Boys and men, from twelve to sixty, gleefully pelted the boat while the policemen on board scampered for cover.

"My poor ferry boat," Hannah said softly. At this point, the skipper, who had not signed up for being pelted, and fearing for the damage to his boat, not to mention fearing for his life, turned the *Hannah* about and scooted back to Liverpool, closely followed by the second boat. Sergeant Major O'Toole shouted a great "Hoorah" and everyone cheered their victory.

That worked out well, Hannah thought. Nobody badly hurt and little damage to the boat.

"They'll probably now take the train, so we'll head them off at Park Station," the sergeant major said.

"Wait," Hannah said. "Not a good idea. A policeman might fall on the rails and break his neck. Then we'll have the army comin' in. Don't want to fire on our own troops now, do we, Sergeant Major?"

"No sir. I mean ma'am."

"Better still, go to Woodside Station, where the central control for the underground railway is. Take the place by force and shut down the entire rail system. Don't use violence if you can avoid it. Then report back to base at the park entrance. You've done a fine job here, Sergeant Major."

"Yes sir. Sorry, yes ma'am," Sergeant Major O' Toole said, as he saluted. Hannah smiled and saluted back, hoping she had done it right.

As the rioters marched away, flushed with determination, Hannah shook her fist at the retreating ferry boats. "Go back to Norway, yer hairy-arsed bastards!"

◆

Throughout Thursday the riots continued. Local hospitals overflowed with protesters and police, although protesters would only attend the hospital if their injuries were serious. After medical treatment they were likely to be arrested for rioting.

From the North End to the Morpeth dock, the entire dock area was under siege. Rioters pelted police patrols with bricks and emptied piss pots on them from upstairs windows. They stretched wires across the roads to hinder their progress and removed manhole covers to catch the unwary. All the shops on Grange Road West stood smashed and looted. The riots made headlines in all the evening newspapers, even on the BBC Radio, Six O'clock News. The causes and political implications of the riots were discussed by professors of sociology, although no mention was made of people starving.

◆

Chief Inspector Mathew Baker pulled his police car over to the side of Laird Street and stopped behind an army lorry, which a police sergeant was searching.

"What have yer got for me, Sergeant?" he asked.

"This lorry left the docks about noon, sir, carrying munitions. The driver swerved to avoid a group of rioters being chased by police and hit a telephone pole. No major damage to the army vehicle. The driver is being treated at the general hospital for minor injuries."

"Please, God, don't tell me the rioters made off with guns and explosives!"

"No, sir," said the Sergeant. "The rioters kept running. Out of curiosity, I opened a couple of wooden crates in the back of the lorry to see exactly what it was carrying." The sergeant removed the top from one of the crates.

"Looks like ammunition to me," said the chief inspector, "though antiquated Great War stuff."

"These three crates at the back all contain the same thing, but I decided to open a crate at the front of the lorry, just on a hunch, and guess what I found?" the sergeant asked, quite pleased with himself.

"Bibles?"

"No, sir." The sergeant grinned. "Cigarettes and whisky! My guess is that these three crates in the back are just to fool anyone who gets nosey. The rest of the crates contain contraband. It appears that we've stumbled upon that nationwide smuggling ring the London police warned us about."

The chief inspector examined the driver's paperwork, consisting of the manifest, the authorization certificates, and the customs documents. "These all look in order. Who else knows about this besides you and me?"

"That constable over there," the sergeant replied.

The chief inspector called the constable over. "Now listen boys, here's what you do. Make it look like no one has touched these crates. Constable, get the driver from the hospital, put him back in his lorry, and send him on his way. Sergeant, go put on your civilian clothes. I'll give you my unmarked car, and then you follow that lorry. I want to know where he goes." The Sergeant and the Constable nodded.

"One other thing. Tell absolutely no one about this, understand? It's good to see someone doin' some police work in this town, instead of crackin' some poor bastard's head open."

◆

Running clashes between police and rioters continued throughout Thursday evening, with Alf Richards leading the charge. Hannah stayed home closely guarded by Peter, who adamantly refused to let her out the house, knowing she would be a prime target for the police.

"Maybe you don't want me to leave the house," Hannah said to Peter, "but I don't see how yer gonna stop me."

"Yer not too auld for me to put you over my knee and give you a good spankin'," Peter replied.

"Promises, promises," Hannah said.

Friday saw a lull in the disturbances, while both sides licked their wounds and took stock. Very few people ventured onto the streets. Most of those who did were workmen boarding up smashed windows.

A group of unemployed protestors guarded the park entrance, which had become the rioters' headquarters, and no police chanced going near.

Chief Constable Driscoll took the opportunity to have warrants issued for the arrest of those he determined to be the ringleaders of the riots. Meantime, Hannah and Alf met with other NUWM leaders in the Ram's Head. They agreed that the worst was probably over, and that Alf and Hannah should approach the town council on Monday to reiterate their demands. This time without any demonstrators.

Early the next morning, Alf Richards knocked on Hannah's front door. "I told yer not to come here," she said.

"You have to see this," he replied, holding up a copy of the *The Times*, Saturday edition.

Apparently a reporter for *The Times* had been granted an interview with Joseph Stalin in Moscow. Stalin had railed against Capitalism, citing the Depression as the death throes of a corrupt system. He pointed to the suffering of the working class, caused by the greed of the privileged.

Alf read the paper. "It is time for the working class of Britain to rise up against their oppressors, as they have done in Birkenhead."

"He didn't actually say Birkenhead, did he?" Hannah asked in shock.

"I dunno," Alf replied. "Sometimes the press will try to tie us to an imaginary Soviet conspiracy, but this is the *The Times of London*, the paper with the most credibility in the country. So yes, Stalin could have said Birkenhead."

"Why would he single out our town?" Hannah asked. "There are unemployed disturbances in Belfast and Glasgow. The unemployed are marching in major cities like Sheffield and Newcastle."

"Your guess is as good as mine."

"If Stalin has held us up as a shining example of Communism, then we're doomed!"

"We sure are," Alf replied. "Damn you, Joseph Stalin. Damn you to hell!"

◆

All Saturday morning, Chief Constable Driscoll was on the phone, answering calls from people much more important than himself: the home secretary called; the chief constable of Scotland Yard called; the deputy prime minister called. Reports of means test riots breaking out across the country didn't help. Stalin's comment had made Birkenhead seem like the epicenter of the unrest, inspired by a Communist conspiracy. Driscoll assured all of these important people that he had the situation in Birkenhead well in hand, and all he needed was more police. The Russian leader's comment had afforded Driscoll a wonderful opportunity to display his crisis management abilities, filled as he was with lofty aspirations. By 5 p.m., six hundred more policemen had arrived from Birmingham, Manchester, and North Wales.

In town, Saturday was even more peaceful than the previous day. Weekend shoppers filled the Haymarket, and a Tranmere Rovers football game was played without incident.

Quiet determination prevailed at Birkenhead Police Headquarters. Driscoll gave instructions to a roomful of police officials from other areas. He handed out lists containing the names of those to be arrested, and maps of the dockland area, marked with crosses of registered Communists and NUWM leaders.

Sections of the docks were marked off and allocated to different police groups. Arrest warrants were distributed. A convoy of Black Marias drove in from outlying areas and Walton jail was notified to expect many reluctant guests. All police cars and ambulances were ordered to switch their sirens off. This little party was going to be a surprise.

Councilor Frobisher, as usual, was on hand. "Make sure you arrest the Corcoran woman," he reminded Chief Constable Driscoll, "but be careful—she is extremely violent."

At midnight, the police moved in. They hit first at the Morpeth buildings—the poorest dockside flats in town. Police hammered on doors or smashed them in. They beat the occupants with their batons, men and women, some still in their beds. They arrested five men before they moved on, leaving others lying in the street, battered and bloodied.

Policemen rampaged through the dockside streets and smashed every window they passed. They invaded houses indiscriminately and attacked the occupants, regardless of their involvement in the riots. All those named on Driscoll's list were pummeled before arrest.

❖

"Get up and get dressed, Hannah," Peter said, looking out of the bedroom window. "There's one hell of a commotion going on out there." Someone thumped on the front door.

"Don't answer it!" Hannah said.

The door crashed open and baton-wielding policemen poured into the hallway. Peter was halfway down the stairs. They dragged him down the rest, knocked him to his knees, and beat him with their batons. He covered his head with his arms to protect his skull.

Eileen came running down the stairs, in her nightdress, screaming, "Leave him alone! Leave him alone!" A policeman knocked her to the ground and kicked her in the stomach. Hannah burst out of her bedroom, yelling at her other children to get back in their rooms.

She charged down the stairs like the devil's angel and smashed into the first policeman, then delivered a crippling blow to the nose of the second. Hannah grabbed his baton and used it to ward off the third policeman before she gave him a sharp kick in the groin. She heard a noise behind her, swung around and punched a police sergeant, who dropped to his knees.

Then a baton crashed down on the back of her head. She fell to the ground and another baton blow caused her brain to smash against her skull. Hannah disappeared into a dark hole.

❖

Sarah Richards, Alf's wife, peered out of her front door to witness the police beat up her neighbor at the end of the street, while other policemen threw furniture out of his smashed windows. Sarah slammed the door and slid the bolt.

"They're comin' for yer, Alf," She grabbed her husband's arm with a trembling hand. Alf took his wife in his arms and held her tight against his chest. "You can hide in the coal hole," she said.

"I'll not hide anywhere, Sarah." He kissed her forehead. "You know, of all the hardships we've been through together, all the hatred—me the pariah, you the pariah's wife—you've never once complained. Not once. God knows, yer had a right to."

"Please don't talk that way," she said.

Alf kissed her gently on the lips. "This too will pass. I've been beaten before, and I'm as tough as old boots. Listen, when this is all over, wadda yer say we go for a wee holiday, to Blackpool-on-Sea, perhaps, just for a couple of days?" Sarah smiled through her tears.

Alf went outside, locked the door behind him, and rolled up his shirt sleeves. Standing in the middle of the road, he put his fists up in a boxer's pose, as half a dozen policemen charged at him.

◆

Hannah woke up in an ambulance, with Peter's arm around her shoulders. The ambulance was full of battered people, who groaned with their injuries. Impressions of boot studs marred Peter's bloated face. His eye was welted closed, and his hair matted with blood. Pat O'Malley sat opposite, half naked, with purple bruises covering his shoulders and neck.

Hannah placed her hand on Peter's swollen cheek. "My God, what have they done to yer?"

"It's not much," Peter replied. "They call that a beatin'? Bunch of daisies. Those coppers must be Welsh."

"What of my Eileen?" Hannah asked.

"She was on her feet and movin' around when they dragged us out. She'll be fine."

"My head hurts," Hannah said, and fell back into her abyss.

The emergency room at Saint Catherine's Hospital was jammed with victims of the night's terror, closely guarded by policemen. Doctors performed triage, with fractured skulls getting first priority. Hannah was diagnosed with a concussion, the cut on the back of her head requiring twenty stitches, while the lump on the top grew as big as a golf ball. After they were treated, police hauled Hannah and Peter off to jail to join over fifty people already arrested that night.

◆

The next day, Chief Constable Driscoll lolled back in his office chair and congratulated himself on a job well done. He had smashed the Communist conspiracy, so he saw no reason why a promotion to a big city constabulary would not be an appropriate reward, maybe with an Order of the British Empire thrown in. His reverie was interrupted by Chief Inspector Mathew Baker.

"I know you're very busy, sir, but I have some news on the smuggling ring."

"Oh really? What is it then?" Driscoll said with a roll of his eyes.

"It appears that cigarettes, whisky, and perfume—all heavily taxed items—are shipped over to London from America, and then illegally delivered around the country by a tramp steamer. Lorries take the contraband from the Birkenhead docks to an army storage depot in North Wales, where it's distributed to under-the-counter markets in the northwest by army personnel. I've notified the military police, and they're making arrests."

"Good work, Baker. Anything else?"

"Yes, sir. In order for the lorries to clear the docks without inspection, they must have authorization forms stating that they contain munitions and other hazardous material, and they must be signed by the chief customs officer for the port and by the chief constable. Here is a sample of the form and, as you can see, someone has forged your signature. A very good forgery, I might add."

"Hmm, I see," said the chief constable, tapping his fingers on his desk.

"Of course, we must clear you of any involvement," Baker continued. "It's just normal procedure, you understand, and shouldn't inconvenience you much."

"And how do you do that?" Driscoll's nostrils flared.

"With this." Baker dropped a paper on Driscoll's desk. "It's a warrant to search your house, signed yesterday by Magistrate Gaskin."

Driscoll clenched his fists. "You expect to find whiskey and cigarettes in my house?"

"No, probably just a big wad of money squirreled away. But I'm a reasonable man. I can always tell the magistrate that we searched your house and found nowt. He won't know any better."

Driscoll stood up and leaned over his desk. His chin quivered with rage. "You slimy bastard! I'll have you thrown off the force."

"Sit down and shut up," Baker said coolly.

127

"Get out of my office!"

"I don't think so." Baker picked up the warrant. "I'll stay right here to prevent you making any phone calls, while a squad of coppers searches your house. I'd advise you not to aggravate me, because after what you and your gang of roughnecks did to the poor of this town last night, I'm having trouble suppressing the urge to strangle you where you sit."

Driscoll sat back down. "What is it you want?"

"Three things. First, you'll submit your resignation to the mayor in the next hour. You can cite poor health or stress over the riots—I don't care. Is that clear?" Driscoll bit his thumb nail and looked away.

"Is that clear!"

Driscoll managed a slight nod.

"Second, you'll recommend me for interim chief constable, and further recommend that I be made permanent.

"Finally, you will drop all charges against Hannah Corcoran and her husband, right now. You will release them and have them escorted home safely. I'll wait while you make the call."

Driscoll picked up the phone. "Do you have a history with this Corcoran woman, Baker?"

"Yes, she used to be my swimming instructor."

❖

As soon as Hannah and Peter arrived home, aching and weary, they went straight to bed and fell into a deep sleep. Several hours later, Peter was woken by the sound of Father Flaherty knocking at the front door.

"Alf's dead," said the priest. "Beaten to death in front of his house. God rest his soul."

"I won't tell Hannah yet. Let her sleep," Peter said softly.

Father Flaherty, Peter, and Granma White sat at the kitchen table drinking tea. "A fine man was Alf," the priest said. "He'll be in heaven now. God doesn't discriminate against atheists." Peter never spoke a word. "Would you like to tell me more about him?" the priest asked. Peter shook his head and looked away.

When the good father left, Peter took the step ladder from the shed and climbed into the musty attic. Avoiding the mouse traps, he shone his flashlight around until he located a battered wooden trunk. Peter pulled clothes out until he found his old army jacket and removed a dirty handkerchief from its side pocket. It was the same handkerchief that Alf had tied around Peter's mouth and nose during the gas attack. Peter tied the handkerchief around his face. He switched off his flashlight and, there in the darkness, he let the grief wash over him.

He remembered Alf as a boy—cheeky, clever, mischievous—as close a friend as anyone could ever want. He remembered him as a man who had brains enough to climb away from the docks and make an easy life for himself, but he never did. Instead, he chose to spend his life trying to ease the load of others. And they beat him to death for his trouble.

❖

Hannah awoke with Peter sitting on the bed staring at her.

"What is it?" she said. "What's wrong?"

"It's Alf. They've killed him."

For several seconds, Hannah was stunned to silence. "No . . . No . . . No," she cried. She punched her pillow with her left fist, again and again. Swollen with anger, she continued to punch it until Peter threw his arms around her and held her tight. When he let her go, she buried her face in the battered pillow and gave way to hacking sobs.

❖

Outrage over the events of Saturday night spread throughout Merseyside. By Monday noon a huge crowd had gathered at the park entrance, including dockers on strike for the day, shipyard workers who had laid down their tools, working-class people from most of the local factories, even a large group of office workers. They came from all over. The ferry boats were packed solid with sympathizers from Liverpool. It was estimated that over twenty thousand marchers crammed down Conway Street, toward the council meeting in the town hall. They spilled out into the side streets, packed Argyle Street, and spread themselves from the Haymarket to the Abattoir. Birkenhead had never seen anything like it before or since.

George Newell, with his docker representatives, plus Hannah with her head bandaged, were admitted to the council meeting. The atmosphere was subdued. The mayor asked Hannah if she was the sole representative of the NUWM.

"Yes, sir. The others are in prison, awaiting trial."

"Mr. Richards, too?"

Hannah bowed her head. "Alf Richards never regained consciousness and died last night from his injuries."

"I am very sorry," the mayor said.

"The PAC met this morning," the mayor continued, "and made the following recommendations to the council, which we have adopted. Firstly, we will petition the government to abolish the means test—this you already know. Secondly, we shall increase unemployment payments by twenty-five percent. Thirdly, we will allocate 170,000 pounds sterling for work schemes to alleviate unemployment this winter. That's all we can do at present."

"Thank you," Hannah said, in a weary voice. In contrast, the dockers' contingent was elated, rushing outside to announce the victory to the huge crowd, who cheered and waved their banners.

Hannah stood rooted.

"You may think you have won a great victory," Robin Frobisher said, "but we have thwarted your little Communist conspiracy."

Hannah let the comment pass.

"Is there something you would like to say, Mrs. Corcoran?" the mayor asked.

Hannah's bandaged head swirled. She clasped her hands together like a nun. Her voice quivered. "What will happen to the men who murdered Alf Richards?"

The mayor responded, "There will be an official inquiry into alleged brutality by the police."

Hannah's voice turned to ice. "I've heard about your inquiries." Moving her head slowly from one row of councilors to the other, she glowered at them all.

"The crimes committed by the police on the poor of this town last Saturday night, September 13, 1932, will disgrace the name of Birkenhead forever. And you Tory councilors who condoned it, and you Labour councilors who could have prevented it, will bear the shame for the rest of yer lives. Your grandchildren will read of it and be ashamed of their blood."

Hannah turned slowly and left.

Outside, a large portion of the crowd chanted for Hannah to show herself so they could cheer her for the great victory. She stood on the inside of the town hall doors, paralyzed by her emotions.

Mathew Baker stepped forward and put a hand on her shoulder. "Are you all right, Hannah?"

"Good God, Mathew, I haven't seen yer in donkey's years!" She hugged him tightly and kissed his cheek. "Are you the one to thank for getting us out of jail?" He smiled and nodded.

"How did yer get rid of that bastard Driscoll?"

"The same way I got you out of jail!"

Hannah managed a slight grin, quickly replaced with a deep sigh. "No, my old friend, I'm not all right. I'm twisted up inside. I need to punch someone, really hard, so they never recover. So I can say, 'This is fer you, Alf Richards. This is fer you.'"

Hannah opened the doors. The crowd cheered, threw their caps in the air, and chanted "Hannah! Hannah! Hannah!" She walked slowly down the town hall steps, her cheeks streaked with tears. At the bottom of the steps, her husband waited to put an arm around her.

"Take me home, Peter," she said. "This activism is for stouter hearts than mine."

Chapter Eleven

≡ 1932 ≡

Aftermath

A few days later, Peter and Hannah were nursing their wounds when Eileen burst in. "Have you heard the news?" she blurted. "Tomorrow the king is coming to Birkenhead!"

"What king?" Hannah asked.

"*The* King. King George V."

"Why is the king coming here?" Peter asked.

"I dunno. Maybe he feels concerned for his subjects. We've been in the headlines a lot lately," Eileen replied. "Isn't it exciting—we get to see the king."

Peter looked at Hannah. "Best if you stay indoors, what with your head injury and all."

"Fat chance," Hannah said. "Alf and I have got a bone to pick with that fella. I wish it was Churchill, but the king will do."

Peter stood up from his chair. "Alf is dead, luv. We must move on. That blow to your head has knocked you senseless. Stay in the house, out of harm's way. I beg you."

"It's the least I can do for him—for his memory."

Peter's voice went up an octave. "Listen to me, Hannah. You *will* stay in this house."

◆

On September 18, 1932, Birkenhead rippled with excitement. King George V and his entourage arrived around noon at Central Station, where he was greeted by a large, cheering crowd. Most of the unemployed didn't blame the king for the sorry state of affairs. In fact, they thought his appearance meant that someone of importance actually cared about their welfare.

After a reception in the town hall, the king's motorcade toured the dock area, including Price Street, Cleveland Street, and Beckwith Street, all lined by King George's cheering subjects. Although the king smiled as he waved mechanically, he squirmed in his leather seat as he passed the smashed windows, the boarded-up shops, and the uncleared debris—grim evidence of the past week's melees.

◆

"At least let me go and wave at the monarch as he passes by," Hannah told Peter.

"You stay put." Peter glowered at her. "I'm not lettin' yer be famous today, 'cos then yer'll be famous for the rest of yer life, which will be spent in the clink."

"Well, yer can't stop me from going to the toilet."

Peter rolled himself a cigarette, safe in the knowledge that the backyard door was closed tight with a big lock he had installed earlier. After he'd smoked and stubbed out his cigarette, Peter checked his fob watch. The woman's takin' a long time in the loo, he thought.

He went out back to check but there was no sign of Hannah, only her rusty old bicycle leaning against the backyard wall. Peter could imagine the whole spectacle—Hannah climbing up onto her bicycle, one foot on the handlebars, the other on the seat, and then hauling herself up and over the eight-foot wall. He noticed that she had removed the chain from the bicycle and thrown it, God knows where, to prevent him from cycling after her.

"Damn stupid woman!" Peter undid the lock on the back door, darted down the alley, turned on Beckwith Street, and headed for the park entrance. Even in his youth Peter was no Jesse Owens, so he was soon panting like a hot puppy.

The king's motorcade finally arrived at the park entrance, where a sizable crowd had gathered to cheer him on.

"I didn't realize I was so popular," remarked the king, as he emerged from his car. He approached the crowd, held back by a metal barrier and a large contingent of police. Accompanied by the mayor and a couple of bodyguards, the king moved down the barrier, shaking hands and chatting sympathetically with the unemployed.

Gasping for breath, Peter reached the edge of the crowd. He dashed into the Gaumont Cinema across the street from the park entrance, where he quickly found access to the roof. Peter scanned the crowd below until he spotted Hannah, easily recognizable with her bandaged head. The king moved down the line toward her. "Oh my God!" Peter said to himself, as he realized he was too late.

The king stopped to talk to an elderly man standing beside Hannah. "Keep coming, keep coming," Hannah said to herself. She curled her fist behind her back. Her fingernails dug into her palm, and her teeth clenched tight. "This is for you, Alf Richards," she whispered.

A bodyguard abruptly stepped between the king and Hannah. "What is in your hand, madam?"

Hannah took her left hand from behind her back and opened her palm. "Nothing," she replied. "It's just a habit."

"This is Mrs. Corcoran," the mayor said. "One of the leaders of the unemployed."

Hannah found herself face to face with the King of England. Her mouth dropped open, momentarily captivated by his handsome face and his luxuriant beard. He was gallantly dressed in his regimental uniform. He smiled at her. A king smiled at her. She doubted if any man in history looked more like a king. All the same, she didn't bow.

"How, may I ask, did you hurt your head, madam?"

"Last Saturday night, police pulled my husband and me from our bed and beat us with batons, sir."

"Oh dear. Why is that?"

"Because I'm part of an international Soviet conspiracy aimed at destroying your government and institutions, replacing them with a people's republic, spreading the wealth among the working class, and guillotining the aristocracy."

"You are being sarcastic." The king smiled again.

"Yes I am. I apologize."

"There is no Communist conspiracy, I take it?"

Hannah shook her head. "That's just an excuse for the police to beat us. There are about a hundred registered Communists in this town—the most there have ever been, but I'm not one of 'em.

Half of 'em are undercover coppers, anyway. There's not one single Communist elected to your Parliament, so there's no communist conspiracy anywhere in yer kingdom, and unlikely to be one as long as we have a monarchy to glue us all together." The king's smile grew wider, obviously interested in what this unusual woman had to say.

Hannah swept her hand around toward the crowd. "Look at these people. These are the unemployed, the rioters, the ones the newspapers call revolutionaries. Listen to them cheer you. Do they sound like revolutionaries? You see, Your Majesty, all these people want is to work, or just to have a tiny piece more of the pie when work is unavailable. God knows, the piece they started with was meager enough. That's all the riots were about, nothing more. Neither your economic system nor your social hierarchy was ever in jeopardy— not during the General Strike of 1926 and not now." The king's brow furrowed as he considered Hannah's words.

"We did have a Communist leading us, mind you," Hannah continued. "He was gassed in the Great War, fighting for his country. He spent his life trying to help the poor and the downtrodden, but police thugs beat him to death in front of his own house."

"I'm very sorry," the king said.

"Charles II would not have stood for such injustice," Hannah said.

"You know your history," King George said. "Very good. But Charles II had a great deal more power than I." Hannah the Hammer locked eyes with King George V and bent closer to him.

"For God's sake, sir," she whispered, "your people are starvin'. It's not because there's a shortage of food. It's because they can't afford to buy it. Act, sir! I beg you, act! They have no one to speak for them. You're their only hope."

The king looked down at the ground and stroked his beard. Now he looked a great deal less regal. Poor man, Hannah thought, he wants to help but he can't. He's just a figurehead after all.

The king took Hannah's left hand and held it in both of his. "I will do my best, but I want you to know this—if I had to live in conditions like this, I would be a revolutionary myself."

The words etched themselves on Hannah's brain. Hannah bowed. King George V moved on.

When Hannah returned to her house, Peter was waiting at the

135

front door. His face puffed with anger. "Listen closely, Hannah Corcoran. Never, ever, pull a stunt like that again."

"Oh simmer down, Peter. You didn't really think I was going to punch the king, did yer? I'm not that stupid."

A few hours later, a knock came to the door. Eileen answered it. "It's Mayor Jenkins," she yelled.

"Is the king with him?" Granma White asked.

"No, just the mayor."

"Well, this is our day for dignitaries. Are we not lucky?"

The major refused the cup of tea Hannah offered. "What did you whisper to the king?" he demanded, his face radish red. "I heard you lecture him, but I didn't hear the whispers."

"Well now, I asked him to loan me five shillings until Thursday. He said that he would love to, but he was stony broke. Apparently, his old lady doesn't give him his pocket money until Saturday night."

"What did he say? I want to know."

"Calm down," Hannah said. "I didn't cast aspersions on you or your gang. I asked him to do everything in his power to ease the plight of the unemployed. He said, 'If I had to live in conditions like this, I would be a revolutionary myself.'"

"If that's true," he said, "we have to get it into the newspapers. It paints the town in a much better light." The major's color was returning to an insipid pink. "By the way, the king said you were a real hotspur, whatever that means."

Granma White piped up. "He's talkin' about Sir Henry Percy the Hotspur, the impulsive and rebellious medieval knight."

The mayor grinned. "Hannah the Hotspur. Well I never. It's better than Hannah the Hammer, I suppose. You're a woman of wonderment, that's fer sure. Just stay out of trouble, for the love of God, for a week at least."

◆

To respect the fact that he was an atheist, no church service or Mass was said for Alf Richards. He was cremated at Landigan cemetery; the urn containing his ashes was placed with other urns in a semi-circle on the cemetery's grounds. Her eyes moistened, Hannah gripped Peter's hand and knelt down to speak to Alf's remains.

"Guess what, Alf? We won! We beat those buggers. Tonight there'll be children goin' to bed with food in their bellies, because of you. There'll be fewer little wooden coffins, because of you. Yer brought self-respect back to the working class of this town. One day there'll be a statue of you erected in Hamilton Square. Count on me fer that. Future generations will know that a hero of the people once lived here."

Peter bowed his head. "I'll never forget what you did for me in Ypres, auld mate. And don't you worry—we'll look out for Sarah."

That evening, a candlelight march was held in Alf's honor. More than ten thousand people marched from the park entrance down Conway Street to the town hall and around Hamilton Square. They marched back to the park entrance, where eulogies were delivered by Alf's brother and by George Newell, the dockers' representative. They used Alf's battered, old tin megaphone and his rickety soapbox.

The next day, the *Birkenhead News* reported that a "crowd" had gathered in remembrance of Mr. Richards, who was cremated earlier in the day. An editorial concluded:

> *While we are loathe to speak ill of the dead, it must be pointed out that Alf Richards, a known Communist, was the chief ringleader responsible for agitating the unemployed into rioting and looting. Had he not resisted arrest, the police would not have had to use deadly force. The law must be strong enough to suppress Communist propaganda at a time like this. With the passing of Mr. Richards, the town will hopefully revert to the normalcy of law and order.*

Seething with anger, Hannah tore up the newspaper and threw it in the fire grate. Throughout the marches and riots, the articles in the *Birkenhead News,* written by reporter Tim Philcox, and supported by editor Donald Griffin, were heavily slanted against the unemployed. They were filled with references such as *illegal aggression, violent disorder, alien political forces,* and *Communist vanguard.* Attributing the cause of the unrest and violence to Alf Richards was, to Hannah, an unbearable affront to his memory.

❖

The Cock and Bull in Argyle Street was a pub favored by the staff of the *Birkenhead News,* so it was no surprise to find editor Donald

Griffin knocking back a pint after work several times a week. As usual, he went to the men's room to relieve himself before he headed home to his family. He didn't give much notice to another person coming into the men's room as he stood there, urinating. With a quick move, the person grabbed the back of Griffin's head and slammed his face into the ceramic tile wall. Donald Griffin let out a muffled cry as he dropped to the floor, banging his head on the urinal as he fell. His assailant quietly exited.

❖

Back at police headquarters, Sergeant Billy Grant flipped through his notebook.

"What's the doctor's report?" Chief Constable Mathew Baker asked.

"Mr. Griffin has a smashed nose, broken teeth, and a black eye. He may loose the sight in his eye. I checked on Hannah Corcoran. She was at a church meeting in Saint Lawrence's all evening. A dozen people can vouch for her, including two priests. I also checked on her husband. He was at the Ram's Head at the time of the attack, according to the barman and Pat O'Malley."

"Peter wouldn't hurt a fly," Baker said. "And it's not Hannah's method. She prefers to use her left hook, and she wouldn't attack from behind."

Sergeant Grant continued. "It happened so quickly, Griffin didn't get a glimpse of his assailant, and no one in the crowded pub remembers seeing anyone follow him into the men's room. We have nothing to go on except, strangely enough, something that the assailant apparently stuffed into Griffin's pocket."

With obvious disgust, the sergeant held up the object between his finger and his thumb. It was a filthy old handkerchief.

Two days later, the body of Tim Philcox was found floating in Morpeth Dock, with his throat cut. The wooden handle of a docker's hook hung from his shoulder, with the metal hook embedded in the back of his neck.

❖

All the people arrested on the night of September 13, except for the so-called ringleaders, were released on the grounds of insufficient evidence. The fifteen ringleaders, except for Hannah, were tried by a jury selected from the middle-class city of Chester, fifteen miles away. Every one of the accused entered the courtroom showing some sort of injury. When they explained they were beaten by the police, they received little sympathy from the jury and none at all from the judge. They were all found guilty of conspiracy, despite the fact that there was little evidence against them. For some of them, being a member of the Communist Party was evidence enough.

Several of the accused claimed that upon arrest, the police placed rocks in their pockets to frame them for violent acts. It seemed the verdicts were a forgone conclusion, though. They were all sentenced to one to two years hard labor. Given that these men were malnourished for several years before their imprisonment, it was no surprise that the sentence of hard labor resulted in a sentence of death by heart attack for four of them.

Indeed, when a road tunnel was dug under the River Mersey the following year, many of the workers, so long unemployed and undernourished, died of heart failure on the job. Among them was Teddy Riley, the next door neighbor to Peter and Hannah.

An inquiry was held, behind closed doors, into the accusations of police brutality on the night of September 13. Family after family gave evidence of being roused from their beds and beaten with police batons. The verdict of the inquiry was never made public and no indictments were brought against any of the officers involved.

As if to even things up, the murder of Tim Philcox and the assault on Donald Griffin were never solved.

A few weeks later, as they lay in their bed waiting for sleep, Hannah whispered to Peter, "Do yer know who killed Tim Philcox?"

"No, but I have my suspicions," he replied. "I had nowt to do with it."

"I never asked yer that, Peter," she said. "I would never ask yer that."

Chapter Twelve

=== 1936 ===

Little Jimmy Kelly

Hannah sat at the hospital bedside of her estranged sister, Peggy Kelly, and wished to God that things had been different between them. Peggy held Hannah's hand in a tight grip, despite the weakening effect of the pneumonia that wracked Peggy's frame. She demanded an answer to her request. "Promise me, Hannah. Promise me you'll take care of little Jimmy."

Hannah wanted to burst out, "No, I'll not take care of your grimy little wretch of a kid. How dare you ask me!" But she stayed silent, holding in her feelings—never an easy task for her.

Resentment between the sisters ran deep—indeed, ever since they were kids and Hannah donned the role of mother when Granma White went blind. Peggy hated being bossed around by her older sister, without considering the fact that Hannah was forfeiting her own childhood. Peggy plotted with her brothers to foil Hannah at every turn. For her part, Hannah resented her sister for never taking any responsibility for the family. Even as adults, Peggy assumed that Hannah would take care of Granma White, as she had always done, even when Hannah was destitute. The rift between them was beyond repair.

Two years previously, Peggy's husband had died when he fell from staging in the shipyard. Now Peggy's days were numbered, and as a last act of defiance, as Hannah saw it, her sister was leaving her with one more child to raise—one more body to clothe and one more stomach to fill. Hannah could place ten-year-old Jimmy Kelly in an orphanage, but that was not considered the Catholic course of action. Morals dictated that she accept the boy into her nest.

"Of course I promise to take care of him. I'll raise him as my own," Hannah said at last.

◆

After her sister's death, Hannah tried in her heart to feel grief but none existed, and that consumed Hannah with guilt. When little Jimmy Kelly sat around the dinner table with his new family for the first time, his feet not touching the floor, Hannah stared at the boy and saw Peggy.

"Do you eat much?" she asked with pursed lips.

"Mother!" Doris cried.

The boy looked up. "I like cake," he said in a subdued voice.

Hannah's sarcasm was whittled sharp. "Well then, we'll have to be sure there's plenty of cake in the larder." Hannah continued to stare at him. A mess of black curls reached over his ears. His clothes were grubby, to say the least, and his table manners didn't exist. What an unpleasant little guttersnipe he is, Hannah thought. "When was the last time yer had a bath?" she asked.

"Fer God's sake, Mother! There's no call for this," Doris said. "The boy's mother is barely cold in her grave." A heavy silence filled the room.

Little Jimmy bowed his head. "Why?" he said, barely audible.

"Why what?" Hannah asked.

"Why did Jesus have to take me mam?" Little Jimmy closed his eyes for a moment, then burst out crying. Hannah covered her mouth with her fingers. Doris jumped from her chair and grasped the boy in her arms.

"Don't cry, young feller." She held him tight to her bosom. "We'll all look after yer, the whole family—me, yer Uncle Peter, yer Auntie Hannah, yer cousins, and yer grandma. You're part of our family now. There's love aplenty and cake in abundance."

Hannah remained silent.

By all accounts, it was easy to love little Jimmy. He had a round head, like a cabbage, with a grin that swept across his face as sweet as marzipan. He could charm you with that grin alone. A happy-go-lucky lad, there was little he wouldn't do to please. Before long, he had wriggled his way into the heart of every family member except

Hannah. Eileen christened him "The Lovely Lad," unable to resist tousling his curly black hair or smacking a wet kiss on his cheek.

Granma White taught little Jimmy all the old Irish songs, so they could sing them together when the mood took her or when there was gin in the house. "Did yer ever wonder why Welsh people always seem to be so dour and miserable?" she asked Jimmy. He shook his head. "It's because they love to sing, but they don't have any good songs. Sure, they have 'Men of Harlech' but that's about it. God gave all the good songs to the Irish, and the Welsh never forgave us."

"There's a Welsh lad in our class called David, and he always seems happy," Jimmy replied.

"Well, there yer have it. I'm wrong again." Granma White tousled his hair.

Sometimes they would say the rosary together; Jimmy used the white-beaded rosary that Granma White had put in the bottom of his Christmas stocking. "He brightens my every day," the blind lady declared.

"Why doesn't Auntie Hannah like me?" he asked his grandmother.

"Don't worry, she'll come around," she answered, with her usual reassuring smile.

Even Vera loved the little feller. He helped her with her chores and followed her around. For Vera, he was the son she almost had.

To Steven, little Jimmy was a godsend. Although they never became close friends, Jimmy happily deflected all the girls' pampering away from his cousin. For his part, Steven ensured that Jimmy, small as he was, wasn't bothered by the school bullies.

Every evening when Peter arrived home from work, he gave little Jimmy his tobacco tin and a two-ounce packet of Old Holborn cigarette tobacco. The tin held the cigarette papers and all the stubs of roll-your-own cigarettes that Peter had smoked that day. Jimmy removed the small amount of tobacco contained in the stubs and rolled it into a new cigarette. He then rolled the new tobacco into cigarettes for his uncle's consumption the next day. Each cigarette held just the right amount of tobacco—not too fat, not too thin, tapered at the end just right, and closed tightly with a quick flick of Jimmy's tongue. "Better than perfect," Peter announced.

While everyone else rejoiced at this wonderful addition to the family, Hannah remained distant. The best she could muster was an occasional begrudged nod of approval, which Eileen interpreted as chinks in Hannah's armor of resentment, but eventually it was Granma White who broke through.

Granma White and Hannah were knitting together in the back room, while the rest of the family was occupied elsewhere. Granma White put her hand on Hannah's knee, which indicated to Hannah that her mother was about to impart something of importance. "God has blessed us with an angel from heaven, and yer can't continue to treat him like a bad rash. I understand why yer still harbor bitter feelings against your dead sister, and I blame no one but myself. It was my duty to dispel the bad blood between you two when yer were mere children. God forgive me, I should have tried harder. So now I'm asking yer to forgive me and relish this one wonderful gift your sister has given you."

A week later was Hannah's birthday and the whole family gathered for a shoulder-of-lamb dinner, with carrots, turnips, and roast spuds so crisp they had no equal. Eileen had made a delicious strawberry trifle.

"If you only had a small amount, would it be called a trifle trifle?" Lilly asked.

"If you put mushrooms on it, then it would be a truffle trifle," Grace said.

"And then if you had a small amount of that it would be a . . . trifle truffle trifle!" Lilly and Grace yelled in unison.

Hannah opened her gifts: a new umbrella, a history book on the monarchs of England, a pinafore that Vera had made herself, and a woolen spectacle case knitted by Doris. Little Jimmy leaned over the table and handed Hannah a small box wrapped in tissue paper. She opened it to display a cameo broach.

She gasped. "This is beautiful. Is it Wedgewood? It can't be Wedgewood!"

"Sure is," Doris said. "Second-hand but it's still Wedgewood. I took Little Jimmy to the pawn shop by the market, and he picked it out himself. He used up all the money that he earned from his paper round." Hannah was speechless.

"I love you, Auntie Hannah," Jimmy said. "You took me into your family, and you all look after me and make me happy." Hannah stared at Little Jimmy. Little Jimmy stared back. Everyone else stared at Hannah, waiting for a reaction. Then, a single tear slid down Hannah's cheek.

"Come here, you little twerp," she said. Little Jimmy rounded the table and Hannah gave him a hug that forced every bit of air out of his lungs. Everyone applauded, and life in the Corcoran family was back on an even keel.

◆

In September 1933 Peter was promoted to foreman. It meant more money, fewer hours, and no more manual labor. He had been slogging away on the docks for more than twenty years, and his back was close to breaking. He swapped his thick woolen jersey for a white shirt and plain green necktie, his working men's trousers for creased pants, his heavy coat for a tweed jacket purchased from a stall in the market, and his boots for polished brown Brogues. But he still wore his flat docker's cap to let everyone know he was a dock laborer at heart.

Hannah was ecstatic. "I love yer all the more, if that's possible," she said. "But I must tell yer what Terry McCartney told me back in the shipyard days—all foremen are registered bastards."

Raised by his grandparents, Peter never knew his mother and father and had always suspected he was illegitimate. "Where do I register?" he replied.

◆

The following Sunday was as warm as the devil's tongue, so the whole family spent the day at Moreton Shore. In all his short life, Jimmy had never been to the seaside. He wadded in the ocean, searched for crabs among the rocks, played football with Steven and Peter on the sand, and ate ice cream and candy floss. Hannah watched with delight.

"C'mon, Jimmy," Eileen said. "I'll teach yer how to swim. You too, Mother."

"No thanks," Hannah said. "I tried it once and I didn't like it."

Like everyone else, Hannah couldn't resist tousling Little Jimmy's curly hair. He never bothered to comb it, because sooner or later someone would tousle it. To Jimmy, Hannah became a hero who could win any scrap, solve any problem, and lead any charge. He loved to go to the shops with her, because people would nod to her with respect. It made him feel special. These were good times.

One day Hannah took Steven aside. She explained to him, in the most apologetic of tones, that although he was slated for the priesthood, she felt Jimmy Kelly was a tad more pious and might make a better priest. Not that Steven was a bad son or anything like that, and without doubt he was a good Catholic boy, she assured him.

"You know best, Mam. I'll do whatever you ask of me. If it will help Jimmy in his road to the cloth, I'll give up my alter boy position to him."

"Thank you, Steven. You're a fine son." When Hannah left, Steven uttered a sigh of relief that could be heard in the next county.

◆

After school, Jimmy Kelly would often accompany Vera when she walked Kim around the park. One summer day in 1934 he came home alone in a right state. His hands were covered in blood. Dark red blotches stained his school blazer, and his little body trembled. Eileen let out a fearful shriek.

Hannah came running from the kitchen. "Holy Mary, mother of God!" Hannah pulled open his blazer, ran her fingers through his hair, spun him around to examine his back, and bent over to check his legs. She spurted out questions. "Where are yer hurt, Jimmy? Where's Vera? Who did this to yer?"

"It's not my blood," Jimmy said. "It's Kim's blood. A big dog attacked him. Vera and a park warden took him to the vet by park station."

"I'm away," Hannah said to Eileen. "Clean up the boy." She pulled off her apron and shot out the door.

Vera had calmed down a wee bit by the time Hannah reached the vet's clinic. Kim lay on his side on a metal table, emitting a pitiable whine, while Vera stroked his head.

"It's bad, Mam," she said in a quivering voice. "Very bad. My poor boy."

"His left rear leg is broken," the vet said. "He has severe laceration to his neck and back, and half of his right ear is bitten off."

"Can you fix all of that?" Hannah asked.

"Yes, I can splint the leg and stitch up the wounds. But there's nothing I can do about the ear, and we'll have to keep him here for probably a week. It's going to cost a bit."

"How much?"

"I'd say twelve shillings, easy."

"Twelve shillings! God love us, I can't afford that."

"Then it's best we put him down," the vet said.

Vera yelled, "No! No! Please Mam, yer can't do that."

"I surely won't," Hannah said. "You fix him up, Doctor. I'll get the money, never you fear."

"I'll need some collateral," the vet said, stroking Kim's head.

"Here, take this." Hannah sucked the knuckle of her finger and tugged on her wedding ring, but time had swollen it in place. She pulled and twisted to no avail—it was entrenched in her flesh.

"Stop!" the vet said. "I'll trust you for the money."

◆

That evening, Vera noticed the back page of the *Liverpool Echo* lying on the kitchen table. "That's him!" She pointed to a picture of a professional boxer. "And that's the other man, behind him. They were running in the park with their dog, a big German type that attacked my Kim without provocation. They laughed when I begged them to call off their dog. If it wasn't for the park warden, Kim would have been mauled to death."

Hannah picked up the paper. She learned that a major boxing match was scheduled for two days hence between the contender, Johnny Murphy from Liverpool, and the reigning middleweight champion of Britain, Henry Hancock from the East End of London. It was to be fought in the Liverpool Auditorium. Hancock's trainer was the other man in the picture. The fight was billed as Cockney versus Scouser, but there was little hope for Johnny Murphy to come out of the bout in one piece, as Hancock had never been beaten. He bore the sobriquet "Henry Hancock, Hard as the Hogs of Hell."

Hannah mulled over the paper. "Says here that he trains at Samson's gym in Birkenhead to avoid the boxing fans in Liverpool, whose constant attention would distract him from his mission to retain the title. Also says he likes to run in Birkenhead Park, where he's less likely to be bothered. Well, Mr. Henry Hancock," Hannah announced, "you're about to be bothered."

❖

Hannah headed to Samson's Gym on Cathcart Street, marching to the cadence she repeated in her head: *Hard as the hogs of hell, hard as the hogs of hell.* Passers-by scrambled out of her way. You didn't want to slow down Hannah when she was on a mission, and her eyes burned with resolute fury.

When she arrived at the door of Samson's Gym, a few boxing fans had gathered, along with a reporter and photographer from the *Birkenhead News*. The doorman was none other than Pat O'Malley.

Hannah gave Pat a cursory hug. "So, Pat, yer the doorman, are yer? Keepin' the hordes at bay?"

"Just 'til the big star has left town," Pat replied. "What are you doin' here, Hannah?"

"I've come to collect some money he owes me."

"Are yer gonna clobber him?"

"It's a possibility."

"Ah, Hannah, yer know I can't let yer in."

"Don't see how yer gonna stop me, Pat."

"I'll loose me job."

"Better than loosin' yer teeth. C'mon, Pat, you've only got two days left, and you were lookin' for a job when you found this one."

Pat sighed as he opened the door. "You owe me, Hannah Corcoran."

The inside of the gym was even more a man's domain than the Garrick Snug. The smell of sweat drenched the air. The place heaved with serious tension, where white-skinned men in wet vests and long shorts punched leather balls, skipped ropes, lifted barbells, boxed shadows, and flexed their muscles with masculine pride. Hannah could not help but feel a twinge of eroticism. A big, hairy fellow came up behind her.

"Who are you?" he growled.

"I'm the mother of Johnny Murphy. I've come to ask Mr. Hancock not to hurt my lad too much."

"Good luck with that," the hairy man said. "He's the feller in blue shorts, sparring in the high ring."

Hannah watched from the side of the ring, as the two men shot punches at each other. She yelled up at Hancock, not once, but twice. He ignored her, so she grabbed the ankle of his sparing partner as he spun by, causing him to tumble to the canvas.

"What the Hell!" Hancock said. "Who the hell are you?"

"I'm Hannah Corcoran. You let yer dog maul my dog in the park—damn near killed the poor animal. So you owe me twelve shillings for the vet's bill, plus the cost of my nephew's blazer, covered in blood. Second-hand I'll grant yer—let's call it a shilling. My daughter's coat is ruined, too. It's a hand-me-down but needs replacing, nevertheless. Say two shillings. In total, that's fifteen shillings yer owe me."

"Get this baggage out of here," Hancock said.

Fred Samson, the gym owner, appeared and put his arm around Hannah's shoulder. "C'mon, missus, on yer bike." He pulled her toward the door.

This is gonna be tricky, Hannah thought. She quickly computed her next move. First off, Hancock was a professional boxer, so she probably only had one shot, if that. Second, he wore protective head-gear that covered his cheeks and chin and protected his eyes. There was no margin for error. The punch must be spot-on target. She prayed to Saint Anthony to guide her fist.

Hannah spun away from Fred Samson and walked back to the ring. She bent over and climbed through the ropes. Hancock was talking to his sparing partner, with his back to Hannah. He never saw her coming, but his sparing partner did. He yelled to Hancock to look out, causing Hancock to turn around to his left.

But the fist was already in flight; there was no avoiding it. If he had turned to his right the blow would have struck him on the side of his padded cheek, with little damage. But Saint Anthony was involved in this little brouhaha, so the fist scored a bull's-eye straight into his nose, then veered off slightly to his left eye, protected or not. There was the usual splat, accompanied by a sharp crack that caused a tremor to run through the onlookers.

A sharp, stinging sensation shot from Hannah's wrist to her hand. She winced and jammed her fist under her armpit. Henry Hancock bounced off the ropes and fell to the canvas. A torrent of blood poured from his nose.

Hannah couldn't stop herself. She straddled his body and pointed down at him, saying "A one. A two. A three—" Then all hell broke loose. Men jumped into the ring and some jostled Hannah around, while other men protected her, Hancock being unpopular with many members of the gym.

Hancock's trainer knelt over him and announced that the boxer's nose was well and truly broken, and his left eye was swelling up like a cow's udder. He declared that the title bout would have to be cancelled or at least postponed. He bellowed at Hannah, "You just cost us a thousand pounds! You witch!"

Only the pain in her hand stopped Hannah from slugging him, too. She hoped her wrist was just sprained and no worse.

"It's fifteen shillings that's owed," Hannah said.

"I'm gonna call the police and have you arrested," the trainer replied.

"Not a good idea," shouted Pat O'Malley from the door. "I've a reporter and photographer from the *Birkenhead News* outside, and I've a mind to let them in. Can you just see the headlines? 'Henry Hancock, middleweight champion, knocked senseless by middle-aged housewife.' I think that would make the national newspapers, don't you? Now, make way for Hannah to leave."

"I'm not leavin' without my fifteen shillings," Hannah said.

"You must be Hannah the Hotspur," Fred Samson chimed in. "I've heard about you." He pulled two pound notes from his pocket and thrust them at Hannah. "Here, now get the hell out of my gym."

Hannah pushed a pound back at him. "Fifteen shillings is owed. I'll be back with yer change." She sauntered to the door, past big burly men, some of whom cheered her.

Pat O'Malley winked. "Done and dusted, Hannah."

Hannah smiled and turned to address the room. "Hard as the hogs of hell? Ha! More like soft as a soggy sausage!"

◈

The incident was replete with recovery. Kim recovered from his injuries. Hannah's wrist recovered in time for the fist's next performance. Vera and Jimmy Kelly recovered from the trauma of it all. But poor Henry Hancock never quite recovered from the humiliation and lost his title soon after, never to regain it.

Chapter Thirteen

≈ 1938 ≈

Doris and George Hamm

Being a picky eater was about the only fault that could be found with Doris. The rest of the family had almost finished their evening meal, while Doris pushed her peas lazily around the plate with a fork, her pork chop half eaten, the mashed spuds hardly touched. She glanced at her wristwatch again. When Hannah mustered up a scowl, Eileen could see that her mother was about to give Doris another rebuke regarding her poor appetite, so Eileen headed off her mother.

"Are yer goin' out again tonight?" Eileen asked her sister. Doris nodded. "With the same bloke?" Doris nodded again. "When do we get to meet this mystery man you're datin'? He honks his horn and you go runnin' out like a little pixie, off to God knows where. Why don't you bring him in? Are yer ashamed of us? Not that I blame yer, of course."

"All fair questions," Hannah said.

"No, Eileen, you're the only one I'm ashamed of," Doris said, and she and Eileen chuckled in unison. "I'll bring him in when I'm ready for you lot to meet him, hopefully soon."

"Sounds serious," Hannah said. "C'mon Doris, throw us some crumbs."

Doris responded with a mischievous grin. "All right, I'll tell yer. His name is George Hamm. He comes from Portsmouth, down South, but he works at the Birkenhead Shipyard." She paused to survey the face of everyone at the table. "And he's asked me to marry him!"

The whole table stopped eating, except for Steven.

"Bloody Nora!" said Eileen. "What was your answer?"

"Language," Hannah said. "Well girl, don't keep us all in suspense!"

"Yes, I said yes! But I told him he would have to first ask permission from my father." Hannah glanced at Peter. They both smiled faintly. "As if," Peter whispered.

"Where does he live?" Vera asked.

"He lodges at a house in New Ferry."

"That's in Saint Anne's parish. Such a lovely church for a wedding," Hannah said, with a cheesy grin.

A lump came to Doris's throat. She blurted, "He's not Catholic, Mam, he's Protestant."

All eyes swiveled to Hannah, then to Doris, then back to Hannah. Eileen, Steven, and Lilly bowed their heads in the expectation of an explosion. Vera looked affronted and Grace simply gulped. Peter looked away. Hannah held Doris in a frozen glare.

Eventually, Hannah said in solemn tone, "We need to talk, daughter."

A matter as serious as this required the discussion be held in the parlor. Only three were present. Hannah and Doris sat at opposite ends of the room, like boxers between rounds, while Granma White sat in the middle by the fireplace, a silent spectator, reserving her opinion for as long as she could hold it in.

Hannah started out in a mildly sarcastic vein. "Tell me about his religion again, so I can better absorb it."

"He's not Catholic. He's a Protestant," Doris answered.

"And he comes from where?"

"He comes from Portsmouth in Hampshire, down South. Why are you asking me to repeat everything?" Doris was doing her best to stay calm.

"And you want to marry him?"

"Yes Mam, I do."

"And his name is George Hamm. What type of name is Hamm? He sounds German to me."

"No, he's English from Hampshire. Hamm is from Hampshire. Do you see?"

Granma White suppressed a giggle.

Hannah sighed. "So you want to marry a Protestant from the South. What type of Protestant is he?"

"I don't know, Mam. What types are there?"

"Do you mean to tell me you don't know what type of Protestant this man is that you want to marry? Well now, you've got your Anglicans, your Lutherans, Wesleyans, Baptists, Episcopalians, Pentecostals, Presbyterians, Quakers, Methodists. . . . Good God girl, there are more types of Protestants than hairs on a cat. These people can't make up their minds. Now Catholics, on the other hand, are simply Catholics. There is only one type of Catholic, one type of Church, one true religion."

"I don't think he's a fervent Protestant." Doris fidgeted, scratching the back of her ear.

"None of them are, dear. It's a wishy-washy religion at best. Look, if I allow you to marry outside the faith, it sets a precedent for your sisters, don't you see? It gives them license to go off and marry a Hindu or a whirling dervish or any old Chinaman that comes along."

"I'll take the Chinaman," Granma White said.

There was a moment's silence while Doris searched for a rebuttal. "He'll convert. I know he will. Of course we'll bring the children up Catholic. C'mon Mam, this is Doris you're talking to." She leveraged her status as the most mature among Hannah's daughters.

"Do yer love him?"

"Oh, yes!"

"And why?"

"Oh God, where do I start? He's charming and polite. He's educated and well-spoken. And interesting, not like the usual boys I meet around here. He has a soft, lyrical voice, and he's mature. He's mature, but he still has a good sense of humor, even for a Southerner." Doris paused. "And he loves me enough to want to marry me."

Hannah continued to fish. "How's he fixed?" she asked, rubbing her thumb and her forefinger together.

"He's a professional engineer—an expert on submarines. That's why he's here, working in the shipyard. He has his own motor car, he smokes fancy cigarettes, and he has all his shirts made special."

"Sounds bloody near perfect, if you ask me," said Granma White.

Hannah looked at her mother in disapproval, then continued with the interrogation. "Where did you meet?"

"At a dance in Liverpool."

"Is he a good dancer?"

153

"He's okay."

"Is he handsome?"

"Not really. He's ten years older than me, a bit overweight, slightly balding, but he's no Quasimodo."

"Does he have a good singing voice?"

"I don't think so," Doris said, puzzled.

"Okay, let's get a look at this southern Protestant of yours, but I'll make no promises, yer understand." Doris beamed with delight. "One other thing," Hannah added. "If I disapprove of him, what will you do?"

"I'll not marry without your consent, Mam." Whether Doris was sincere or not, it won the debate.

❖

If Eileen was the smart one, Vera the meek one, Lilly the pretty one, and Grace the flighty one, then without a doubt, Doris was the sweet one. Selfless and unworldly, warm and gentle, no one could call her clever or vivacious. What made Doris rare was her sweet disposition. Whenever trouble brewed between Grace and Vera, Doris would step in to smooth grated emotions. She even had the ability to calm Hannah when she boiled over. Without a doubt, Hannah admired her more than any of her children.

Doris had a thin face with high cheek bones but without those roses that made Lilly and Grace sparkle. Her body was lithe, almost fragile, which she dressed in the smartest of clothes. Doris had a passion for clothes. She worked in the ladies clothing department of Beatty's Department Store on Grange Road and used all her spending money, including her lunch money, on the latest fashion. She kept her hair neatly coifed, plus she knew how to understate make-up to its best effect. George Hamm took an instant shine to her.

On their first date, to impress her, George took Doris to a fancy restaurant in Liverpool. The waiter asked her how she would like her steak cooked, so she told him sweetly that he could either fry it up or put it over the hob until it turned brown. The waiter looked at George, then back at Doris, then back at George.

George laughed. "Oh Doris, you're such a card." He looked back at the waiter. "I think she likes her steaks medium, don't you dear?"

"Oops," Doris said, after the waiter left. "Did I commit a major dining blunder?"

"Afraid so. It was wonderful!"

"I might sound a bit working class," she said, "but it's just a front to ward off gentlemen who want to marry me for my money."

"I can't imagine," George replied.

Doris nodded. "In point of fact, I'm independently wealthy. My parents are in the iron and steel business. My mother irons and my father steals!" They both bubbled with laughter.

The waiter in the corner glanced at them. "Love's young dream," he mumbled.

After a couple of months of stepping out together, Doris was convinced that she had found her permanent beau and, much to her overwhelming delight, George was equally enamored with her.

It was a submarine that tempted George to move to the Northwest. Birkenhead Shipyard had won a contract from the Royal Navy to build the latest, state-of-the-art sub—one of the new T class, HMS *Thetis*. George's reputation preceded him, and the shipyard welcomed him with open arms. But he soon became homesick, for he found Merseyside grimy and damp, and he had difficulty understanding the broad accent of the locals. He thought of returning south, until he met Doris, which changed his outlook dramatically.

She was not like most of the middle-class Southern girls he had dated, with their snobby pretentions wrapped in delicate sensibilities. He found her basic honesty charming. Her vulnerability created a great need in him to take care of her.

◆

The meeting between Hannah and George Ham had to be carefully orchestrated, or so thought Doris. After all, it was her future happiness at stake. In this endeavor, she enlisted the help of Eileen, who knew the quirks and pitfalls of Hannah's complex and unpredictable mind better than anyone. George, Doris, and Eileen met in the lounge of the Monks Ferry Pub in Oxton. It was a dry run, with Eileen shooting questions at George. Most of them were loaded with stumbling blocks to prepare him for the showdown with Hannah.

Eileen told him there were four things about Hannah he should be aware of. "First, she will want to know that you love Doris—that you will make her happy. Let her see it in your eyes. Second, she is a sucker for a compliment, so polish her ego but don't overdo it. She'll know when she's being patronized. Third, don't say anything that comes close to bad language. My mother doesn't care for swearing. She often swears herself, but she'll never admit to it."

Eileen suggested that George tap dance around the religion issue and exaggerate the importance of his job, without seeming to brag. She told him to lie if he had to, because Doris was worth it. Eileen took a breath. "I'll take another gin and tonic if you're buyin.'"

The three of them settled down to a fresh round of drinks. Eileen continued her advice. "Bring whiskey or tobacco for my Dad and brandy for my Granma. Other than that, there isn't much more to tell you. Just be yourself—that will carry the day."

"Thank you, Eileen," said George. "If you are anything to go by, I look forward to being part of your family."

"Now that's charm," Eileen said.

"You said there were four things?" George asked.

"Oh yes," answered Eileen. "If the meeting doesn't go well, and my mother hides her left hand behind her back, get the hell out of the house as fast as your legs can carry you and hightail it back to Hampshire!"

❖

Come the big day, Hannah ensured everything was ship shape and Bristol fashion. The house was cleaned top to bottom, and the stoop was scrubbed. There was real toilet paper in the lavatory instead of past copies of the *Birkenhead News*. Fresh holy water filled the vestibule vial, and the glasses were clean and shiny. Hannah had warned Vera not to take the expression "spit and polish" too literally.

Doris bought some little cakes from a bake shop in the market, the kind you can eat with one bite, because George once said that he liked them. And there were chocolate fingers and little triangular sandwiches of potted shrimp spread.

"Is the king coming back to visit us?" Granma White asked.

"I need a drink, so I'm off to the pub," Peter said, rising from his old chair.

"You'll sit where you are," Hannah said, putting her leg out as if to trip him. "This feller is coming here to ask for your daughter's hand in marriage, and it'll defeat his purpose if you're not actually here. Do you see that?"

Peter grumbled and sank back in his chair. The sound of a car pulling up and the car door slamming made everyone bubble with expectation. Doris thought she might faint out of nervous stress. "Please be kind," she asked her family.

"Fat chance," Grace said. Now fifteen, Grace had inherited Hannah's impishness. She leaned against the piano and smoothed out the ruffles of her new burgundy dress.

Doris opened the front door. "Why, it's Mr. Hamm, isn't it? What a surprise."

One thing I like about these people, George thought, is their sense of humor. He kissed Doris's cheek and could feel her nervousness. "It'll be all right, sweetheart, you'll see." In one hand he held a bunch of bright flowers and in the other a brown canvas bag. Doris ushered him toward the parlor, passing the vial of holy water, which he glanced at. He said, "Am I supposed to . . ."

"Don't worry about it," Doris said.

George entered the parlor and took a deep breath. The gathered Corcoran-Luxton clan sized him up, such that he felt like an anarchist standing in front of a jury of policemen.

"This is George," Doris announced. "This is my dad, and this is Granma White. These are my sisters: Vera, Lilly, and Grace. Eileen you already know, and here is Jimmy Kelly, my cousin. My brother Steven is out playing football." Lilly and Grace made mock curtsies. "And this is my mother."

"Ah, Mrs. Corcoran," George said, moving to her chair. "I'm so glad to meet you at last." He handed her the flowers. "Oh, and before I forget, Percy Thompson sends his love."

"My Lord, Percy Thompson." Hannah cracked a wide smile. "What a lovely fella. It must be well over twenty years. Such pleasant memories."

"Who the hell is Percy Thompson to be sending you love?" Peter asked.

"Oh relax, man," Hannah replied. "He was the foreman that hired me at the shipyard. He was promoted because of me."

"Well, now he's general manager, and when I told him I was coming to visit, he explained how important you were to his career," George said. "You're a legend in the yard. They talk of the time you clobbered Roger Dalglish, and the time you saved the chief constable from drowning."

Hannah ate it up. She put her hand on her chest and smiled demurely. "That was such a long time ago."

Lilly whispered to Grace, "Boy, he's good."

"What's in the bag?" Lilly asked aloud.

"Money!" said Grace. Eileen tapped her sharp on the back of her head.

"A little refreshment for you, sir," George said, as he shook Peter's hand and gave him a bottle of whiskey.

"Johnnie Walker!" Peter exclaimed. "George, you're a fine gentleman."

"I told you our dad would sell one of his daughters for a bottle of whiskey," Grace said, in slightly more than a whisper.

"She's not his daughter," Vera said.

"Ah, stifle," said Grace.

"Enough," said Hannah.

George handed out a bottle of expensive brandy to Granma White, a big box of Cadbury's milk chocolate assortment to Lilly and Grace, some American murder magazines to Vera, perfume to Eileen, and two tickets—one for young Steven and one for Jimmy Kelly—for the next home game of the Liverpool football club.

Lilly declared, "It's like Christmas!"

George, Hannah, and Peter talked and laughed for a couple of hours, while Granma White stole some of Peter's whiskey, Hannah stole some of her brandy, and Jimmy Kelly stole some of the girls' chocolates. Vera went to her room to read her magazines, and Doris floated with joy.

The meeting couldn't have been more successful, and the subject of religion never came up. All were in a jovial mood, helped in part by the drink. George, sensing a victory, thought it would be a good time to take his leave.

"Thank you for the company. I've had a wonderful time. I see now where Doris gets her warmth and her wonderful Scouser sense of humor."

The expression on Hannah's face changed dramatically to grim aloofness. "We're not Scousers. Scousers are from Liverpool. This is Birkenhead—different people, different background, different values. In fact, it's quite an insult to call us, or my daughter, a Scouser." Hannah got to her feet as her voice moved up an octave. "We don't like to think we are better than other people, but in this case we are. Scousers are ill-mannered and generally stupid. So stupid in fact, that when other people call them Scousers, they don't even know they're being insulted."

George glanced around at what was now a room full of serious faces. Doris appeared distinctly nervous. He looked back at Hannah, who glared at him. Her left hand moved behind her back.

George gulped. "Look, I didn't mean to insult anyone. I thought it was acceptable to say you were Scousers. I mean . . . " He hesitated and looked bemused. "Wait, you're just pulling my leg!" Hannah burst out laughing, and then everyone else did, too.

"See, I told you my family is strange," Doris said, as she walked him to the car. "Do you still want to marry me?"

"Of course I do. Your whole family seems like decent and interesting people."

Doris gave him a mock punch to his shoulder. "I'm not just a person. I'm a Scouser!" They embraced, and Doris returned to the house.

Immediately Hannah threw her arms around her daughter. "That's my girl, that's my girl! He's a fine man and a good catch, all right. A man with prospects, a man who knows what he wants and is going to get it, not some docker's son who'll never have two farthings to his name. You'll be as happy as a flea on a goat. God love the pair of yer. Now, Lilly, get on that piano. Let's have a knees-up and a bit of a sing-song. Vera, pass me that brandy."

❖

Two months later, Doris and George were married in Saint Lawrence's Church, and a fine spring marriage it was. Young Father Michael, Father Flaherty's protégé, presided. George's best man was dapper Harold Owen, a friend and fellow engineer at the shipyard. Doris's sisters were bridesmaids, pinked and blued and flowered. In her wedding dress, Doris gleamed like polished brass.

George's parents and younger brother travelled up for the wedding from Portsmouth, and they seemed pleasant enough. His plump mother carried more fat than a Zulu Queen, in stark contrast to Doris, who disappeared when she stood sideways. His father, short and precisely built, turned out to be rather dull.

No one asked George's parents if they were disappointed that their son had married below his class, so to speak, because no one cared if they were disappointed. Heaven knows what they thought of the Irish wedding reception. Held in Saint Lawrence's club hall, it was rambunctious and loud, with dancing, singing, boozing, and toppling over. At one point, Doris noticed a look of angst on their faces, as if they had stepped into a third-world jungle during a bizarre religious ceremony, just before the human sacrifice.

Lilly and Grace jitterbugged with anyone who cared to join them. Eileen found a suitable two-step partner. Doris hovered above the floor like an angel, and Peter was called upon to sing. He started off with his old favorite, "Barefoot Days," followed by "I'll Take You Home Again, Kathleen," then "Carrick Fergus," which everyone joined in. He was about to dive into "Danny Boy," until he received a scowl from Hannah that said "enough is enough." She knew he was powerless to stop himself once he got going. He came down from the stage and gave Hannah a big kiss on the lips, right there in front of everyone. All applauded.

In a corner of the reception hall, Granma White and Father Flaherty were getting sozzled together, neither having been known to turn down a drink.

"Will you not have another whiskey, Father?"

"Not for me, Granma White. Thank you, but I've had enough now."

"Ah, go on, have another. It's a wedding."

"No, I've early Mass in the morning. Thank you, Granma White."

"Ah, c'mon, just a wee drop of whiskey. It'll do no harm."

"No, no, I can't. All right—just a small one then, just one more if you'll join me."

"Will you not have another drink, Father?" And so it went, until the priest could hardly see, and the blind woman could hardly stand.

Hannah was deeply happy. Bad times were behind them. Everyone had work. There was money coming into the house, and her second-born child, her sweet Doris, had found a good man. She cried joyful tears and thanked God for his blessings.

◆

George and Doris spent a blissful honeymoon week at Southport-by-the-Sea, before moving into their house in Upton, a middle-class suburb of Birkenhead. A small brick wall surrounded the front garden. In the center grew a lilac tree whose fragrance was so strong that passers-by would dally for a few seconds to delight in its scent.

Doris had moved up a couple of rungs on the social ladder. That was not the reason she married George, and no one who knew her expected any change in her personality.

She remembered Hannah had once told her that when Karl Marx was asked if he wanted to eliminate the middle class, he replied no, he wanted to eliminate the working class. Hannah added that no one should ever be ashamed of being working class, but if the opportunity arose to become middle class, you shouldn't be afraid to take it, just as long as you remembered where you came from. In Doris's new life, she was proud of where she had come from but didn't particularly want to go back.

Each morning Doris would pack a lunch for George, adding a little love poem that she composed—a different one each day. Then she left for her job in the dress shop, and he left to work on his new submarine. To Doris, nothing could be more perfect than those halcyon days of marriage. But perfection didn't last long, for there were ominous clouds on the horizon. Once again, the sound of distant drums could be heard wafting across the River Rhine.

◆

As usual after dinner, Hannah was listening to the radio, and Peter was reading his newspaper. Either way you looked, the news was dominated by the impending war with Germany.

Hannah had heard enough. "That old warhorse is snortin' again," she said with a growl. Peter put his paper down. He didn't relish the thought of having to listen to Hannah complain about Winston Churchill every single day for the duration. "Churchill's not even in the cabinet," he said.

"Don't matter. It's his handiwork. That fat Tory bastard is workin' behind the scenes. He's started another war, right enough." Hannah picked up her knitting.

"Did it ever occur to yer," Peter said in a tired voice, "that the Germans might have something to do with startin' these wars?"

"Why would the Germans want to start another war with us?"

"Because they lost the last one and they're still mad."

"So it's kinda like a rematch," Hannah said.

◆

With war clouds overhead, George's new submarine, HMS *Thetis*, took on a new importance. In April 1939, the navy towed it up to Scotland to perform its trials on the River Clyde. George traveled with the sub, and Doris stayed with Hannah because she didn't want to stay in her house alone. When George returned, it was evident something troubled him. Doris made him a steak and kidney pie for dinner, after which they strolled to the Sportsman's Arms for a drink. Sitting at a quiet corner table, she placed her hand on his.

"What's bothering you, luv? The trials didn't go well?"

"No, they didn't," he replied. "First off, there was a problem with the steering. The mechanism for turning the rudder was reversed, so when you turned to port, the ship went to starboard and vice versa."

Doris laughed. "I could see where that might be a bit of a problem." George frowned. "I'm sorry, luv. I didn't mean to make light of your worries," she said.

"Then, when we tried to dive, the forward hydroplanes jammed, so we had to abort the whole thing."

"But isn't that what the trials are for? To uncover the problems?"

"Yes, but minor problems. These are major problems. They should have been found by the shipyard and navy inspectors long before the boat was launched. This is shoddy workmanship, and I'm concerned that this boat was rushed forward because of the impending war."

◆

The *Thetis* returned to Merseyside, and the date was set for a diving trial in Liverpool Bay. On the Saturday following the trial, a dinner dance was planned for all those involved in the construction of the new submarine. It was to be a grand affair, to be held in the Kirkland Dance Hall, with over 700 people attending. Doris bought a new frock for the occasion, which she had seen in the window of one of her store's competitors. It was Bavarian blue with white lace frills around the hem and sleeves, set off by a matching lace shawl, a sweet little purse, plus real nylon stockings.

On the morning of the trial, Doris didn't make George his usual lunch because he would be on the submarine all day, and there would be a reception when the trial was over. When she kissed him goodbye, she could sense his stress. "You're worried," she said.

"Everything will be fine." As he hugged her, she took the opportunity to slip the usual little love poem into his jacket pocket. It's not the best one I've ever written, she thought, as she watched him walk down the path to his car. But there will be others.

Chapter Fourteen

≡ 1939 ≡

Submarine

At 10:00 a.m., June 1, 1939, His Majesty's Submarine *Thetis*, sailed from the Birkenhead Shipyard to complete its trials, escorted by the tug boat *Grebecock*. In charge was Commander Gary Bowyer, a stocky, round-shouldered matelot in his late forties, who had spent most of his career underwater. A humorless man, he was fiercely loyal to the navy.

For the trials, *Thetis* carried 103 men, 50 more than her scheduled complement. The extra men included six naval submarine officers slated to be future commanders of T class submarines, two caterers who would handle the post trials reception, and a River Mersey pilot. The rest of the extra men were employees of the shipyard: fitters, plumbers, electricians, other tradesmen, naval architects, and engineers like George—all of them civilians.

Workmen considered it an honor to be part of the trials of a new ship, particularly a new class of warship, for it meant they had been selected by the bosses as the best of their trade. Commander Bowyer projected a quiet optimism to the workmen, but George Hamm and his best man, dapper Harold Owen, plus many of the crew who had sailed on the first trials, harbored concerns that the problems uncovered during those trials may not all have been resolved.

The sleek new submarine, a giant black sea monster, glided out into the calm waters of Liverpool Bay, where the air was sharp with the salty smell of the Irish Sea. Passing Egremont Promenade, the best place on the river to watch ships come and go, onlookers waved and cheered to the officers in the coning tower. The little tug

Grebecock came puffing up behind, like Sancho Panza scampering after Don Quixote.

At 2:00 p.m., thirty-eight miles out of Liverpool, fourteen miles off the coast of North Wales, Commander Bowyer signaled the *Grebecock* that *Thetis* would commence a slow dive. The air was forced out of her tanks and her main vents opened, but try as she might, she couldn't obey the dive command. The submarine's bow struggled to break below the surface, like a child learning to swim, tottering on the edge of the swimming pool. A degree of apprehension shuddered through the naval officers on board.

The commander called the engineers around him. "I thought this problem had been resolved," he said, glowering at George, although he knew that the responsibility and expertise of the diving systems belonged to Harold Owen, the engine specialist. Commander Bowyer had taken a dislike to George on the first trials, because George made a few suggestions on how the trials should be conducted. Bowyer believed that no captain should be expected to stomach advice on how to run his boat, particularly from a civilian. In contrast, Bowyer befriended Harold Owen for no reason other than they were both of Welsh stock.

"The boat is too light in the bow," Harold said. As the sub carried no torpedoes, he suggested to the commander that he should flood a couple of torpedo tubes to add extra weight—not an unusual procedure in submarine warfare. Commander Bowyer ordered that outer hatches of torpedo tubes five and six be opened. Still, *Thetis* would not dive.

The commander's body stiffened even more. "Now what?" he asked.

"I believe the dive should be aborted," George replied.

Commander Bowyer glared at George. "No, we will not abort, Mr. Hamm. Not until we have explored every possible reason for this submarine's failure to dive. There are five more submarines like this in the pipeline, and we may be building the same failure into each one. War is on the horizon, so time is of the essence." The commander ordered Lieutenant Brown to check if the outer hatches of torpedo tubes five and six had indeed opened.

Running through the inner hatch of each torpedo tube, a test-cock was installed, which consisted of a small pipe and a spigot. If water came out when the spigot was opened, it would indicate the torpedo tube was flooded. When Lieutenant Brown opened the test-cock, only a small trickle appeared, indicating that number five torpedo tube was empty.

The insides of torpedo tubes are subject to the corrosive effects of seawater, so they are painted with bismuthic enamel. What Lieutenant Brown didn't know was that the inlet to the test-cock had been painted over, plugging it up with half an inch of enamel. The outer hatch of torpedo tube number five was indeed open to the sea. Also, the lieutenant didn't know that attached to the test-cock was a small metal rod called a rimer. Its purpose was to be pushed into the test-cock to clear any obstructions. He didn't know this because it was not included in his training. Instead, assuming that tube number five was empty, he opened the inner hatch to determine if there was still a small leakage from the outer hatch, which had been detected on the earlier trials.

Seawater came gushing in. Frantically, the lieutenant and another crew member tried to close the hatch, but one of the locking bolts got caught between the hatch and the hatch seating. They raced to the second compartment but that hatch also jammed. Finally they managed to close the hatch of the third compartment.

Unaware of the problem, Commander Bowyer impatiently put the submarine in hard-dive mode. With her two forward compartments now filled with tons of seawater, *Thetis* plummeted, bow first, to the sea floor.

The impact knocked George over, along with many others in the crowded vessel, causing some minor injuries. The hull remained intact, but the underwater communication equipment was damaged beyond repair. HMS *Thetis* settled on the sandy sea bottom, 160 feet below the surface.

Lieutenant Brown, with a quavering voice, reported back to the commander with the bad news. The commander, arms crossed, glared at him with fierce anger. For an eternity, no one spoke.

Finally, Commander Bowyer looked at Harold. "Is there any way that—"

Harold interrupted. "No, sir. No way. If there was just one compartment flooded then, yes, we could surface again, but not with two. We will need help from above."

"In more ways than one," George added.

Under normal circumstances *Thetis* carried sufficient air to last for thirty-six hours, but because she had twice as many men on board, the air supply was reduced to eighteen hours. Two escape chambers protruded from the hull, one forward, one aft, but the sub was in water too deep for them to be of use. Heavy trepidation descended on the men—all they could do was to wait and hope.

On the surface, the crew of the tug boat had watched the submarine struggle to dive, then suddenly disappear. A naval officer, Lieutenant Colchester, together with a telegraph operator, acted as observers and liaison between ship and shore. The officer confessed to being somewhat alarmed by the sub's diving problems but was not alarmed enough to act. Instead, he waited for the submarine to reappear, although he was not aware of how long the trial dive was supposed to take. After three hours Lieutenant Colchester was concerned enough to send a telegraph to submarine headquarters in Gosport, Hampshire, 300 miles south, to inquire how long the *Thetis* dive should take. But he never marked the telegraph urgent. He didn't want to cause alarm.

The telegraph didn't arrive until 5:30 p.m. at the Gosport post office, where the telegraph delivery boy was busy fixing a puncture on his bicycle. As no urgency was assigned, the message didn't reach its destination until 6:15 p.m. The submarine had been down for almost four hours.

❖

Throughout the time the submarine had been down, the men on board could feel the boat moving with the tide.

"We must have drifted at least a mile from our diving point," George remarked to Harold. "Plus the tug must have drifted even further. How the hell will any rescue party know our location?"

Harold put his head in his hands. "Yes, and darkness is closing in."

❖

News of the lost submarine quickly spread through the shipyard and then throughout the town. Doris had decided to work late to help with the inventory, because she knew George would also be working late. On the bus home, she overheard a conversation between two women seated in front of her.

"A brand new submarine on its trials, down with all hands," said the first woman.

"Surely they can get it back up," said the second woman.

"Excuse me, what's this about a submarine?" Doris asked. The look of anguish on Doris's face alarmed both women.

"That new submarine, *Thetis* I think it's called, went out today and disappeared. That's all I heard, luv. I'm sorry."

Doris yanked the bus's emergency cord above her head as she sprung from her seat. The driver jammed on his brakes, throwing everyone forward. An old Morris sedan behind screeched to a stop, swerving to avoid colliding with the bus.

"I must get off," Doris cried, as she ran the length of the bus, jumped off the platform, and fell onto the pavement. A young man got out of the Morris to help her to her feet.

"Are you all right, luv? Why did you jump?"

"Yes, I'm all right," she gasped. "My husband . . . that submarine . . . it can't be true . . . I must get to the shipyard."

"C'mon then, I'll drive you," offered the kind stranger.

When they arrived at the shipyard gates, a large crowd had already gathered. Doris was so distraught she almost forgot to thank the man as she jumped out of his car. She turned back. "Thank you, so much for your help."

"It was nothing. Look, do you have family in the area? I'll go and fetch them, if you like."

"Yes, that would be very kind." She gave him Hannah's address.

Doris pushed her way through the crowd. "What news? What news?" she cried.

"Nothing," replied another wife. "These buggers won't tell us anything."

◆

On board the *Thetis*, Commander Bowyer tried to keep spirits high. He assured the men that as soon as the submarine failed to resurface after its scheduled half-hour dive, the navy would have initiated a rescue plan called "Operation Subsmash."

George whispered to Harold, "What a load of bilge water." Harold nodded. They were both aware, as was Captain Bowyer, that such a plan was in name only. The Royal Navy was not renowned for its contingency procedures; those in charge preferred to sail by the seat of their britches, hoping all the pieces would fall into place when the time came. Commander Bowyer, however, could not have conceived of the ineptitude and sheer bloody-mindedness about to be exhibited by his fellow officers involved in the attempt to save the lives of himself and his crew.

◆

Upon receipt of the telegram from Lieutenant Colchester, the submarine headquarters eventually took action. The admiral was out sick so Captain McIntyre took charge. He alerted all surface vessels, aircraft, and submarines in the area to head at once to Liverpool Bay. He then left to take command, traveling by duty vessel, the destroyer *Winchelsea*, as per naval regulations. He should have gone by train or even aircraft, instead of the old, slow destroyer. His expected arrival in Liverpool would be six hours after the air on *Thetis* was due to run out.

Before he left, McIntyre sent a signal to HMS *Tedworth*, a specialist diving vessel crucial to the rescue effort, to proceed immediately south to Liverpool. The *Tedworth*, however, was on the River Clyde in Scotland, 200 miles north of the River Mersey. And her crew was ashore playing football. On receipt of the order, the *Tedworth* had to sail 70 miles up the river to a coaling station because her coal holds were empty. It took four hours to perform this operation. By the time *Tedworth* was scheduled to arrive in Liverpool Bay, she too, would be too late to take part in any rescue attempt.

◆

Back at the gates of the shipyard, the crowd was slowly dispersing as the evening wore on, leaving mostly relatives and parish priests to keep vigil. The kind young man arrived back with Hannah, Peter, Eileen, and Lilly, who all comforted Doris as best they could. They had brought flasks of tea, sandwiches, and blankets.

Hannah grabbed the young man with the car by the lapels. "What's your name, son?"

"Bobby Flynn," he replied.

"Well Bobby, you're a saint, a good Samaritan. We thank you, and God love yer."

"It looks like I'm quite involved by now, so I'll be glad to drive people back and forward all night, or you can use my car to get a little sleep when you get tired." Hannah kissed him on the cheek.

She strode to the shipyard gate and ordered Peter and the girls to hoist her up, so that her head was over the top of the gate. A policeman on the other side ordered her to get down or he would arrest her.

"Listen carefully, sonny boy," she said. "Go get Percy Thompson. Tell him Hannah Corcoran is here, and he better get his backside out here right now, so he can explain to these poor people what the hell is goin' on."

A few minutes later, the policeman appeared at a side entrance, beckoning Hannah to follow him. Percy Thompson beamed when he saw her.

"Is that you, Hannah? How long has it been? Twenty years?" Percy gave her a tight hug. "You look as young as ever."

"So you're the head boss now, you sly old dog."

"With the events of today, anyone who wants my job is welcome to it," Percy said. "Are you still punching people?"

"Only if they ask for it." Hannah turned serious. "Listen Percy, my son-in-law is on that sub. People here need to know. It's the not knowing that's driving us crazy."

Percy put his arm around her shoulders. "This is what I know. The sub hasn't resurfaced, and we don't know why. Neither do we know the sub's location. The air on board will last until about mid-morning, not much longer. The navy has ships coming in from all over, so there will be a full-scale search throughout the night. I'm pulling in all the experts I can from our side, but I'll tell you this, Hannah, it doesn't look good."

Hannah's brow furrowed. "Thanks Percy. Thanks for the truth." She turned to go.

"Hey, Hannah, I could use your help," he called after her. "I don't have the time to keep coming out to update folks at the gate. You could be my spokesperson and keep them informed. They know and trust you."

"I'll help in any way I can. First, maybe we can get some hot tea out to those people."

❖

Throughout the night, the submarine moved with the tide, buffeted by the sea like a child's toy. Lieutenant Brown, wracked with guilt for opening the torpedo tube, volunteered to swim out of the escape chamber, around to the bow, and try to close the open hatches. Commander Bowyer dismissed the suggestion as impossible.

The men were crammed together in the living spaces, and George was pushed up against a lanky young sailor as they both tried to find a comfortable spot to spend the night.

"Do you think we'll be rescued, mister?" the sailor asked.

George didn't want to give him false hopes. "I don't know, son. I just don't know. They have to find us first, and they don't have much time."

"What will it be like," the sailor asked, "if we die here? Will we just fall asleep when we use up all the oxygen?" His tone was nonchalant, as if asking for directions to the nearest pub.

George shrugged and shook his head. He thought of Doris and how frantic she must have been when she heard the news. I hope Doris doesn't grieve for too long, he thought. I hope she finds someone else who will love her as much as I do. He thought of them dancing together, gliding as one around the floor to a foxtrot, the ballroom lights shining off her hair, the scent of her rose perfume—her body, warm and vibrant, pressed against his. Just one year they had. Just one year together. It didn't seem fair. He bowed his head and held his hands to his face to cover his sorrow.

"Sorry, mister. I didn't mean to upset you," the young sailor said.

A crusty old tar, crouching opposite, overheard their conversation and leaned over. "We'll suffocate—that's how we'll die. Like someone is holding a pillow over yer face. Like you're being slowly strangled."

The sailor shifted in his space. "Can we make it faster?"

"Sure, we could fill the sub with water through the escape chambers," the old tar answered. "That would quickly raise the level of carbon dioxide, and we'd suffocate in no time, long before we drown."

The young sailor took a small photo from his pocket and held it to his lips. "Do you want to see a picture of my wife and little girl?" he asked George.

"No, I don't think so," George replied. "Wait, yes, let me see it." George took the picture and forced a weak smile. "Your little one has your blond hair and your dimpled chin. She's lovely." The sailor looked pleased and nodded in agreement.

"That's enough talk now," George said. "We're wasting oxygen."

◆

Hannah followed Percy along a corridor leading to the company boardroom. Photographs and paintings of famous ships built by the shipyard hung along the corridor: HMS *Birkenhead*, CSA *Alabama*, HMS *Ark Royal*. . . . She stopped. There it was on the wall—a photo of her in her workman's overalls, flanked by Percy Thompson and John McGregor, taken over twenty years earlier. Percy turned around.

"I look so young, so fresh," she said.

"I'll never forget that day you burst into my office, like a clap of thunder, and demanded a man's job, at a man's wages," Percy said. "You brimmed with purpose and courage—there was no way I could refuse you."

Hannah allowed herself a smile as memories flooded her head. "It was hard work," she said. "Hard to the bone. I remember the blisters on my hands, the aching back, total exhaustion that wracked every muscle. Every night I slept like the dead. But I also remember the good times, watching those warships slide down the slipway—ships that Terry McCartney and I help build.

"Remember when I punched those louts and saved Mathew Baker? I'd swagger down the quay and big burly workmen, men made of steel and ropes, would hail me like I was a queen. Working here transformed my life, and it's you I have to thank for that, Percy Thompson."

Percy grinned. "Your work did us both a world of good."

The shipyard's boardroom was acting as the war room for the emergency. Hannah walked into a beehive of activity. About a dozen men, managers and foremen, barked instructions down the phones or mulled over charts of Liverpool Bay, trying to calculate, using the speed and direction of the tides, how far the submarine had drifted. Workmen were installing direct phone lines. Two men in dark suits huddled in a corner, wrapped in serious discussion. The tension in the room was so palpable that no one took notice of Hannah's presence.

◆

The closest navy ship to the stricken submarine, the destroyer HMS *Brazen*, was fifty-five miles away. With all her stokers feverishly shoveling coal into the boilers, she raced to the scene, to the location of the tug, *Grebecock*. The sun was down and a bright moon took its place. At 9:25 p.m., one of several RAF aircraft scouring the area, spotted the *Thetis'* marker buoy, with a bright flag attached, bobbing in the water. The navigator relayed the position to the *Brazen*, which was just one mile away. The RAF navigator, knowing what was at stake, recalculated the position of the buoy to be certain but erroneously came up with new coordinates. HMS *Brazen* steamed off to search seven miles south, in the wrong direction. More precious time was wasted.

◆

At 10:00 p.m. Hannah returned to the gate to update those keeping vigil. In a voice quivering with relief, she informed them that the submarine had been located ten miles off the Welsh coast, and that ship, boats, and tugs were racing to the scene. A great cheer went up. What she didn't know was that those vessels were heading to the wrong area.

"As soon as there's any development, I'll be right back out." Hannah hugged Doris, then went back to the boardroom.

About 1:00 a.m., into the boardroom strode Rear Admiral W.T. Wade, accompanied by several naval officers and sailors, armed with rifles.

"I'm taking over command of this operation," the admiral declared.

"Like hell you are," Percy replied. "This is our submarine. It hasn't been officially handed over to the navy."

"It became the navy's submarine when it was launched," the admiral shot back. "Not to mention when the government paid you 375,000 pounds for what appears to be a badly constructed boat. I'm not here to argue with you. If you want verification of authority, you can call the first sea lord right now, but be warned, he won't be happy being woken at this hour."

Percy Thompson stepped down. He updated the admiral: Boats had arrived in the area, containing divers kitted out, as well as welders, fitters, and drillers. Nine private airplanes waited to take off at first light, volunteers all.

"They haven't located that marker buoy that was spotted over three hours ago. They must be searching in the wrong place," Percy said.

"The navy has its own ships in the area. We don't want too many damn amateurs bungling around," Admiral Wade said. "The submarine could have been sabotaged. Let me tell you, security in this shipyard is a disgrace. There is a war coming, so Nazi saboteurs and spies, I'm certain, are already deployed. Clear away that crowd from the main gate, for a start." Percy bit his tongue.

"Who is she?" said the admiral, pointing at Hannah.

"She is my spokesperson, plus she represents the families of the shipyard workers on board the *Thetis*."

"She goes," said the admiral.

"She stays," said Percy.

"I'm not going anywhere," Hannah said, "and neither are the people at the gate."

At that point, into the room burst a character straight out of a Dickens novel. Snowy-white hair hung down to his shoulders. Mutton chop sideburns framed his fat, ruddy face and pockmarked nose. His huge gut hung like a dead dog over his belt. He plopped himself into a chair, lit a cheroot, coughed, and spat up into a handkerchief.

"Ernie Cox is the name. Salvage contracting is the game. Heard you fellers have lost a submarine, so me and my crew sailed over from the Isle of Man to offer our services."

"We have our own salvage people en route," the admiral said. "Thank you, but we will not require your services. Too many cooks, you understand."

"Listen, sailor boy, when it comes to salvage, I have more experience in my left testicle than you have in your whole damn navy." Ernie Cox stuck his face into the face of the admiral; his foul-smelling breath caused the admiral to pull back. "When it comes to organization, you lot are like a one-legged man at an arse-kicking party."

With glee, Ernie Cox reminded the admiral that when the German navy surrendered at the end of the Great War, the British fleet escorted the German ships up to Scapa Flow Naval Base in Scotland. Then, through incredible lack of diligence, they allowed the Germans to scuttle their entire fleet to prevent the British navy from getting their hands on it. More than fifty German warships went down.

"I bet you navy boys don't like to be reminded about that little balls-up." Cox sniggered. "Well, me and my crew hauled up thirty-two of them Jerry ships, and let me tell yer, it's a lot more complicated than throwin' a couple of ropes under the ship." Cox turned to Percy. "Find that submarine and if it's still intact, I'll bring it up with the men alive—guaranteed. That is, if they still have air to breathe."

"You got it," said Percy.

Hannah got up to stretch her legs, which gave Ernie Cox the opportunity to slap her bottom. "Hey sweetie, I need some whiskey. Do me a favor and search through these management desks. One of them is bound to have a bottle of whiskey stashed away."

Hannah bent down and stared into his face, gnarled and battered by a hundred angry storms. "If I find some whiskey, I'll drink it myself. If you ever touch me again, it will be you that needs salvaging."

Ernie Cox laughed. "At least find me something to spit into."

Hannah winked. "I'll be right back with the admiral's hat."

❖

On the stricken submarine, sleep was trumped by anxiety. Men prayed silently. Some wrote goodbye notes to loved ones and tucked them into their tobacco tins. A few workmen demanded the navy rum store should be doled out, so they could face death half sozzled. In an attempt to lighten the ship, Commander Bowyer had the drinking water and diesel fuel pumped out.

"Wait! Wait! What was that?" George stood up in alarm. "Did

you feel that? The stern is moving. Can you feel it?" Everyone did. The stern was moving slowly upwards. The commander's actions appeared to be working. The rear of the ship slowly inched its way toward the surface, while the bow stayed rooted to the sea floor. Soon, the sub was at an angle of forty degrees. Men desperately grabbed any hold they could to prevent falling backwards.

The commander announced that they had broken the surface, and the stern was probably sticking out of the water by about twenty feet. A great cheer rung through the submarine. George did a quick calculation in his head: We are in 160 feet of water, the sub is 270 feet long, at a 40 degree angle—yes, 20 feet sounds right. He pushed his way forward toward Commander Bowyer and yelled to get his attention.

"Commander, the rear escape chamber should now be only about sixteen feet from the surface. We can start getting the men out."

Bowyer growled at more advice from George. "Yes, but what do they do when they reach the surface? We don't know if there are any boats there to pick them up. It's still night up there. They might never be found. We will wait 'til dawn."

❖

Doris stayed all night at the shipyard gates, while the other girls took turns as Bobby Flynn provided a shuttle service to Hannah's house and back. The new day was bright and calm as hot tea and muffins were passed around. A new, larger crowd had formed. The gates opened at 6:00 a.m. to allow workmen to enter. At 7:50 a.m. Hannah appeared and the crowd went silent. She had more news for them.

"At about 7:45 a.m., a search plane spotted the stern of *Thetis* sticking twenty feet out of the water, twelve miles off the Welsh coast at Holyhead. Rescue boats will soon be there, and I'm sure they'll get the lads out in no time." She assumed it would be a reasonably easy task. "That's all I know right now—I'll keep you posted." The crowd cheered, and wives and mothers hugged each other and cried tears of relief. Hannah clasped Doris's thin body to hers. "Keep the faith," she whispered.

❖

Upon reaching the submarine, the rescue crew banged on the

hull with heavy hammers. The noise reverberated throughout the submarine's structure.

"They've found us! They've found us!" Men yelled. Sailors jigged. Workmen knelt to give thanks. Others cried with relief. George hugged Harold and tousled the hair of the young sailor. Immediately the rescue boats communicated with the sub, using Morse code, while rescue crews tied thick ropes around the stern of the sub to hold it in place.

Commander Bowyer, who had not displayed any emotion throughout the ordeal other than optimism, now decided to use the escape chamber and asked for volunteers. The escape procedure was complex and harrowing. Two men would stand inside a small metal chamber, wearing breathing masks, while the hatch behind them was closed. The chamber was then completely filled with water until the inside pressure reached the pressure of the water outside. The men would then open the outside hatch and escape to the surface.

Adjustments would have to be made to their flotation devices as they left the chamber. They would be breathing pure oxygen that could cause them to throw up in their masks and choke. The oxygen would only last for five minutes. Because the procedure was fraught with danger, only four men volunteered. Commander Bowyer picked Captain Osram and the hapless Lieutenant Brown as the guinea pigs. The escape went without a hitch, and Osram and Brown were soon hauled into the rescue boats.

Now more men volunteered, but the process had taken so long that this time, four men went into the escape chamber. Something went wrong—either the outer hatch jammed or the men panicked—but all four drowned in the chamber. Commander Bowyer abandoned the use of the chamber and decided to let the rescuers get the rest of his men out. The time was now 8:25 a.m.

❖

In the shipyard, there was no shortage of ideas as to how to perform the rescue in the short time they had left. All the expertise and equipment they would need had been on stand-by throughout the night. The simplest method would be to cut a large hole in the stern with oxy-acetylene torches and pull the men out one by one. Welders in boats were already at the site.

The method favored by most experts in the war room involved divers running cables under the submarine, tethered to two salvage ships on either side. These ships would then tow the submarine into shallow waters until the coning tower appeared, and then the men could walk to safety: Men and sub would both be saved.

A coast guard vessel, the *Beacon*, equipped with heavy-duty lifting equipment, was just a few miles away at Holyhead, with divers already on board. The admiral announced that more navy ships had arrived.

Ernie Cox pulled his bulk out of his chair, his jowls quivering in exasperation. "No, no, no!" he yelled, splattering saliva over his shirt. "There's only one way to do this. First you gotta get that coast guard ship to hold the sub steady with the thickest ropes they have— small boats won't be able to hold it for long. Meantime, you drill a small hole in the stern and pump in compressed air at fifty psi. This will immediately provide the men with breathable air. It might make some of the older men sick, but it won't kill 'em. Don't attempt to move the submarine under any circumstances! As it is now, that sub is extremely unstable. It's at the mercy of the tide, plus it has loose water swirling around inside and tanks still filled with air. Any false move by those rescue boats could cause the submarine to twist, which would cause it to loose its slight buoyancy and sink. If it does sink though, the crew will still be alive because of the new oxygen. No matter what, we can proceed to bring the entire sub to the surface."

"Then what's the best way to do that?" Percy asked.

The old salvage man continued. "Not with divers. We gotta get the water out of the sub to stabilize it, by continuing to pump in compressed air for five or six hours. The air will force the water out, and the men can close all the open hatches. Once the vessel is stable, the crew can bring it to the surface. It can be towed to shore on the next tide, intact."

"That's just a theory," the admiral said.

"I've done similar work a hundred times," Cox responded.

"How can air force out water?" Percy asked.

"Given the right pressure, air will go through anything, even watertight hatches."

Percy Thompson scanned the faces of the people in the room, looking for someone who might have a rebuttal, but no one spoke.

"How long will it take to get your crew out there?" he asked Cox.

"My boat with a 100 cubic foot capacity compressor and drillers on board, left at 8:00. It's 8:40 now—they should be there."

"How long will it take for them to drill the hole, tap it, and begin pumping in air?"

"Fifteen minutes, twenty tops."

Terry McCartney and I would have drilled that hole in five minutes, thought Hannah.

"We'll do it your way, Cox," said Percy, handing him the phone. "Tell your crew they have the go-ahead."

"Not so fast," Admiral Wade chimed in. "The navy will make the decision." He got on the phone line he had routed directly to Admiralty House in London, and explained the situation quietly to a superior. He wrote something down on a piece of paper, which he stuffed into his trouser pocket.

"They'll get back to me," he said. "They understand the time constraints."

Everyone in the room sat back, their eyes focused on the clock, except for Hannah, who paced around in a tight circle. The minutes ticked by without mercy: 9:00, 9:10, 9:15.

At 9:20 most of the men answered the tea break bell, in a need to ease the tension. Remaining in the war room were the admiral, Percy, Hannah, Ernie Cox, a telegraph operator, and two armed sailors.

"Make the call to Cox's crew," Hannah said to Percy. "Give them the go-ahead. Time is up."

"No you don't," the admiral ordered.

◆

In the *Thetis*, the lack of oxygen was starting to take effect. All the men exhibited disorientation and suffered cringing headaches. Slowly they began to lose their strength. As time dragged on with no apparent action from outside, Commander Bowyer asked Harold Owen if he wanted to take a shot at using the escape chamber.

"Why not?" Harold answered. "Better to die trying to escape than to sit here waiting."

179

"Take someone with you," Bowyer said.

Owen looked over to his friend. "What do you say, George? Want to give it a try?"

George thought for a few seconds. He looked at the young sailor. "Take him. I don't have the strength to stand."

Owen and the sailor got out successfully, but after that no one had any strength left to open and close the hatches. George Hamm put his hand in his pocket and found Doris's note. He knew it was there, and he knew it was time to read it. He closed his eyes, kissed the note, and returned it to his pocket.

❖

"For pity's sake, Percy, make the call," Hannah pleaded.

"If he touches that phone, shoot him!" the admiral said to the two sailors.

Hannah looked at the clock: 9:35. "For the love of God, make the call!"

Percy picked up the phone. A sailor leveled his rifle at him. Hannah grabbed the barrel with her right hand, as her left fist flew into the sailor's face. He staggered backwards onto the other sailor. She turned to face the admiral, who backed away toward the window. She punched him full-square in the nose. His head jerked backward, as it smashed through the glass.

Ernie Cox bounced in his chair, yelling with the excitement of it all, and encouraged Hannah to hit the admiral again. The second sailor, having regained his balance, leveled his rifle at Hannah.

"Make the damn call!" she yelled at Percy, who quickly picked up the phone again. The second sailor leveled his rifle at Percy, as men ran back into the room. Hannah approached the second sailor and pushed her chest into the rifle barrel.

"Is your mother still alive?" she asked.

"Get back or I'll shoot," he said.

Hannah pressed further. "When you tell your mother that you shot a mother of seven because she was trying to save her son-in-law, how do you think that will go over?"

Behind her, Percy put the phone down. He heaved a heart-broken sigh. "Too late. The *Thetis* broke free of one of the rescue boats and disappeared below the surface."

It never resurfaced.

Hannah bent over the admiral, still groggy on the floor. His white hair was dyed red from the blood seeping from a gash in his head. She took the piece of paper out of his pocket and read it aloud.

"Under no circumstances should the submarine be damaged."

She gave the paper to Percy. "I don't understand."

"Neither do I," he replied.

Ernie Cox pointed at the admiral. "That bastard never looked at this as a rescue mission. It was always about the sub."

Men were tending to the admiral, applying towels to staunch the bleeding. "Pity you don't let the bastard bleed to death," Hannah said. She turned to go. "I need to inform the people at the gate."

"No you don't. I'll do it. This is my shipyard—my people built that boat. It's my duty to tell them," Percy said, with a heavy voice. He sat down and placed his forehead on the table. Hannah put a hand on his shoulder.

"You did all you could, old friend." With head bowed, Hannah left.

"She punched an admiral." Percy sighed. "They'll put her in prison."

"No they won't," said Ernie Cox. "Because you have a piece of paper in your pocket that will damn them all to hell."

At 10 a.m. Percy Thompson appeared at the shipyard gates, holding an official update. His voice trembled as he read it.

❖

Two days later, Doris entered the clothing store where she had bought her dress for the ball. She held a shopping bag, with the dress inside. She wore no make-up; dark rings underlined her eyes. Her shoulders were bowed. Her face was as gaunt as ever. She looked down at her skirt and fastened a button she had missed.

She remembered how excited she and Eileen had been, just a few days earlier, trying on dresses and giggling like schoolgirls. Before, the store had looked inviting. It was bright and colorful and smelled of semi-expensive perfume, but now it looked gaudy and ostentatious. There were few customers. Off to the side, a cluster of four women, all about Doris's age, all held shopping bags like hers. They watched her with grim expressions as she approached a shop assistant and pulled out the dress.

"Yes, madam, may I help you?"

"I wonder if I could. . . . I wonder if you could. . . ."

The middle-aged shop assistant, a bit busty, with too much eye shadow asked, "You want to return that dress, dear?"

"Yes." Doris looked down at the floor.

"I understand. Do you want your money back, or do you want to replace the dress with a black one?" the shop assistant asked, as kindly as she could.

"A black one? Yes, I suppose a black one. May I replace it?" Doris's voice was no more than a whisper.

"Yes, dear, of course you may. Please wait with those ladies and someone will be with you shortly."

Doris approached the four women, who watched her and then lowered their heads. One of them, a redhead, looked up at Doris, and then so did another woman, and another, and finally the last two. For a brief moment the eyes of all five women locked together, sharing a common grief. Then it was gone.

"Would you like a cigarette?" The redhead asked Doris.

"No thanks," Doris said. "I don't. . . . Wait, yes, I'll take one. Why not?"

❖

Condolences came in from all over the world for the *Thetis* tragedy, including one from Adolf Hitler himself. Just two months later, Hitler invaded Poland, causing Britain and France to declare war on Germany. Lieutenant Brown was on leave at the time. Dressed in his naval uniform, he sat alone in a corner of a quaint pub in the equally quaint seaside village of Cornwall, where he was born. He knocked back hard cider as he stared out the window at nothing in particular. He drank glass after glass until he reached a clarity of mind that often comes with intoxication.

Lieutenant Brown staggered out of the pub. He drove away in his secondhand Aston Martin, weaving erratically and racing around winding, Cornish lanes as if he were in the Le Mans Grand Prix. He swerved off the road, onto a footpath he knew well. With his foot hard down on the accelerator, he ignored the warning signpost. His car hurtled down a grassy slope, smashed through a wooden fence, and shot off the edge of a cliff.

For a second, the car hung in the air like a paper airplane, until it plummeted, turning as it went, and smashed upside down onto the rocks below. Atlantic waves broke over the wreckage as if it had always been there. HMS *Thetis* had claimed her hundredth victim.

Chapter Fifteen

=== 1940 ===

The Battle of Beckwith Street

For the first six months of World War II, nothing much happened. The British called it the "phony war," but by the end of 1939, things certainly heated up. The army recruitment office on Grange Road, that had processed thousands of lads during World War I, was open again for business. Between the wars it was a co-op butcher's shop, appropriately enough.

❖

Hannah and Vera had been looking for little Jimmy Kelly all day until they found the note he left on Hannah's pillow. Hannah gasped as she read it.

"Oh my God! He's run off to join the paratroopers! He wants to do his bit. He says he loves us all and will see us again when the war's over, which will probably be soon."

Vera turned on the waterworks. Hannah frantically searched through the top drawer of the big set of drawers on the landing, looking for little Jimmy's birth certificate, but to no avail.

❖

A long line of lads standing outside the recruiting office on Grange Road made way for Hannah as she barged past them. Inside, she marched up to the counter to face off with a big recruiting sergeant, with a brown, unkempt mustache and fat, red cheeks.

"Jimmy Kelly of 57 Beckwith Street. Seventeen years old. Underage. I want him back right now!"

The sergeant flipped through some paperwork. "His birth certificate said he's eighteen. His teeth looked good, so in he went."

"Do yer show these boys how to alter their birth certificates, or do you actually alter them yerself?" Hannah asked.

"Where's yer patriotism?" asked a corporal, sitting at a desk, processing recruits.

"Where have yer shipped him off to?" Hannah asked the sergeant.

"That's confidential information. Listen, missus, this war is startin' to heat up, so soon there'll be conscription and yer lad will be in anyway. Now or three months from now, what's the difference?"

"I promised his mother on her deathbed that I'd take care of him, so I'll cut off his toes before I let that fat Tory bastard take him for cannon fodder."

"Yer holdin' up the war, missus, so best if yer just bugger off," the sergeant said.

"I'm off to the town hall, then," Hannah replied. "I ought to be talkin' to the farmer, not to his pig." Hannah swung around and headed for the door but stopped in front of a lad in the line.

"Mike McIntyre, what the hell are you doing here? Does your mother know?" Hannah turned to the sergeant. "This boy is only sixteen! His mother will be out of her mind with worry."

"I'm joining up," the boy said.

"Like hell you are." Hannah seized him by the ear and dragged him toward the door.

The sergeant came out from behind his desk. "Yer can't do that!" He grabbed Hannah's shoulder and swung her around. The sergeant could have grabbed either of Hannah's shoulders, but he chose the right one. In retrospect, it was a poor decision, because the momentum of Hannah being swung around added to the ferocity of the blow that shattered the sergeant's nose. He tottered back to his desk, plopped down in his chair, and fumbled around in the desk drawers, while nose blood dripped onto the birth certificates.

The corporal quickly picked up the phone. Hannah strode over to his desk. "Hey, patriot, who yer callin'? Yer mother?"

"The police," he answered.

Hannah pressed her finger on the receiver. "Yer know, patriot, there's nowt would give me greater pleasure than to punch yer right square in your gob for your part in this filthy business. But I'm not gonna." She took her finger off the receiver. "Imagine the headlines in the *Birkenhead News* tomorrow. 'Mother manhandled by army recruiters while attempting to regain underage son.'"

The corporal put the phone down. A startled look took over his face as he stared past Hannah to the sergeant. The sergeant's eyes were glazed over and blood still seeped from his nose. Hi army issue revolver was pointed at Hannah's head.

"Don't be stupid," she said, and walked out, pushing Mike McIntyre in front of her.

❖

Hannah sobbed her way to sleep that night. She had explored every avenue to get the lovely lad back: She visited the town hall to harass councilors, wrote to members of Parliament, wrote to the newspapers, and left no bureaucrat unturned. She even wrote to the prime minister, who by that time was Winston Churchill.

"Yer might have had more luck with the prime minister," declared Granma White, "if yer hadn't addressed yer letter to the fat Tory pig at 10 Downing Street!"

"Oh, Ma, you know I didn't. Would've liked to, but I didn't."

❖

As it turned out, the army life was not for Jimmy. Basic training was far beyond his ability to endure, having spent the previous seven years being mollycoddled by Hannah and her girls. So Jimmy ran away from the paratroopers back home to Hannah's house. Hannah greeted him with a sharp lecture about the anxiety he had caused, then she hugged the breath out of him, ruffled his curly hair, kissed his cheeks, and hid him in the attic.

Soon the army came knocking in the form of burly Sergeant James Calhoun, together with little Corporal Timmy McKay of the Royal Military Police—an Ollie and Stan couple if ever there was one. Sergeant Calhoun's magnificent, granite chin jutted out proudly to underline his masculinity. What a wonderful target, Hannah thought. Corporal McKay, half-hidden behind the sergeant, looked puny and awkward in his army uniform. Sergeant Calhoun stated, in the same bullying tone that had served him well so far, that he had reason to believe a deserter might be hiding in the house, and that said deserter must give himself up, tout bloody suite.

Unwarned and unprepared for the fist of doom that curled behind her back, the poor man put his thick hand on Hannah's chest, and pushed her aside as he strode over the threshold. The left hook shot out like an angry cobra, perhaps the most devastating blow that Hannah had ever delivered. The fist, carrying all the anger that Hannah had accumulated over several weeks, hit the target square on. The poor man's jaw was dislocated and his hefty male ego destroyed forever. Sergeant Calhoun collapsed onto the Blue Angel.

"You'll pay for any damages," Hannah said. With the sergeant sprawled in Hannah's hall, Corporal McKay shakily considered his options. If ever there was a time for a strategic military withdrawal, it was now.

"Best get yer sergeant to the hospital," Hannah said.

◆

Captain Sebastian Walker, of the Royal Military Police, stormed out of the emergency department of Birkenhead General Hospital, having just been debriefed by his stricken sergeant. The debriefing took a while, given the man could hardly speak due to his facial injury.

The captain barked at his driver to head immediately to Birkenhead Police Headquarters, where he filed a complaint against Hannah Corcoran for assault and battery and demanded that she be arrested immediately. The Birkenhead constabulary hadn't heard anything so hilarious in a long time. They howled with laughter, which only added to Captain Walker's fury.

"What kind of policemen are you?" he yelled. "We're at war! Wartime desertion is a capital offence and harboring a deserter is a major crime. I can't afford to lose my best sergeant to some Irish biddy wielding a rolling pin!"

The policemen stopped laughing when Chief Inspector Mathew Baker appeared from his office. "It was a fist," Baker said quietly.

"What?" Captain Walker said.

"It was her fist, not a rolling pin."

"How do you know? How can a fist do so much damage? My sergeant says she hit him with something she held behind her back."

"That's right, but it was her left fist behind her back, not a rolling pin. During the riots of 1932 she doffed three out-of-town policeman who were attacking her husband, and the poor men have never been the same since. Furthermore, for your information, she's not an Irish biddy—she's a respected activist."

Chief Inspector Baker raised his voice. "You call yerself a soldier? Don't yer think you should have scouted out the enemy before yer went chargin' in? Yer let those two fellers walk into an ambush—they were totally outgunned by Hannah's fist. Anyone around here could have told yer that. It would take at least a platoon of soldiers to get past her vestibule, but you'll not be using my men to do it. We've got better things to do than drag some poor lad out of his house so you can take him away to shoot him, when yer should never have let him sign up at his age in the first place." Baker pointed to the door.

"If you want to shoot someone, go find some Germans. Now, get the hell out of my police station!"

◆

Captain Sebastian Walker, his anger a stream of bubbling lava, returned to Hannah's house the next day with a lorry full of military policemen. What followed was a little-known battle of World War II that military historians commonly refer to as the battle of Beckwith Street.

Before they left the barracks, the captain briefed his men. He explained that the objective of this sortie was two-fold. Firstly, apprehend the deserter, one Private James Kelly, and bring him to justice. Secondly, arrest his adopted mother for aiding and abetting a deserter and for assault and battery on a military policeman. Through inside information, the captain told his men, he knew the deserter was still in the house. He was also informed from the same source that Hannah and her family knew they were coming.

The captain explained that his strategy was to mount a frontal assault on the enemy's front door, whilst feigning an attack on the backyard through the back alley, thereby forcing the enemy to divert her forces to the rear, as Napoleon did at Austerlitz.

In addition, some of his men would move in on the flanks from

the backyards of the houses on either side, thus performing an encir-
cling movement, as Hannibal did at Cannae.

Finally, he would hold a few men back in reserve with ladders,
in case the conflict required a scaling assault on the upper story, as
Wolfe did at Quebec. The captain's men looked at each other and
rolled their eyes.

Captain Walker, now pumped with adrenaline and military passion, outlined the tactics to be adopted, striding back and forth, his
swagger stick under his arm. "Batons are to be used liberally and with
force, as most of these people are of Irish blood so have thicker skulls
than normal. If the deserter attempts to escape, he can be shot. His
mother might come at you with a rolling pin, in which case extreme
force must be used to subdue her."

The captain's inside information was from one of his men, who
dated Becky Cavendish, whose best friend was Pauline Donnelly, who
was an old school friend of Lilly Corcoran, who was one of Hannah's
daughters, so all the information that Becky gave her soldier was
carefully fed through the pipeline by Hannah.

Little Jimmy Kelly was no longer in the house, having left immediately after the corporal took the sergeant to the hospital, and was now
hid in the basement of Saint Lawrence's Church. Hannah, however,
was planning a welcome for the military police.

❖

The army lorry pulled up outside 57 Beckwith Street and dis-
gorged Captain Sebastian Walker with twenty of his men, armed with
batons and side arms. The news had spread throughout the parish,
so an interested crowd had already gathered. It included a reporter
and photographer from the *Birkenhead News,* who had received a tip
about possible shenanigans in the docklands, much to the chagrin of
Captain Walker. With the crowd jeering them, the MPs approached
the front door, but they slowed to a standstill when they saw what
was in front of them. Sitting on the stoop, in her usual spot, was
Granma White, smoking her clay pipe, surrounded by a group of
nuns who had been recruited from the Convent of the Little Sisters
of the Poor.

"Clear those people out of the way," ordered Captain Walker, but once again, the men hesitated. One of the men asked the nuns to please leave, but the nuns stood silently firm. One of the nuns handed the MP a rosary.

"They block our approach," stormed the Captain. "Pick them up and carry them away if you have to."

"Beg pardon, sir," a sergeant said. "But a lot of our men are from this area and bein' Catholic, they would be loath to manhandle a nun. This crowd is Catholic, too, so the situation could easily turn nasty."

Sister Winifred, Mother Superior, handed the captain a rosary and told him in a soft Irish lilt, that if he was ever sent off to fight the Germans, all the nuns would pray to the Blessed Virgin for his safe return. "But there are no Germans here, only women, children, and old men," she said. "Are you sure in your heart that you are doing the right thing?"

Captain Walker was sure. He posted half of his men at the front to ensure no one left by the front doors or windows. He led the rest of them around to the back door, where another surprise awaited him. The door was heavily barricaded such that it would take a lot more than a couple of stout shoulders to budge it, and the walls on all sides were topped with thick coils of barbed wire, which some dockers, who shall remain nameless, had borrowed from the dock wall the previous night. Hannah had watched as they installed it on her wall that morning and wondered how it was possible to steal barbed wire.

Captain Walker was running out of options. He returned to the front of the house and informed his men that if they couldn't go in the front door or in the back door then, damn it, they would go through the windows. The ground story windows were still guarded by the nuns, but the upper story windows were fair game. The captain called for the ladders. As his men fetched the ladders, all of the upper story windows opened and out of each popped the head of one of Hannah's daughters. They waved to the MPs below and blew kisses.

"What are those ladders for?" Grace called. "Have you boys come to elope with us?"

"I'll take that one," said Eileen, pointing to a big corporal.

"No, he's mine," shouted Lilly, who then threw something out of the window at him.

"What was that projectile?" yelled Captain Walker. Then another one shot out of another window, barely missing the captain's head. "Good God! What the hell was that?" It rolled over to the feet of onlooker Pat O'Malley, who picked up the object and held it high for all to see: a light green oval covered in spikes, larger than a golf ball, smaller than a cricket ball.

"It's the fruit of the horse chestnut tree." Pat said. "And inside is a beautiful, shiny conker nut. Did you never play conkers when you were a boy, Captain? Hannah's girls went out at the crack of dawn this morning to collect them in the park, where the horse chestnut trees flourish in abundance."

Before the Captain could reply, conkers flew out of every window, aimed at the MPs below. The crowd laughed and jeered at the soldiers who attempted to set up their ladders while dodging conkers. It was entertainment on a grand scale, but poor Captain Walker was beside himself with anger and befuddlement.

At that point, a siren wailed and a police car forced its way through the crowd. Out jumped Chief Constable Mathew Baker. He yelled at both sides. "Stop this! Stop right now before someone gets their eye poked out!"

Captain Walker was quick to remind the chief constable that the military police had jurisdiction over the civilian police during wartime. The inspector shrugged and pointed out how ridiculous the captain would look in the *Birkenhead News*, dodging conkers. "Give me some time to talk to Hannah. Maybe we can get things resolved," Baker suggested. Captain Walker reluctantly agreed, given that his battle plan had failed miserably so far.

Baker approached the house and shouted out to the girls. "Tell Hannah I want to speak to her before this situation gets out of control."

Eileen poked her head out of a window. "I'd say the situation is pretty much out of control already, Chief Constable."

Hannah poked her head out of another window. "I'm right here, Mathew. Come on in, but you'll have to climb one of the ladders to the upper windows. The front door is blockaded from the inside."

Chief Constable Baker climbed the ladder and disappeared into the house. "What the hell is goin' on, Hannah?"

"I thought maximum publicity was the way to keep the boy home," Hannah replied.

"Well, yer wrong. It only escalates the situation."

"Mathew, you look so manly when yer angry—it's quite intoxicatin.'"

Baker scowled at her. "Quit yer flirtin', missus. You're in deep bother. The way I see it, I have to arrest yer for the assault on the military police sergeant. We'll have to somehow get the charges dropped in the courtroom."

"Keep talkin'," Hannah said.

"Did he provoke you?" Baker asked.

"Well, he pushed past me to get into the house."

"Did he touch you?"

"Yeah, he pushed me out of the way."

"Ha! Then we've got him."

Baker shakily climbed back down and approached Captain Walker. "Here is the situation. Hannah agrees to give herself up to me, not you, on the understanding that she be taken before a civilian magistrate on the charge of assaulting yer sergeant. She will not be charged with abetting a deserter, since yer have no proof of that, plus if the lad was ever in the house, he's long gone by now."

The chief constable called over the reporter from the *Birkenhead News*, putting a fatherly arm across his shoulders. "Robert, my friend," he whispered, loud enough for Captain Walker to hear. "I don't want to see any of this in the paper tomorrow. If I do, you will never get another piece of inside information from the Birkenhead police on any subject, ever again. Send all the pictures to me, for insurance purposes. Do you understand?" The reporter nodded.

A short while later, the crowd cheered Hannah as Chief Constable Baker escorted her to his police car and drove away. Now that the show was over, Captain Walker felt he had won a partial victory, although he couldn't understand why he didn't feel better about it. The crowd dispersed, leaving young boys to collect all the conkers.

Hannah spent the night in the Birkenhead town jail, with a plate of scouse for dinner, washed down with a bottle of brown ale supplied by Doris. Later she played cribbage with the jailor, complaining only once. "Yer can't get a decent cuppa in this place!"

❖

The next day Hannah stood in court before Magistrate Braydon Jones MBE, a humorless Welshman renowned for being partial to the tipple. He had been brought in from Chester, twenty miles away, by Inspector Baker, as most local magistrates had knowledge of Hannah and her fist and might hold a bias against her. Magistrate Jones had plenty of his own biases, however, being a prudish stuffed shirt, hostile to the Irish and in no mood to show any sympathy to deserters.

The court was packed with Hannah's clan, friends, and supporters, all shouting and jeering like it was a Tranmere Rovers football game. They quieted down when Magistrate Jones threatened to clear the courtroom.

A bailiff read out the charge of assault and battery. The magistrate asked the black-eyed, bandaged Sergeant Calhoun to recount the incident, but the sergeant still couldn't speak because of his broken jaw. His prepared statement was read aloud by Captain Walker. The magistrate then asked Corporal McKay for his account of the incident.

"There appears to be a discrepancy between the two versions," the magistrate said to the corporal. "You state that the woman hit the sergeant with her fist, while the sergeant said she employed a weapon. Which is it, man?"

"She hit him with her fist, sir. I saw no weapon." The corporal's voice was shaky. Fortunately for Hannah, he had been brought up to tell the truth and thought, especially in a court of law, this was the safest course of action. Sergeant Calhoun shook his head and grunted under his bandage.

"Did she have anything inside her fist when she hit the sergeant?"

"No sir. Her fist was empty both times, best I could tell?" the corporal's voice still shook as he knew there would be repercussions back at the barracks, for telling the truth.

"How many times, Corporal, did she hit the sergeant?"

"Just once, sir."

The magistrate looked over at Hannah, then back at the sergeant, then back at Hannah.

"Do you mean to tell me that this little woman punched this big hunk of a man and knocked him senseless?" He shook his head. "Incredible."

"Well, when she punched him, he fell over a bicycle in the hallway, which may account for the cut on his head," Corporal McKay said.

Magistrate Jones then turned his attention to Hannah. "Well, woman, you had better tell me your side of the story."

Hannah cleared her throat. "My name is Hannah Corcoran. You can call me Mrs. Corcoran or you can call me madam, but you have no leave to call me *woman*. I'll show you respect if you show me respect, then we'll both get along famously."

The magistrate was taken aback by this assault on his manners. "Very well, *Mrs. Corcoran*, pray tell us what happened. By-the-by, isn't Corcoran an Irish name?"

"Yes sir, it is."

"The Irish are neutral in this war, are they not? Which means they don't care who wins?"

"I wouldn't know what the Irish care about, sir."

"I thought you said you are Irish? Which is it, woman—I mean Mrs. Corcoran?"

"I said my *name* is Irish. I was born and bred in Birkenhead, which makes me English."

Magistrate Jones mopped his brow. "Just tell me what happened."

"Well sir, those two soldiers came thumpin' on the door, lookin' for little Jimmy Kelly. Before I could tell them to shove off, they barged in, and the big one—that one over there—molested me, so I clocked him in self-defense. Simple as that." A sudden tension fell over the proceedings.

"Did you say he molested you?" The magistrate's voice deepened, while muffled cries came again from behind the sergeant's bandage.

"Yes sir, I did. He grabbed my breast," Hannah said. "My girls were in the house—I had to protect them."

"This is a serious accusation, Mrs. Corcoran. Did anyone witness this assault?"

"Yes sir, that soldier saw it." She pointed at Corporal McKay. Sergeant Calhoun frantically scribbled on a piece of paper and passed it to the magistrate.

"Sergeant Calhoun maintains that he pushed you out of his way, but you are lying about being molested." The magistrate turned to Corporal McKay. "Did you see the sergeant push Mrs. Corcoran?"

"Yes sir."

"Where did he push here?"

"At the entrance to the hallway, sir."

"No man! Where on her body did he push her?"

"On her chest, sir."

"On her chest or on her breast?"

Hannah chimed in, "On most women, they're in the same place." A roar of laughter erupted from the crowd.

"That's enough," said the magistrate. "Corporal, is it possible that the sergeant's push to her chest could be mistaken for a grab of her breast?"

"I suppose so," the corporal replied, scratching his head. Sergeant Calhoun and Captain Walker both shot him angry looks.

"I know the difference between a push and a grab, sir," Hannah said, taking the opportunity to reinforce her case. "I know that big feller was coming at me with bad intentions. I know my five daughters were in the house. I know the next day a lorry load of his friends came back, swinging clubs and carrying ladders." Hannah was on a roll. "What sort of men are these? What sort of soldiers would accept a boy into their army, barely seventeen years old? God help this country if we have to rely on these people to defend us."

"That's enough, now." Magistrate Jones twirled his gavel for a few seconds. "The problem is that I'm not sure what the truth is here. As for the deserter, whatever his age, we have a war to fight, so we all must be prepared to make sacrifices. Mrs. Corcoran, do you have anyone who can vouch for your character?"

"That would be me." Up jumped Father Flaherty. "My name is Eamon Flaherty, and I have been the parish priest at Saint Lawrence's Catholic Church for nigh on thirty-five years. I've known Hannah Corcoran since she was a wee bit of a girl, and a finer woman you'll never meet. She attends Mass three times a week, she helps clean the church, she collects money for the Little Sisters of the Poor, and is always available to help a parishioner in need.

"She is tough—yes, no doubt about that, but she has had to be tough. When her mother turned blind and her father died, she took over the family and brought up her brothers and sister virtually alone, and she still a girl herself. She has six children, and when times were tough she worked at the shipyard as a laborer. When her sister died, she took in little Jimmy Kelly as one of her own." The priest took a breath.

"Yer talk about sacrifice. Her first husband was killed at Jutland in the Great War. Her brother was killed at the Marne. Her second husband was gassed at Ypres. Her son-in-law went down on the *Thetis*. I think that's sacrifice enough."

Magistrate Jones pressed his hands together to form a steeple and placed them in front of his mouth. He drew a deep breath. "All right, I'm dismissing any charges against this woman. Mrs. Corcoran, you are free to go."

Hannah smiled faintly, while the court cheered.

"Thank you, sir, thank you, but what about him?" she said, pointing at the sergeant. "Does he get off scot-free? Can I not bring charges against him?"

"That's preposterous!" yelled Captain Walker.

"Sit down and be quiet, or I'll have you ejected," the magistrate said. His brow furrowed in thought. "I'll consider your request, Mrs. Corcoran, but right now we will take a tea break. Be back in fifteen minutes."

Hannah, flanked by Peter and Father Flaherty, filed out of the courtroom and stopped when she passed Pat O'Malley, standing next to Mathew Baker.

"Done and dusted, Pat?" she asked.

"Done and dusted, Hannah."

"Attagirl," Mathew added.

❖

Out in the corridor, Hannah came face to face with Captain Walker and his two men. She pulled the corporal toward her and whispered, "You're a good lad for telling the truth."

"Well, at least we have the deserter in custody," Captain Walker said. "At least we have that."

"What! You have Jimmy Kelly?"

"Gave himself up last night." The captain smiled a smile of victory.

"You evil bastard!" Hannah's left hand slipped behind her back.

Peter grabbed his wife's arms and held her fast. "What will happen to him?"

"Well, he won't be shot, but he'll go to a military prison for a long time—five years, maybe ten."

"If Hannah drops the charges against yer sergeant, can he forego the prison?"

"I think I can arrange that, but he'll still be in the army."

"Then it's agreed." Peter marched Hannah away, his arm around her shoulders. "It's the best we can hope for, luv," he told her. "The best we can hope for."

❖

Jimmy Kelly went back to his regiment after spending just a month in the stockade. It wasn't long before the phony war turned into a serious shooting match. Little Jimmy Kelly died on the side of a hill on the island of Crete, with a German bullet in his stomach and his grandmother's white-bead rosary in his pocket.

❖

Hannah climbed the stairs to her room. She sat on the bed and held the Wedgewood broach Jimmy had bought for her with his pocket money. Lilly and Grace came in and sat next to her.

"Would you rather be alone?" Lilly asked.

Hannah shook her head. "My heart is broken. So young—I can't believe he's gone."

Lilly and Grace wrapped their arms around Hannah. A mother and two daughters, their foreheads touching, wept an ocean for little Jimmy Kelly, the lovely lad.

Chapter Sixteen

≡ 1942 ≡

The Grass is on Fire

Lilly Corcoran's childhood sweetheart, Chris McKenna, came back from Dunkirk on a stretcher, bandaged and bloodied, all shot through. A month later he got up from his hospital bed in the middle of the night and, for no apparent reason, climbed out of the window and fell two stories to the street below.

The doctor proclaimed that with his injuries upon injuries, Chris would not live out the week. The priest came to administer the last rites and the army paid to bring Chris's mother and Lilly all the way down by train from Birkenhead in Cheshire, to Slough in Buckinghamshire. Despite its purpose, nineteen-year-old Lilly felt exhilarated by the journey, for it was the first time she had left Merseyside.

Sitting by Chris's bed, holding his hand, with tears on her cheeks, Lilly agreed to his proposal of marriage. After all, the poor boy was close to death—it was the least she could do.

Maybe it was the prospect of a life as Lilly's husband, or maybe it was the extra special care that a pretty young nurse bestowed on him, but Chris had the impertinence to recover, slowly but surely. Lilly was furious. In the sport of dating boys, the game was suddenly over before she had warmed up. To every handsome young soldier, sailor, or airman, she now had to hide the stigma of being spoken for.

One year later, Lilly considered this predicament as she paced outside the dance hall, smoking her last cigarette while waiting for her sister Grace to show up. Damn Grace, she thought, so selfish, never thinks of anyone but herself, not even her own sister, her best friend. Grace was still free to play the field, to flirt. Jealousy warped

Lilly's mind. She had considered writing to Chris to break off their engagement, but that really wasn't an option. A good Catholic girl didn't send a "Dear John" to a wounded soldier in wartime, without the fear of being shunned by every soul in the town.

Grace finally made her appearance from the darkness of the side of the dance hall, hair disheveled, lipstick smudged. "Hi Lil. Everythin' all right? Yer not mad at me or anything, are yer?"

Lilly turned on her sister. "Where the hell have you been? The dance was over twenty minutes ago, so what the hell were you and that soldier doin' all that time? We've missed the last bus, for God's sake."

"We were just neckin', that's all. Jeez Lilly, you sound like our Mam. I'm sorry we missed the bus. We'll just have to hoof it home—won't be the first time. It's only a couple of miles."

"Gimme a cigarette," Lilly said. "What if there's an air raid? What will we do then?"

Grace looked skyward. "Look at that moon. It's too bright for them Jerries to make an appearance. They're afraid that our lads firin' their anti-aircraft guns might accidentally hit them."

"Better not say that to Eileen, working a searchlight every blessed night."

Grace shrugged. "Anyway, if there is an air raid, the worst the Germans can do is kill us, and if they kill me and not you, then yer can have my navy blue frock."

Lilly grinned. "If they kill you and not me, I'll have all your clothes."

"Our Mam will kill us both for comin' home late. What's worse?" Grace asked. "Bein' killed by the Germans or bein' killed by our Mam?"

"Good question," Lilly said. "I'd say it's a toss-up."

The sisters set off up Bidston Road, with their arms intertwined, puffing away on their Woodbines. *My two pretties*, Hannah liked to call them. Grace, just eighteen, had the smoldering allure of a gypsy dancer, sultry one moment, mischievous the next, and a magnet for any boy within eyesight. Lilly, two years older, was the real beauty. Although all of Hannah's children had inherited her beautiful, jet black hair, it was Lilly who most resembled Hannah when she was a girl—the same violet, flirtatious eyes, the same arresting smile. The sisters skipped along and talked of boys and clothes and the factory where they worked. The factory had once produced margarine but now manufactured ammunition. Mostly they talked of boys. They had drawn black lines down the back of each other's legs, using ash from the grate, to give the illusion they wore nylons. Such was the practice when the price of nylons made them out of reach. The lines generally worked, except when it rained.

As the girls continued their trek, three hundred German bombers, Junkers and Dorniers, had already taken off from France. They followed a course down the English Channel and rounded the tip of Cornwall.

◆

The girls reached the crest of Bidston hill and could just make out the shadow of the windmill in the distance, outlined by the moon. A cool spring breeze blew off the Mersey. Spread out below them lay the port of Birkenhead, barely discernable under the strict rules of the blackout.

They briefly discussed taking a shortcut through the pine woods but then discarded the idea as daft. It was common knowledge that the ghost of Maggie Fletcher, who had been murdered there more than sixty years before, haunted the place. Instead, they turned toward Oxton, past all the mansions were the nobs lived. They made enough noise, just for the mischief of it, to wake the dogs, who in turn would wake their owners.

◆

The German bombers continued north in tight formation, over the Irish Sea and up the coast of Wales. They preferred to fly the western coast of England on their missions to the Northwest, rather than across the eastern coast, which was a shorter distance. If they had to ditch their planes and parachute out, they would most likely be picked up by the neutral Irish rather than the English, whose reception was generally frosty.

◆

An army lorry drew up besides the girls and slowed down. "Do you ladies need a lift?" shouted the driver. Grace looked inside the back of the lorry at the half dozen soldiers seated there. Some of them appeared drunk. "C'mon girls," one shouted, "don't be shy."

"No thanks, boys, we need the exercise," Grace replied.

"Suit yourself," the driver said, as he drove off.

Lilly and Grace continued down toward the town, passing the north end of Birkenhead Park.

◆

The German bombers were now over Caernarvon Bay in North Wales, indicating to the British radar tracking stations that their target was probably in the Northwest, or Clydeside, and not in the industrialized Midlands. A second wave of two hundred German bombers, twenty minutes behind the first wave, following the same flight path, was also under close scrutiny. A thousand telephones rang declaring action stations throughout the Merseyside and Greater Manchester areas. Two hundred thousand volunteers, men and women, hurried to their stations. Squadrons of British fighter planes scrambled, including a Czechoslovak squadron stationed in Birkenhead's Arrow Park.

◆

The piercing wail of the air raid siren stabbed the silence of the night. Lilly and Grace stopped dead in their tracks. "Jeez, Lilly," shouted Grace above the screech, "now what do we do?"

Lilly's heart quickened. She took a deep breath. "Let's hope it's a false alarm. If it's not, then it usually takes about twenty minutes between the alarm and when the bombs fall. I don't think that's enough time to reach the Beckwith Street shelter, even if we run."

"What about the shelter on Claughton Road, by the Roxy Cinema? That's closer."

Great shafts of light sliced through the night sky. The two girls took off their heels, stuffed them into their coat pockets, and ran down Upton Road toward the Claughton Road shelter. They ran on the empty road to avoid any debris or dog mess on the pavement.

The few remaining lights of Birkenhead disappeared, as if a wizard had waved a magic wand. As the sisters got closer to the shelter, they heard the distant bark of anti-aircraft guns. This was no false alarm.

Lilly stopped abruptly. "Ouch, ouch. I've cut my foot on something sharp." She lifted her foot up for Grace to remove a small sliver of glass from her sole. Lilly put her shoes back on and the girls continued to run, though now a little slower.

◆

The German planes veered hard right at Anglesey, heading toward Liverpool Bay. Search lights, anti-aircraft guns, and barrage balloons forced them to gain altitude.

"River Mersey ahead at one o'clock," said the co-pilot of the squadron leader's bomber. The squadron leader peered intently out of the cockpit window and shook his head.

"That's not the Mersey. That's another river. Those aren't city lights. And those docks and ships in harbor are made of wood and canvas. They're not real, but models made to trick us into dropping our bombs on empty fields. I've fallen for that trick before, but not this time!"

◆

Being young and athletic, Lilly and Grace reached the Claughton Road shelter with time to spare. The warden, an old man, as they all were, stood at the iron door and signaled them in. The tail of his white shirt was pulled out over his trousers, a common practice to prevent being hit by vehicles during the blackout.

◆

The squadron had now reached the real River Mersey. "Target ahead, bomb doors open," said the German squadron leader.

◆

"Come on in, ladies, quickly—we have some room left." The sickly smell of vomit and diapers seeped out of the shelter door. Grace grabbed Lilly's arm. "No, let's keep going."

Lilly pulled her arm free. "What is it, Grace?"

Grace's voice was frantic. "I don't know—just a feeling. Please, Lilly, please, let's keep going to the Beckwith Street shelter, where our Mam and Doris will be."

They both began to run again. The warden yelled after them,

"You're crazy! You'll never make it to Beckwith Street. That's down by the docks. Can't you hear them Jerry bombers?"

❖

"Bombs away!" said the German bombardier.

Lilly and Grace crossed Claughton Road and entered the top end of Exmouth Street at the same moment the first bomb fell at the bottom end.

❖

Hannah stewed as she paced up and down by the door of the Beckwith Street shelter. The explosions outside, deafening through the iron door, caused the whole shelter to shudder. Plaster fell from the ceiling, while children crouched in fetal positions on their mothers' laps. Babies wailed and women swayed back and forward reciting the rosary.

In Bidston dock, the shallowest of all the Mersey docks, a light cruiser, HMS *Dido*, blasted away at the German bombers. The recoil from her guns caused the *Dido's* keel to bang against the muddy bottom of the dock, sending vibrations throughout the ground of the entire Birkenhead Docklands. Not knowing the cause of this phenomenon greatly added to the anxiety of people locked in the shelters.

"Good God, can you hear that?" Hannah asked. "They're trying to kill us all in one night! My girls are out there!"

"Don't worry," said the warden, none other than Chunks Cavanaugh. "They're smart girls. They'll find shelter."

❖

The first bomb hit the Ramsey's fish and chip shop at the bottom of Exmouth Street and blew it into oblivion—haddock, cod, chips, mushy peas and all. Though they were a good hundred yards away, the girls were knocked over by the force of the blast, as if they had run into a plate glass window. The next bomb landed on the co-op grocery just two doors down from Ramsey's. Grace jumped to her feet, cursing like a sailor. She pulled Lilly up by the collar of her coat and dragged her to the doorway of Mrs. Mack's newsagent shop. But the space was taken by a sailor and his girlfriend hunkered down, his arms wrapped around her in reassurance.

Lilly and Grace dived into the doorway of the bicycle shop next door, stooping down with their hands over their heads. Bombs fell all around them with deafening explosions. The sky rained bricks, pavement, and glass. They huddled in their little sanctuary as the world destroyed itself two yards away. Lilly screamed. It was over in no more than the time it took to recite three Hail Marys, but the terror was branded into Lilly's brain. Even in her dotage she could close her eyes and replay the experience vividly.

Grace peered out into the street. "Holy Jesus! Exmouth Street is an inferno. C'mon, Lilly, we better get out of here!"

"I'm not going anywhere," Lilly said, still trembling.

Grace pulled out a couple of cigarettes, lit them both, and gave one to Lilly. "Pull yourself together, Lil, we're still alive and kickin'. Those buggers missed us." Grace's eyes showed no fear. She acted as if she had just been on a roller coaster ride, as if she enjoyed being close to death.

They finished their cigarettes. "Well, you can stay put," Grace said, "but I'm goin'. Yer know, that's probably just the first wave." With that, Grace darted out of the shop doorway, with Lilly close on her heels.

Burning debris still fell around them, shot up by pockets of ignited house gas. Burning buildings lit the sky, and the fires spread along the rows of the attached tenements. Somewhere in the distance a woman screamed.

The girls decided to run back to the shelter at Claughton Road, when a warden running the other way stopped them.

"Where have you come from?" he asked.

"Exmouth Street," Grace said.

"Is it hit?"

"It doesn't exist anymore. Where have you come from?"

"Grange Road is fine but Oliver Street is clobbered. It looks like the entire dock area from here to the river took the brunt." Just then another warden joined them.

"Hey, Charlie," he said, "I've just heard that there's more on the way. Where are you girls headed?"

"To the shelter on Claughton Road."

"Oh no, you're not. It took a direct hit. Nobody will be left alive inside there."

Lilly grabbed Grace's coat lapel. "God Grace, how did you know it would be hit? How in hell did you know!" Grace just shook her head.

They then decided to try and make it to the Beckwith Street shelter before the next wave of bombers and ran down Claughton Road again, looking for any side street that wasn't on fire and could take them down to the docks. Eventually they turned down Parkfield Avenue with the Convent of the Little Sisters of the Poor on one side, and a row of houses with front lawns on the right. They were the only houses with gardens this close to the docks.

But it was too late. The terrible cacophony of destruction began again. They crossed the street, searching in vain for shelter. On the small lawn of a house with peeling paint, a few bushes at least gave the illusion of shelter. As they jumped the fence, an explosion knocked them both off their feet again.

Lilly landed face down on the lawn, thrown like a wet rag. She lay there reciting the Lord's Prayer in quick breaths. Her heart pounded. Her body shook and her painted fingernails dug into the soft earth. She turned her head and faced shards of burning debris littering the lawn.

"Oh my God! The grass is on fire! Grace! Where are you? For God's sake, where are you?"

"Stop yellin'. I'm over here behind the bushes. Are you all right?"

Lilly crawled along the grass, avoiding the burning debris, and ducked under the bush where her sister sat, resting on one hand. Blood streaked down the side of Grace's face and neck. She stared down at her left leg, reddened with blood from a gash on her thigh.

"Bollocks, bollocks, bollocks! Would you look at that?" Grace said. "Ruined. My best coat ruined, and I only just bought it! You can't get blood out, you know that. If I ever get my hands on that Hitler feller, I'll punch him worse than Mam ever punched anyone!"

At that moment, the front door of the house creaked open and a dark figure of a man appeared on the steps, silhouetted by the flames of the burning convent. The figure appeared to have no legs. Lilly stared at the apparition in horror. Her ability to handle the anguish she had suffered that night was all used up. The macabre sight pushed her over the edge. She fell to the ground and curled into a fetal position like a boiled shrimp. She covered her head with her arms, breathing through her teeth, while around her trembling body the grass continued to burn.

The figure shouted, "Is someone out there?" A woman appeared behind the man, towering over him.

She gasped at the sight across the road. "Holy God in Heaven! The convent's been hit!"

"I think there's someone on the lawn," the man said.

"Over here by the bushes. My sister Lilly and me. I think we need some help."

The couple approached them. The man seemed to walk fine on the stumps of his legs. The woman bent down. "You're Hannah Corcoran's girls, aren't you? Are you hurt?" Grace recognized the woman, Mrs. Williams, from church. She knew that her husband had lost both his legs in World War I, but no one had ever seen him because he never left the house.

Mrs. Williams scanned Grace's bloodied thigh. "You're gonna need this wound seen to, luv. Is your sister hurt, too?"

Grace shook her head. "I think she's just in shock. A cuppa and a cigarette might help."

"Help my sister first," Lilly said. "She's blood all over."

Mrs. Williams took the girls into her house to clean up Grace's wound. The place was dark and dank and smelled of camphor and bleach. The furniture, the rugs, and even the lamps were Victorian dark brown. Pictures on the wall displayed long-ago battles in sepia tone. Mrs. Williams bandaged Grace up as well as she could.

"Best get her to the shelter, where they'll have first-aid kits. You've not far to go now," Mrs. Williams said to Lilly, who had regained some of her composure, thanks to the tea and the cigarette.

"Do you think you can walk?" Lilly asked Grace.

"Of course I can. For God's sake, stop fussin'."

"Don't yell at me," Lilly answered. "It's your fault we're in this mess. If we'd caught the last bus or taken a lift from those soldiers we'd be safe by now!"

"Right," said Grace, "and if we had gone inside that shelter, we'd both be dead!"

"Where are the rest of your sisters?" asked Mrs. Williams.

Lilly answered, "Vera is sitting with Granma White. Eileen is on searchlight duty and Doris is in the shelter with our Mam. Thank you for your help—we'll be off now."

"Here, take this," Mr. Williams said, and handed Grace a walking stick with a horse's head handle.

The terror returned to Lilly as they left the comparative safety of the house to enter the inferno that the town had become. She fought the urge to run back and bang on the door. With one arm around her sister, Grace limped along as best she could to the Beckwith Street shelter. It was converted from an old iron works, with a deep cellar closed tight by a large steel door. Lilly picked up a brick and banged it against the door.

"Open it," Hannah said, inside the shelter.

"Now listen, Hannah," said Chunks Cavanaugh, "you know I can't. It's against the law to open a shelter until the 'all clear' is sounded."

"Open it. I won't ask again."

"Don't you think about punching me, Hannah. I'm family, remember."

Hannah's left hand curled into a fist behind her back. "It's family I'm missin'—Lilly and Grace. They're your family too." Chunks, considered "not all there" by many, was smart enough to know that if he didn't open the door, Hannah would—after she'd belted him.

"Douse all lights," he shouted and then pulled the door open.

When Lilly helped Grace inside, Hannah gasped at the blood on Grace's coat.

"It looks worse than it is," Grace said, as they lowered her down on a mattress. Chunks fetched the first aid kit.

"It's a nightmare out there," Lilly said, her heart still racing. "Claughton Road, Oliver Street, Price Street, St. Anne Street, Exmouth Street, Parkfield Avenue, the Roxy—everywhere is ablaze."

"What about the brewery on Oliver Street?" asked an old man in a corner.

"Clobbered," said Lilly.

"Thank God for that," he said. "The beer was rubbish."

Doris sat next to Lilly and gave her a cigarette. "Are you okay, Lil?"

Hannah turned sharply to Lilly. "She looks okay to me. What I want to know is why didn't you look after Grace like I told you? Why didn't you get home earlier? Look at the state of your sister! She could have been killed!"

Lilly couldn't hold back her tears. "Why do you always pick on me? How am I supposed to control her? She's an adult and will do whatever the hell she likes. I'm not the mother, you are. What should I do when she doesn't heed me? Punch her? That's your answer, not mine." Lilly's sobbing continued unabated. The shelter occupants were stung to silence as they watched the tense little Corcoran drama play out.

"Stop that blubbering," Hannah yelled. She grabbed Lilly by the shoulders and shook her like a bag of laundry.

Doris stepped in. "That's enough mother. Can't you see she's been through a terrible experience?"

Having been on edge all evening, Hannah made the sudden leap from anger to remorse that often characterized her unpredictable emotions. She began to cry, too. She wrapped her arms around Lilly. "I'm sorry, my sweet. You're safe now, with your family. I'm sorry. You brought your sister home through the air raid, that's the main thing."

"We took shelter in Mrs. Williams' house on Parkfield Avenue, right opposite the convent. It took a direct hit," Grace said. "Lilly was a brick—she helped me get to safety."

"What?" Hannah exclaimed. "What did you say, girl? Not the Little Sisters, surely?"

"Which shelter do they go to?" Doris asked.

"They don't," Hannah answered. "The nuns go into the convent cellar. We've got to help them. Who is with me?"

While all of the adults in the shelter were concerned about their own homes, the thought of not helping the sisters was a hard bullet to chew, even if it meant the risk of leaving their youngsters in someone else's charge. After all, nuns were one step closer to God than any of them. About a dozen people raised their hands—mostly housewives.

"Now, Hannah," Chunks Cavanaugh said. "I can't open the door again. I'll be reported."

Hannah's left hand went behind her back. Doris put her arm around the warden and whispered to him. "I've seen the left hook in action, Uncle Chunks. Don't take the chance."

Chunks Cavanaugh flung open the door.

Chapter Seventeen

≈ 1942 ≈

The Blitz

Hannah and her group emerged from the shelter to the shock of the Apocalypse in full fury. The sky glowed bright scarlet from the destructive power of thousands of bombs that had rained down on Merseyside that night. It was bonfire night from hell. The Devil's Circus had come to town and gone haywire.

Everywhere was action. Fire engine bells clanged. Bulldozers scraped debris off the roads. Makeshift ambulances fought their way through the rubble. Fire wardens scurried hither and thither. Incendiary crews banged on the doors of burning houses. People were running somewhere, anywhere, to escape the nightmare. The very air was afire. It seems like the end of everything, Hannah thought.

A frantic woman stopped Hannah's group. "Have you seen my boy, Gerald? Twelve years old, gray shirt, wellies, gray pants. He ran out of our Anderson shelter looking for his dog. Number 11, St. John Street." She pleaded with her eyes. "Help me. For pity's sake, help me."

Hannah put her arm around the woman's shoulders. "If we see him, we'll fetch him. Someone is bound to spot a lad alone."

Further along, a double-decker bus lay on its side, still smoldering. The sickly smell of its burning tires choked their throats as they passed.

"Look! Mum, look!" yelled Doris, pointing to the south. Flames and sparks shot into the sky from down by the docks. Hannah winced. Looks like the Vittoria Dock, she thought, where Peter is a warden. Please God, keep him safe. For a moment Hannah stopped in her tracks, mouth half open, while anxiety creased her face.

No one could read Hannah better than Doris. "You keep going

to the convent, Mum, and I'll find my dad. I'll check on Granma and Vera on the way." Doris pushed her mother slightly forward.

◆

At the Vittoria Dock, a freighter half-laden with goods bound for Saint Petersburg had taken a direct hit. The deck amidships was ablaze, and men on board scrambled to reach the gangway through the flames and smoke. On the quay, dockers acting as auxiliary firemen hastily rolled out their hoses, while others tended to the casualties of the explosion. A tall bearded man with a thick neck and a weather-worn face, uniformed as a Merchant Navy officer, barked out orders. Seamen forced their way up the gangway, against the heat, to bring the wounded down.

Peter Corcoran charged up the quay through a veil of black smoke, grasping a long-handled axe in each hand. As he passed, the officer grabbed him.

"What are those axes for?" he demanded. "Who the hell do you think you are, the last of the Mohicans?"

"We gotta cut loose this ship," Peter said. "Let go of me."

The officer tightened his grip. "Oh no, you don't. I'm the captain of this vessel and those are my crew on board. We'll get the men off and douse the fire from the quay."

Peter struggled. "Why were these men on board? They should have been in shelters."

"Repairs," said the captain. "We were due to sail on the morning tide. Anyway, who the hell are you?"

"I'm the fire warden for this dock. These warehouses are full, and we can't risk the fire spreading to them. I'm sorry about your men, but I'm going to cut this ship loose and let the fire boats deal with it. Your men will have to jump in the drink."

"So where are these fire boats?" the captain demanded. Peter knew all the fireboats were over on the Liverpool Docks, overwhelmed with burning ships. There was little chance of cutting one free for Birkenhead.

"Can you feel the wind change?" Peter asked. "Soon sparks from your ship will reach the warehouses. You've lost this vessel, yer gonna have to face it."

"What about the wounded still on board?" said the officer, still holding Peter fast.

Peter thought, where is your left hook when I need it, Hannah? I have no option but to give this feller a Merseyside kiss. Peter head-butted the officer, who fell backwards, freeing Peter from his grip.

Two sailors appeared on the deck of the burning ship. "No more wounded," one of them shouted.

"Get ashore right now," Peter yelled.

"Wait, I hear someone below," one of the sailors said, and disappeared through a hatch.

"Bollocks!" Peter remarked.

The ship was moored to the quay with three thick ropes tied around black metal bollards—forward, amidships and aft. Peter grabbed a nearby docker, gave him an axe, and ordered him to cut the forward line. Then taking aim at the line astern, Peter struck hard at the rope around the bollard—then struck again and again. Sparks flew off the axe as it hit the bollard, until it cut the rope through. He ran to the line amidships, where the heat was intense, to perform the same procedure.

"Stop him!" yelled the captain, his nose still throbbing from its encounter with Peter's forehead. Two sailors ran at Peter but stopped abruptly when he swung his axe at their heads, like a Viking berserker.

"I'll slice yer noggins clean off if yer come any closer! I've got to cut loose this ship. I don't wanna, but I have no bleedin' choice."

The line amidships gave way and the ship slowly drifted away from the quay, stern first. The gangway, still attached to the ship, dragged along the quay until it reached the end of the dock and swung with a crash against the side of the stricken vessel.

The sailor who had gone below reappeared, holding another sailor upright. "Smashed leg," he yelled.

Peter yelled back. "Heave him over the side, then jump in yourself. We have boats in the water to fish you out." On cue, two motorized dinghies, manned by dockers, sped from across the dock. When the wounded man hit the water, two dockers in a dingy jumped in and hauled him to safety, as well as the other sailor.

The captain stared in doleful silence as he watched his burning ship drift away.

"I'm truly sorry," Peter said, "but the contents of these sheds are vital to the war effort."

"What's so important? Are the sheds full of munitions?" the captain asked in a saddened voice.

"No, it's Spam. Spam from America."

"You mean the tinned meat? Are you serious?"

"Yes, sir. I'm deadly serious." Peter replied. "It's our secret weapon. It's the main source of nutrition for the whole country—without it we'd starve. Our servicemen rely on it and now that the Russians are on our side, their armies will fight on it. You see, the German's don't have Spam. Without Spam, we can't win this war."

❖

Hannah, with her small group from the air raid shelter, had reached the remains of the convent. Firemen and wardens battled the flames. Rubble was everywhere. Heaps of red bricks, concrete, glass, dust, and smoldering wood were all that remained of the Parkfield Avenue end of the convent. The Claughton Road end still stood, three stories high, but it spat flames and heavy smoke from its windows.

"What are you lot doing here?" asked a gruff warden with three stripes on his arm.

"Did you find any sisters?" Hannah asked.

"Not a one. They shelter in the cellar of their chapel, and that heap over there is all that's left. I doubt there's one left alive."

"There's only one way to find out." Hannah scrambled over some bricks, but the warden grabbed her and pulled her back. "Not a good idea, missus." He turned to the group. "This whole place is unstable. That wall could come down any minute. See that depression by the wall? That triangular piece of metal sticking out is very likely a fin of an unexploded bomb. When the wall comes down, it could set it off—it's much too dangerous to go near. Besides, everything is still red hot. There's nothing can be done."

"Well, get a bomb disposal squad over here." Hannah said, folding her arms.

"Are you kiddin'? They're as scarce as petrol coupons. Their priorities are army depots, airfields, railways, and docks. Not convents. Jerry is deliberately droppin' unexploded bombs because they cause more disruption that way, and some of them are booby trapped. After their training, those poor bomb disposal officers have a life expectancy of three weeks."

At that moment, Father Flaherty appeared on the scene, with Father Michael in tow. "Holy God in heaven!" said the older priest. "Are any of the sisters spared?"

"We don't know yet—we're going to dig for them. How many were there? I mean are there?" Hannah asked.

"Twenty-seven nuns, five novices," replied the priest. "The entrance to the cellar was in the corner of the chapel, over in that far corner. That's the best place to start."

Soon they were joined by Peter Corcoran and Doris, along with a dozen dockers armed with picks and shovels. Hannah hugged her husband. "Yer shouldn't be here. You'll be in deep trouble for abandoning your post."

"It's all under control down at the docks. When we heard the convent was hit, I couldn't have stopped the men coming here even if I wanted to. If another wave comes we can get back fast enough."

"You should all go somewhere else," the warden said. He explained to the new group the dangers involved. "I'm just tryin' to save more lives. There is nothing you can do for the sisters. Why not help at another site? There are plenty to choose from, but I can't allow you here."

"What's yer name?" Hannah asked.

"Jones," he said. "Warden Jones, from Rock Ferry."

"God is looking at yer right now, Warden Jones. He's testing you, so when yer get to the gates of heaven he's goin' to ask, 'What did you do to save my daughters?' Now, get out of my way afore I strike yer down."

"The warden's right," said a young mother. "It's too risky. If that wall comes down, it could kill us all." The sentiment was shared by others in the group, who slowly began to back away.

"Give me yer gloves," Hannah said to the warden, whose face was reddening with anger.

"You need to slip back to the asylum, missus, before they realize you've gone."

Hannah's left fist took its place on its launch pad.

"That's Hannah the Hotspur," Peter said. "I strongly advise yer to give her your gloves." Warden Jones took of his gloves and thrust them at Hannah's chest. "There, go and get yerself killed."

Hannah scrambled to the top of the heap of rubble. She picked up two house bricks, one in each hand, and threw them aside. She picked up two more and turned to the group, fierce determination in her eyes.

So there stood Hannah the Hotspur, in her faded green coat and her worsted, calf-length skirt, with an old woolen scarf around her neck. She balanced on the rubble, legs akimbo, a brick in each hand, illuminated by the burning building in the background. The sight seared itself into Peter's brain. For the rest of his life, this image of Hannah would be perfectly preserved. How could a man not love a woman like this? He joined Hannah on the heap. After him came Doris, then the two priests, and finally, the dockers and the housewives.

Warden Jones shook his head. "All right, I'll have the firemen hose down the chapel area, so you won't burn yer hands, but I'll take no responsibility for any of yer."

The group dove in, pulling debris from the mound that once was the chapel. The heat of the smoldering building next to them reddened their faces and made it difficult to breath. Once they had uncovered the steps to the cellar, it didn't take long to find the first victim—a young novice with a sweet face and a crushed body. One hand still clutched her rosary. Two more nun's bodies were soon recovered. A solemn silence descended on the diggers. Then at last they heard a muffled cry for help from the rubble below.

"Someone's still alive!" a docker yelled. Despair turned to elation as everyone doubled their efforts. They finally reached the bottom of the cellar steps but found the way blocked by a heap of broken bricks. Warden Jones dug at the bricks with an iron bar, creating a hole through to the other side. He put his arm into the hole, and an old wrinkled hand grasped his.

"Thank you, Jesus, thank you," the nun said, wheezing.

"How many of you are there?"

"Maybe twenty. Some have fainted for lack of air. Some are badly hurt. Some have gone to the Lord, I think."

"As soon as we make a hole big enough, all that can walk must get out on the double. We will get the rest after them. Do you understand?" asked the warden.

"God bless you, my son. You are not a minute too soon. I will stay with the injured."

Sister Winifred, Mother Superior of the Convent, stayed in the cellar until all the nuns still alive were helped out.

"Everyone clear away!" the warden demanded. "The outside wall could collapse any moment. Get out now—we'll recover the deceased later."

When Sister Winifred finally emerged from the cellar and her eyes got used to the light, she gasped in horror. "Look what they have done to the convent! It's destroyed! The barbarians!"

"We'll rebuild, don't you worry," Father Flaherty said.

"I might have known you'd be here, Father." She put her arms around him and wept. "And Hannah and Peter Corcoran, of course. Who else would risk their lives? God bless you all."

The nuns sat on the pavement, comforting the injured, awaiting bulldozers to clear pathways through smoldering wreckage so the ambulances could reach them.

Warden Jones yelled "Run! Everyone run!"

The south wall of the Convent tottered and collapsed. People scattered up and down Parkfield Avenue. The wall fell straight, in a cloud of dust, and then seemed to bounce, hurling bricks everywhere. Luckily, it failed to ignite the unexploded bomb. Peter ran with Hannah hot on his heels. He tripped on a brick and went sprawling on his back. Hannah fell on top of him.

"Are you all right?" he asked.

She nodded. "But we've got to stop meeting like this." Hannah jumped up and looked around. "Is anyone hurt? Is everyone accounted for?" There was no immediate reply.

"Father Flaherty. I don't see him," Father Michael said. The rescuers scuttled back to the mound of bricks.

Hannah discovered a black trouser leg that stuck out from a heap of bricks. "Oh God! No!"

"Over here," someone shouted. "He's unconscious but he's alive."

"Who is it?" Hannah yelled back.

"Father Flaherty."

"Then who is this?" Hannah asked.

Rescuers uncovered the owner of the black trouser leg to find Warden Jones, barely alive. At that moment, the "all clear" sounded.

◆

Hannah crammed into an ambulance with Father Flaherty, the injured nuns, and Warden Jones. One of a convoy, they drove far out into the Wirral Peninsula, to the only remaining hospital that wasn't swamped with victims.

"Tell me what you know," Hannah said to the ambulance driver.

"God Almighty," he said. "All of Merseyside got totally clobbered. Almost every street in the docklands is hit. Not just Birkenhead— Wallasey, Bebington, even Heswall and Neston. Liverpool is a total inferno. There are three ships on fire in the docks and a couple more in the river. Factories, railway stations, army depots—you name it. Casualties will be in the many thousands. Who knows how many will be homeless. This was the worse raid yet. Where is God? I ask you, where is God?"

◆

The scene at the hospital was total pandemonium. Ambulances couldn't get close because of the congestion; injured people lay on the lawn outside, for there was little room inside. Locals brought hot tea and biscuits to those victims and their loved ones, who patiently waited to see one of the doctors or nurses. The medical staff was beyond exhaustion.

Hannah volunteered to help bring the wounded in off the lawn to spaces in the hospital corridors vacated by the treated or dead. The injuries ranged from broken limbs and concussions to serious burns. Their cries cut through Hannah like a scalpel. Some had already died for lack of attention.

One young woman, with a blue bump on her forehead and what appeared to be a fractured fibula, held a shawl tight around her body. Hannah asked her to remove the shawl to determine if she had any more injuries. Slowly she unwrapped it, to reveal a baby of no more than three months. The baby's head lolled on one side. Her eyes were the same green as her mother's. Hannah had never seen eyes so green and never would again.

"This is my sweetie, Annie. They tell me she's dead, but I don't believe that. People can be so mean. She can't be dead. What would I tell my Eric when he comes home from the war? Can you please help her?"

Hannah gulped. She took the baby from the young woman. There was no breath, no pulse. "Stay here until someone comes to get you," Hannah said.

Back in the emergency room, a doctor quickly confirmed the baby's death. Hannah sat cross-legged on the cold hospital floor, holding the little body tight against her chest.

"Are you all right?" a nurse asked her.

"I'm not going to weep," Hannah said. "I'm as tough as they come. I can deck any man you care to name, big or small. I can pull nuns out of smoldering graves. I can drill a half-inch hole in four inches of Sheffield steel in five minutes." Hannah held the baby tighter. "I'm known far and wide as someone you mess with at your peril. I know death. I've washed a hundred dead bodies. That's how tough I am. So I'm not going to weep."

The nurse leaned over her and took the baby from her. "Here, take this," she said, and handed Hannah a clean handkerchief to dab her eyes.

Throughout the night, ambulances delivered more casualties. Hannah did her best to comfort the relatives. She spotted Nelly McVeigh from Watson Street, whose soldier son gave his life in North Africa, not a month before. Now here the poor woman was with her seriously injured grandson.

"A direct hit on my dead son's house," Nelly said, her face distorted with grief. "His wife, Agatha, his wife's mother, and her young daughter—all killed. If this boy doesn't survive, the whole family will be wiped out, except for the baby."

"Baby?" Hannah asked.

"Just four months old, found in her crib under the bed with not a mark on her. I suppose I'll have to rear the poor little tyke and me at my age, with a dicey ticker."

"A baby girl. Where is she?"

"In the waiting room with my daughter."

Nelly led Hannah to the infant in the crowded waiting room.

217

"May I?" she asked, and picked up the baby to examine her. She smiled at the green of her eyes. Close enough, she thought. "Are you going to adopt this child?" Hannah asked Nelly's daughter.

"I have three of my own," she replied. "I can't provide for another."

"Nelly, it seems neither you nor your daughter can take care of this baby, and I can't say I blame yer—times are tough enough. There's a young woman in this hospital whose baby just died that looks a lot like this one. She's out of her mind in anguish. What do you think?"

Nellie and her daughter spoke to each other in distressed whispers. Finally, they both nodded. "As long as she gets a good home," Nellie said.

Hannah found the young woman in a side ward. "She's not stopped asking for her baby," the nurse told Hannah.

Hannah placed the child in her arms. "Here she is, your little Annie."

"This isn't my baby," the young woman said, shaking her head. "These are not her clothes. My Annie's eyes are greener."

"We changed her clothes. This is your Annie." Hannah's voice was insistent. "Do you have milk?"

"Yes, but—" Hannah interrupted. She grasped the young woman's hand and held it firm. "Look into my eyes. This is your baby. Do you understand?" There was a pause.

"I understand," she replied softly. She cuddled the child.

"You can't do this," the nurse said. "It's wrong. There are procedures. There are documents. There are hospital rules."

"On a night like this, there are bound to be hospital mix-ups," Hannah responded. "Besides, there were just too many coincidences. Too many pieces fell into place. I didn't do anything nurse, because on a night like this, God is making the rules."

The nurse managed a slight smile. "All right, I'll say nothing."

◆

By 4:00 a.m., the hospital refused entrance to any more ambulances, which were sent even further afield. Hannah curled up in a corner of the waiting room and fell sound asleep. Two hours later, a nurse woke her to ask if she was there with the priest and the nuns. Hannah nodded.

"Two of the nuns didn't make it, I'm afraid. Two more we've admitted with serious injuries. The rest have minor injuries and can leave. The priest has a broken arm and a head injury but he'll recover."

"God bless you," said Hannah. "And the warden named Jones?"

"He passed away. I'm sorry."

Hannah emerged from the hospital to a morning sun obliterated by smoke. She and the discharged nuns rode back to Birkenhead in a furniture delivery van, acting as an ambulance. Passing through the village of Irby, the van slowed down where a small crowd had gathered outside the police station.

"Stop the van," Hannah, said, curious to know what the commotion was about. She got out and asked a bystander, "What's goin' on?"

"A Ju 88 was one of the bombers shot down last night, and landed in a field a couple of miles back. Three of the crew got out, one of them wounded, and they escaped into the woods, but the Home Guard caught them this morning. They locked them in the police station, and now the army's here to pick them up."

Hannah pushed her way to the front of the crowd. First down the police station steps came a stretcher with the wounded man. Then two German airmen came behind, their arms held tightly by soldiers, shuttling them to the army lorry. The first German was no more than a boy, barely nineteen, typically Teutonic with a fresh face and straight blond hair. The second was twenty-five at the most, with a defiant arrogance about him. As they passed, the crowd just glared at them in quiet anger.

Hannah stepped in front of the older German, her left hand behind her back. The fist of retribution flew with such ferocity that her feet left the ground, and the sound of the ensuing thud sent a gasp through the onlookers. The blow knocked him clear of his captors, and he collapsed like the wall of the convent he may have bombed. He lay face down with his arms stretched out to either side, hemorrhaging from his nose. He was quickly pulled upright by the soldiers on either side, who dragged him to a lorry. No one uttered a word— not the other prisoner, not the police or the soldiers, not a person in the crowd. They all stood stunned by the violence of the blow.

After Hannah got back in the van, someone in the crowd said, "That must have been Hannah the Hotspur."

❖

During the Blitz, Granma White refused to go to the shelters. She would sit in her room throughout the attacks, but not alone, for Hannah insisted that she and each of her children take turns sitting with the old lady. Only Eileen was exempted from this duty, because Eileen, independent and reliable as ever, had joined the Women's Army Corp and spent every air raid on searchlight duty.

By the standards of a later time, it might seem cruel that a mother would put her children in such danger because of the vagaries of an old woman, even though they were all full grown. Times were different then—it was the elderly, not children, who were the focus of the family. Children, while they were cared for and nursed, loved, and grieved over when they died, were, to put it bluntly, replaceable. It was unusual in those days for all the children of a large Catholic family to reach adulthood, given the quality of medical attention available and the number of childhood diseases that flourished.

This time it was Lilly's turn to sit with Granma White when the sirens screeched, only a week after the night Lilly and Grace were caught outside in that terrible air raid. Lilly's pride still stung from the treatment she had received from Hannah in the shelter.

Granma White sat on her bed and Lilly snuggled up next to her, the room lit by a single candle, with the blackout curtains pulled tight. Vera's dog snored on the rug.

"How many hats do you have, Granma? I've only seen you wear that one." Lilly pointed to the dresser, where her grandmother's black hat was outlined by candlelight.

"Just one."

"Then why do you call it your best hat?"

"You prefer I call it my worst hat?"

Lilly laughed. She thought a minute, and then asked, "What's it like being blind?"

She regretted saying it as soon as the words left her mouth. She was afraid she had gone too far, for they had never talked of it before.

Granma White seemed unfazed. "Hmm, you know, I've been blind so long, I rarely recall the time when I could see. Being blind allows your imagination to do the seein' for yer, so you see only what you choose to see. You see good things, rarely bad. You never see ugly, you only see beauty. I see Mary and the angels all the time."

"What does an angel look like?" Lilly asked.

"They all look like my grandchildren! I'll tell you what it's like to be blind—fetch my Longfellow book."

Lilly took the book off the shelf. It smelled like an old stuffed doll she once had.

"Now go to 'The Song of Hiawatha,' the introduction, and go down to the eleventh stanza."

Lilly took the book over to the candle and read.

> That the feeble hands and helpless
> Groping blindly in the darkness
> Touch God's right hand in that darkness
> And are lifted up and strengthened

"Do you understand?" her grandmother asked.

"Not really," Lilly replied. "Perhaps you need to be blind to understand."

"Perhaps."

In silence, Lilly stared at her grandmother's wrinkled face, and wondered if she would ever be as clever as this old woman.

"You're staring at me," Granma White said.

"How do you know?"

"I can sense it." Grandchild and grandmother exchanged smiles.

"Why are you and my mother so different?" asked Lilly, snuggling up again.

"Are yer still angry with her?"

"Yes, she shook me and embarrassed me in front of all those people. And it was all Grace's fault we missed the last bus, not mine."

"She loves you, Lilly."

"Then she should find a better way to show it."

Granma White leaned over and gently stroked the ringlets that cascaded down to Lilly's shoulders. "They say you're the prettiest of them all." She ran a gnarled hand down the side of Lilly's cheek. "Your mother holds you to a higher standard because of your beauty. She had hopes that you wed someone in the same mold as George Hamm, which is why she is so upset that you promised Chris McKenna you'd marry him—a docker's son with no prospects."

"I thought he was going to die," Lilly replied.

Granma White smiled and nodded. "Personally, I think you can do far worse. He's a fine young man, handsome too, I hear. He always stops for a chat and lights my pipe without complaint. I think. . . . Can you hear that? Here they come!"

The drone of distant aircraft and the bark of anti-aircraft guns stopped the conversation cold. Lilly curled up closer to her grandmother, who put a reassuring arm around her.

"Be still, my sweet one," she whispered. "All will be well." The ominous noise grew louder.

"Why are they trying to kill us?" Lilly asked. "What have we done to them? I don't know any Germans. My dad says they're aiming for the docks, but the anti-aircraft guns make them fly higher, and when they're low on fuel, they just drop their bombs anywhere."

"Not so," Granma White said. "Those Jerry fly boys are deadeyes. They boast about it in their beer gardens back home. Remember, we're very close to the docks, and sometimes they aim for very specific targets. Take the fish and chip shop on Exmouth Street for example. Not many people know that Adolph Hitler lived in Liverpool for a year in 1912, and even fewer know that he once took a day trip on the ferry over to Birkenhead. He walked around the market before he stopped in at the Ramsey's fish and chip shop for a haddock, three pence worth of chips, and some mushy peas. Now, everyone around here knows that old man Ramsey will short change yer, but Hitler wasn't to know that. He didn't realize it until he got back to Liverpool and was mad as a box of frogs. So when the Blitz started, he told fat old Goering to make sure Ramsey's chip shop got flattened."

"True story?" Lilly asked.

"Cross my heart." Granma White raised her hand across her large bosom.

"What about the convent?" Lilly asked. "What did the nuns do to Hitler?"

Granma White thought for a second. "Nowt. They did nowt. But those Jerries are all Protestants, and they know that Birkenhead, though mainly Catholic, has more than it's fair share of Orangemen. So the word went out, 'If you've got to drop a bomb on the town, aim for the convent.' Why? Because you'll be hard pressed to find a Protestant in a nunnery."

"You know what, Granma?"

"What?"

"You're so full of baloney!" Granma White gave Lilly a playful squeeze.

All at once the planes were overhead, and the world was filled again with the whine of the bombs and teeth-jarring explosions. The walls of the house shook to its foundations, shattering windows. Lilly closed her eyes and held her breath, clinging to her grandmother, who quietly recited the rosary. The floorboards heaved. Cracks travelled along the plaster of the walls like thin snakes. A picture of the Sacred Heart above Granma White's bed fell down.

With a terrifying crash, part of the bedroom ceiling caved in. Plaster, wood, and pieces of roof slates rained down around the two women. A great flash of fire shot up from the floor to the ceiling, and stifling smoke filled the room.

Lilly grabbed her grandmother's arm and bustled her to the door. She half dragged her down the stairs, afraid she might trip and cause the pair to hurtle head-over-heels to the bottom. When they reached the hallway, a thunderous banging came to the front door. Lilly opened it and two fire wardens burst in.

"Where is it?" asked the first warden sharply.

"Up one flight, first room on the left," Lilly said.

The warden raced up the stairs two at a time, fire extinguisher in one hand, sledge hammer in the other, with amazing sprightliness for an older man.

"Who else is in the house?" asked the second fireman.

"No one, just me and my blind grandmother here."

"Take your granny out to the middle of the street—be careful of falling debris. Keep away from houses. Lucky for you we were passing when that incendiary hit." He ran up the stairs after his fellow warden.

"And a dog!" Lilly shouted after him. "There's a black dog named Kim."

Lilly led Granma White into the middle of the street. Bombs were still exploding somewhere in the distance—maybe Liverpool, maybe Manchester. The sky was on fire again. Shards of burning wood littered the street. Small gas leaks exploded and clouds of choking dust blew off the river.

"We can't stay here! We're too vulnerable!" Carefully, Lilly led her grandmother down the street into a back alley, easing her backwards until the old lady could feel a brick wall. A black dog ran across the front of the alley, panting, in a state of raw panic.

"That's Vera's dog!" Lilly said. "Kim, Kim, come here boy," she yelled, but the dog was too terrified to respond. "I have to get Vera's dog. You wait here—I'll be right back."

"Don't leave me," Granma White said and gripped Lilly's arm.

"Don't worry. I'll come right back."

"Please don't leave me here."

Lilly ran out of the alley into the street, yelling the dog's name. Her yelling grew fainter the further she ran, until it stopped altogether. Granma White pressed her palms against the wall behind her. Fear, such as she had never felt before, overwhelmed her. Where was she? She could feel the heat of the fires, so hot she began to sweat. She could smell the burning houses, but what should she do? Should she stay here? Should she walk back to the house? In which direction? Her cane was in the house. She might trip and fall on some burning piece of wood. For the first time in her blind life she felt totally alone and helpless. She had no frame of reference, standing in the middle of hell. She struggled in her pockets to find her rosary, but that, too, was in the house.

"Lilly, Lilly, for God's sake, come back," she pleaded. She sensed someone coming. Footsteps on the cobbles. A woman's footsteps. "Lilly, is that you?"

"Yes, it's me. I'm coming, Granma," Lilly said, pulling the dog by his collar. "I caught Kim. I'll slip my belt through his collar as a leash." As Lilly drew near, she stopped, aghast. Her grandmother's mouth was open and her whole body quivered in fear.

"Oh God, I'm so sorry! I never should have left you." Lilly grasped the old lady and whispered "shush" in her ear and patted her back like a crying baby. "It's all right now, Granma. You're safe now. I'm safe. Kim's safe. It's all over."

❖

A half hour later, Hannah and the girls returned from the air raid shelter to find Granma White with her composure returned. She occupied her usual place on the stoop, smoking her pipe and sipping brandy from a beaker. The front door was wide open to allow the smell of burnt wood to waft out.

Hannah shrieked. "Lilly! Jesus, Mary, and Joseph, where is my Lilly?"

"She's inside, unharmed and safe. We were fire bombed," Granma White said, as if it happened every night. "More precisely, I was fire bombed because the damn thing landed smack dab in my room."

Hannah bent down and grasped her mother's arms. "Are you all right, Ma?"

"A bit shaken, but not a scratch."

Lilly emerged from the house to be greeted by hugs from her mother and sisters. Vera started to cry but recovered when she pulled Kim to her chest and allowed him to lick her tears.

"Here's the damage," Lilly said. "The parlor windows are blown out. There's a big hole in the roof and in Granma's ceiling. The carpet's burnt, plus most of the bedclothes. The bed is singed, as are the walls, but the floorboards look sound. Most of Granma's clothes are drenched in fire retardant, and a lot of her books are gone. Inside the dresser drawers looks good, but the top of the dresser is badly burnt."

"My best hat?" Granma White asked.

"It's a goner," Lilly replied.

"We can replace carpets and clothes," Hannah said. "I just thank the Lord that you're both unharmed."

"Your daughter saved my life," said Granma White. "I panicked but she didn't."

"We were lucky those fire wardens were right there when it happened. You should have seen how quickly they put out the fire," Lilly said, diverting any praise away from herself.

"Well, that's the end of the bombing of Birkenhead. We won't see those Jerry fly boys again," Granma White said. "Hitler has at last destroyed what he was after."

"And what would that be?" Hannah asked.

"Why, my best hat, of course!"

Chapter Eighteen

≡ 1945 ≡

War's End

It was a grand night for an ambush. The moon was new and the sky was coal-tar black. The waves broke on the northern French coast just loud enough to mask the low hum of the engines of two British Motor Torpedo Boats (MTBs) lurking in a desolate cove. The crews of the MTB—only twelve sailors in each—stood motionless and silent at their stations, senses honed on detecting the sight or sound of their quarry. French partisans had reported that two Vichy French cargo ships, escorted by a German destroyer, had been spotted sailing up the coast toward the Cherbourg Peninsula.

Nineteen-year-old Steven Corcoran, the torpedo operator on MTB 212, crouched at his station, trying to muffle a cough. Like all his mates, his mind was focused, his body tense. He knew from experience that when the action began, if it happened at all, it would be deadly pandemonium, over in seconds. The job required a lot of nerve.

◆

With conscription looming, Steven had voluntarily joined the navy to avoid the other services. Hannah realized it would be futile to try to prevent him, so she stuffed a rosary into his pocket, together with a picture of the Sacred Heart. With her arm clutched around Peter's waist, she watched the train pull out of Lime Street Station in Liverpool, carrying her only son off to Winston's war against the Hun. She vowed to herself that if he didn't come home in one piece she would hunt down the fat Tory and pummel him until his beady eyes popped out.

If one imagined a young Peter Corcoran, made him a bit taller, a bit leaner, added a dash of charm, but kept the calm persona, mixed with an occasional burst of Hannah's feistiness, then that would be Steven.

At first, Steven was assigned destroyer duty, escorting Liberty ships across the Atlantic. They ran the gauntlet of German U-Boats in an almost exact reenactment of the First World War scenario. He greatly welcomed his transfer to an MTB flotilla, preferring the role of predator to that of prey.

The crews of MTBs were the British Navy's unsung heroes of World War II. They patrolled the English Channel, fighting off German E-boats, attacking enemy convoys, landing secret agents, escorting commando raids, and even raiding enemy ports.

They were equipped with two torpedo tubes and generally had three machine guns for defense, although their main defensive attribute was speed. They sliced atop the waves at an exhilarating forty knots—nothing on water was faster. Their strategy was stealth. They sneaked up on their prey, let loose their torpedoes, then got the hell away as fast as their powerful engines could take them.

While the battleships of the Home Fleet spent much of the war at anchor in Scapa Flow, these tough little mosquitoes patrolled the English Channel, the Adriatic, and the Mediterranean. They menaced anything, big or small, that they deemed a threat. The crews cared little for navy traditions, discipline, or protocol, let alone dress code. Regular naval officers called them "scruffy little pirates," a sobriquet that suited Steven and his mates just fine. To the British Admiralty they were expendable, and huge numbers of these men were lost. But their role in the war effort was vital.

The navy simply assigned MTBs an identification number, but the sailors who manned them gave each a woman's name, usually from a mother of one of the crew. The name tied the young sailors together like members of a football team, like they were brothers of the same blood and the boat was the woman who gave them birth. MTB 237 was named the *Christine*, after the skipper's mother, and no one was going to argue with that. But there were several candidates for MTB 212. Once Steven explained to his shipmates the phenomenon that was Hannah's left fist, flashing out of nowhere to deliver a deadly strike, the similarity was too obvious to ignore. So MTB 212 became *Hannah II*, because the original Hannah ferry boat still chugged daily across the Mersey.

◆

The two boats, the *Christine* and *Hannah II*, had been hiding for over an hour. The crews were beginning to think it could be a false alarm or that maybe other MTBs further south had already engaged their quarry. But then the noise of large engines broke the calm of the night, followed by the dark outline of two cargo ships chaperoned by a sleek German destroyer, which steamed slowly and quietly past the MTB's hiding place. Steven's heart beat faster as he tried to control his heavy breathing. He knew from experience that this would pass soon. He pulled his rosary from his pocket and kissed the crucifix.

With barely a whisper, the *Christine* engaged her engines and emerged slowly from the cove, followed closely by *Hannah II*. They were like two crocodiles sliding into a river with their unsuspecting prey in sight. They maneuvered behind the destroyer, on the assumption that enemy lookouts would be less vigilant when looking astern.

All at once, loud voices were heard from the German ship. A searchlight scanned the water behind it, locking in on the *Christine*.

"Damn, they've spotted us," said Lieutenant Blake, the commander of *Hannah II*. The fresh-faced young man, a junior tax attorney in civilian life, was barely older than the young men he commanded.

"Brace for action!" he ordered.

Steven grabbed two stanchions while digging his heels into the bulkhead. He knew that everything now would depend on the reactions of every sailor on the boat. Each man had a specific job to perform, which dovetailed into the next man's job, and the smallest mistake could mean the death of them all.

The two MTBs thrust their engines into high gear, causing the boats to shoot out of the water. With a fierce roar, amid a wall of spray, they raced away at full speed out to sea. The *Hannah II* followed the *Christine*, in order to get a good run at the midship of their enemy. The searchlight stayed locked on the *Christine*, as tracer fire from the destroyer and the cargo ships stabbed the darkness.

The skipper of the *Christine* swung his boat around and headed back in a zigzag pattern toward the cargo ships, using his speed to increase his chances of scoring a hit. His sister boat followed the same course. Abeam to the first cargo ship, four hundred yards away, the *Christine* fired her torpedoes. At the same moment, a 20mm shell hit the *Christine* amidships, exploding her fuel tanks and blowing her apart. The crew of *Hannah II* watched in horror as the bodies of their comrades were flung into the air among the wreckage.

"Cut the engines," ordered Lieutenant Blake. "Observe complete silence." *Hannah II* slowed to a drift. Steven heard the skipper whisper to his number two that the enemy might not realize there was a second MTB.

The searchlight from the German destroyer scanned the water again, joined by searchlights from shore batteries. A loud explosion suddenly lit up the night sky, as one of the errant torpedoes from the *Christine* struck the first cargo ship astern. The crew of *Hannah II* stifled a cheer, as their boat continued to drift toward the destroyer, but the explosion had exposed their position.

"Steady lads," the lieutenant said with sharp resolution, now that his boat was at right angles to the destroyer's bow.

"Fire both torpedoes."

In an automatic reaction from a hundred real and practice drills, Steven fired off both torpedoes. The two metal assassins shot through their tubes and splashed into the waves.

Lieutenant Blake jammed his three Stirling engines—1,400 horse power apiece—to full power. Again, with a tremendous roar, the boat took off like a greyhound. The officer swung it around in a tight arc, almost capsizing it, away from the destroyer and out to sea.

With its bow out of the water, *Hannah II* dashed over the swell as it now became the target for all the destroyer's guns, the guns of the one cargo ship, and those of the German shore batteries. The boat's three machine guns fired back at the destroyer's main deck in an attempt to unnerve their gunners, but *Hannah II* was now, in effect, one big plywood and mahogany fuel tank, and a couple rounds of machine gunfire could destroy it. Lieutenant Blake knew, however, that whatever the fate of his little boat, his torpedoes had been fired so close to the destroyer that there would be no time for the enemy ship to avoid them.

Both torpedoes exploded squarely on the destroyer's hull. Two sheets of flame shot skyward, outlining the darkened French coast behind.

Through the spray on either side of *Hannah II*, the number two peered through binoculars at the devastation they had left behind. "Two direct hits amidships," he yelled. "Good shooting, Seaman Corcoran."

Now out of range, Lieutenant Blake began to breathe again. "Damage report?"

"No damage evident, sir," the number two replied.

"Casualties?"

"No casualties, sir. All crew accounted for." He paused as his voice turned solemn. "Except for all our mates on the *Christine*. Wait, where is Steven Corcoran?"

"Seaman Corcoran, report!" Lieutenant Blake said.

"Steven, where the hell are you?" the number two roared. A grim silence descended on the crew.

"Down here," answered Steven, scrambling around on his hands and knees near the wardroom hatch. "I'm looking for my front tooth that got knocked out when we gunned the engines."

"Seaman Corcoran reports a front tooth missing, sir," the number two said, which raised great amusement among the crew.

"Don't worry, Seaman, we'll get you a false tooth." Lieutenant Blake grinned.

"That *was* a false one, sir. I lost the real one last year in a football game."

When they reached harbor, a reception committee of their peers cheered the crew of *Hannah II*. A senior officer saluted each sailor as he came ashore. He explained that French partisans had witnessed the encounter and reported that the German destroyer had definitely sunk.

"Yes, we bagged ourselves a Jerry destroyer tonight," Lieutenant Blake said. "But we couldn't have done it if the crew of the *Christine* hadn't sacrificed themselves." There was a short silence.

"Double rations of rum all around," said the senior officer. "Let's drink to the crews of the *Christine* and *Hannah II*."

◆

Steven spent the rest of the war on *Hannah II*, patrolling the English Channel. The little boat even took part in the Normandy invasion, escorting landing craft as they approached the shore.

When the war finally ended and he was demobilized, Steven took the train home to find his mother and father standing on the exact spot in Lime Street Station where they had stood when he left four years earlier. Behind them had gathered the rest of the family, so there were hugs and tears, and slaps on the back, and joy all around.

"Have yer been standing here all the time I was away?" Steven asked Hannah, his arms wrapped around her.

"So we have," she replied. "The station master kept bringing us Birkenhead Brewery pale ale and sardine sandwiches."

"Where is your front tooth, Son?" Peter asked.

"Lost at sea. The navy quacks promised to give me a new tooth, but I think they had more important priorities."

"Well, the first order of business is to get your teeth fixed," Hannah said. "You'll not find yerself a good Catholic wife if yer teeth look like a row of bombed houses."

❖

With the end of another war, a multitude of servicemen came home to find the country bankrupt again. The blitz had left thousands in Birkenhead homeless and a new large cemetery full.

Lilly had reluctantly married her soldier. Eileen had married Bobby Flynn, the lad who was so helpful when the *Thetis* went down. Doris moped her way through each day, and Vera hadn't changed at all. With all the paychecks coming into the house during the war, Hannah had accumulated quite the nest egg, although with such harsh rationing of virtually everything, there was not much to spend it on. Still, it felt so good, this new prosperity. For the first time in her life, she didn't have to fret about food, clothes, and rent.

The war had taken George Hamm, Jimmy Kelly, friends, and neighbors, but Hannah thanked God that Steven had returned home without a scratch. Sitting at the kitchen table, Hannah watched her son scoff down a plate of beans on toast. He hasn't changed, she thought. Like his father, war hadn't altered his personality. He was the same bright-faced lad, full of quiet humor and level-headedness.

"Tell me about the war," Hannah said. While Vera made some tea, Steven told Hannah of the night they sunk the German destroyer and how they had named their little boat after her. Hannah expressed delight and assumed the demure look that came whenever she received a compliment.

"Mother, look at Granma White!" Vera said.

Granma White had poured her tea into her saucer, blew on it, but had completely missed the teacup as she poured it back. The tea soaked into the rug. Hannah gently took the cup and saucer from her mother.

"I think you're tired, Ma. Why don't you go for a lie-down?" Steven and Hannah helped Granma White up to her room and put her to bed.

"I'll stay with her awhile," said Hannah, as Steven left. She brushed a white lock of hair from her mother's forehead. "You've not been well all week, Ma. It's been so bloomin' hot."

"It's my time," Granma White said softly.

"Nonsense, Mother. You're just under the weather. I'll send Vera to fetch the doctor."

"No doctors. Please, no doctors and no blubbering, because if you start blubbering then I will, too. When I meet my maker I have a feeling my sight will be restored, and I don't want my eyes to be all sore and bloodshot before him." Hannah couldn't help a smile. Granma White's breathing grew weaker and her chin drooped. She grasped Hannah's hand.

"I'm ninety years old, so I've had a good outing. But my life would have been unbearable without you, daughter. You were my eyes and my strength. You provided me with everything I needed, and you helped raise my children."

"And you helped raise mine, while I went off to battle the world."

The old lady wheezed. "You gave your children all your affection in the time you had to spare, and you let me supply the rest. I'm grateful for that. There's one last thing I want you to do for me as soon as I'm gone." Hannah held her ear to her mother's lips as she whispered, until she felt her mother's grip loosen on her hand. Granma White's jaw fell open and her heart stopped beating. Hannah placed her head on her mother's chest, like a child would, with hot tears running down her cheeks.

Then Steven knocked on the door. Hannah asked him to bring up Vera's long scarf that she wore when she walked the dog on cold days. Steven returned and looked at his grandmother. Her eyes were closed but her mouth was wide open. "Is she? . . ."

"Yes," Hannah said. She wrapped the scarf around her mother's head, over the top and under her chin. With one hand holding her shoulder and the other the scarf, Hannah and Steven tugged tightly on the scarf until Granma White's jaw pulled shut. "That's better." Hannah said.

"Now tell Vera to go to the phone box on the corner and contact Doris, Lilly, Eileen, and Grace at work. Tell them to come straight here when they're finished. No spouses, just the direct family." Steven looked at his mother with a puzzled expression.

Hannah continued. "You go and buy four bottles of wine from the off-license. Take the money from my purse. Then tell your father to come home right away—he's working at the Blue Funnel Line." Hannah's voice was calm but low and sad. Steven held his mother in his arms and kissed her forehead. "I'm so sorry," he muttered.

Hannah sniffled. "She was ninety years old—it was her time. No fuss, no pain. She missed her teacup and slipped away. My mother, my best friend, just slipped away."

❖

By 6:00 p.m. all Hannah's children had gathered in the parlor. Each in turn went up to Granma White's room to pay their respects, so the house was awash with sorrow. Lilly and Grace went to the local chippie and brought back supper for everyone. When they had finished eating, Steven opened the wine.

"You never drink wine with greasy chips. It's considered an insult to the chip maker," Steven said, trying to lighten the mood a little.

Vera continued to cry. "No more tears," Hannah said.

"Vera is not going to stop crying," said Grace. "She can't help it."

"I suppose so," Hannah replied. "For the rest of yer, here is what I want you to do. We will toast the life of your grandmother and then

I want each of you to recount a memory you have of her, amusing or interesting, but not sad. It was her last request."

They drank a simple toast.

"I'll go first," Steven said. "When we were kids, Granma White told us when they fired the one o'clock gun on Bidston Hill we had to duck our heads down low so the cannonball wouldn't hit us. To this day, whenever I hear that gun, I automatically duck."

"Me too," said Doris.

Grace laughed. "Me too. She told me they fired the gun to signal that it was time for her afternoon nap."

"I remember when we were kids we would kneel between her legs, with a newspaper on her lap," Doris said, "while she ran a nit comb through our hair. She would comb out those nits so we could pick them up and throw them into the fire to hear them crackle."

"We all remember that." Lilly grinned.

"What a nasty thing to remember," Grace said.

"It was no disgrace. Every kid in the town had lice in their hair. Every house had a nit comb," Hannah said.

"I took her to confession every Saturday," Eileen said. "And I wondered what sins an old blind woman, who sat on a stoop all day, could have possibly committed in a week. One day I held my ear up close to the confessional door.

'Bless me Father, for I have sinned,' she said. 'It has been a week since my last confession.' And then she said, 'I'd like to place a shilling each way on Hard Nose in the fifth at Sandown Park, and half a crown to win on Speak No Evil in the sixth at Chester.' Then she opened the confessional door and said, 'Did you get all of that, Eileen?'"

"I've heard that story before," Doris said.

"I don't believe it," Grace said, cocking her head on one side.

"I *can* believe it," said Hannah.

They raised their glasses to toast her again.

"My turn," Grace said. "When we came home from school, she would be sitting on the stoop, waiting for us to run errands for her— to go for tobacco or a newspaper, or sometimes to the Wellington Arms for a flagon of pale ale. We would try to sneak past her on the stoop, but she would grab our legs as we passed. Somehow she always knew we were there."

"I have one," said Vera, who had stopped crying at last. Surprised, all eyes turned to her.

"When I ran away from the convent, I came home, but you weren't here, Mam, only Granma. I asked her if you wanted me home again. She told me that you were sick with worry and that you had half the Liverpool police out looking for me. She said you would give the world to have me back.

"Granma White knew that all my life I wanted a dog, but you always said you didn't need another mouth to feed, dog or human. So she told me to go down to the animal shelter and pick out a nice, friendly dog, not too small, not too old. Then she told me to come back in half an hour, when you would have returned, and ask you if I could come home again and bring the dog with me. She said I should tell you it followed me home. Granma called it 'leveraging my advantage.'"

Hannah laughed. "Why, that old rascal."

"Speaking of dogs," Lilly chimed in. "When that incendiary fell on the house during the blitz, I left Granma White in the alley next to the chip shop while I went looking for Vera's dog. She begged me not to leave her. When I got back she was terrified, shaking like leaves in the wind." Lilly hesitated. A lump came to her throat. "There were many times I needed her, times when she comforted me. Yet the one time she needed me, I let her down. I feel so ashamed." Lilly broke into tears, jumped up from the table, and ran upstairs to her grandmother's room.

"I'll go," Peter said, as he went upstairs to comfort his daughter.

"More wine, anyone?" Steven asked.

"Your turn, Mam," said Eileen. "Tell us something we don't know about our Granma."

Hannah thought for a moment. "You all know yer grandmother didn't have a violent bone in her body, not like some members of this family." Everyone grinned. "Well, this happened before she went blind. There was a teacher in Saint Lawrence's school—a heartless old bastard who enjoyed smacking us kids around. One day he slapped me hard for something trivial, such that when I got home, the outline of his hand was still on my cheek. The next day, your grandmother came into the classroom and, without a word, slapped him back in front of all the kids. It was fierce enough that it knocked his dentures clean out of his mouth."

"Which hand?" Grace said.

"Have a guess," Hannah said.

◆

With the end of the war came a general election. Winston Churchill, riding high on his success as a war leader, believed it to be a foregone conclusion, particularly as he was running against Labour candidate Clement Atlee, whom he considered a weakling.

Churchill was making a pre-election speech on the radio, which Hannah half listened to while she knitted. Peter was reading the newspaper.

"Mr. Atlee is a very modest man. Indeed he has a lot to be modest about," Churchill said.

Hannah cracked a smile. "You have to hand it to old Winston—he certainly has a way with words."

Churchill was still seeing Communists under his bed. He was all empire and anti-Socialist, lauding the praises of pre-war conservatism. His distinctively prophetic voice continued. "Socialism is the philosophy of failure, the creed of ignorance, and the gospel of envy— Its inherent virtue is the equal sharing of misery."

Hannah stopped knitting. "Are you listening to this old windbag, Peter? The bastard assumes that Socialism causes misery, as opposed to misery forcing you to embrace Socialism. This man, who never knew a miserable day in his life, who was born into wealth and power, wants us to vote for him so his kind can keep their boots on our necks."

"He was a great war leader. We wouldn't have won without him," Peter said with a sigh.

"Maybe, but his time is over. He's a relic, a dinosaur. The service men and women coming home from this war, and us working-class civilians who have lived through it, demand that the old social system be thrown out like a bin-full of filthy rubbish."

Churchill continued. "Atlee's cradle-to-grave welfare state would require a Gestapo-esque body to implement."

Hannah jumped out of her chair. "Did you hear that?"

"Me and millions of other people," Peter replied.

"He compared the Labour Party to the Nazis, the people that we have been giving our lives to defeat for the last six years. I can just see the headlines in tomorrow's papers—'Churchill declares Atlee a Nazi!' He just lost any working-class folk who were thinkin' of voting for him because of his wartime leadership. The silly old bastard has just shot off his own balls!" Hannah did a jig in the front parlor.

Churchill lost the election in a landslide.

◆

The next day, Vera answered the knock on the door. "Mam, it's a nun from the convent," she yelled.

"Well, show her into the parlor, for heaven's sake, while I put the kettle on."

"It's Mother Superior," the nun said, sipping her tea like it was a treat. "She's very ill and has asked to see you."

"How old is she?" asked Hannah.

"No one knows for sure. It would be impertinent to inquire, but she must be at least seventy."

Hannah and the nun walked back to the convent together. Hannah had never been in the temporary convent they'd built four years earlier, after that terrible night back in 1941.

In her nun's cell, a bleak featureless room that smelt of camphor and oil of cloves, the mother superior lay on a wrought iron bed, with a thin mattress. A single small window, aided by a bedside lamp, dimly lit the place. It was clear to Hannah, as she held Sister Winifred's withered hand, that the mother superior was one step away from meeting her maker.

"I'm going to the Lord soon, Hannah. If he doesn't know what you did for my nuns during the Blitz, then he certainly will by the time I've finished talking to him." The old nun managed a weak smile. Hannah smiled too.

"I have one last favor to ask of you. I want my body clean before the Lord. I don't want my nuns to clean me. It wouldn't be seemly. Of course, I wouldn't want a man to touch me, so I'm hoping you, in your loving way, could do me the honor." Her voice petered out.

Hannah hesitated. "It's been many years since I prepared a soul for burial, but the honor would be mine."

◆

A week later, Sister Winifred was buried in a small corner of Landican Cemetery that was reserved for the nuns. Unlike the rest of the cemetery, it was unkempt and overgrown, which angered Hannah.

"This is a holy place but it looks like Boot Hill," she said, and promptly sent Eileen off to complain to the cemetery management. Hannah and Peter, together with Sister Mary, the new mother superior, walked around looking at the names of nuns on the gravestones—women who had devoted their lives to helping the sick, the poor, and the aged.

"There would be a good few more graves here if you and your husband hadn't risked your lives to dig us out of that cellar—mine included," Sister Mary said.

The funeral party made their way back to the bus as it began to rain. I'm making too many trips to this cemetery, thought Hannah. She shuddered to think who might be next. Father Flaherty had taken ill, and Mathew Baker had retired from the police due to bad health. Both would be terrible losses. But there was another potential loss on the horizon, so dreadful she dared not even think of it.

"Please God," she whispered. "No more."

God wasn't listening.

◆

Eileen lifted the black veil from over her face, patted her eyes with her handkerchief, and picked up a handful of dirt. She tossed it in the grave, onto Doris's coffin. The rest of the mourners followed suit until the coffin was covered. Hannah, in a near state of collapse, was being supported by Peter and Steven.

Although Doris had lived six years beyond George Hamm, everyone agreed she died when the *Thetis* went down. That day the sparkle in her eyes disappeared and never returned. In some ways she was the same old Doris—the epitome of calmness, as sweet as a fresh peach, a caring person who could be counted upon. The only person she didn't much care for anymore was herself. The Doris who was always so mindful of her appearance lost interest in fashion and rarely wanted to socialize. Worst of all, she barely ate, despite the protests of her family. Her face became tight, her body pathetically thin. Her sisters tried all they could to "snap her out of it," but it became clear that part of Doris was lost forever.

Eventually, tuberculosis, the scourge of humankind, came calling, and Doris had little fight in her body to turn it away. She spent some time in a sanatorium, but the disease came back. There was little anyone could do.

❖

It had taken the navy three months to locate the stricken *Thetis* off the coast of Anglesey. Not wanting to perform the odious task of bringing out the badly decomposed bodies, the navy brought coal miners from South Wales. They had experience in removing dead comrades from cave-ins.

The navy then refused to transport the bodies of shipyard workers back to Birkenhead. Instead, they buried them at Anglesey, many miles from their families, such that their graves would barely see a flower from one year to the next.

❖

The funeral group walked slowly back to the cars. Hannah stopped and turned back to look at the grave.

"Are we doing the right thing?" she asked her family. "Should we have buried her in Anglesey, next to her husband?"

Peter had had this discussion with Hannah a dozen times already. "Remember, Hannah, Anglesey is so far away she would hardly ever have flowers on her grave. Here in Landican Cemetery, she will always have flowers. You know how much Doris loved flowers."

Chapter Nineteen

═ 1949 ═

Distress

Four years after the death of Granma White and Doris, Hannah was still not herself. One of the few things that brought her pleasure was music. She bought a large gramophone—a piece of furniture really, with shiny veneered wood and two top drawers that slid apart. When it went on the fritz, Grace suggested that a girl she worked with had a boyfriend, Ricky Lambeth, an electrician at English Electric, who might be able to help. He installed two new vacuum tubes, and in no time Perry Como crooned again in Hannah's front parlor.

Hannah tried to pay Ricky, but he would only accept the cost of the tubes. Still, she managed to stuff a couple of pound notes into his pocket before Grace showed him to the door. What Hannah didn't see was that Grace stole a kiss from him.

"What a nice feller," Hannah said.

"Handsome too, don't you think?" Grace answered.

"Very handsome."

"And clever."

"Very clever. Where's he from?"

"He lives in Rock Ferry."

"No, I mean what country is he from?"

"He's English. Born and bred in Birkenhead."

"Grace, you know what I mean—he's black."

"He's not black, Mother. His skin is brown, because his parents are from Ceylon. His father jumped ship years ago and married a Ceylonese woman already living here."

"This feller's girlfriend yer work with—what color is she?"

"She's white."

"Stupid girl," Hannah said.

◈

The following week Hannah was shopping in the market when she was approached by Annie Beatty, known for poking her nose where it didn't belong.

"It's none of my business, Hannah, but I hope you know that the black feller your Grace is seein' got a girl from Woodchurch Road pregnant."

"You're right, it is none of your business, yer nosey auld sow," Hannah replied.

Grace knew the jig was up when she arrived home that night to be met by the sour stares of her parents, stewing at the kitchen table.

"You've got less sense than God gave a turnip," Hannah started out. "People are talking behind my back, behind your back. They think you're a tart."

"Mother, yer said yourself he was a nice feller, handsome too. All the girls fancy him. And you should see him dance."

"I expect he has a lovely singing voice as well," said Hannah.

Grace nodded. "He could be a professional."

Hannah buried her head in her hands. She gritted her teeth in a futile attempt to control her temper.

"Besides, I don't care what people think," continued Grace.

Hannah slammed her hands down on the table. "Damn it, Grace, everyone cares what people think!"

Peter spoke at last. "What about the girl from Woodchurch Road he got pregnant?"

"He told me it wasn't him," Grace said.

"But it could have been?" asked Hannah.

"Look, Grace, luv, think what you're doin'," her father said. "Yer a good-lookin' young woman with a pleasant personality and a fine catch for any young man. Why go lookin' for bother?"

◈

The more family and friends tried to pry Grace away from Ricky, the more she stuck to him. The unhappy situation came to a head at Vera's birthday party when the whole clan had gathered at Beckwith Street, in-laws included. Because of her meekness and her quiet devotion to Hannah, Vera was unwittingly marginalized by her siblings. Usually she sat in a corner and said little, like a servant, so it warmed Hannah's heart to see that everyone had shown up, bearing gifts and making a fuss over Vera. Hannah took the occasion to wear her new floral dress, claiming that she needed to replace most of her clothes, as they seemed to shrink with age. Peter, on the other hand, had hardly changed through the years. Eileen called him the Dorian Gray of the Birkenhead Docks. He wasn't sure what that meant, but he took it as a compliment.

The birthday bash moved along fine, with wine, beer, and food in abundance. Hannah had purchased a large marzipan birthday cake from the co-op and carefully sliced it up: small pieces for the grandkids—Eileen's girl and Lilly's two, and a small piece for Vera's dog—Kim, black lab number three.

As Hannah cut slices for the adults, Grace proudly announced that she and Ricky were to be married. The banns were already posted in Saint Anne's Church. The table was stunned to silence.

Hannah was the first to speak. "You willful, wicked girl!"

"You're disgracing our family," Eileen added.

Grace stiffened. "I love him, and I intend to marry him. The color of his skin or his family background doesn't matter to me, so why should they matter to you? This is 1949, not the middle ages."

"It matters to everyone else, right or wrong." Hannah took a deep breath. "This is not about him, this is about you. When you're out with him, everyone will stare at you, like you're a leper. No neighbors or friends will want to know yer. You'll be ostracized. Your love for him and his love for you, if indeed he has any, will be tested every single day. Yer don't have the strength to handle that, Grace—not for the rest of your married life. You might be happy with him now, but sooner rather than later, that happiness will disappear."

"Then I'll show you, won't I?" Grace replied.

Hannah's tone turned sharply from pleading to sour, as she addressed the whole room. "I forbid any of my family to attend this wedding!" Peter dropped his chin to his chest.

Grace reached across the table and put her hand on Lilly's. "I'll be honored, Lilly, if you will be my matron of honor."

Lilly, taken aback, breathed in heavily and let out a sigh. She glanced at her mother, then back at Grace. "Of course I will. You're my best friend, as well as my sister. I'll not abandon yer."

Grace turned next to Eileen. "I want nothing more to do with yer," Eileen said. She gathered up her husband and daughter, kissed Vera on the cheek, and left the house.

"So Vera, will you come to the wedding?" Grace asked.

"I'll do whatever our mam says," Vera mumbled.

Grace sneered. "Isn't it about time yer started thinking fer yourself?"

"Leave Vera alone!" Hannah jumped in.

"What about you, Steven?" Grace asked her brother.

Steven paused while he scratched his head. "I think you're making a huge mistake. This feller yer want to marry has probably taken abuse, because of his race, all his life. He was almost certainly taunted and bullied at school, so by now he's gotten used to it, unless it's twisted him up inside. But you're not used to it. In either event, as our mam says, you'll never be happy."

"Are yer coming to my wedding or not?" Grace folded her arms.

Steven shook his head. "I'll have to think about it."

"I know this much," Grace sputtered. "If Doris was alive, she'd come."

At this, Hannah flared up out of her chair, which caused everyone else to stand. She rounded the table to point a finger two inches from Grace's face. "No she wouldn't. She would tell yer exactly the same as we're tellin' yer!"

"Calm down, now," Peter said, placing himself between Hannah and Grace, putting his arm around Grace's shoulders.

"I've met this feller. I've had a drink with him in the Garrick Snug, and he seemed like a decent bloke to me. Still, I hope that you change your mind because your mother is right. You're choosing a life of strife. But if yer can't be deterred from marrying this feller, as yer father, I'll give yer away. That much I promise."

Hannah bit her upper lip. She glared at Grace with moisture-glazed eyes. "There's a big suitcase under my bed. Fill it with your

243

things, and get out of my house. If you marry this man, never come back!"

"You can stay with me," Lilly said.

"That might be best," Peter said. "At least for a couple of days, until tempers cool."

Grace turned to her mother. "I love you Mam, but you're a bigot. That's all this is about—bigotry."

As Grace left, Vera called after her, "Thanks for ruining my party."

❖

Hannah simmered all evening without saying a word to Peter. In bed that night, she broke her silence. "Do you think I'm a bigot?" she asked.

"There's some bigotry in all of us," Peter replied.

Hannah pouted. "So, you think I'm a bigot."

"Look, Hannah, I believe you have Grace's best interests at heart, but you're also concerned about what people will think of yer, having a daughter who marries a colored man. Only you can decide how much bigotry is involved."

Still angry, Hannah changed the subject. "Why didn't you support me in front of the family?" she demanded.

"Yer left me no choice." Peter sat up in bed. "Grace is not going to change her mind, even if the whole family disowns her. Couldn't you see that? And one other thing—Grace is my daughter, too, and this is my house as well as yours. You should have thought about that before you threw her out."

❖

Grace and Ricky were married at Saint Anne's, as planned. The congregation was small, to say the least—Ricky's parents, his sister, his best man, Grace's friend, Lilly, and Chris. Peter Corcoran gave away the bride. The couple went to live in Lilly's house until they could afford a place of their own.

Peter knew that the chasm that Grace had dug between him and Hannah would take time to close, but he had no doubt that close it would. Such was his faith in their bond. Still, the atmosphere at 57 Beckwith Street remained frosty as an igloo for weeks.

❖

It was a sad day in the Birkenhead Docklands. The entire parish turned out for the funeral of Father Flaherty. He had been Saint Lawrence's parish priest for more than fifty years and had performed his duties better than his Maker could ever have expected. Protégé Father Michael, in the eulogy, cited the dead priest's compassion, humility, and dedication to his parishioners.

The old priest had suffered with a terrible disease for almost two years. When the pain was upon him, which was most of his waking hours, his wrinkled old face contorted and his frail body trembled. Hannah would sit with him and feed him barley soup. She would mop his forehead and hold his head when he winced, praying to Saint Lawrence to ease his suffering. In his more lucid moments, when the pain killers kicked in, Hannah and Father Flaherty would reminisce about the good times, which often were not so good, but had grown such in their memories. Sometimes they would say the rosary together, and she would give him a little tipple of whiskey when it was over.

"Father, do you remember the night of the swaying congregation?" Hannah asked.

The priest chuckled. "Now, that's a Christmas Eve I'll never forget."

On Christmas Eve, every pub on Merseyside would be chock full of Christmas revelers, and when the pubs closed everyone would stagger to the churches to attend Midnight Mass. Even those sinners who never saw the inside of a church all year wouldn't miss Midnight Mass. And every intoxicated soul sucked a Victory V throat lozenge.

This traditional remedy for colds and sore throats had been around longer than anyone could remember. It worked simply by setting your mouth on fire. The lozenge consisted of sugar, linseed, chloroform, the devil's own gum, and cannabis. It was probably the last ingredient that made it so popular. The pungent smell from a Victory V would make the eyes water of anyone within ten feet. It was used by those who wished to mask the smell of drink. This usage became so common that if you were sucking a Victory V, it was assumed you had a skinful of ale.

On the Christmas Eve in question, Saint Lawrence's reeked of Victory Vs, because the congregation didn't want the Lord to think they had come to celebrate the Holy Sacrament as drunk as a publican's parrot. The church was packed to the rafters, and everyone present was pleasantly sozzled, including Father Flaherty. Even the alter boys stole a few swigs of wine before it was consecrated. "Oh Come All Ye Faithful" never sounded so feisty as when sung by three hundred tipsy souls. Father Flaherty gave one of his cracking sermons, full of hope for the future, peace on earth, and good fortune at the bookmaker's window. As he spoke, he swayed backward and forward in the pulpit and his words were a bit slurred, but then so were everyone else's.

Halfway through his sermon, the good father noticed that the entire congregation was swaying, too, not independently but to his rhythm. When he swayed forward, the congregation swayed forward; when he swayed backward, they did, too. It was an involuntary reaction, as though they were all on a boat together in a heavy swell. When the priest stopped swaying, the congregation also stopped. When he started up again, so did they. The phenomena continued throughout the Mass.

"It was truly bizarre," Hannah said. "Like robots wired together."

❖

When death finally ended the priest's agonies, Hannah realized that she had loved him like a member of the family. He had been a mainstay in her life, a consistent source of faith-based advice mixed with good old-fashioned common sense. He never seemed to judge people, just took them for what they were and left them better than before they knew him.

At the priest's viewing, Hannah held his vein-riddled hand, kissed his forehead, and slipped a small bottle of Irish whiskey into the pocket of his vestments, in the unlikely event that God turned out to be a teetotaler. She remembered how he would ask every time she went to confession, "How many poor souls have you punched this week, Hannah?"

"Not a one, but the week is not over yet, Father," she would answer, and they would both snicker.

Landican cemetery was jam-packed with cars spilling out onto the road. No bishop within a hundred miles could have garnered such a send-off. Over a thousand mourners came to say goodbye to the old priest, but none more distraught than Hannah. The man was a saint, she thought. I just don't understand why God allowed him to suffer so much at the end.

◆

A few days later, Hannah knelt in the confessional, a small wooden lattice window between her and Father Michael. She was having trouble getting her words out.

"What is it, Hannah? What's troubling you?" the priest asked. "Have you punched someone again?"

"No Father, it's not that. I'm upset because. . . . Well, I'm beginning to doubt my faith. I can't understand why so many people, so many good people, have to suffer."

Father Michael gave a nod of empathy. "It's God's way of testing us like he tested his son. I know the death of Father Flaherty was very difficult for you, but he is with the Lord now, so we should rejoice for him."

"It's not just the good father. It's Doris, it's George Hamm, it's Alf Richards, it's little Jimmy Kelly," Hannah said.

"Well, Jimmy Kelly died in a just war. He was one of God's warriors fighting evil. He knew that he had to go back in the army."

Hannah was confused. "What do you mean, he knew?"

"Well, we talked about it right here when he hid in the basement. I told him it was his duty to give himself up—that the Nazis were the devil's legions, and it was his Christian duty to fight them. He knew in his young heart it was the right thing to do. I'm sure that you must have been very proud of him."

Hannah's mouth dropped open. "You talked him into giving himself up? Good God, man, he was only seventeen years old! You sent him away so those Tory bastards could have him killed! What type of priest are you?"

"No, no Hannah," he said. "You don't understand."

But it was too late. Hannah's left fist smashed through the wooden grill into his face. She stormed out of the confessional, pushed past the startled parishioners, and strode down the aisle to the altar. She looked up at the familiar Jesus on the cross.

"Are yer happy now that I've punched a priest? The lovely lad—he was just a child. Explain to me why you let that happen. And Doris. She wouldn't hurt a fly. My sweet Doris. Why did she have to suffer?" Hannah was yelling now, her voice echoing through the church. "And what about Alf Richards? What did he ever do to you? Or George Hamm, for that matter? And tell me why you let the good father suffer for so long? The agonies of that wonderful man lasted for two years. Yours lasted for only two days. Explain that to me.

"So what's the plan? I'm entitled to know. How does this all fit together? I'm assuming yer have a plan, because if there's no plan, this whole existence is just a damn big waste of time!"

Hannah felt a hand on her shoulder. It was Father Michael, whose right eye had swelled to a dark gray.

"Hannah, please listen to me. God tests us in—"

"No more listening! You can keep your God and your religion. I've had my fill of them both."

Hannah swung around and marched out of Saint Lawrence's Church without looking back. She wandered in a daze, her emotions all haywire. It wasn't until two streets later that the pain of wood splinters in her left hand registered enough for her to pull them out. Every so often she stopped and put her hand over her mouth, then continued to walk. She felt as lost as her blind mother had done on that terrifying night of the blitz. Except for Hannah there was no wall for protection.

She passed Winnie O'Connor and Mary O' Neil, who greeted her. Hannah looked straight through them and continued walking. "Good God," Winnie said. "She looks like she's seen a ghost."

Hannah continued aimlessly until she reached Grange Road, full of Saturday shoppers. Passing Woolworths, she spotted Grace and Lilly on the other side of the road, sharing a joke. Grace had been married for six months, and Hannah had never spoken her name since.

Look at that Grace, Hannah thought, all smug and willful. Grace, the last child born, the one I lavished with the most time and love. She never had to live through the hard times. She never had to lift a finger to clean or to cook. Selfish, ungrateful girl. And what do I receive in return? She split my family, she affected my marriage, and she made me so mad at the world that I punched a priest.

The sisters stopped when they saw their mother crossing toward them. From the look on her face, it was clear she wasn't looking for reconciliation. Hannah strode straight up to Grace and slapped her hard on the side of her face. Grace screamed and staggered back against the glass window of W.H. Smith's book store.

"You split up my family, you vixen!"

Lilly yelled, "For God's sake mother, leave her!" Grace sat on the book store step and wept, while her mother screamed at her.

Passersby, repulsed by the scene, moved quickly away as Hannah continued her tirade. "I gave yer everything you ever needed, but it wasn't enough. You had to split my family. You wouldn't listen to anyone. I punched a priest because of you!"

She stopped abruptly, glowered at Lilly, and left as sharply as she had come. She stopped about twenty yards away and glared. Grace still crouched on the ground. Lilly had never seen such a look on her mother's face. The anger in her eyes was now gone, replaced by despair, as if she suddenly realized what she had done but didn't believe it. Her lips quivered but couldn't find the words. She closed her eyes, bowed her head, and walked slowly away. Lilly wanted to run after her, but Grace needed her more.

❖

Mathew Baker hammered on Hannah's front door. Vera answered, and he could see from the redness of her eyes that her waterworks had been turned on for a long spell.

"She's not here," Vera said. "She came home about two o'clock for a cuppa but then left on her old bicycle. She's not been seen since. They're out looking for her." Vera dabbed her eyes.

Peter came home then. He'd been all through the park, without a sign of Hannah, and anxiety creased his forehead. Soon Eileen showed up, having searched around the market, but she, too, had no luck finding her mother. Mathew, Peter and Eileen sat at the kitchen table while Peter poured a tot of whisky all around.

"What the hell happened?" Mathew asked. "She could be arrested for each of those assaults today."

Peter drank his whiskey down in a single gulp. "She's been walking on the rim of a volcano for the last few days, and I guess she finally fell in. She's not been stable since the old priest died, and now she has it in her head that she was responsible for Doris's death."

"Huh?" Mathew's face narrowed in confusion. "Doris has been dead four years."

Peter explained that six months before Doris died, Hannah had washed the body of Sister Winifred—against her better judgment—who also died of TB. Hannah believed she carried the disease back to Doris.

"That's ridiculous," Baker said.

"It's possible but not likely," said Peter. "Doris, in her depressed state, was susceptible to disease. She had to catch TB somewhere, and Hannah did spend some time with the old nun before she died. Mind you, the disease is still active in these parts, so Doris could have caught it anywhere."

"Where did she come up with this idea?" Mathew asked.

"She picked up a medical book in the library. Mathew, she's walkin' on broken glass. We have to find her."

The two men considered the possibilities of her whereabouts that hadn't already been explored. "You take Bidston Hill," Mathew said. "I'll take Egremont Promenade."

"Oh no," Peter said. "I'll take Egremont—"

Mathew interrupted. "I insist." Both men knew that although the promenade was a favorite place to watch ships or for couples out for a moonlight stroll, it was also a place for those who wished to end their lives. The sea wall was high, with no access to the water except by boat. Once you climbed over the railings and stepped off the wall, there was no turning back.

◆

Hannah sat on a wooden bench at Egremont Promenade, just feet from the railings, staring across the Mersey at the Liverpool skyline. She listened to the tide rhythmically buffet the sea wall. The squawk of the seagulls and the rich smell of the ocean reminded her of joyful days—honeymoons and sweet summer scenes, days out at the seaside, building sand castles with the kids, and wading in the cold sea up to her knees. Two benches down, an old tramp tried to sleep, while a young couple locked arm in arm strolled past, glancing at Hannah. In the background, a Cunard freighter glided in with the dusk on the evening tide. The lights along the promenade sprang on, and across the river, lights on the Liverpool office buildings twinkled to life, like fairy lights on a Christmas tree.

Hannah slowly regained her equilibrium. She floated above herself to look down on the mangy cur she now believed she was. She stared at the railings, where two weeks earlier, a young woman jilted by her fiancé had climbed over to take the fatal plunge.

I wonder how difficult that decision was for her, Hannah thought. The agony that young woman felt must have been insufferable, like the shame and guilt I feel now. I killed Doris and now I've lost Grace. I punched a priest. What a miserable lump of human garbage I am. How can I look anyone in the eyes again?

Hannah pictured herself climbing those railings. Much easier than going over the wall at the shipyard. Just one step and the guilt would be gone for ever.

She turned when a car pulled up behind her bench. Mathew Baker got out and sat down beside her. "Mind if I join you?"

"Mathew, have you come to arrest me?"

"I'm retired. I can't arrest anyone anymore. You've had a bad day, old girl."

Hannah put her hand on her forehead. "I'm so ashamed." Mathew put a reassuring arm around her shoulders; she rested her head on his chest.

"All your life, Hannah, you've carried a heavy load. Today you stumbled. Your judgment was warped by grief. People will understand."

"No they won't. They'll think of me as a dangerous lunatic. I've ruined my reputation. All that I've achieved, now bursts like soap bubbles." She paused. "Did you know I caused the death of my sweet Doris?"

"Peter told me. What a harebrained notion. Have yer been thinkin' about climbing over those railings?"

Hannah sighed. "I've not ruled it out."

"If you jump in that river, I'll tell you this for nowt—I'm not goin' in after yer. I never did learn to swim."

"Me neither." They both managed a weak smile. For several minutes they listened to the tide, without a word spoken, her head still on his chest. She always felt safe when Mathew Baker was around. He was her Lord Protector, her Archangel Gabriel. She could feel his heartbeat.

"Mathew, you never did marry."

"I never found the time."

"And I believed it was because you couldn't have me, and no other woman measured up."

"I thought that was fairly obvious," Mathew said with a grin. "C'mon Hannah, I'll tie yer old bike to my car boot and take yer home. In the morning it won't seem so bad."

The last seagull squawked his last squawk and flew off to wherever seagulls go at night.

◆

Mathew Baker dropped Hannah off at her house, where she ran into Peter's arms. The poor man was frantic with worry. Mathew looked at his watch. Seven o'clock. I don't have much time to do any fixin', he thought. He drove quickly to the offices of the *Birkenhead News* and strode into the office of editor Bernie Bramburg.

"Bernie, my friend, when do the presses roll?" Mathew asked.

"Nine o'clock." Bernie, a flabby, ambitious character, leaned back in his leather chair, hands behind his head, brimming with smugness. He took a puff of his cigarette and blew smoke rings. "I've been expecting you, Baker."

"I've brought yer a terrific story for tomorrow's headlines. Yer gonna love it," Mathew said, and plopped himself down on a wooden chair.

"I already have a terrific story. Hannah the Hotspur, champion of the poor and downtrodden, heroine of the docklands, brutally attacks priest in a confessional and savagely slaps her daughter in Grange Road. Front page stuff." Bernie smirked. "I love it."

"Hearsay," Mathew said.

"There are witnesses. You're not chief constable any longer, Baker, so you're not gonna get that old witch out of *this* jam. You won't influence this newspaper ever again. That's what I hate about you—always trying to manipulate people, doin' deals, callin' the odds like some slimy racetrack tout, digging up the dirt on people to use for yer own ends. Get yer arse out of my office."

"Fine, I'll take my news to the *Liverpool Echo*," Mathew said with nonchalance. "Do you want to know what it is before I leave?"

"Impress me then, you old fake."

"Do you remember when Tim Philcox was murdered right after the riots? What am I thinkin'? Of course you do. You and he were reporters together, and best mates, I seem to recall. Well, new evidence has come to light. The new chief constable is an ambitious feller and solving a seventeen-year-old murder would be a big feather in his cap."

Bernie shifted in his chair. "Well, you couldn't solve it. Yer didn't solve much."

"Oh I know who did it, all right—the only person with a real motive."

"And who would that be, pray tell?"

"Johnny Dermot."

"Hah! Dermot was killed in a bar fight almost twenty years ago. He was a drunken bum."

"I know that, but he was also a violent bum. He slashed the throat of Philcox and dumped him in the river because someone paid him to."

"And who would that be?"

"You! According to your ex-wife, Dolores, you paid Johnny Dermot to kill Philcox because she and Philcox were having an affair. You told Johnny to put that docker's hook in his neck, to make it look like dockers killed him because of his slanderous reports during the riots. The only thing that docker's hook told us was that dockers didn't do it. No docker's that stupid to leave a calling card." Bernie rose to his feet. "Sit down, I'm not finished." Mathew relished the moment, watching Bernie cringe. The two men glared at each other in stark hatred.

"All right, let me hear the rest of your bullshit story," Bernie said, as he sat down.

Baker continued. "Actually, that docker's hook belonged to yer old man, who once worked on the docks. That's what Dolores told me when she came to see me, right after you dumped her for Shirley Higgins. My God, was she ever choked up with anger. She told me yer came home drunk the night of the murder. You beat her up and admitted that you had her boyfriend killed."

"Yer full of crap, Baker," Bernie said, swiveling back and fro in his chair.

Mathew continued. "She claims that yer threatened to kill her, too, if she ever ratted on yer. I have a signed statement, which I keep in my safe at home. Dolores has since emigrated to Australia, but the statement's still here. What's up Bernie? You've gone all pale."

"So why didn't you arrest me if yer had the proof?"

"At the time, we didn't have enough proof. It was your word against the word of a woman scorned, and Dermot was killed in that brawl just a week after. But guess what? Dolores is back from Australia. I had a drink with her the other day, and she wants to know why you weren't prosecuted. There's enough evidence to reopen the case. Even if you're not convicted, the headlines in the *Liverpool Echo* will read '*Birkenhead News* editor under suspicion for murder.' Top that, Bernie, if you can."

Bernie stood up again. Anger creased his face. Mathew clucked. "Nothing about Hannah in the newspaper. Right? I said right!"

"Right," Bernie hissed through his teeth.

"Good. From now on, do as yer told, little man, and keep yer gob shut."

One down, two more to go, Mathew thought.

❖

The first thing to greet Mathew Baker when he walked into the Birkenhead registrar's office the next morning was the bright smile of Ruth, the receptionist. "Good Morning, Chief Constable. How's retirement? What do you do with all that spare time? We miss you in here."

"Mornin' Ruth. You look as gorgeous as ever. I spend my days standin' at the corner of the street, shakin' my fist at passing motorists. Is he in?" Ruth nodded and pointed back toward the registrar's office.

"What you're asking me to do could cause me to lose my job," said

Registrar Dennis Allsop. "Plus, it's illegal. I can't believe an ex-chief constable is asking me to break the law!"

"Don't get yer undies in a tangle, Dennis. All I'm asking is fer you to make one copy for one day. After that you can destroy it."

"Sorry Mathew, too risky."

"All right, if you won't do that for me, do this—look me in the eye, pretend I'm your wife, and tell me you're not bumpin' young Ruthie out there."

Dennis Allsop gulped.

"One copy, one day," said Mathew Baker as he turned and left. "I'm off to see a doctor."

◆

Peter finally persuaded Hannah to see Dr. Morgan in order to get something to calm her nerves. He insisted he accompany her. As they were leaving the doctor's office, Peter asked the doctor how difficult it was to pass tuberculosis on to someone. Hannah scowled at Peter. She didn't want to discuss that problem with anyone. The doctor explained that you usually had to be around that person for a long period of time.

"Why do you ask?" the doctor said.

"Could Hannah have carried the disease back to our home after being with Sister Winifred for an hour?"

"I told you I don't want to talk about it," Hannah said.

"It's very unlikely," replied the doctor. He paused. "If you mean the mother superior who died about four years ago, I seem to remember treating her for pneumonia, not tuberculosis."

"The *Birkenhead News* said she died of TB," Hannah said.

"Well, we all know how reliable that particular source of information is," the doctor replied, raising his eyebrows. Peter nodded in agreement.

"The best way to be sure is to go to the registrar and look at the death certificate," the doctor said, giving Peter a sly wink. Doctor Morgan pulled Peter aside and whispered, "Tell Baker he and I are square, okay?" Peter nodded. As they walked away, Hannah asked Peter what the doctor whispered to him. Peter told her that the doctor wanted him to be sure that she took the tablets he gave her, not being convinced that she would.

❖

Hannah asked Ruth, the receptionist, for a copy of Sister Winifred's death certificate.

"Sorry, madam, we don't do copies unless you are a relative. You can write to Somerset House in London, explaining why you need it. They will likely send you one, but there will be a fee."

"Can you just let us look at it then?" Peter asked.

"I'll ask the registrar. Back in a jiffy."

Ruth returned with the nun's death certificate and laid it out in front of Hannah. *Cause of Death: Pneumonia.* There it was in black and white.

Peter put his arm around his wife. "Feel better now?" Hannah managed a smile.

"Well it's too late for me to go to work," Peter said, "so why don't I treat you to an ice cream sundae at Olivetti's? Then we'll go to the matinee at the Savoy. It's Fred Astaire and Ginger Rogers."

Hannah and Peter trundled away. Dennis Allsop took the certificate from Ruth and tore it in little pieces. "Not a word to anyone," he said.

❖

Father Michael looked out from the pulpit at a packed congregation for Sunday High Mass. They were standing ten deep at the sides and the back of the church, hoping to hear the priest address the issue that people had been talking about all week. Father Michael didn't disappoint.

"I have some explaining to do," he said. With that, the priest described how Hannah had come to him bewildered and looking for spiritual guidance. The suffering of Father Flaherty, the deaths of her daughter, her mother, her son-in-law, and her adopted son had caused her to question her belief in her religion.

"I know many of you here have suffered similar losses because of the terrible war and have struggled with the same doubts, so you can understand her frame of mind." The priest took a deep breath. "But I was wrapped in my own agenda, so I failed to see the torment in her soul. Instead, I threw oil on the fire, and Hannah reacted by striking out at the source of her distress.

"The fault was mine, not Hannah's. She taught me a lesson that I sorely needed, so judge me, not her. I hope she forgives me. I pray she comes back to the church."

◆

But Hannah didn't come back. She apologized to Father Michael, of course. He accepted her apology with a new-found piety, of which some of his parishioners were skeptical. On the other hand, they forgave Hannah simply because she was Hannah, the town heroine, because of all she'd done for the town over the years. She still could not, however, rationalize the deaths and suffering of so many people close to her. Instead, the energies she had once expended on her religion, she now directed to supporting the Labour Party.

◆

Hannah knocked on Lilly's front door on Claughton Road.

"Mam," said Lilly, surprised. "Come on in."

"How are you?" Hannah asked in a sheepish voice.

Lilly hugged her mother. "All the better for seeing you."

"I've come to see Grace," Hannah said softly. Grace appeared from the front room. Mother and daughter stared at each other for several seconds in the vestibule, the tension thick as tar.

"Well?" Grace said finally, arms folded.

"I don't have enough words to tell you how sorry I am," Hannah said. "I'm here to ask you to forgive me, although I would never blame yer if yer couldn't." Tears welled in her eyes.

Grace bowed her head. "I know yer suffered under a lot of stress and grief. Of course I forgive yer—it's all in the past and forgotten." There were several more moments of silence before Grace put her arms around her mother. "Do you remember when I was a kid and I would jump on your lap? Do you remember what I would say to you?"

"Yes, of course I do. You would say, 'Tell me again why I love you.'"

"Well," Grace said, "tell me again why I love you."

"You love me because no one loves you more than I do." Hannah hugged Grace so hard she begged for air.

Chapter Twenty

≡ 1959 ≡

The Snug Revisited

Hannah had not set foot in Saint Lawrence's Church for ten years—not since she punched Father Michael. She did attend christenings and marriages in other local churches, plus the occasional funeral. Then one day, on her way to the shops, she stopped at the gate of Saint Lawrence's for no reason she knew, other than her corns were acting up. She peered into the front lawn, at the statue of the Blessed Virgin, at the grass that needed cutting, at the old moldy gravestones. Nothing's changed, she thought.

As Hannah passed through the gates and approached the church's big wooden doors, something stirred inside her—a memory of Father Flaherty's winning smile and the warm feeling of belonging. She took the large black metal ring in her hand, twisted it, and pushed one side of the doors open. Like walking on ice, she stepped inside.

Once through the entry she halted. She took a deep breath to savor the familiar smells of sweet incense and candle wax that forever linger in God's house. To her left hung the poor box, near the board displaying the notices of marriage banns. She fumbled in her purse, then dropped some coppers into the box, thought a moment, then dropped in some silver.

To her right was the baptismal font, where memories poured over her like holy water on a baby's head: first Eileen, then Doris, then Vera, Lillian, Steven, and Grace—tiny babies dressed in white—beautiful babies with rosy cheeks, the fruit of her womb. My Doris, poor Doris, she thought.

Hannah dropped a shilling in the candle box and placed the lit candle on a side altar. She moved slowly past the rows of pews she had cleaned so often, so long ago. A few parishioners knelt in prayer. She knelt in the fist pew and focused on the Savior up on the cross.

"Lord, the last time I was here I may have said a few words to yer that came out more harsh than was meant—words I regret. You reckoned I was tougher than I am, although you've seen me weep often enough. Still, yer tested me and I failed. I've wandered in the wilderness, confused, without my religion to shore me up, for too many years. I'm back in yer flock if you'll have me."

Hannah didn't realize she was whispering loud enough to be heard. A young priest appeared and stood a few feet away from her until she glanced up at him.

"Are you all right?" he asked in a pleasant Irish cadence.

She weighed him up. No more than twenty-five, she thought, so young, so handsome, he might have been little Jimmy Kelly, the lovely lad.

He bent over and quietly said, "Is there something weighing heavy on your soul? I'm Father John. Would you like me to hear your confession?"

"Father, the last priest who heard my confession received a black eye for his trouble, to my everlasting shame."

"Why, you must be Hannah!" he declared. "I've heard so much about you. Father Michael, now a bishop no less, once told me that the black eye was a sort of epiphany for him. You made him realize that he held a false set of values, too concerned about the material, not enough about the spiritual."

Well, at least something good came of that particular incident, Hannah thought.

"You lectured King George V, I heard. Is that true?"

"It is, to be sure. He taught me something. Do you want to hear it?"

"Of course."

"He told me if he had to live like us he would be a revolutionary. It made me realize that we're a product of our hereditary and our environment, neither of which we have any control over. We don't choose our parents or whatever situation we're born into. Our values are instilled in us by others, so the only free will that truly exists is that which is dictated by the soul." Hannah paused. "For example, if I was born into the same circumstances as Winston Churchill, I shudder to say, I would behave like Winston Churchill."

She got up from her knees and sat on the wooden bench. I don't remember these benches being so hard, she thought. The young priest sat next to her.

"You see Father, to make a long story medium, the only things that can change us are traumas—events that make us reassess our basic foundations. They twist us around and head us off down a different road."

"You mean like getting punched in the confessional?" Father John asked.

Hannah grinned. "I wonder how many of my punches have changed lives for the better. You should have seen the looks of utter shock on their faces. Maybe it was the trauma they all needed."

"What was your trauma, Hannah?"

"My life has been one continuous, boiling trauma. I've leapt from hurricanes to volcanoes to cyclones. From World War I, to the Spanish flu, to the general strike, to the Great Depression, to the food riots, to the Blitz. I've survived the death of loved ones and beatings by the police. But it was the trauma of watching Father Flaherty suffer and the death of my dear daughter Doris that drove me away from my religion."

"And what's brought you back?"

Hannah shrugged. "Truly, I don't know. Maybe the saints and angels are bored and want to see the left hook in action again. I'll let yer know when I find out."

The priest helped Hannah steady herself on her feet. "Before you go, you should know that you are the reason that all the confessional grills in every Catholic church in this country have been changed from wood to metal."

They both couldn't help but laugh. Hannah walked slowly back down the aisle.

"One other thing," the priest called after her.

She turned. "What is it?"

"God welcomes you home."

◆

After a hard day's toil on the Cathcart Street docks, loading cartons of leather shoes into the hold of the steam ship *Patrocolus*, bound for Bremerhaven, Steven spent the evening cycling around Oxton and Upton, pushing Labour Party pamphlets into middle-class letter boxes. It could have been considered an exercise in futility, as both of these wards of Birkenhead were predominately conservative, but as a general election and local elections were on the horizon, Steven felt that every voter should hear the Labour Party message.

This was one aspect of Steven's personality that delighted Hannah. For sure, he had inherited his father's laissez-faire attitude to many things. But he was pure Hannah when it came to feeling the injustice and oppression that the working class of Britain still had to endure. The dream of a welfare state was taking much longer to become a reality than Hannah had hoped.

"If you feel so strongly about it, why don't you run for town councilor?" Hannah asked her son.

Steven looked up at the ceiling and grinned. "Maybe I will. Will you help me, Mam?"

"Try stoppin' me." Hannah said.

Mother and son outlined a plan. Unfortunately, all of the Labour party candidates had already been selected by that time, so Steven would have to run in an uncontested conservative ward, which meant that he would have virtually no chance of winning. Still, Hannah thought it would be a terrific learning experience for Steven, plus it would get his name known for when the next election rolled along. They could expect no funding from the Labour Party, whose resources were best expended on battles that could be won. Hannah happily ordered a new checkbook.

Steven chose to run in the ward of Oxton, against the incumbent, Ernest Frobisher. Not only was he the head of the Conservative Party in Birkenhead, he was the grandson of Robin Frobisher, Hannah's old nemesis.

Hannah allowed herself a hearty chuckle. "It'll really frost old Frobisher's knickers when he learns who is pitted against his grandson. Let's give that auld devil and his spawn a run for their money!"

Hannah enlisted the family, whether they liked it or not, to knock on doors, hand out pamphlets, plant placards in people's gardens, and accost strangers in the street. They used Hannah's reputation when they could, as time had faded the incident in the confessional. Yet her exploits as a champion of the working class, who literally pulled no punches, had been embellished and magnified with each telling. Eileen designed a poster that read:

YOUR PARENTS MARCHED WITH HANNAH THE HOTSPUR DURING THE GREAT DEPRESSION. NOW VOTE FOR HER SON TO FINISH THE JOB.

It did Peter's heart no end of good to see his family engrossed in the election drive and how it brought Hannah and Steven tight together. Hannah wrote speeches for Steven, listening while he practiced. She shot awkward questions and coaxed the right answers out of him, sometimes with a motherly smack on the back of his head.

Hannah enjoyed knocking on doors, handing the householders a pamphlet and urging them to vote for the Labour candidate, which often sparked the type of political argument that she enjoyed. Hannah was about to stuff another pamphlet into another expensive letter box, when she stopped and thought, hmm, I recognize this house. And I recognize that wall, where I once stood and urged the crowd not to throw stones through the windows. What a day that was!

She knocked on the door. Ernest Frobisher, the Tory candidate, opened it to the sight of Hannah the Hotspur, mother of his opponent, grinning from ear to ear.

"You're not going to win, you know, so I don't know why you're wasting your time and money," said Frobisher, with a haughtiness that revealed his family background.

"Is your grandfather at home, sonny boy?" Hannah asked.

"He is."

"Tell him his old friend Hannah Corcoran is here. Tell him to come to the door, and if he lets me punch him once in his gob with my left hook, then I'll withdraw my son from this race."

"Good Lord. My grandfather is ninety years old. He's in a wheelchair!"

"That's all right," Hannah said. "I'll kneel down!"

◆

Come the day of the election, Hannah was astir early and peered out the window at a foreboding September sky. "Looks like rain," she said. Massive gray clouds had dragged an immense baggage of water across the Atlantic and dumped it without mercy on the west coast of England. By 8:00 a.m. it was teeming up a storm. Hannah looked out the window again. "It's a deluge," Hannah said with a wide smirk. At noon, angry thunderheads bellowed; sheets of water blew down the street. The rain abated somewhat in the afternoon but then started up again by early evening.

Eileen and hubby Bobby Flynn picked up Hannah and Peter in their little Morris Minor to take them to the town hall to await the election results. Vera was squished in the middle, sniffling away.

"What's the latest?" Hannah asked.

"Well, everywhere is flooded." Eileen said. "Cars are stranded in the Mersey Tunnel, which has closed down. Many roads are closed, too. The trains are still running, though they're all running late."

Hannah was ecstatic. "It's a walk in the park," she said to Steven when they arrived at the town hall. "It's a breeze, a foregone conclusion. It's tinned peaches with clotted cream. It's Marmite on toast. It's a roasted leg of lamb with mint sauce and big dollops of mashed potatoes covered with melted butter. Butter, mind you—not margarine."

"Crazy old lady," Steven said. "The rain might help us a bit, but we're still twenty-to-one outsiders."

"Don't you get it?" Hannah replied. "No one is going to show up for Frobisher. The middle class doesn't like getting wet. The working class doesn't care one way or the other. They're used to it. The working class gets up at 6:00 a.m., then walks to work and votes on the way. Or they cycle to work, but either way, they get wet. The middle class goes by car to get to work by 9:00 a.m. They'll get stuck in their cars coming home, and then it's too late to vote. Or if they do get home on time, they're not gonna go out again in this storm to vote in a one-sided election. Get it now?"

Steven won by twenty-three votes.

Hannah's clan hooted and hollered inside the town hall. To Hannah, the rain was divine intervention. Now she realized why she had gone back to her religion.

"You're not suggesting that because you went back to the church a month ago, God provided the rain?" Steven asked his mother.

"You have a better explanation?"

"You really are a crazy old lady," he murmured, putting his arm through hers. Hannah smacked him playfully on the back of the head.

"Hey, yer can't hit me—I'm a councilor."

"Well, Councilor Corcoran, don't forget what yer promised your mother."

"I remember. A statue of Alf Richards in Hamilton Square. It's a done deal."

Steven and his mother walked arm in arm out of the town hall to discover the family, like a bunch of drunken Gene Kellys, jumping and singing in a large puddle at the bottom of the steps. Hannah spotted Ernest Frobisher pushing his grandfather in a wheelchair.

"I'll just go to thank them for a good clean contest," she said.

"It's customary for the losing party to first congratulate the winners," Steven said.

"Then we'll take the high road," she replied.

Hannah raised her eyebrows and gave Ernest Frobisher a weak smile. "I'd just like to thank you. It was a fair and clean contest—"

Robin Frobisher cut her off. "Don't get too smug, Corcoran," he wheezed. "Your victory won't last. We'll never let your kind run this country. We'll put you back in your place soon enough, and you'll thank us for it."

Hannah noticed how feeble he looked. What a blow this defeat must be to him, she thought, knowing he would die powerless in a socialistic country. She felt like saying, "Listen to me, you old Nazi bastard. Us 'Commies' are in charge now, so you better get on home and pack, because tomorrow you and your grandson here are off to the gulag." But she didn't. In the end, she was victorious; there was no point in being cruel.

◆

A month later, Grace stooped in the telephone box at the end of Farnham Drive, fumbling for coins in her purse. The pain came again, causing her to let out a silent scream and her body to stiffen. She ran her finger down the telephone book looking for a taxi company close by. She dialed the number and silently prayed, "Not now, God, not now." But it was too late for prayers.

Her water broke and ran down her legs. That was the moment, she realized later, when the last vestiges of her love for Ricky Lambeth disappeared. My mother was right, she thought.

Ricky was making good money at the new Vauxhall plant in Eastham, enough for them to buy a semi-detached house in middle-class Oxton. But a mixed-race couple could find no more welcome in suburbia than they could down by the docks.

They rarely went out in public together, because people stared or averted their eyes like they do when they see a deformed person. Grace often felt like saying, "Who the hell do you think you're staring at?" But she never did. She smoldered inside and found no outlet. As their bickering increased, Ricky spent more time in pubs than at home. Even the birth of two beautiful baby girls failed to slow the deterioration of their relationship.

So there she was, in a telephone booth about to give birth. Her two children were alone in the house, while Ricky boozed it up in the Garrick Snug with Chris McKenna, Lilly's husband. They had lived on Farnham Drive for over a year, yet there was no one she could ask to mind her children, even in her current predicament.

The taxi arrived. "Where to?" asked the scruffy looking driver. Grace felt a contraction as she hoisted herself into the taxi, which stunk of cheap whiskey.

"Where to?" he asked again in an agitated tone.

"I'm having a baby. I'm in labor."

"The hospital?" he asked.

If I go to the hospital, she thought, who will look after my children?

"Fifty-seven Beckwith Street," Grace said. "Down by the docks."

❖

Vera answered the knock on the door.

"There's a woman in my taxi, says she's in labor. She hasn't paid me," the driver said.

Hannah and Peter came running. Vera and Peter helped Grace inside, while Hannah gave the driver a pound note.

"I don't want anyone having any damn babies in my cab, missus. I need other fares tonight. Besides, they make a right mess on the back seat."

Hannah held out her hand. "Where's me change?"

"What about a tip?" the driver asked.

"Here's a tip for you, Sir Galahad. Take a bath now and then."

As her family bundled Grace upstairs to the spare bedroom, Hannah asked, "Who's looking after your children?" Grace shook her head.

"Where's Ricky?" Hannah asked. "Wait. No need."

Hannah sent Vera running to fetch Mrs. Hesketh, the midwife on Watson Street. She told Peter to prepare for a birth, if he could remember how, while she set off on a quest.

A soft drizzle refreshed her face as Hannah retraced her steps of forty-three years previous, except this time she bypassed the Conway Arms. When she reached the Garrick Snug, she hesitated before she entered. Not a brick had changed in all that time—not a lick of paint applied, not a window cleaned.

She wondered who was in there. She closed her eyes.

Who is that standing at the bar? My God, it's John Luxton, as handsome as ever! And there is that nasty Welsh butcher in his bloody apron, standing next to the couple of young louts from the docks. Haughty Roger Dalglish is trying to impress that pompous Spaniard, Richardo. There's the violent football player talking sports with Henry Hancock, Hard as the Hogs of Hell. In the opposite corner the German pilot is squished between the agent provocateur and the burly military policeman. And there in the middle of it all sit Father Michael and Admiral Wade, looking mighty uncomfortable.

"Are yer goin' in?" Hannah said to herself. "Or are yer gonna stand out here all night?"

Hannah went in, as brazen as you like. As before, she was assaulted by thick acrid cigarette smoke. The place was full of dockers and ship-yard workers, with faces chiseled by years of toil. And again, all eyes turned to Hannah.

"Holy God," the barman said. "It's Hannah the Hotspur. No women allowed in—"

"Gob shut!" Hannah demanded.

Chris McKenna and Ricky Lambeth were immediately filled with trepidation; both wondered the same thing—which one of us has she come for?

Hannah moved slowly through the men, and stopped at Chris first. She could hear his breathing. He met her gaze.

"Who's looking after your kids while Lilly's working at the Savoy Cinema?"

Shakily Chris answered. "They're old enough to look after themselves. Besides, there's always Ginnie Williams next door if there's a problem."

Hannah moved on until she reached Ricky. Anticipating a blow, Ricky shuffled backwards. Hannah's left fist was already behind her back—a sixty-seven-year-old fist. Retirement had aged it—thick, blue veins crisscrossed its back. Wrinkled, thin skin stretched over bony knuckles. The arm muscles that powered it were blanketed by flab and had lifted nothing heavier than a wee grandchild in years. My punching days are over, she thought, and I'm not going to mar my record with a miss in front of all these men, right here in the place it all started. She lowered her hand to her side.

"I'm not gonna punch yer," Hannah said, contempt in her voice. "Yer wife is in my house, giving birth as we speak. Yer two young kiddies are at home with no one looking after them. Get your sorry arse out of this pub, and get home right now before I change my mind and hammer yer stupid. You too, McKenna."

Ricky and Chris moved sheepishly through the crowd of men without looking back. Among the Snug's patrons, it was debatable which was the more humiliating—to be decked by Hannah or to be thrown out of a pub by her.

As Hannah followed her son-in-laws out, she spotted Pat O'Malley leaning against a wall, rolling a cigarette.

"Didn't notice yer, Pat," Hannah said. "How long have you been standing there?"

Pat gave Hannah a toothless grin. "Oh, since about 1916."

Chapter Twenty-One

≡ 1972 ≡

Passing of the Hook

With the aid of Vera, Hannah pushed herself up from the front pew of Saint Lawrence's Church. With one arthritic hand on Vera's arm, and the other on a plain walking stick, she waddled down the aisle toward the church door. She never made it. Her left leg collapsed first, and then the right. Vera grappled in vain to hold her up. Hannah's weight was too much and her daughter too frail.

❖

Hannah hated hospitals. She had no problem recommending them to others, but she would never go near one herself. She couldn't bear the thought of handing over control of her body to strangers. Nevertheless, she found herself in a bed of the geriatric ward in Saint Catherine's Hospital. She stared up at a large white clock on the wall opposite and watched the red hand sweep away the seconds left in her life.

Between the top of the clock and the ceiling was affixed a small wooden crucifix, with Himself nailed in his familiar agonizing pose, knees bent, head bowed to one side. The obvious symbolism of a Christ in pain looking down on one of his children, joined in suffering, was lost on Hannah. To her, the statue was just an annoyance, because it reminded her that soon she would have to explain to her Maker why she had clobbered the priest. She prayed to Saint Anthony to smooth the way.

As one might expect, Hannah was not a model patient. Some of the hospital staff had never heard of Hannah or her infamous left hook, so Eileen felt it necessary to warn the nurses not to get too close. She suggested that if they needed to give her mother a pill, it would be prudent to stand at the end of the bed and throw the pill at her, in the hope that she would catch it in her mouth.

Of course, Hannah was far too weak to present a threat to anyone anymore. The hook had not made an appearance in over two decades, not since she clobbered the priest. That incident, together with all the other appearances of the famous left hook, passed into local folklore, to be recounted at family get-togethers. The grandchildren would stare at their cuddly old grandmother, wondering if everyone was talking about the same person.

"Look," Eileen said, handing her mother a copy of the *Birkenhead News*, opened at page three, "you're in the paper."

Hannah fumbled for her glasses and read aloud:

SOCIAL ACTIVIST HOSPITALIZED

Hannah Corcoran, of Beckwith Street, known as one of the leaders of the unemployed during the protest marches of the Great Depression, collapsed in Saint Lawrence's Church last Tuesday and is undergoing tests in Saint Catherine's Hospital. Mrs. Corcoran, 80, also known as "Hannah the Hotspur," was the first woman laborer to work at the Birkenhead Shipyard during WWI.

Hannah chuckled. "Fame at last. If they come looking for an obituary, send them to Lilly's boy. He knows the whole story."

As she stewed in her hospital bed, Hannah told every visitor, doctor, and nurse, in a voice that faltered, "This place used to a workhouse, back before the Great War. I always swore none of my family would end up in a workhouse. I don't want to die here. I want to die in my own bed. Take me home. Hey you, yes you, in the white coat, fetch my clothes—I wanna go home."

Hannah had many visitors, but none more frequent than Vera. Every day, Vera, after walking her black lab, Kim number four, would ride the bus to the hospital. She sat in the visitors' room, tucked into a corner like a pixie, and waited for the bell to ring that signaled the morning visiting hour had arrived. Then she would wait throughout the afternoon until the evening visiting time was over, hoping to catch a ride home with one of her mother's other visitors.

Occasionally the nurses would take pity on Vera and allowed her into the ward to sit next to Hannah, after the doctors had finished their rounds.

"Come closer," Hannah said, holding Vera's hand tight. "There's something I need to say to yer. I'll be going to God soon. . . ." Vera began to cry.

"Stop that! Stop that now, girl. You're always cryin', for God's sake."

"You can talk. Where do you think I get it from?"

Hannah handed her a tissue. "Listen to me, Vera. You have been the best daughter a mother could wish for, but I never understood why you never warmed to Peter. I reckoned you were jealous of him and baby Grace, but only you know the reason. I never tried to change you."

Vera began to cry again. "I don't want yer to go, Mam. I don't know what I would do without yer."

Hannah continued. "Now I'm asking yer to do something special for me. I want yer to look after my husband, as you've done for me. I want you to cook for him, clean and care for him in his old age. He's a good man. You don't have to love him, just keep him from hardship and loneliness until he joins me." A lump came in Hannah's throat, but she didn't cry. "Promise me you'll do this."

"I promise," Vera said.

"Now, go and buy yourself a cuppa tea and a cheese sandwich in the cafeteria." Hannah slid a pound note into Vera's hand. "And stop cryin'." Vera, with the help of a black lab named Kim, would keep her promise to her mother.

The next day, Grace accompanied Vera to the hospital. Grace had been designated by the family to find out from the doctors exactly what was ailing their mother.

The medical staff poked and prodded Hannah. They stuck tubes in her, took samples, conferred with each other in whispers, and then left. Hannah despised this affront to her dignity. The doctors never felt it necessary to inform the patients or their families about the procedures or what they thought the problem might be, or even what cure, if any, would be pursued. After all, they were doctors and the patient and other people, well . . . were not. They never shared information until all the tests were conducted, all the data gathered, all the opinions considered, and then not until they could squeeze a few precious minutes out of their schedules.

This was particularly true of consultants—the elite of the medical profession. Consultants roamed the hospital wards like grand viziers in the Sultan's palace. They were aloof, dour, and unapproachable.

Such a man was Hannah's consultant, Charles E. Dundas, MD. The good doctor was a man of refinement. He loved the theatre and good French wine, sitting, as he did, on the board of the Liverpool Symphony Orchestra. His suits were tailored and he considered himself a cultured person of selective tastes. He preferred his patients to be of the paying kind—well bred, educated, successful, and cultured, instead of working-class people, to which the Socialist government made him devote some of his precious time.

Not that he had anything against the great unwashed. After all, one has to have the working class to perform many necessary labors. It was just that he felt their stupidity so difficult to tolerate—and their smell, of course. Were they so poor that they couldn't afford soap? Doctor Dundas often thought that he should have emigrated to America when he was younger. That's where the money was. At fifty-one, he could have retired by now.

That evening, Hannah's bed was surrounded by a clutch of visitors. There was Peter, Eileen, Pat O'Malley, and Vera, of course. Grace sat down by the nurses' desk, waiting to talk to the doctor. She had been there since 9:00 a.m. The head nurse had assured her that a doctor would speak with her that day, despite the fact that they were so busy. Grace waited anxiously on the hard wooden bench, thumbing through dog-eared magazines. She had waited through until noon, when Lilly relieved her so she could grab a sandwich and a cuppa.

Grace's vigil continued throughout the afternoon. Every hour or so, the head nurse would inform her, "Doctor Dundas is very busy today—emergencies, you understand. I've told him you are here."

At 6:00 p.m. a distinguished, balding man in a dark suit strode past Grace without giving her a second look. The nurse called after him. "Doctor, oh Doctor, there is someone. . . ." He ignored the nurse and continued walking toward the elevator.

"Is that him?" Grace asked.

"That's him," the nurse replied, her face scrunched in disgust.

Grace jumped up and ran after him. She reached the elevator doors as they began to close. The doctor gave her a cold stare, making no attempt to keep the doors open. Grace turned to the stairs, and skipped down them as fast as she could, until she fell and scraped her knee. By the time she caught up with him, the doctor was out the door, halfway across the lawn, headed toward the reserved parking lot.

Grace grabbed his shoulder. "Doctor, I need to know about my mother."

He pulled away from her and looked her up and down, with obvious contempt. "Do not touch me," he demanded. "Look, what do you want? I've had a long day and I'm on my way home. I'll see you on Tuesday, perhaps."

"I've been waiting all day. Please, sir, I need to know what you've found." Grace's tone was frantic, pleading.

The good doctor heaved a deep sigh. "All right, who is your mother?"

"Hannah Corcoran. Ward seven."

"Hannah Corcoran? Oh, yes—I remember. The cranky old woman. She has cancer."

"What! What did yer say?" Grace gulped for breath.

"Are you deaf, woman? She has cancer. Her body is riddled with it. She has a month at best." Grace's mouth fell open and her breath came in gasps. "Is that it? Can I go now?" the doctor asked.

Without warning, Grace found her left hand curled behind her back, forming a fist. It flew out like the devil's angel and smashed into the face of Charles E. Dundas, M.D. He tottered backward clutching his nose, then fell forward, face down onto the grass.

Grace held up her fist and stared at it with awe. She had never hit anyone in her life. She looked down at her victim and stood over him like a heavyweight boxer who had just delivered the knockout punch.

"You arrogant, unfeeling bastard!" she said. Remembering something Hannah had once said, she knelt down next to the moaning figure on the ground. "You can call me Mrs. Lambeth, or you can call me madam, but you have no leave to call me woman."

◆

Up on ward seven on the third floor, Pat O'Malley, peering out the window, had witnessed the whole event.

"Quick, quick, Hannah you've got to see this! Eileen, grab that wheelchair. C'mon Peter, let's get her out of bed." They hauled Hannah into the wheelchair and took her over to the window, where she could look down at the scene below. A big man in a dark suit was kneeling on the lawn, head bowed. A few people were gathered around him.

"That's your doctor!" Pat said with a chuckle.

"What wrong with him?" Hannah asked.

"Not sure, but my guess would be broken nose and bruised lower eye socket."

"Who did it?"

"Your youngest, Grace," Pat said proudly.

"Which hand?"

"Why, the left of course."

"Who would have thought it? The hook has passed to Grace, of all people—my darling Grace!"

Meantime, Grace had returned to the third floor of the hospital. She passed the same nurse at her desk, still holding a telephone to her ear. She put the phone down and yelled at Grace, "Hey, someone just clobbered Dr. Dundas. Was that you?"

Grace nodded. "I couldn't stop myself. He said my mother was riddled with cancer, a month to live, as cold as if he was ordering another brandy."

"I would have paid to see that," the nurse said. "But they've called the police, you know. You'd better make yourself scarce."

Grace's face scrunched up in anguish. "I want to see my mother."

"Follow me." The nurse took Grace into a small room full of white uniforms and kitted her out as a nurse, complete with white shoes and the nurse's identity badge.

"Why would you risk getting in trouble?" Grace asked.

"I know about your mother," the nurse said. "My dad marched with her during the food riots. He told me about her bravery and how she and your dad were beaten by the police. She's a heroine in my eyes, and I'm sorry she's so ill."

◈

Grace hid herself behind a curtain at the end of her mother's ward and looked around furtively. She beckoned her father. Peter looked surprised by Grace's disguise, but her solemn expression caused him to walk slowly over to her, and with each step his heart sank further.

Grace held Peter's coat lapel. "Cancer," she said quietly. "Cancer all over. A month at best." Peter dropped his jaw and bowed his head. Just as slowly, he walked back to Hannah's bedside. He grasped Hannah's hand, and the look in his eyes told her everything.

She smiled. "So be it." Grace came up behind her father. "Good God, girl, what are you wearing?" Hannah asked.

Grace sat on Hannah's bed and held her wrinkled left hand. "I punched your doctor, but I wanted to see you before the police come looking for me."

Hannah uttered a weak chuckle. "That arrogant toad deserved it. Thank you. You saved me the trouble. What did it feel like?"

Grace bowed her head. "It felt good. My God, it felt so good!" Everyone around the bed laughed.

"Well, the hook is yours now, Grace. Use it sparingly, use it for good, use it to protect your family. Aim for the right cheekbone and don't let them see it coming. Find yourself a guardian angel, if you can." At that point Steven arrived. "Well, speak of the devil," Hannah said. "If Councilor Corcoran can't keep you out of jail, nobody can."

"What's going on?" Steven asked.

"Someone punched your mother's doctor," Pat O'Malley replied.

Steven put his hand on his head. "Oh God, Mother, no!" The group burst with laughter.

Hannah turned to Peter. "Get me out of here, Peter. Let me die at home, in my own bed."

"All right, my love. Vera, fetch her belongings. Eileen, bring your car around to the front. Pat and Lilly, get Grace out of this place before she's arrested."

As the others left the room, Hannah asked Peter, "So how long do I have?"

"A month, maybe more," he said.

"A month is time enough to wallow in my memories."

Peter brushed a wisp of silver hair from her forehead. "Tell me one."

Hannah's eyes brightened. "I remember when I chased you around the windmill, and you stopped abruptly so I'd bump into you. Then you stole a kiss."

Peter smiled as tears welled in his eyes. "I was nervous as a schoolboy."

"Your turn," she said.

"I'll never lose the image of you standing atop that heap of rubble during the Blitz, a brick in each hand, with the convent blazing behind you. You stood firm, full of courage and defiance, like the figurehead on the bow of an old sailing ship, plowing through a stormy sea."

"My sails are tattered," Hannah said. "I've weathered many a storm, but I never would have survived without you by my side."

Peter bent down and held her tightly. His tears soaked into her hospital gown. "They ought to write a book about you," he whispered.

"Get Lilly's lad. He likes to write."

"Ready?" Peter asked.

"Ready," Hannah replied. "Take me home, husband."

Author's Note

The Town of Birkenhead today is a shadow of its former self, with hardly a ship in port. The docks resemble a ghost town, destroyed by containerization. The shipyard is closed down, a victim of persecution of the trade unions. But Birkenhead is coming back, driven by a new generation with strength of character inherited from the people who inspired *Hannah's Left Hook*.

Though parts of the story are based on actual events, this is a work of fiction. The following sources helped me shape the story:

Birkenhead at War 1939–1945, Ian Boumphrey (Ian and Marilyn Boumphrey, 2007).

HMS Thetis: Secrets and Scandal, David Roberts (Avid Publications, 1999).

Idle Hands, Clenched Fists: The Depression in a Shipyard Town, Stephen F. Kelly (Spokesman Books, 1987).

Life at Lairds: Memories of Shipyard Working Men, David Roberts (Avid Publications, 1993).

The Admiralty Regrets: The Story of His Majesty's Submarine "Thetis," C.E.T. Warren and James Benson (George G. Harrap & Co., 1958).

The First World War, John Keegan (Random House, 1998).

The Great War at Sea: A History of Naval Action 1914–1918, A. A. Hoehling (Thomas Y. Crowell, 1965).

Yesterday's Britain: The Illustrated Story of How We Lived, Worked and Played in this Century, Reader's Digest (Readers Digest Publications, 1998).